The Perfect Love

Ida Heartthrobs Book Two

BETHANY
MONACO SMITH

First edition floral discreet paperback January 2025

ISBN 978-1-963450-16-3

Editing by Lacey Braziel at On the Page Publishing

Cover Design by Bethany Monaco Smith

For more information about this book, visit the author's website.

www.bethanymonacosmith.com

About The Perfect Love

The Perfect Love is an emotional small town college romance featuring a curvy, feminist FMC healing from past trauma and a sarcastic, overprotective cinnamon roll MMC healing from loss. Their love story builds slowly but it's full of delicious tension and heat.

The Perfect Love is a complete standalone. Though it is part of the Ida Heartthrobs series, these books are only loosely interconnected and don't need to be read in a specific order.

Trevor is a side character from both the Freaking Love and Friends Like This series. You don't need to have read either of those, but if you have read Friends Like This, please note The Perfect Love takes place over the same time as Married Like This/Together Like This and the first half of Heartbreak Like This. Keep reading for trigger warnings and a character list.

Are you ready to fall ass over tits for Trevor and Chelsea?

Meet the Characters

Because Trevor is a side character in two other book series, there are lots of side characters in this one. I did my best to introduce them slowly and not make it overwhelming, but if you need clarification, you can jump back to this page at any time.

THE LOVEBIRDS TIED TOGETHER BY AN INVISIBLE STRING:
- Trevor Matteny

- Chelsea Winters

CHELSEA'S FAMILY:
- Robbie- uncle who is more like her big brother

- Gene- father

- Hilary- stepmother

- Gran- her badass maternal guiding light

Trevor's family/friends:
- Liz- mother

- Hyla- best friend/chosen sister

- Nick- best friend

- Mitch- father

The seven housemates/best friends:
- Amanda Hamilton

- Sarah McKinley (Trevor's ex)

- Rae (McKinley) Cooper

- Aaron Cooper

- Joel Wilkinson

- Mackenzie (Mackie) Montoya

- Miles Hyun-Hansen

The other Ida Heartthrobs (mentioned):
- Jesse Wilkinson (Joel's brother)

- Jamie Henderson (friend & Amanda's boyfriend)

Trigger Warnings

IF YOU'RE LOOKING FOR possible triggers in this book, this page is for you. If you're not, you can skip this page and dive into the story.

trigger warnings may contain plot spoilers

The FMC in this book is recovering after rape, and thus rape and sexual assault are heavy themes for this book. Other than brief retellings of her story, her rape is not on page. *Other triggers in this book include:* heavy discussions of loss & ongoing grief, suicide attempt (non main character-slit wrists, not described in heavy detail), alcohol/medication overdose (non main character).

If you are a victim of sexual assault or rape and need support, help is always available. Please reach out. In the United States call 1-800-656-4673

Any updates or changes to this information can be found on my website: www.bethanymonacosmith.com/triggers

To all the women who have been through hell and let their healing shape them into a beautiful badass version of themselves

and to the men who say...
CITYTTBABYATB

1

Beautiful Badass

Chelsea

ONE DAY, WHEN I have children, I want to be able to tell my daughters a man did not break me. The world did not break me. I fought back, and I'll keep fighting.

Which is why I'm loading up my cute little Prius, ready to take on the world—or at least a new town. *Setting off on an adventure.*

Just call me Bilbo Baggins.

If Bilbo had been motivated by healing from past trauma and a quiet feminine rage burning softly in the background like a well-stoked fire.

I load my large, bright purple suitcase into my trunk and shove it closed, inhaling the lake air. I'm trading one lake for another with my college choice, but I'm hoping that will help me feel more at home.

My dad looks at me hesitantly. "Got everything? Are you sure you don't want me to drive you?"

I let him pull me into a hug while channeling my inner strength. That strength has been my survival and the closest thing I have to the old, confident version of myself.

"I'm sure. I'll be okay. Part of the reason I chose to transfer to SUNY Finger Lakes and move to Old Lake Town is because Uncle Robbie will be right there." Literally. My uncle owns a small apartment house and will be two floors down from me if I need him. Safety while not compromising my independence.

I get why Dad's worried, though.

I spent four straight months in bed, two more angry while I clawed my way out, and the last three picking up the pieces. Not healed but heal*ing*. I'm on a journey to reclaim the best parts of the old me while building the person I'm becoming.

New college. New focus. Fresh start. Hopefully everything I need to stay out of the space I was in and let myself take chances and meet new people, find new friends. Even if there are some things I'll never do again. And that's okay.

I'm okay.

And when I'm not, I will be.

I'm resilient even in the moments when I don't feel that way.

Or at least that's what my therapist says.

Yeah, healing is a journey.

My phone goes off, and I pull it from my back pocket only to find a group text from my supposed best friends asking why I didn't go out with them last night.

Getting away from two insufferably unempathetic people is just another bonus of moving almost three hours away.

When your life falls apart, you learn quickly how strong your friendships are. Unfortunately, I learned mine were as fragile as a mediocre white man's ego.

Which is why I ignore my text, put my phone in my purse, and set that in the backseat. I want nothing but fantasy audiobooks for the next three hours of my life.

Morally gray fae book boyfriends are better than real world men. *I said what I said.*

My dad looks me over and nods. "Okay. Call me when you get there. And again this weekend. Or text me. Just... let me know you're okay."

My stepmom, Hilary, steps up next to him and takes his hand. "She'll be okay, honey."

We share a quick hug, but don't linger, though I appreciate her support.

Hilary is nice and a perfect match for my dad, but they didn't start dating until I was sixteen, and they got married when I was eighteen, so we've never had a deep bond. Which is fine. I never craved a maternal figure. Mostly because I already had one.

"Of course she'll be all right." Gran pulls me into her arms. "You rose out of the darkness, and I'm incredibly proud of how you continue to fight. Don't take shit from anyone. And don't let anyone steal your power or your peace. You've earned both."

"Thanks, Gran. I love you."

"Love you too, sweetheart." She lets me go. "Have fun. Try to knock the patriarchy down a peg or two whenever you can."

I laugh at that. "I'll do my best."

My grandmother has always been my maternal, fuck-the-patriarchy guiding light. My biological mother was never involved in my life, and I don't blame her.

She and my dad weren't serious when she got pregnant, but he offered to support her. Her parents pushed her not to have an abortion, so she gave things a shot with my dad, but within a few months of having me, she knew motherhood wasn't for her. She signed away her rights and left me with my dad. She wasn't a bad person, but she felt trapped into a life she didn't want, and I fully respect her choosing herself. She never popped back up in my life or made things confusing for me, and I grew up surrounded by love, so I have no complaints. I hope wherever she is, she's living the life she wanted for herself, because we all deserve that freedom. That choice. I'm grateful I'm here, but I wouldn't want any woman to be forced into any situation or decision they didn't want.

I've always felt that way, but it's stronger now. The desire to help, protect, and empower other women has always been woven into my DNA, but my personal experiences have heightened that. Which is why I have an internship focused on helping, empowering, and advocating for women lined up.

This is me taking my life back, and I'm ready for it.

"I'll call you tonight, and then I'll call again on Wednesday after my first day at my internship. And I'll text like crazy. Promise."

"I guess I can live with that," my dad says.

I kiss his cheek and throw my arms around him again. "Love you, Daddy."

"Love you too, kiddo. Drive safe."

"I will."

I grab my giant water bottle from the roof of my car and get settled in the driver's seat.

A ripple of emotion burns in my chest as I look back at my house and then at my dad's smiling face, but I take a deep breath and close my eyes, centering myself.

I may not be as carefree, wild, or upbeat as I once was, but I'm slowly finding those things again.

And I'm strong. I can do hard things.

At least that's what Glennon Doyle says.

This is the *right* thing, and I'm going to put my positivity pants on and believe it will lead to great things. It has to because I have karma on my side, and the universe is her best friend, which means the universe is totally on my team too.

It's about time.

"How much money did you spend at Target?" my uncle Robbie asks the second I'm through the front door of his apartment.

He's ten years younger than my dad, and since my dad had me young, that means he's young enough to be my older brother.

"Almost as much as I spent at the bookstore."

"Textbooks are ridiculously expensive."

I laugh. "Uh, yeah. I meant that cute little indie bookstore downtown. Their romantasy section was huge. Textbooks. Please. I'll get the cheapest used ones I can find online or find someone in my classes to share an account with for the ebooks."

"Ah, right. How could I forget? You need bat boys and shadow daddies more than anything educational."

I stare at him from across the bright kitchen. It's all white cabinets and light wood tones. Mine is almost the same as his, but the woods in mine are darker and it's one bedroom instead of two.

"You can get away with it because you love the bat boys and shadow daddies almost as much as I do, but I beg of you, *never* say 'shadow daddies' in front of my father or I might spontaneously combust in embarrassment."

"Now you're just giving me ways to harass you." I stick my tongue out at him, but he nods to the table behind me. "Let's eat. I'm starving."

We sit down together at the small table and Robbie sets a large bowl of pasta and a container of meatballs in front of us.

"Eat."

"Where's the garlic bread? If I'm going to carb load, I need to do it properly. Thirty percent pasta, seventy percent garlic bread."

"Thanks for making me a homemade meal, Robbie. You're the best ever. I'm so glad I came to live here. I'll even wash the dishes to show you how much I love you."

I do a slow clap.

"Excellent feminine voice. You should consider voice acting."

He just arches a brow and I roll my eyes.

"Fine. Thank you so much for making me food. Now, seriously. Where's the garlic bread? If you tell me you didn't make any, I'll have to dock a star on your review on Yelp."

The timer on the oven beeps, and he stands. "If you had to choose between shadow daddies or garlic bread, which would you choose?"

I stare at him blankly. "Shadow daddies feeding me garlic bread. Duh."

He opens the oven and pulls out a tray of my edible boyfriend—garlic bread.

"That wasn't a choice."

"Uh, yeah it was. I heard them both in the same sentence. That means they go together."

He sets the tray on some hot plates on the table, and I quickly yank three pieces off, burning my fingers along the way, but it's a helpful reminder not to shove it in my mouth yet if I want to taste it rather than burn half my taste buds off.

I dig into some pasta, and silence takes over the room as we both eat.

But the silence doesn't last long.

"So, speaking of carb loading, are you going to play volleyball this year?"

I lift my head with my fork halfway to my mouth. "Wow. What a subtle transition. But also, what does carb loading have to do with volleyball?"

"Don't athletes carb load?"

"Yeah, like hockey players and football players who are running—or skating, whatever—for hours at a time."

"Potayto, potahto. Are you playing?"

Volleyball isn't exactly a sore subject, it just feels like a different life since I've done it, which is strange because it used to be one of the biggest parts of my life.

"No. My paid internship at Promise Advocacy is going to take up a lot of that kind of time, and that's what I'd rather be doing. I might see if there's a rec league on campus though. I miss it."

"Sorry. Not trying to be a bummer."

"You're not. It's another part of me I want to find again."

"Not to be totally sappy, but I'm proud of you."

"Yeah, wallowing for almost a year before finally facing life again is something to be proud of." I shove a bite of garlic bread in my mouth.

"Bullshit. And do not even talk about yourself like that. Got it? I don't care if self-deprecating humor has always been your thing. You've worked really hard to be where you are and make it through something tough. Don't talk shit about yourself."

I trill my lips. "Fine. Now stop being sappy."

He kicks my leg under the table. "If you insist. Now, I made you garlic bread. Where's my dessert?"

I smile in relief. My therapist would tell me I need to take compliments like that and believe them, but I'm not in therapy because I have my shit together, so I'll continue to avoid that topic and suck at taking compliments.

I get up and grab my bag, then pull out two cookie sandwiches from the coffee place downtown. They're both chocolate chip M&M cookies with frosting in between. Vanilla for me, chocolate for him.

"I love you."

"Well, duh. You're contractually obligated to as my uncle."

He grimaces. "First, I thought we agreed you don't refer to me as your uncle because I'm too young and hot. And second, I don't recall signing a contract for that."

"Well, you did. So it doesn't count."

He waves his hand. "Contract or not, no one ever said I had to *like* you. But I do. So again, stop with the self-deprecating shit."

I chuckle. "Is it sad that my"—he pins me with a look, so I stop myself from using the word *uncle* again—"father's much younger brother is my best friend?"

He raises his cookie sandwich and taps it against mine. "Nope. Because you're mine too."

I glance over at my bag again, where my phone is with still unread texts from my supposed "best" friends.

A moment of bliss hits and a chill runs up my spine, making me smile. This is where I'm supposed to be. I'm supported and I'm ready to take on the world again—or at least one little chunk of it.

After we finish eating, I head back up to my apartment, ready to set up the hundreds of dollars' worth of blankets, pillows, and accessories I got at Target, and my new bookcase for all my new book boyfriends. They need a safe place to live.

Since I'm a strong, independent woman, I told Robbie I could put it together by myself. And I'm doing the damn thing, but also getting distracted and wondering if my book babies can survive living on my coffee table until tomorrow.

My phone goes off, and I grab it, seeing yet another text in my group chat with my friends.

Guess I should deal with it so I can move on. I'm not going to cut them out of my life or anything, but I'm choosing distance, so I don't choose raging on them and burning our thirteen-year friendship to the ground.

Bridget: Girl, you totally missed out on all the cute boys last night. Why didn't you come out with us?

Lex: Yeah! We needed one last girls' night, and you ditched us.

I didn't respond to those, so now I have two new ones.

Bridget: And now you're not answering. Don't you love us anymore?

Lex: Don't make me send you a picture of my pouting face.

I sigh and type out a response.

Me: I told you I needed to finish packing last night, and I didn't answer because I've been getting settled in at my new apartment.

The three little dots appear immediately.

Lex: Well, you should've packed last minute this morning.

Bridget: Yeah. We wanted to see you before you moved hours away. I still don't understand why you had to change schools. We were all within an hour of each other before. Now you're stupidly far away.

I don't even know how to answer that. Or explain why I've avoided going out with them all summer. Because the thing is, I've said it. But they don't like my answer. Or they don't understand it. They don't understand why I can't get over it.

I mean, apparently, I was just supposed to let it roll off my back.

It was only a little rape.

Tears prickle in my eyes.

All it took was one night to destroy my life. One night of not paying attention to my drinks. One night of my college friends ditching me. One night of mistakenly trusting a guy, who then used me and discarded me like I was a disposable toy. One night for my body to stop feeling like my own and for my life to change forever.

I'm not over it.

Sometimes, I think I never will be.

And my "friends" don't even bother trying to understand that.

All they did was pick on me and treat me like crap because I wasn't fun anymore.

I want to rage at them. I want to scream about what selfish, unempathetic people they are. That they should consider themselves lucky they have no idea how I feel. I want to tell them to fuck off.

But I don't want to create more turmoil in my life.

Our hometown of Birch Lake is small, and rifts run deep. I don't want that.

For half a second, my thumb hovers over the button to delete and block the conversation, but I don't click that either.

Instead, I take a breath, then type a response.

Me: Because this is where I need to be.

Then I put the conversation on mute, play an audiobook through my Bluetooth speaker, and finish setting up my bookcase.

This is my home now.

This is my life now.

And even though I'm messy at best, still crawling out of the darkness and afraid to be around the opposite sex, I'm doing the damn thing.

I'm going to live my life and be the most beautiful, badass version of me I've ever been. That's how I win.

2
Pretty F*cking Spectacular

Trevor

"HAVE FUN LIVING WITH seven other people, potentially hearing your ex have sex with one of your closest friends, and... oh, yeah. Don't forget to wrap it before you tap it."

I stare dryly at my sister. "Remind me again why I like you."

"Because I'm your favoritest person in the whole world."

Hyla's warm brown eyes dance as her sun-kissed blonde hair rustles in the wind. Her smile and her words are a playful mask of the pain I know she's feeling.

She's my sister in every way except biology. We've known each other since we were born. My mom is the mom in her life, and if Hyla would ditch her shit-tacular parents, my mom would adopt her in a heartbeat. She's had a rough time lately—the last few years, really—but so have I. We've been each other's ride-or-die for our entire lives. Through her shitty parents, and plenty of heartbreak and loss. Leaving her the first time for college two years ago was tough, but after all we've both been through in the last six months, leaving her this time is harder, even if she will be a lot closer to Mom.

I pull her into a hug. "You are my favorite person."

"Excuse me. What about me?"

Mom's all smiles with her hands on her hips, but I know she has a hard time letting me go too. We survived the worst together. I'm glad she and Hyla will have each other when I'm not here.

But this is the moment I second-guess going.

I'm transferring schools this year. I could've gone somewhere closer to home, but I still wanted to explore more, and experience life outside my tiny town of Ida. So I'm moving to a different tiny town and into a house with seven of my friends.

At least it has a sweet view of the lake.

"Stop with that look," Mom says. "This will be good for you. You need a breath of fresh air, and where better to get that than right by a beautiful lake?"

Right. Forgot my mother is a mind reader.

I shift from Hyla's arms to Mom's and hold her close.

"I love you."

"I love you too, honey." She clears her throat to pretend her voice doesn't break.

Whose bright idea was this, anyway?

Oh, yeah. Mine.

This is supposed to be my fresh start. A chance to start over. New school. New major. New life plan, even if the wounds from the old one are still healing.

Still, I don't *need* to do this.

I want to.

That's harder for me to admit because of my character *not-a-flaw* of always putting the important people in my life first. If anyone says it's a flaw, they can suck it, because caring about the people I love will never ever be a bad thing. I'd go to jail or an early grave for Hyla or my mom—even a lot of my friends—and I'm good with that. It's who I am. And, if I'm honest, who I am is pretty fucking spectacular, so there's no need to change.

Hyla would smack me in the back of the head if she caught me saying that, but for being unbiologically related, she'd totally say the same shit.

Mom lets me go, then pinches my cheek.

"Mother, why?"

She laughs. "Because you'll always be my baby."

Then Hyla sings the Mariah Carey song of the same name from behind me, and yeah, I'm ready to leave.

"And on that off-tune note."

Hyla mock gasps. "How dare you? I have a stunning voice."

"Stunning's a word for it."

She slugs me in the arm. "Okay, you can leave now. I'm tired of you already."

But she can't even manage the words without tears filling her eyes.

I wrap her in another hug.

"Sure you don't want to come with me?" Hyla recently took a break from college, but I'm sure she could easily find a job in the college town I'm moving to. "We could get bunk beds."

She snorts a laugh.

"'Cause hearing you hook up is high on my list of priorities." She blanches. "And living with my ex-girlfriend who I still have feelings for and sometimes hook up with even though I shouldn't sounds like a dumpster fire waiting to happen." She wraps an arm around Mom. "I'll be in good company here. Plus, someone has to keep an eye on her."

I slowly nod. "True. But probably not you." I look between them. "I'm not sure who's the bigger troublemaker and who's the instigator."

"Depends on the day." Mom pulls me in for another hug. "Be good. Take care of yourself. Don't forget to smile," she whispers. Those words almost fucking break me. At the worst of times, she whispered them to me. A reminder to keep going, keep seeing the brightness in each day, even when it all feels dull and cloudy.

Which is a lot of the time lately.

Nope. Not going down that road.

I glance toward my car. Only one road I need to head down now. I already loaded up most of my shit into the moving truck my friends hired.

It's going to be insane living with seven of them—including my ex. But we were friends first and we're friends again, and I'm over the love we once shared. She ended things because she knew it wasn't the right fit. Sure, we could've *made* it work, but forcing something to work isn't what you should do at seventeen. Now I'm grateful for it because I know she was right.

As long as my room isn't next to the one she'll be sharing with her boyfriend—or whatever he is to her—I'll be fine.

"Stop standing there looking all melodramatic," Hyla says. "We love you, but you've got a life to live. Go have fun. Party. Fall in love—or lust. And I promise I'll be up to visit soon."

"You better." I toss a hand through my curly hair. "Okay, I better get on the road. Love you both."

"Call me or I'll call you and be extra annoying," Mom says sweetly.

"Oh, I know."

"Hey!"

"I mean, I love you!" I blow a kiss in their direction and climb into the car.

They wave as I start my car and drive away from the large country-style house down the long gravel drive and past the gate at the end of it.

It's not until I'm about to turn out of the driveway that I remember I have one last stop to make.

An important one, but also the hardest.

I need to say goodbye to my dad.

Pain radiates through my left leg and hip as I break above the lake water and suck in a breath. Swimming is supposed to be low impact, but I guess moving boxes for an hour, plus racing my friends down the dock over and over before jumping into the lake were not low impact activities. I grip one of the posts of the dock as I hobble out of the water.

It's moments like this where I swear I can feel every fracture in my leg. I can pinpoint the exact spots where the breaks were, where rods or pins were put in, or where pieces of me were cut away and replaced with new ones.

A knee and partial hip replacement wasn't on my bucket list for my sophomore year of college, but neither was losing control of my snowboard and bouncing off a few trees.

I may have won the battle, but I still lost.

Lost the future I was planning for myself. A shot at playing baseball professionally. Now, I have to live with never playing again. Not like that. Sure, I'll probably play in some rec league with my friends one day, but it's not the same.

I wince my way up the stairs, limping like I'm still freshly recovering.

"You okay?" Amanda Hamilton leaps out of the Adirondack chair she's sitting in and comes over to me.

Amanda is the most recent addition to the craziness that is this friend group. While I consider them some of my closest friends, the six of them still goofing around on the lawn have been ride-or-die since they were six years old. Amanda, who lives in one of the nearby towns to Ida, New York—where we all grew up—met them during their freshman year of college and quickly became the long lost seventh member of their little group. But since she's newer, she's not part of the hive mind as much as the rest of them.

Amanda and I hit it off quickly because she's feisty and funny and doesn't take anyone's shit. She also speaks fluent sarcasm. All essential things for a solid friendship with me.

She's also a mother hen, and wraps her arm around me, guiding me to a chair next to the one she vacated.

"I'm okay. Just did a little too much today." Sometimes I let myself forget everything, then I have a moment like this and realize that's impossible. "One day, I'll age into my body, right?"

She laughs. "Exactly. And when you do, you'll be a step ahead of us because you've already had your knee replaced. You'll be running circles around us." Her face softens. "Want a beer?"

I toss a hand through my hair. "Yeah. Thanks."

She nods, and returns a second later with a beer for me and a hard cider for her.

"So, how are you feeling about being here? New school? Living with the hive mind?"

She leans back in her chair and puts her feet up on the railing. I stare out at the lake and take it all in.

"Pretty good. I'm excited for the possibilities. I'm not sure I'll ever stop being bummed about losing my shot at going pro or just playing for longer, but it is what it is, and I'm refusing to let baseball go. I already asked Aaron and Joel to put in a good word with their coach. I can't play, but I want to be involved with the team."

"I'm sure you'll find a way. Just turn on the annoying Trevor charm."

"Rude. I'm never annoying. Fabulous is the word you're looking for. Maybe incredible."

"Obnoxious. Over the top."

"I think we must be speaking different languages."

She laughs. "Totally selfish, but I'm glad you're here. We always had the most fun when you and Hy would come to visit us and we'd spend a weekend here. Now we get to live like that all the time. Minus Hyla, but she'll just have to come visit."

"I tried to get her to come."

"She needs to find her own path. And her and Mackenzie sharing a house would be complicated."

"I know."

Amanda rolls her eyes. "You can't solve Hyla's problems for her, so focus on yourself. Channel your egotistical side. Weren't you just telling me how great you are?"

"Stupendous, really."

"That's how you should hit on girls. Just walk up to them and tell them you're stupendous and they should be honored to spend time in your presence. I promise it'll work."

"Sounds very effective at getting me slapped."

"Oh, did I say it would work? I meant it would work at entertaining me."

"I hate you."

"Lies."

"How's Jamie?"

I swear hearts appear in her eyes at the mention of his name, but then her face falls a little, and she swallows hard. "He's ahh... he's fine."

"Mands."

"What? He's busy and fine."

"You can talk about it. How's he settling in with the Knights?"

Amanda bites her lip, still looking unsure. Her boyfriend, Jamie, was drafted by the New York Metros right out of high school. He's currently settling in with the triple-A team near our hometown, The Binghamton Knights.

"He's having a great time. He was worried about settling in, but he's killing it."

I elbow her. "It's okay to talk about it. Better than okay. It's hard for me, but I'm happy for him." I never had as much raw talent as he did. Jamie is two years younger than us, but his talent as a pitcher is next level. "And you deserve to be the proud girlfriend."

"What about you?"

"I don't think Jamie's looking for a proud boyfriend."

She ignores my comment and continues on. "Are you hooking up or looking for something serious? I figure I should know for when someone sees me with you and inevitably asks. I mean, obviously I'll warn them you're much more of a pain in the ass than your looks could ever give away, but if they're still interested..."

"Eh, as soon as I play the crippled card, I'll have them falling at my feet."

She pins me with a look, and I laugh.

"Come on. You know I wouldn't do that. Not exactly proud that I fucked my chances at a dream career."

"You haven't answered me."

Almost got away with it.

"I don't know. I guess I'll see what happens."

I take a swig of my beer and look back out at the lake.

If Amanda knows I'm lying—which there's a good chance of—she doesn't call me on it.

It's not like I'm ashamed to say the truth, I'm just not sure exactly what the truth is. I'm not choosing celibacy until I find my perfect match, but I'm over the hook up scene. It was never really me to begin with.

I swore off love for a bit after Sarah and I ended. I wallowed, uninterested in dating anyone for a while, then swung in the opposite direction and fucked my way through my freshman year of college. Sophomore year I was still hooking up, but more focused on baseball until my accident.

Most of the guys on the baseball team at my old school would've given me shit if I hadn't been. Granted, most of them were pricks, but it's part of the toxic culture that can come with sports. If we say we want love or a serious girlfriend, we're pussies. We're supposed to fuck the nearest girl who's interested and then discuss those girls in the locker room.

That kind of toxicity is one thing I'm happy to be done with because none of that ever settled right with me, and it's not what I wanted. It's also why I never became close with most guys on the team—the ones I got close with were both quieter and in relationships. Most of the guys were only good to party with, and that got old fast. Even my former roommate—who I thought was a good friend—was like that, and ditched me as soon as he found out about my accident.

That's all part of why I decided to come to SUNY Finger Lakes with a horde of my friends.

Coming out of one of the darkest seasons of my life, I wanted to be surrounded by people I trust and respect, who will support me while I figure my shit out—and on my bad days.

Everything I've gone through recently was a reminder of what really matters and who I am. That's a guy who thought he found the love of his life, the girl he was going to marry, at thirteen years old. I *wanted* that to be the case.

It's ingrained in me. I like caring for other people. I like being in a relationship. There's nothing like the connection of loving someone and having them love you back.

Maybe it makes me a sap.

Pathetic.

Even naive.

But if last year forced me to do anything, it was to accept what I want out of life and go for it. I have more clarity about what I want for the future, and while I'm not expecting my perfect love to magically appear, I'm choosing to live my life and actively work toward the things I want.

I lost a piece of the future I thought I'd have, but I didn't lose everything, and more importantly, I refuse to lose myself.

3

Sparkly Rom-com Journey

Trevor

I WALK DOWN THE stairs of the lake house and into chaos.

Not surprising when I live with this many people. Surprisingly, I haven't heard any of them fucking yet, so the walls must be nice and thick.

When I round the stairs into the kitchen, my eyebrows shoot up.

Miles has Joel in a headlock, while Aaron leans against the counter, sipping on coffee like nothing else is happening. Mackenzie—who we all call Mackie—is sitting on the kitchen island, tossing little pieces of bacon at Amanda for her to catch in her mouth.

I go straight for the coffee pot. Aaron makes the best coffee.

I've barely poured my cup when Amanda calls out from behind me.

I spin around as a piece of bacon flies toward me. I lean forward and catch it in my mouth with ease.

"How did you do that? I've caught like two in ten minutes."

"Baseball player."

"Didn't realize you catch balls with your mouth." Mackie grins. "I'm sure there's a sex joke in there somewhere."

I take a spot leaning against the counter next to Aaron, who is laughing, then I look around. "Hold up, where's your fiancée?"

I tease him with the word because he's been extra obsessed since they got engaged a few months ago.

"She and Sarah left early this morning. I'm riding in with Joel."

"And did you have to have your faces surgically separated?"

"You're hilarious."

"We're all twelve years old on the inside."

Joel breaks free of Miles's hold, quickly stands, and gives him a titty twister before dashing away. Miles chases after him around the couch in the living room.

"As evidenced." Aaron takes another sip of his coffee. He's by far the most laid back of the three guys. Miles is aggressively type A and Joel is soft-spoken but more dramatic.

I smack his shoulder. "Aren't you supposed to be the mature one? Seeing as you're getting married in two months."

"Don't get him started," Miles says, walking back into the kitchen and grabbing a bottle of water from the fridge. He hands one to Joel, who is right behind him.

"Yeah, he'll tell you exactly how long down to the minute."

"Only because I have a countdown timer going," Aaron says.

"And you're obsessed with your fiancée," Mackie sings.

"Are you surprised by that? You're the ones who insisted *for years* we were in love."

"Because you were. Dumbass." Joel hoists himself onto the counter, and I laugh as Aaron gives him the finger.

Yeah, we're definitely still twelve, but I wouldn't have it any other way.

Aaron smacks my chest. "Hey, are you going to talk to Coach M today?"

The room is suddenly silent as everyone waits for my response.

"Yeah. I'm going to stop in before my first class."

"Good."

He's been on his own journey with baseball after injuring his hand senior year of high school. He was all set to play ball in college. He's an incredible pitcher. He's finally getting the right treatment now and hopes to pitch again this year, but for the last two he's been an amazing coach. Aaron was the first to jump in and encourage me to find a different future that still involves baseball.

Some people don't get it. *Just walk away. It's a part of the past.* But when something is ingrained in you to your very core, when it's your coping mechanism and your stress reliever, you can't just walk away.

I'll never be able to play like I used to, but I'm determined to still be involved with the team.

Baseball is a part of me, and it always will be.

I'm a chickenshit.

All I need to do is walk inside the athletic building, go up to the third floor, and knock on the head baseball coach's door.

For some reason, my feet don't want to move.

It's almost like if I go up there, it's the final acknowledgment that I'm never going to play again.

That's stupid as fuck, because that's been obvious since I was lying in a hospital bed, unable to get up to take a shit by myself.

I'm not someone who gets nervous easily. I'm extroverted, friendly, and too confident for my own good. But this is hard. It feels a little too much like swallowing my pride. Or begging. Not things I'm used to doing.

Someone walks past me into the building, and instead of following them, I pull my phone from my pocket and text my best friend back home, Nick.

Me: Tell me to stop being a chickenshit.

The three little dots appear in an instant.

Nick: Stop being a whiny little scaredy cat, put your big boy boxers on, and go do whatever thing you need to do.

Me: You have such a way with words.

Nick: You're stalling.

Me: You don't even know why I'm asking.

Nick: Irrelevant. If you're asking me to give you a push, it's because it's something you want to do. Since I'm not there to hold your hand, you'll just have to be brave and do it on your own.

Me: Like you'd hold my hand.

Nick: Yeah, no. That's reserved for when you're almost dying in the hospital. Right now, I'd give you a shove. Or drag you by the ear.

Me: Leigh's rubbing off on you.

Me: Do NOT make a sex joke about your wife. She'll know and yell at both of us.

Nick: Then stop texting me and go do the thing. Seize the day. Carpe diem. Hakuna matata. Live laugh love. Insert applicable mantra here.

I laugh at that. That's what I wanted when I texted him—for him to pull me out of my head.

Nick can act like a five-year-old to cheer me up and get me out of my head, or he can settle in for a lengthy conversation about the complexities of life. It's what makes us such good friends. And he's always shown up for me whenever I need him.

Me: Okay, you've convinced me.

Nick: Excellent timing because a toddler meltdown is imminent, and I need to go.

Me: Have fun with that.

Nick was a teen dad, but life worked out how it was supposed to for him. He and his wife are insanely in love, and he's a great dad. I almost envy him. Not the teen pregnancy part, but how happy he is with his life. He proves every day that it doesn't matter if you're young, you can find your person and start a beautiful life with them.

And that's enough sappiness for me this morning.

As if I'm running from those thoughts, my feet start moving and I finally make it through the doors of the building. The coach's office is easy enough to find, and I quickly knock on the door before I can second-guess myself.

"Come on in."

I push the door open and see Coach M behind his desk. I saw him from a distance last year when I came up for a couple of games, but I've never met him before. Aaron mentioned me to him, though, so I'm not showing up out of the blue.

He looks up, his piercing gaze instantly connecting with mine, sizing me up. I stand tall, letting him break eye contact first.

"Can I help you?"

"I hope so. My name's Trevor Matteny, Aaron—"

"Ah, Cooper's friend. He mentioned you'd be stopping in. Come sit."

Coach M is in his late forties with a serious look in his eyes, but the laugh lines around his mouth tell me it's all a hard-ass coach act.

"Thanks for meeting with me."

"No problem. So, Aaron didn't tell me much about you, only that playing isn't an option anymore, but you'd like to be involved with the team in some way."

"That's the gist. I was playing D1 ball for Syracuse and was supposed to be looking forward to the draft about now, but my dumb ass went snowboarding with my friend in January and bounced off a few trees."

"And the doctors were definitive about you not playing again?"

"There's only so much rehabbing you can do with a fully replaced knee, a partially replaced hip, and an entire leg that's held together by rods and pins. Moving boxes the other day took me out, so anything beyond a pick-up game with my friends is out for me."

He nods slowly. "I'm sorry to hear that, and I understand the desire not to lose something that's woven into who you are. It's why I offered Aaron the coaching position. What exactly are you looking for? I don't have any paid coaching positions available, but I'll always take volunteers."

"I don't know exactly. I'm studying sports management now, and I guess I was thinking—well, I was thinking I'd take whatever I can get. Ideally, I'd like to see the behind the scenes of the team, maybe? Something working with you or the other coaches. And yeah, I'd love to be involved with practices and stuff. I don't need anything paid, but the locker room, the field, the game calls to me. I'm not ready to leave it behind."

I shift in my chair, again that sensation of begging crawling up my spine, but then Coach M smiles.

"How long did you play?"

"Pretty much my whole life. It's something my dad introduced me to at a young age, and I fell in love with it."

"From the behind-the-scenes things, what are you hoping to get from that? Just being close to the game or preparation for your future?"

"Both, I guess. I'm leaning toward wanting to work with some kind of sports development or management, maybe in a school or college or even a minor league team."

He nods and claps his hands together. "I have some ideas, but I want to look into a couple of things. Can you stop in tomorrow morning around the same time?"

"Yes, sir."

I stand and extend my hand to his.

He shakes it, a smile coming through.

"I'll see you tomorrow."

"Thank you."

The second I'm outside his office, I let out a whoosh of air. I did it, and to my surprise, I feel lighter now. I don't think I realized how much facing this reality and finding a way forward was weighing on me. Not that it's a magic solution to the trauma I caused myself and am still healing from, but it's progress, and that's the whole point in this fresh start, *Eat, Pray, Love*, sparkly rom-com journey I'm on now.

With that weight off my shoulders, I set off to find my way across campus and make today my bitch.

4

Book Boys Are Better

Chelsea

TODAY HAS NOT BEEN what I was expecting.

I anticipated some uncertainty, some anxiety, and probably for something small to trigger me. But today has been... great.

I've liked my classes so far, but the shining star of the day has been Promise Advocacy.

From the second I walked in the door, I knew I was safe.

It wasn't one specific thing, but a low-key vibe. Maybe it's the quiet space with calming music or the comforting maternal energy, but whatever it is, it's working. If I'd had a place like this to go after I was raped, maybe I wouldn't have crashed and broken as badly as I did.

Promise Advocacy is a safe space for women who have faced sexual assault, sexual abuse, or rape. A main focus there is outreach, working with local high schools and the college to provide resources and education to help prevent sexual assault and rape and to give girls and women who have been through it a safe place.

They're killing it.

A lot of it has to do with the director, Kristen. Up until today, I'd only spoken with her over video call, but she has a decisive yet calming presence. When I applied for this internship—which is extremely competitive, and I got lucky that one of the interns from last year transferred schools so there was an availability—I told my story. It was the first time I'd written out what happened to me and let that story out, but it felt good, and my past experience—horrible as it was—is probably part of what made me a good fit to work here. They have peer counselors and support groups and they want their staff to come in understanding the gravity of the work they do. I get it. And I still need that support too.

Like she knew that, Kristen was waiting by the reception desk to meet me when I walked in, and when we got back to her office, she asked if I was okay. She genuinely cared about what my experience was and where I was at in the healing process. She also reminded me that Promise's services are open to me too. I was lucky growing up that I didn't have to work crappy jobs because I helped at my family's campground, but I've heard of the toxic work environments friends and classmates have had to endure, and it's obvious Promise isn't anything like that. Even though I spent most of the time there today being shown around and meeting people, I already had that feeling of belonging. It's where I'm supposed to be. It's where I can make a difference and help others.

Every experience today was a positive one, and it all left me feeling fantastic. Like the old version of me. The one who was always upbeat, outgoing, and ready for some fun.

Which must be why I'm driving off campus to a lake house a girl I met three hours ago invited me to.

Although, to be fair, I met her at Promise, where she also interns. Rae McKinley was one of the first people Kristen introduced me to today. Rae has been working there for the last two years, and was the one to show me around and introduce me to everyone there. She took it a step further by offering to introduce me to her best friends—all seven of them, who she lives with.

I immediately said yes, then second-guessed it. But when I clarified to make sure it wasn't a party, her eyes met mine, and a moment of understanding passed between us. We don't know each other's stories, but we've lived each other's pain. Then she told me whether I joined her tonight or not, their house is a safe space. It only took her a few minutes to understand what I needed to hear and genuinely care in a way my supposed friends back home couldn't do over the course of nine months.

Hearing Rae talk about her friends, how they grew up, and her adorable relationship with her fiancé solidified my decision as the right one.

I want to make new friends and let the playful side of me out again. I'm following her there, so I have my own car and can leave whenever I want to. Rae said this would be like a family dinner, which also made me feel more comfortable. Still, I texted Robbie the address the second I had it. My gut says I'm safe, but I'm still going to be careful, pay attention to my surroundings, and stay away from alcohol.

Not that avoiding alcohol is difficult. I've been doing it since I was assaulted.

Before everything happened, I was a party girl. Always down to have a good time. I've never liked getting wasted, but getting a little tipsy, dancing with random guys, and maybe hooking up was what I looked forward to. And meeting new people. I always loved that.

The night I was assaulted was different, though. I always used the buddy system, either with my volleyball teammates or my suitemates. But the teammates I went out with that night were both fawning over some hockey player, and they both ditched me to go hook up with him *together*. Which would've been fine... if they'd told me. Instead, one minute they were looking out for me, and the next they were gone.

A guy who seemed fun and into me played pool with me, and we had a couple of drinks and kissed, but somewhere along the way, he slipped something into one of my drinks, and now everything about that night is hazy and muddled.

After what he did to me, I wouldn't leave my dorm for two days or talk to anyone. I was catatonic and finally the RA called my dad. It wasn't until both he and Robbie were there that I admitted what happened. They took me to the hospital, and I had a sexual assault exam and bloodwork done. They got some DNA, but it didn't match anyone in the system, and unsurprisingly, my bloodwork showed trace evidence that I was drugged. Which explains why my memory from that night was too blurry to give any defining details of the guy—besides short blond hair and hazel eyes. Without much more to go on, nothing ever came of it.

After all that hell, my dad took me home, and I spent the next few months refusing to do anything but hide in a dark bedroom.

I'm still battling the shame of not fighting for myself sooner. My therapist told me no two people have the same process, and I was handling it the best I could, but that hasn't stopped my guilt. Or the shame around being the rape cliché. Drunk girl at a party.

Nope.

I am not going there tonight. I refuse to. I'm going to have fun because Rae seems like a fun mix of endearing, sweet, and totally spicy, and if that's any indication of her friend group, I think we'll get along great.

As I follow her car into the driveway, my mouth literally drops staring up at the massive house. She said her friend's dad owns the place. He must be loaded. Because *holy shit.*

I climb out of the car, taking in the huge deck and large windows.

Rae smiles sheepishly as she walks over to me. "If I remind you that eight of us live here and share the space, will it seem less over the top?"

I laugh. "I don't think that's possible. I swear I'm only a little jealous."

"Well, when you see how obnoxious we can be, this big house might suddenly seem small."

She leads me up the stairs to the deck, but before we get to the front door, someone calls out to her from the driveway. Rae turns and a smile lights up her face as a short blonde hurries up the stairs toward us. She's got an overstuffed messenger bag on her shoulder with a stethoscope hanging out of it.

Rae introduces the girl as her sister, and my gaze bounces between the blonde with blue eyes—Sarah—and Rae with her chestnut hair and golden hazel eyes.

My surprise must be evident because Sarah says, "Looking for the resemblance?"

Whoops. I laugh. "Kinda."

"I'm adopted."

Rae wraps her arm around Sarah. "Yep. We were best friends first, then the universe decided I get to keep her forever."

That reaffirms my gut feeling about Rae. She's clearly the type of person who cares deeply for those close to her—and likely people she barely knows at all.

Rae rests her head on Sarah's shoulder, and Sarah kisses her head. I smile watching the interaction. *Family dinner.*

"What do you think?" Rae asks. "Ready to meet everyone?"

"Bring it on."

It sounds like it's going to be chaotic, but I'm up for the challenge. If anything, I'm too intrigued to leave now.

Rae swings the front door open and my breath catches again as I look around the large open space with shining hardwood floors and a fancy kitchen.

"Damn."

"It's pretty awesome," Sarah says.

"Looks like the party has already started." Rae leads the way across the room to the sliding doors that open to a large back deck. "Hey." The second she's on the deck, everyone stops to look at her. "I brought some fresh blood. This is Chelsea. I work with her at Promise. She just transferred here, so I thought I'd bring her over to meet everyone and hopefully gain some new friends."

And there are a few—though not all of them—sitting out here.

Manning the grill is a tall guy with long-ish but well-styled black hair and an easy smile. "Hey, nice to meet you. I'm Miles." He gestures with the spatula he's holding. "I'm the resident cook around here."

"Rude! I help!" a thin girl with curly brown hair yells from the far end of the outdoor table. "I'm Mackenzie. Nice to meet you!"

The girl next to her, who has long strawberry blonde hair, smiles brightly. "Hey, I'm Amanda. I'm the most recent addition to crazy town. Hope you'll stick around and join us. Although, once they have you in their clutches, there's really no getting out."

I can't help but laugh at that. These are my kind of people. The kind I would have gravitated to if I'd met them at my previous college. Fun, relaxed, but wild around the edges. And the love they all have for each other is palpable, even when their words are nothing but sass.

Rae points across the table toward a boy with light brown hair, and I wonder if it's her fiancé. "And that's—"

"Well, well, who do we have here?" The smooth, indulgent voice that dances through the air sends a chill up my spine.

Rae spins around. "A new friend, so be on your best behavior."

"No promises."

I spin to face him, and *holy shit.* I thought this house would be the most gorgeous thing I'd see tonight. I was wrong.

The guy I'm praying isn't Rae's fiancé is tall and mostly lean, but with defined muscles, especially his arms. A mop of curly brown hair sits atop his head, mussed in the sexiest way, and his brown eyes, so dark they almost look black, meet mine. His expression changes and those eyes light with something like recognition. And happiness. I swear pure joy is radiating off him.

My cheeks heat—fuck, my whole body flushes—and I can confidently say I haven't felt anything like this in a long time. I haven't *wanted* to. This butterflies-whirling-in-my-stomach, sugar rush, cotton-candy-in-my-brain feeling.

Anything having to do with guys has been a big hell no for me for a while now, but I think this guy has broken me.

"Hi," I breathe, still drinking him in. He's gorgeous, but there's something else too. Like there's a tether to my soul, and he's tugging on it, pulling me closer.

Okay, maybe I've been reading too many fantasy romance books.

The concept of mates is fictional, right?

What am I thinking right now? And, oh god. Please don't let him be Rae's fiancé. Wouldn't be the best start to a friendship with her if I go all starry-eyed over the guy she's madly in love with.

He steps forward and holds out his hand.

"Nice to meet you. I'm Trevor."

I don't remember what Rae said her fiancé's name is, but I know it wasn't that. She told me about her friends earlier and for some reason, his name stuck out, maybe because she mentioned he transferred here this year too.

My fingertips brush his palm as my hand slides into his and little electric charges dance on my skin before shooting down my spine and then straight to my heart.

What is happening right now?

Is this real?

Am I still breathing?

But his warm hand wrapped around mine feels too real to be a dream, so I snap back to reality, find my brain again, and introduce myself. "It's nice to meet you. I'm Chelsea. Rae said you just transferred up here this semester. So did I."

His smile goes from bright to downright devastating. He finally lets go of my hand, and while I immediately miss the warmth of it, at least I get to hear his voice again. "Maybe we can get to know campus together."

"I'd like that."

There's a small twist in my gut. I'm not sure if it's excitement or fear. Would I want to spend time alone on campus with this guy I don't know? I mean, there's *something* happening between us right now, but I've trusted too easily before. Yet, I'm still staring at him, fucking captivated.

Before anything else can happen, though, a very different smooth voice sounds.

"Hey, beautiful."

This one does nothing for me, other than make me look at Rae because it's obvious *this* is her man.

Rae's all swoony-eyed as she strolls over to him. "Hi, Ace."

I don't think Ace was his name either, but did it start with an A? Aiden? No. Aaron. Or Ace, apparently. I'm sure there's a story there.

Despite how enamored I am with Trevor, I can't tear my gaze from Rae... until the two of them start kissing. *Really* kissing.

Next to me, Sarah stifles a laugh.

"Are they always—"

"This nauseating?" she cuts in. "Yep."

"But it's better than them being whiny, emotional messes."

I glance over my shoulder at the guy across the table, whose name I still don't know.

Rae sticks her middle finger up at him as she pulls her face from Aaron's and turns around.

"Oh, yeah. Chelsea, this is Joel," Sarah says. "He's—" Then her cheeks go pink and she sputters for the right words about who he is. Which makes me think there's something going on there.

Rae steps in to save her. "His family owns the house."

Joel feigns offense. "That's all I am to you?"

Rae rolls her eyes. "He's also like my very annoying brother and was my first best friend. We're where this little group began. The OGs." She holds out her fist across the table.

"The OGs." Joel bumps her fist in return, and I stifle a laugh.

I'm definitely getting the family vibes here, and if I hadn't been introduced to Sarah already, I'd have assumed Joel was Rae's brother.

"And they never let us forget it." Aaron takes Rae's hand and leads her around the table. He drops into a chair next to Joel, and instead of pulling out a chair for Rae, he drags her down onto his lap. Which makes the hearts in her eyes get bigger.

"Absolutely nauseating," I whisper to Sarah. Even if the clear love between them makes something burn inside me.

I love romance stories for a reason.

"Chelsea." That silky voice draws my attention away from everyone else.

And speaking of romance... Trevor pulls out a chair for me, then offers me his hand to help me sit down.

What the freaking what?

My first boyfriend was a sweet and adorably nerdy guy. He lived next door. He was thoughtful, but he never did anything like that. He opened my car door, even pulled out my chair, but the way Trevor waits until I'm sitting and pushes the chair in gently is just different.

Another warning bell goes off in my gut.

It could be an act.

Smooth, charming boys can also be liars.

But Rae wouldn't be friends with that type of person, would she?

I take a deep breath and try to channel the old me. The one who didn't inherently not trust people. I can take this as it comes and see what happens.

Then he says my name again, and my brain goes haywire for a second.

"Chelsea, can I get you something to drink? We have beer, wine—"

"Something non-alcoholic?" I try to keep my voice from sounding squeaky. It's not exactly a test—I have no plans to drink tonight—but his reaction will be telling.

"You like fruit punch?" he asks.

I laugh because that was the last thing I was expecting. "Sure."

"I'll be right back."

"Hey, what about the rest of us?" Joel calls after him.

"Fuck off. You live here."

I bite my lip to keep from laughing. Definitely family vibes.

The banter continues, but I'm realizing I just let a guy leave the room and get me a drink. Which goes against my major rule of never letting someone I don't know incredibly well make me anything to drink.

It's not like he can put alcohol in it because I'd be able to taste it.

But...

This is a safe space.

That's what Rae told me.

If she's been through something similar to what I have, she wouldn't take those words lightly.

When Trevor returns and sets the drink in front of me, I unconsciously look at Rae first. Her eyes meet mine and she gives me a reassuring smile as she drops her gaze to my drink.

Pushing past all my fears, I keep a smile on my face as I reach for the cup and take a drink.

Again, I want to laugh. It tastes delicious and not unlike something I'd have at a kid's birthday party. Not that there's anything wrong with that.

"Ooh. That's really good. What is it?"

"Fruit punch and tangerine seltzer." He shakes the can in his hand. He's not drinking either. I'm not sure if I want to take that as a good sign or bad, so I shut my brain up and focus on the moment.

"It's delicious. Thank you."

"Hey, the meat is about ready. Someone want to grab all the rolls, condiments, and sides?" the tall one with dark hair says. Miller? No. Miles.

"I'll get them," Rae volunteers.

Sarah jumps up too. "I'll help."

And apparently that's code, because suddenly all the girls are offering to help and I'm being dragged inside with them.

In the kitchen, Rae goes right to pulling food out of the fridge as Sarah helps, but Amanda looks at me.

"What is happening between you and Trevor?"

My cheeks heat again. So that insane tension was obvious to everyone else too. Great. The girls all look at me, and while that lack of trust rears its ugly head deep in my gut, I've always craved strong female friendships. I thought I had them, but it's become clear I don't. This little group? There's a connection between them that's surprisingly deep, and I think this is them inviting me into it.

I swallow and look around at them before answering. "I don't know. I swear when I saw him, it felt like my heart stopped. Obviously, he's drop-dead sexy, but when he touched my hand, I felt this—"

"Tingly feeling? Like you've always known him and like you'll know him forever?" Rae asks.

Is she in my brain? Is there actually a hive mind thing here? "Yes. How did you know that?"

Rae's eyes light up as she glances out the window at Aaron. "Been there. *Still* there."

"I feel like I'm getting way ahead of myself. I just met him. But damn it, I want to *know* him. I'm so glad you invited me here tonight." I blow out a breath, my words surprising me. Because I do want to know him. And after everything, that's terrifying.

Rae laughs. "I had a feeling about you. Guess I was right."

This is my chance. To quell my fears. To make sure I'm safe.

"Is he a good guy? I mean, you all seem pretty nice, but he's not a jackass player who's going to break my heart, is he?" I go for a twist on the truth. Rae has an idea of what I've experienced, but I'm not ready to get into that yet. Still, it doesn't stop me from lowering my voice and letting a hint of my vulnerability shine through. "I've been through enough."

I'm surprised when Sarah is the one who speaks. "Trevor is *amazing.* Truly. He can pick up girls, but he doesn't play them. He has never been that type."

"Yeah, we don't hang out with those types of guys." Rae squeezes my arm, her eyes meeting mine as she answers the subtext of my question.

"Sometimes you just date them to avoid your feelings for the love of your life," Mackenzie deadpans. Though I have a feeling she's talking about an actual player and not my experience.

Rae rolls her eyes hard. "It's been four years! I was sixteen." She shakes her head and looks at me. "Some things will *never* die."

"Nope," Amanda teases. "And I didn't even know you then."

"Anyway," Sarah continues. "Trevor is caring and the absolute best boyfriend."

My eyes go wide and I almost jolt back. "There's nothing going on with you guys, is there? It seemed like there was something between you and Joel." I really, *really* don't want to be messing with some other girl's guy. And that would make him a total dick. But they barely paid each other any attention so...

Amanda laughs at my words and then at the way Sarah mutters, "Something."

I relax a little, but Amanda keeps pushing at Sarah. Lots of sister energy here, even between the ones who aren't siblings.

"What was that?" Amanda asks. "It was a little garbled."

"Shut up. We're not talking about Joel. We're talking about Trevor." Sarah meets my gaze. "There's nothing going on with Trevor anymore, but we were each other's first... everything. I'm not saying that to freak you out. He's incredible, but it wasn't the right fit for us. We're good friends now, but that's all. And if you need reassurance about that..." She glares at the rest of the girls, who are enjoying this way too much. "I might possibly have feelings for Joel."

"Surprised you didn't choke on those words," Mackenzie says.

Sarah ignores that, her gaze coming right back to me. "Trev's been hurt, too. But I promise, he's one of the good ones."

There's something about the emotion of her voice as she speaks that makes me believe it, and it puts me at ease to the point that I almost feel bad for asking now.

"Okay. Thanks."

Miles sticks his head in the door. "You guys done with your girl talk? I'm fuckin' starving."

"Coming," Rae calls. She shoves something into everyone's hands and we make our way back outside and sit down.

Trevor's smile is bright and almost childlike as I join him again. Miles passes around plates, but Trevor grabs mine.

"Anything here you're not interested in?"

"It all looks great."

Then he dutifully fills my plate with a bit of everything.

"Can I have a little extra potato salad? It's my favorite."

"Of course." He grins as he adds more to my plate and sets it in front me. "Let me know if you want more of anything."

Something hits me at that moment. He didn't get me a drink for any other reason than to be thoughtful. It's so stupid that it makes me want to cry, but I'd forgotten—or maybe stopped believing—that guys like that exist.

"Thanks."

I wait until his plate is full and sitting in front of him before I start eating. An easy conversation bounces around the table as they discuss the first day of classes.

I settle in and enjoy the delicious food. And the company.

It's cozy and relaxed. Rae called it a family dinner because these people *are* family to each other.

Trevor's arm rests over the back of my chair, and after a moment, his fingers twirl through my hair. That ridiculous tingly, sparkly feeling floats through me again, and combined with the comfort of this place and these people, my fears fall away and the playful side of me comes out again.

Trevor shifts in his chair, moving the tiniest bit closer to me, and I take it as an invitation.

Slowly, I rest my hand on his thigh. He tenses for half a second, then relaxes and gives the slightest tug on a strand of my hair.

I grab my drink and take another sip, trying to cool myself down because I can see myself getting into trouble with this boy. In the best possible way.

Trevor

I don't know what's happening.

When I let my idea of the future shift from baseball and on to other things I wanted, I wasn't expecting the universe to drop my dream girl at my feet.

This *almost* makes up for the tree thing.

When I saw Chelsea standing on the deck, all long wavy-curly auburn hair and the kind of curves I can imagine my body pressed against, it was like seeing my fantasy come to life. But then our eyes met and her hand touched mine, and for a second, I believed love at first sight was a real thing.

I'm not stupid enough to believe I'm in love with her, but the connection was instant—and that's leaving the physical attraction out of it.

Though she seemed a little shy or uncertain to start, as she settled in, she opened up and I got to see the spicier side of her as she quipped about Aaron and Rae's PDA along with the rest of us, ribbed Sarah for the way she was looking at Joel, and casually teased Miles about how particular he was being in setting up the logs in the fire pit.

Between hanging out with everyone and now the two of us alone, we've been sitting by the fire for hours now.

"No way you've read *A Court This Cruel and Lovely*," Chelsea says, standing up and inspecting the marshmallow she's been roasting. She gave everyone a whole tutorial on how to make them when the fire first started dying down to coals.

When I asked her how she knew the perfect way to roast a marshmallow, she smiled and told me she wasn't going to reveal all her secrets and that I had to work for those.

That playful smile of hers hits me square in the chest every time I get to see it.

I put another marshmallow on my stick and rest it on the edge of the fire pit.

"Tell me you're not going to say something sexist about how men can't read romance novels."

She rolls her eyes as she sits back down in the chair next to me and pulls her marshmallow off the stick.

"No, but it's not as popular as some of the bigger ones out there like *A Court of Thorns and Roses*."

"I've read that series too."

She purses her lips as she stares at me, then a knowing smile spreads across her face. "You started reading romance books with a girlfriend. Sarah?"

My eyes dart to her and I almost drop my stick into the fire pit. "She told you about us?"

"It came up in passing."

She takes a bite of her marshmallow, and it takes everything in me not to stare at her lips as she licks some of the stickiness off them.

"How long were you two together?"

"A few years."

Her eyes go wide. "Really? When did you break up?"

"Almost four years ago. We started dating pretty much as soon as we were allowed to—around thirteen. Then we broke up halfway through junior year of high school. Took a bit, but we're good friends again now." I rotate my stick to get my marshmallow evenly browned, since the queen of marshmallow roasting is sitting next to me. "For the record, you're wrong, though. I didn't start reading romance books with Sarah. Mysteries were our thing. I don't typically read basic romance. Usually it's fantasy stuff because my mom and my sister read a lot of those types of books, and I got tired of them trying to drag me into their conversations when I had no idea what they were talking about. It started with *ACOTAR* and it's been all downhill from there," I say with a grin. Mostly because that series was the base level of enjoyment, but I've actually found several really great series since then. *A Court This Cruel and Lovely* being the start of one of them.

"That's kind of adorable."

I groan in response and she laughs.

"So, you have a sister?"

"Kind of. It's not biological, but we grew up together as best friends and my mom pretty much raised her in all the ways that matter. We consider each other siblings. Her name's Hyla, and you'll probably hear her mentioned, especially if you hang out with the girls more. She and Mackenzie have a history."

Chelsea tilts her head. "Is that your not-so-subtle way of letting me know she's not a threat?"

"Not exactly, but I know how people can be about male-female friendships. Aaron and Rae are a perfect example of why people could be concerned, but Rae and Joel are the perfect example of not needing to be concerned at all. Even Amanda asked if Hyla and I had ever hooked up." I pause, swallowing back my nausea because *ew*. "But we've always had a sibling relationship."

"And you have your own little book club with her and your mom. So cute."

Her wild eyes dance. I've never seen anything like them before. They're mostly blue, but close to the pupil they're brown.

"Yes, we've established I'm *adorable*. What about you?"

She flips her lip out in a pout. "Are you saying I'm not adorable?"

"Only one of the many words I could use to describe you. But I meant what got you into fantasy romance?"

"I'm putting a pin in the *what other words you could use to describe me* question that's on the tip of my tongue. I've always loved romance in general because, no offense, book boys are better than real ones."

My eyebrows shoot up, but I bite my lip, holding back a smirk. I'll take that challenge.

Then Chelsea continues. "Romance is a genre written primarily by women for women. So they know what their audience wants. They give us a healthy representation of reliable men, who are not infallible, but work hard to be good humans. That's a lot more than we get from most men in real life. Romance is a safe place. I've been leaning heavier into fantasy lately because..." She sighs and drops her voice, looking at the fire. "I've needed more of an escape from reality lately."

I reach over and run my hand down her arm. "I get it."

We haven't talked about why either of us transferred here, and I'm not in a rush to do that. Tonight is about getting to know each other, feeling things out, and seeing if the crazy connection we felt can actually lead somewhere.

She turns toward me, her lips parting slightly, and it takes all my willpower not to stare at them. Before she says anything, a shiver runs through her.

I stand up and hold out my hand. "We should head inside. The fire's dying down and now that the cool fall air is creeping in, nights get chilly."

She uses my hand to pull herself up, and I grab the nearby bucket of water to douse the fire. Then we head inside, passing Amanda, Mackie, and Miles sitting on the back deck on the way in.

Rae almost fell asleep sitting on Aaron's lap by the fire, so after apologizing to Chelsea, she let Aaron take her upstairs. Chelsea didn't seem to mind, and we sat by the fire together talking as everyone else slowly left.

Joel's in the kitchen as we pass by, but Sarah went upstairs a while ago. She's in the accelerated nursing program and already working her butt off.

"So much warmer in here," Chelsea says happily.

"There are a ton of blankets too, if you need one."

"Thanks."

I grab two bottles of water and join her on the couch.

"So, what were we talking about?"

"How much better fantasy men are than real men."

Joel snickers as he walks by, and I throw my middle finger up at him.

"You're determined to hurt my feelings, aren't you?"

"Just making sure you know I have very high standards. If you're not going to kill your way across a continent to save me, is it really true love?"

I groan. "Ugh. Now I have to take up murdering people? Impossible standards."

She laughs, and God, I love that sound. Even if the way it pierces my soul scares me.

She throws her legs up on my lap, making herself comfortable in the corner of the couch.

"Is being a footrest another standard I have to live up to?"

"No, but it's a plus." She looks around the lake house. "I guess I could give you a bonus point or two for having such a sweet house, especially with the lake view."

"Even if it's not technically my house?"

She smirks. "We'll ignore that."

"Didn't get enough good views growing up in Birch Lake?"

She briefly mentioned her hometown earlier, but she didn't say much else about it.

"Birch Lake isn't as big as this one, and our house wasn't on the water, though I spent every summer by the lake."

"With your friends?"

Her lips pull flat for a half a second, then she shakes her head. "No. With my dad and his family. They own a campground and cabin rental company. I spent most of my time riding around in a golf cart with my dad or my uncle—who is more like a big brother to me."

"We camped a few times at Birch Lake when I was a kid. Mom loved vacationing there because it was close to home, but still felt far away. The first year, I had my heart set on tent camping, but it was this disastrous trip because it poured most of the time. The tent leaked. My mom wasn't thrilled, so the next few years we went, my dad rented a cabin instead."

Her brows lift. "Do you remember the name of the campground? There are a few, so I'll try not to be too offended if it wasn't ours."

"Oh crap. What was it called? I can remember the sign. It had big yellow letters with a beaver, I think?"

She laughs. "Birch's Cozy Cabins. And yes, the sign has a beaver. We call him Buddy."

She's smiling, but I'm... I don't know what I am. Shocked, but in a good way. We camped there every year until I was ten, then everything changed. And Chelsea's family owns that company. She was there.

"Do you think we ever saw each other? Played together?"

Her eyes find mine. "I don't know. I snuck off to the playground whenever I could." She tilts her head. "But I feel like I would've remembered you."

I get a big dumbass smile on my face when she says that. "Why do you say that?"

"Because you're memorable. Your smile. Your charm. Those eyes. I swear, I've never seen eyes that dark before." Then she rests her hand on my arm. "And this. I would've remembered this. How I feel when I'm around you."

I lean in closer. "And how do you feel?"

"Crazy. Wild. Like me again." I don't understand what that means, but I don't have time to figure it out before she continues. "My heart's beating out of my chest. I—"

"Chelsea..." My voice is low and gravelly.

Before I know what's happening, she's straddling my lap, her fingers curling through my hair, her gorgeous face only centimeters from mine.

Her breaths are sharp and uneven. For a second, she doesn't move, but then her lips are on mine, and *fuck*.

Fuck, fuck, fuck.

If I thought I felt a connection before, it's a thousand times stronger now. Her lips feel like they belong on mine. Forever.

I run my hands up her back, still letting her take the lead, but when she skims her tongue over my bottom lip, it's all over.

I push my tongue into her mouth, and I'm officially a goner. Rest in peace me. I've died and am currently in heaven, surrounded by a curvy goddess who makes me forget everything else and feel like I used to.

I clench my eyes shut as I fist her shirt, barely holding in a moan. I've never gotten so turned on so quickly, but Chelsea is like a drug and with each little bit she gives me, I'm desperate for more.

Her soft tongue teases mine, and then she gently bites my bottom lip.

I flex and release my hands, at the edge of insanity as she pours herself into me, taking what she wants and playing with me when she feels like it.

She flicks her tongue against mine, and as much as I try to get my blood to flow anywhere else, it's all headed straight for my dick.

When she shifts slightly on my lap, I'm sure she must feel it, and I pull back, staring at her with lust-filled eyes.

But then her eyes widen, and everything crashes around me.

I don't know exactly what happened. Was it my hardening cock? Because I really tried to prevent that. The rasp in my voice? Because I couldn't stop that if I wanted to.

Genuine fear washes over her, and she scrambles off my lap.

I stand, reaching for her. "What is it? What's wrong?"

She looks around the room in a panic, then grabs her purse from the coffee table. "I—um—I shouldn't have... This was..." she stammers, not making any sense.

"I'm sorry if that was too much. I—"

"I need to go." Her eyes dart to the door.

"Let me walk you out."

"No," she shrieks. Then she clears her throat. "I—I'll be—"

"Everything okay in here?" Amanda's voice is soft as she approaches, Mackie trailing behind her.

"Yes. Uh. I need to get home." She steps closer to Amanda. "Is this, um, a safe neighborhood?"

Amanda glances at me for half a second, then focuses on Chelsea again. "It is, but how about if I walk out with you anyway?"

Chelsea's gaze flits to me, but it's not long enough to lock eyes with her. Then she's turning toward the door. "Yeah, thanks."

"No problem," Amanda says. Her voice is gentle, but firm, and though she seems a little confused, she doesn't seem as confused as me, and I wonder what I'm missing.

I'd never push her—or anyone—any further than they wanted to go. I pulled away because I was worried she'd be uncomfortable.

Once Chelsea and Amanda are out the door, Mackie steps up to me, looking as confused as I feel.

"What happened?"

"I have no fucking idea."

5

Coffee Can Fix It

Trevor

I SLEPT LIKE SHIT last night.

When I get to the kitchen for breakfast, I'm in a grumbly mood. Hyla likes to call it my Mr. Grumpy Pants mood because of course she does.

I slide onto a stool at the kitchen counter, and a moment later, a plate of food and a cup of coffee appear in front of me.

I lift my head and find Rae, Aaron, and Miles staring back at me.

"Thanks."

I take a big bite of the hash browns and eggs. Thank fuck Miles can cook. I mean, I can too, but cooking before school is not high on my list of priorities. For Miles, it's a point of pride that he can feed everyone. Between a home-cooked breakfast and Aaron's coffee, I at least stop scowling.

Still, Rae leans over the counter on her elbows with a furrowed brow.

"Everything okay? After how you and Chelsea were last night, I wasn't expecting a scowl from you this morning."

I stop with my fork halfway to my mouth. Miles and Aaron lean against the kitchen counter, pretending like they're not listening intently for what my answer will be.

They love to meddle.

"It ended a little... weird."

"Weird how?"

"She kinda freaked out and ran off. Wouldn't even let me walk her out."

Rae's lips pull flat, and Aaron's eyes dart to her.

"Oh," Rae says softly, which makes me set my fork down with a clatter.

"Why does it seem like you know something I don't?"

She clears her throat. "I don't... *know* anything. And even if I did, it wouldn't be mine to tell. It would be Chelsea's."

Helpful.

"Well, thank you for that clear as mud assessment."

"Sorry." She squeezes my hand. "For whatever it's worth, I don't think it was about you."

"I'm trying to convince myself of that. Either way... would you—"

"I'll check in with her when I get to campus."

"Thanks." I finally take another bite, then a long drink of my coffee. "And, uh, if you don't think it will upset her, will you let her know I'm sorry if I did anything to—I don't know—make her uncomfortable? I tried... to let her take the lead."

Rae nods. "Of course. Like I said, I don't think it was you." She walks around the counter and pauses next to me, dropping her voice for a moment. "You're one of the good ones."

Then she heads upstairs and the guys both try to pretend they don't want to fawn like mother hens.

I hold a hand up. "I'll be fine, so go find someone else to fuss over."

Aaron puts his coffee mug in the sink. "Good. I just wanted to make sure you're okay before I ditch you." He smacks my shoulder as he walks by. "I'd put on headphones if you come upstairs in the next few minutes. Oh, and good luck with Coach M this morning."

And then he's gone, and it's only the papa bear of their ridiculous friend group staring at me.

"I'm fine," I grumble.

"You said that a minute ago, which means I believe it even less now than I did then."

"I'm a big boy. I can handle rejection."

He shakes his head. "Maybe, but that's not what the look on your face is about—or your conversation with Rae."

"I'm worried about her, okay?"

He stares at me, assessing, then breaks into a smile.

"You've got it bad," he says as he walks away, grinning like an asshole.

"Fuck you very much!" I call after him.

But unfortunately, he isn't wrong. I don't know exactly why or what I think happened, but there's this unsettling drive in me to make sure Chelsea's okay.

I shouldn't be worrying about it. It was one night. It's not my problem.

So why is it that I *want* it to be my problem?

Throughout my shower, I couldn't stop thinking about Chelsea. I wish it had been for dirty reasons, but no. I keep fixating on that mixture of fear and anguish in her eyes. I've seen that look before. Hyla has worn it more times than she ever should've had to thanks to her fucking parents.

The compulsion in me to want to fix that pain in Chelsea is probably not a good thing. We barely know each other, despite our lengthy conversation last night.

I should be focusing on my meeting with Coach M this morning, but since my brain is not in agreement with that, I get in my car with the plan to call Hyla and ask her advice on the drive to campus. In my distracted state, I don't notice her name flash on my screen until the ringtone blares from my speaker, making me jump and drop my phone.

As I reach down to grab it, I smack my head on the steering wheel.

I'm still cursing as I answer. "Are you trying to kill me?"

"Hm. Not high on my list of priorities. I like you too much. Besides, how could I kill you from this far away? Ooh, did an assassin attack you?"

"No, I wasn't expecting a call, and it gave me a nice jump scare." I rub the back of my head and turn my car on.

"Are you unfamiliar with the concept of phones? Or me calling you on them? You really shouldn't be surprised by either, especially not me calling you since you didn't call your mom or me last night to tell us about your first day. Rude, by the way."

Of course.

"Well, I got a little distracted when I met my dream girl and spent the night talking with her."

My phone connects to the Bluetooth in my car so I get full surround sound of Hyla's high-pitched squeak and her following words. "Details now."

I chuck my phone on the seat and pull out of my spot in the driveway.

"Only if you promise to give me some advice when you hear how it ends."

"Uh oh."

As I drive out of the lakeside development we live in, I give Hyla a rundown of what happened.

"Wow. I'm sorry it ended that way. For both of you. It sounds like she's struggling with something."

"Yeah, that's what I was thinking. What I'm not sure about is if I should try to talk to her or see if she's okay. Or if she would just turn and run the other way if she saw me again."

"Who would run from your adorable face?" she says teasingly.

"You mock my pain," I say flatly.

"You said Rae introduced you, right? Odds are you'll run into her again. Take it as it comes. Definitely don't hunt her down like a stalker. *That* would make her run."

"Even with my pretty face?"

"Fun fact: serial killers can have pretty faces too."

"Thanks for that."

I turn onto one of the roads that leads through campus, aiming for the parking lot closest to the athletic building. Since morning practices are over by now and afternoon practices are a while away, it's a fairly empty lot.

"Do you think I'm ridiculous for still caring about her? For being worried? We barely know each other. Should I just let it go?"

I park my car and lean back in my seat, waiting for Hyla's answer.

"You wouldn't be *you* if you didn't care, Trev. It's who you are. And it's how your dad raised you to be. I know you're afraid of caring too much and getting hurt, but we both know you won't be able to let this go. You felt a connection to her, and even if it's fast, that still means something. So don't be a dumbass and miss out on your chance with the girl who could be my sister-in-law one day. This is important."

I sigh and shake my head. "Way to make this all about you."

"Only because if you won't do it for yourself, you'll do it for me. Cause you love me."

I hate that she's right about that.

"Seriously. Do it for yourself. Don't second-guess how you feel. If you see her again, it's okay to check in. Just take it slowly."

"Pretty solid advice. Maybe you should become a therapist."

She scoffs. "Please. I'm too much of a mess to handle anyone else's problems. All you needed was some objectivity. And a kick in the pants—which I am always happy to provide."

"You're so generous. Really."

She laughs. "Well, I guess I'll let you go now that I've done my job."

"Thanks."

"Hey, how was the rest of your first day?"

"Pretty good. I'm on my way to meet with the baseball coach now."

"Good. I'm sure however you end up being with the team, it'll be great for you."

"Thanks, Hy. And thanks for the advice. You were moderately helpful."

"Asshole. Oh, and make sure you call your mom later or she'll be annoyed."

I pause with my hand near the ignition button. "Don't tell her about Chelsea."

"Don't worry. I won't get her hopes up."

"God," I groan. "I shouldn't have told you."

"I'm officially shipping you two now. Chelvor? Oh no, that's a horrible ship name. Trelsea? What's her last name? I need better ideas."

"And on that note, goodbye."

She laughs. "Bye. Love you."

"Love you too, sis."

Then I hang up and throw my car door open. I make it a point to call Hyla my sister regularly. It's the smallest way I have to remind her how important she is to me. She tends to forget she should be important to the people in her life—and herself. No matter how upbeat she sounded on the phone, I know she's been struggling lately. The last time she was like this, things didn't end well, and I don't want her to get to that place again.

As I walk to the athletic building, I put everything else behind me and focus on the present. Baseball. What it has the potential to look like now.

Coach M is waiting for me in his office, and with a bright smile on his face, he looks less like a hard ass this time.

"Matteny, have a seat."

"Morning, Coach."

I do as he said and take a seat, but my legs bounce and I'm drumming my thumbs on my thighs because there's so much nervous energy running through me.

"So, I spent some time yesterday thinking through some options for you. I'm always looking for volunteer coaches to help run practices and work with the players in small groups, but with what you're studying, it seems like a waste to only have you involved for practices. Plus, I can tell how hungry you are to be involved with the team. I want to give you as much of that as possible."

My eyes light up, and his smile gets bigger. It's a shame a coach who cares this much isn't working at a D1 school where he could make an even bigger difference. Most of my coaches cared about the game, but their players... not so much. My coach called me to scream at me after my snowboarding accident. I know what I did was dumb, but to be so angry you need to call and yell at a kid who's already broken is pretty shitty.

"One thing I always need help with is logistics. In my position as head coach, I have to handle everything from babysitting student grades and conduct, to budgeting for the team, to staying up to date on all NCAA rules and regulations to make sure the team and coaching staff are abiding by them. That doesn't even factor in planning out practices and team building opportunities and the behind the scenes of running a team. In the past, sometimes a team captain or assistant coach would take on some of those duties to assist me, but with you here, willing to learn, I'd like to offer you the position of my right-hand man. You'll help me out and learn plenty about the behind the scenes of college sports and team dynamics. If you're interested. The only downside is the pay is shit—by which I mean, it's nothing. I tried to find some room in the budget, but well, if you help me out, you'll see my problem."

"That's fine." I lean forward. "I don't need a paycheck. That sounds awesome. And exactly like what I was looking for."

"Good. And if you're interested, I'd love to have you as a volunteer coach too. You seem to know your shit when it comes to baseball, and I think you could be a positive influence on the team."

I set my jaw to keep my mouth from dropping open.

"You know, you're kind of giving me everything I want. I'm waiting for the inevitable but."

He chuckles. "Didn't you hear the part about no pay?"

"I don't care about the pay at all. I..." I suck in a long breath, letting it all sink in. "Thank you. For all of this. Everything falling apart the way it did... I wasn't expecting to be able to be so involved again, so I appreciate the chance to have baseball in my life again."

He gives a slight nod. "I was twenty-three and playing for a minor league team when I blew out my knee. When they told me I was done with baseball, I said no. Just because I couldn't play didn't mean I was giving up on the sport I loved. I never want to see anyone else have to either. I'm looking forward to working with you this coming season. I'll be in touch when we start coordinating practices, because I'd like you there for that too."

"I'm looking forward to it as well. Thanks, Coach."

He stands up and I do the same, grabbing my bag from the floor before meeting his gaze and reaching to shake his extended hand.

"Take care."

"Thanks. You too."

With that, I leave his office, thoroughly shocked and excited, and hoping it's a sign for a positive day ahead.

Chelsea

"I don't want to go to school," I whine, head resting on Robbie's kitchen table.

"Oof. I haven't had to do this with you since you were seven and Brittany Keller told the whole class you smelled like feet."

I lift my head and glare at him. "Is it necessary to bring that up right now?"

He shrugs. "I'm trying to remember how I got you to go back then."

"Probably by promising me a new book. Or a brownie sundae."

"You've always been obsessed with both. So... you go and I'll buy you a new shadow daddy book? Bat boys? Maybe one with a guy who rides a dragon?"

"I can buy myself books now."

"Okay, I'm out of ideas other than to tell you that you can't quit school on your second day when you haven't even been to half of your classes yet."

My lips pull flat as I stare at him.

I know all this. I know I need to go. But the upbeat energy I had yesterday died an ugly death last night. My stomach still hurts when I look back on it.

Not because Trevor did anything wrong. Because I did.

He followed the signals I gave. I climbed onto his lap. I kissed him. I was about to grind against him when a feeling of complete wrongness washed over me. Shame and guilt mixed together inside me with a hefty dose of discomfort. Then my mind went back to that night, and I realized no matter how badly I wished I could kiss a guy and have fun, I'm not that girl anymore.

Until last night, I hadn't kissed anyone else or had anyone else's hands on me since I was raped.

Then I leaped over all the walls I put up to keep myself safe, only to come crashing down on the other side of them.

It was too much. I'm not ready. But even if I was, I wouldn't have wanted it to be like that. Random hookups were fun in the past, but that was before. Things were different. I was different. I don't know when I'll be ready to have sex again, but when I do, I want it to be with someone I trust and respect.

I wish I wouldn't have gotten so caught up with Trevor last night because he's a good friend of Rae's and I'd love to build a friendship with her. Hopefully she doesn't think I'm crazy after how I ran away from Trevor.

I'm trying not to think about how he might see me now. The connection between us was intense and maybe could've led to something more if I'd handled things differently. Instead, I let myself get caught in the rush of chemistry and lust. Now, here I am. Trying to skip school on my second day.

I'm a freaking mess.

"How about this?" Robbie smiles at me. "Get up, get your stuff, and go stop by the coffee place downtown. I'll put in an order for you. Not to bribe you, but to help give you a good start to your day. Deal?"

I give him a weak smile. "I guess I can do that."

"It's all about mindset. And if you can't get to that place on your own, let some delicious coffee do it for you."

He makes a good point. I don't want to get stuck in this mental space. Yesterday was a good day. Last night derailed things. Coffee can totally fix all that. Right?

I have no idea, but I don't have a choice, so I give Robbie a hug, channel my inner Lorelai Gilmore, and head for the coffee place with the hope coffee can fix me and all my problems.

Okay, maybe Robbie was right.

I'm easily bribed.

But also, coffee is life. Especially when it's this good.

Plus, I put on one of my favorite playlists and drove to campus with the windows down and music blaring. It's a simple thing, but it's always healing for me. Screaming the lyrics while the late summer lake breeze whirls through the window is a soul-soothing, spiritual experience.

Walking across campus, I feel a little more confident again. Calmer, at least.

I'm still jamming to music, and it's hard not to have a *Zoey's Extraordinary Playlist* moment and break into a song and dance routine to *cut!* by Maren Morris and Julia Micheals—which speaks to my soul right now.

I take another drink of my coffee, then look at my phone quickly to double check which building I'm headed to. When I slip it back into my bag and focus in front of me again, I stop short.

Twenty feet away, standing at the edge of a sidewalk near a bench is Trevor Matteny, staring at me hesitantly.

Well, that happened faster than I thought it would.

I don't know what to say to him. Apologizing feels wrong because I did what was right for me in that moment, even if I wasn't clear about why—or anything else.

But since it would be rude or downright ridiculous to walk away now, I give a tiny smile and an awkward wave.

Great.

Slowly, he makes his way over to me, like I'm a wild horse and if he moves too fast, he might spook me. Which is probably fair.

"Hi," he says.

"Hi." I pull my earbuds out and tuck them into my purse.

"I wasn't sure if I should come over to you or not. After last night... I don't want to push you. If anything I did was too far or too much—"

"Trust me. In this situation, I'm the problem. Not you."

Those dark eyes flicker with intensity as he takes me in. "Are you okay?"

Talk about a loaded question.

"I am... I'm just... Last night was..." And I'm speaking in half-sentences again. Brilliant. "I've just sort of sworn off guys," I quickly sputter. Which isn't not true, but it's also not the smartest thing I could've said because if he asks me why...

Trevor's looking at me, amused, and I wonder if every single thought I'm having is visible on my face.

"I can respect that. My intention coming over here wasn't to get a date. It was to see if you're okay." He runs a hand through that sexily messy hair of his, and I swear a part of me melts. Probably the last of my resolve. His jaw ticks, then he continues. "Okay if I'm honest, I also came over here because I can't stop thinking about last night—you. I felt a connection between us. I want to get to know you better, even if all you can give me is friendship. But if you're not interested, that's okay too."

I stare at him for a long moment, replaying last night and trying to figure out what I want. If I can trust him. Sarah said he was one of the good ones, and sure, they were young, but if they dated that long she'd know, right?

"Can I ask you a question?"

He bobs his head. "Sure."

"If I hadn't stopped us last night, what would've happened?"

His eyes narrow and he watches me for a moment like my question is some kind of trick.

"Nothing more than you would've wanted to happen."

"Okay, if I had been up for absolutely anything and you were the one calling the shots, what would've happened?"

Again, his hand goes to his floppy curls. "I would've kept kissing you."

"And that's all?"

"No." He blows out a sigh. "I probably would've pinned you to the couch and deepened that kiss, and if I was really fucking desperate—which I kind of am for you—I might have touched you through your leggings and ground against you a bit. Then we would've laughed that off, and I'd have offered for you to spend the night—just to sleep—or walked you to your car." His cheeks are pink, but his grin comes back. "Where I would've pressed you against the door and kissed you again, made sure I got your number, and asked you on a date."

My eyes widen. Was I expecting him to tell me something more *sexual*? Was I reading too much into it? Either way, I wasn't ready for that level of kissing, but what he described... I think I'd like to get to that place. With him.

"Really?" I breathe.

"I've done the hookup scene. It's not my thing. And nothing about the time I spent with you last night was what I'd do with someone I wanted to sleep with. I don't sit with a girl all night, play with her hair, and ask her question after question because I want to have *sex* with her. I wanted to get to know you. Still do. But like I said, that doesn't have to be as anything other than friends if you don't want more."

But... I think I do want more.

He checks the time on his phone and glances across campus.

"I'm not against going on a date with you." The words fly out of my mouth all at once.

"But you said—"

"I know. And I *had* sworn off guys. Last night I moved too fast. Faster than I should've let myself. But I—you..." I sigh dramatically because this inability to communicate with him thing is really annoying.

He bites his lip and smiles, then moves closer.

"I'd love to take you on a date. No expectations. Let's see what happens. And if it helps, I promise I won't even try to kiss you."

"What?"

"You said you moved too fast last night. If you need to wait on kissing or anything else, I don't mind taking things slow."

My mouth falls open. I really wasn't expecting *that*. But maybe I should've been. He showed me how thoughtful he was last night. That same voice from somewhere deep inside me, the one I kept hearing last night, whispers to me again. *Maybe you can trust him.* I need to try, at least.

"I... I'm not against kissing." I'm really not. Especially understanding his intentions now. Though I still need to go at a snail's pace.

"So, is that a yes to going on a date?"

I don't bother trying to fight back my smile. "You make it really hard to say no."

He holds his hands up. "If you want to take some time to think about it—"

"No. I mean yes." I almost roll my eyes at my ridiculousness. "No. I don't need time. *Yes.* My answer is yes. I'll go on a date with you. But I have a condition."

And holy freaking hotness, the massive smile on his face somehow brightens the already sunny day. If I'd known I'd get to see that, I would've said yes quicker.

"Name it."

"It has to be a daytime date. But no hiking or secluded picnics." I pause and bite my lip. I'm not ready to tell him about *everything* yet. How can I make that more innocuous? "I'm, uh, not much of a nature girl."

He gives me a funny look. "Okay. I can work with that. How about Saturday? We'll have a day date. But you better clear your whole day. We're starting with brunch."

I cock a brow. When he wants something, he really goes for it. But what fun would it be if I just agreed to it?

"I'll be free for the day, but we'll see how brunch goes before I decide if I want more."

That bright smile turns into a smoldering smirk.

"Perfect. So, can I get your number this time?"

I hold out my hand for his phone and our fingers brush as he gives it to me. That same electric jolt from last night hits me. I'm probably giving him emotional whiplash at this point.

I type in my name into the contact info and add a roller coaster emoji at the end, since that's what he can expect from me.

The second the phone is back in his hand, he types something out, then my phone goes off.

With my eyes locked on him, I pull it out of my bag.

Unknown number: Hi.

He shrugs. "Had to make sure you didn't give me a fake number. That might *really* bruise my ego."

With those words and his adorable cheeky grin, he has me smiling and feeling upbeat again.

"I have to get to class soon, but where are you headed?"

"The humanities building."

"Can I walk you there?"

My breath catches. When was the last time a guy offered to walk me to class? Junior year of high school? He's so endearing it doesn't seem real. And that's when I have to shove away the thoughts in the back of my mind that he's messing with me or going to hurt me. My gut says to trust him, and that's what I'm going with.

"I'd love that. Thanks."

Then he does the last thing I'm expecting and pulls my books from my arms, carrying them for me. He's carrying my books. Last night I told him my heart felt like it was beating out of my chest. Now it feels like it's going to burst from how sweet he is.

We walk toward the humanities building, which isn't too far, and my mind replays that entire interaction as well as reminding me how I behaved last night.

Trevor must notice the slight shift in my demeanor, because his gaze burns into me.

"Are you sure you're okay?"

I meet his almost black eyes and hold his gaze for a second.

"Yeah. I'm just... surprised."

"By what?"

"You." I shake my head. "A lot of things. And…"

"Yeah?"

"You didn't ask me why."

"Why what?"

"Why I ran off the way I did last night."

He glances at me. "You said you'd sworn off guys."

"Yeah, but—"

He stops and turns toward me. "Do you want to tell me?"

My voice is quiet when I answer. "Not really."

He shifts his backpack on his shoulder, looking a little sheepish. "I assumed if you wanted me to know, you'd tell me. If you ever want to talk about whatever it is, I'm here to listen."

And just like that, more of my uncertainties melt away.

"Thank you."

"Of course." We start walking again, then he nervously looks at me. "Can I put my hand on your back?"

I let out a whoosh of air and try to keep tears from cresting in my eyes. He's asking for consent to touch me in a gentlemanly way.

"It's okay if not," he says quickly.

"No. It's fine. I'd like that."

He moves slowly, his fingers brushing my low back before his hand comes to rest there. I lean into the touch and smile up at him.

After what happened last night, I couldn't have imagined this. I figured if I saw him again it would be awkward or maybe he'd even avoid me. But he keeps surprising me. And now we have a date planned for Saturday.

How to get a date with the cute boy you're crushing on? Talk with him for hours, flirt with him, kiss him, absolutely panic, run away, and have zero intention of ever seeing him again.

Chelsea's Dating Handbook. Coming soon.

We continue our walk in a comfortable silence, and it only takes us a couple of minutes to get to my building.

When we walk in, the lecture hall is the first door on the left, and I notice Rae leaning against the wall, tapping on her phone.

When she looks up and sees us, she smiles brightly.

Trevor grumbles as Rae puts her phone away and strides over to us.

She opens her mouth to say something, but Trevor pins her with a look. "Don't." When I look at him in surprise, he narrows his eyes. "She meddles."

I laugh at that. "From what I saw last night, all of you meddle."

"Hey, she's got us figured out already."

Trevor cuts another look in her direction, then takes my arm and guides me a few feet away. "I'll text you later? Can I pick you up on Saturday?"

"Yes and yes. Can't wait."

His body relaxes and he gets an adorable aw-shucks look on his face. "Me either. Uh... can I kiss you on the cheek?"

The enamored look in his eyes is so genuine it hurts.

"Yes," I squeak, stomach whirling. My cheeks are red hot, but I don't care.

And when his lips press against my hot skin, my heart beats erratically, and that same tingly feeling I got yesterday shoots through my body. In a lot of ways, I'm terrified, but I want to see where this can go.

With his lips right by my ear, he whispers, "Have a good day. Text me if you want to talk or meet up. Anything."

I reach out and squeeze his hand. "You have a good day too. We'll talk soon."

And what is that sultry lilt in my voice? Who am I?

I'm Chelsea Winters, and I want to enjoy every second of this. Falling for him. Because I already know that's what I'm doing.

He hands me back my books, and with a lingering look, walks away.

I watch him go and literally fan myself because that whole interaction left me overheated and overstimulated—both in the best ways.

"Well, seems like things are good between you two."

I turn to look at Rae, who is smiling mischievously.

"Oh boy, he's right. You do meddle."

"No meddling. He asked me to check on you, but it seems he got to you first."

I look back at the door he walked out of. "Am I totally insane for feeling all swoony and cotton-candy brained over him?"

She laughs. "Nope. I still feel that way."

"And who makes you feel like that?"

We both turn at the sound of Aaron's voice.

Rae shrugs. "Eh. Just this sexy guy I know."

"Where is he? I'll fight him."

I can't help but laugh. "You two are adorable. And kinda gross."

They both shrug.

"It's our thing," Aaron says.

"Do you two have a lot of classes together?" I ask when I realize he's heading to the classroom with us.

"Yeah. Aaron's studying to be a school counselor, so we have the same core classes and try to schedule them together. Way better when you can do a group project with someone you like and trust."

I smile at that. "That's sweet. And it must be nice having a built-in friend in class with you."

She loops her arm through mine. "Now you do too."

Transferring here, I had hopes for what could happen, but kept my expectations low. It wasn't on my bingo card that I'd make a new friend—who comes with plenty more—and meet the sweetest marshmallow of a guy, even if he seems a little growly and grumbly on the outside.

The cynical, untrusting side of me says it's too good to be true, but I actively shut that shit down, beating it to death with positivity because these are good things.

Good things.

Things I deserve.

6
Last First Date

Trevor

"PULL THE PHONE BACK from your ugly mug so I can see your outfit."

"Wow, thank you for that long distance hug, Hy. I'm so glad I called you."

"Yeah, yeah. Less talking, more letting me judge your outfit."

"It's a low-key date," I huff, looking past the phone and at the mirror, not at all worried about how I look. Yeah, even I'm not buying that. In the couple of days we've known each other, it's been a wild ride, and I want this date to be... not perfect. Right. I want it to be right.

That starts with my outfit.

"I like everything except the jeans. Try your ripped light wash ones instead."

I look down at my body, then set my phone on the dresser and find the jeans she suggested. As soon as I've put them on, I realize she was right.

I've got on a simple gray Henley with a dark purple and charcoal checkered plaid flannel shirt over it, rolled up my forearms.

Do I know I look sexy as fuck with my muscular forearms on display? Yes.

Does Hyla tell me the only reason they're jacked is because I have to *service* myself so much? Also yes.

She's so supportive.

"Ah, so much better!" She claps her hands and says, "Shoes..."

"I'm thinking my gray mid-top sneakers."

"Ooh, yes."

I keep talking as I dig through the closet. "How are you doing? How's yoga teaching going?"

"It's fine. I'm okay."

I stand up, shoes in hand, and stalk back to the phone. I grab it and pull it so it's right up to my face. "When you say shit like that so quickly, I know you're lying."

I see the drop in her facade. It's quick, but it's there. Hyla's never had it easy with her family, and these last few years have been particularly bad with her parents. Including her father, the state senator. I usually just refer to him as a prick.

Thankfully, Hyla's moved into her own place away from them, but I worry she's isolating herself too much. She also looks like she's lost weight. The protective side of me wants to try to fix it all.

"Oh, look. Your mom's here and she wants to see your date outfit."

"Hy—"

Then my mom's face fills the screen. Whatever. I'm not letting this thing with Hyla go. She won the battle, not the war.

"Hi, honey."

"Hey, Mom." I pull the phone back so she can see.

"Oh my gosh, you look so handsome."

"You sound like I'm your little five-year-old headed off to kindergarten."

"Because in my mind you still are. But fine, do I need to use a more hip term? That outfit is on fleek. No, snatched. Oh, that outfit ate—"

"Mom, stop. Please. I'm begging you. You're not even using it right." Hyla is behind her, laughing at my pain. "I blame you for this," I call.

Mom laughs, and it's hard to hold on to any frustration when I hear that sound. That laugh kept me going through some of our darkest moments.

"Sorry, honey. I had to. But you look great. I hope you have a wonderful time with Chelsea."

Hyla steps up next to her. "Did I tell you I came up with a ship name?"

"No," I grumble.

"It's still not the best, but I'm going with TreChe. But don't worry, I'll keep workshopping it." She gives me her brightest smile. Annoying me has always been her favorite pastime.

"Fantastic."

"I've got to go, but have a great time. Love you!" Mom says.

"Love you too."

She kisses Hyla's cheek, then walks away.

"I guess I should let you go too," Hyla says.

"Yeah, I need to get going."

"Seriously, have an awesome time. I expect details."

"Yeah, yeah. Anyway, I love you. Take care of yourself. And just... call me if you need anything. Okay?"

Her eyes lose some of their brightness. "I'll be fine. Go have fun with your girl."

"She's not my girl yet."

Hy rolls her eyes.

"Whatever you want to tell yourself. Love you. Bye."

"Bye."

I end the call, take one last look in the mirror, then head out to pick up Chelsea.

The apartment house I pull up in front of is a four-story brick building. It's simple and unassuming, shrouded by trees. Chelsea didn't actually tell me which apartment is hers, but when I get out of the car, I notice she's sitting on the front porch, talking with some guy.

I force my jealousy deep, deep down because that's not the kind of shit Chelsea needs. Unless she's inviting me to be the third part of a throuple, it's not like she's talking to some other guy she's dating.

When she sees me, she smiles and stands up, and I get to spend the entire length of time she walks toward me taking in how stunning she looks.

Like me she's in casual fall vibes because despite it being late August, it's only supposed to be sixty-three today. Last weekend it was eight million degrees. Welcome to upstate New York weather.

Chelsea has on a dark gray tee with the words *Basic Fall Vibes* on it and a graphic of a pumpkin spice latte. She's wearing some lightly distressed jeans with brown boots, and a cream-colored cardigan ties the entire look together. It highlights her curves and her body shape, making her look show-stoppingly gorgeous.

"Hi." Her smile is warm and her eyes are dancing as she comes to a stop in front of me.

I lean down and kiss her cheek. "Hey, babe. You look incredible."

"Thank you," she says on an inhale. Then she skims her fingers up my forearms and leans in. "You look deliciously hot." Her cheeks heat, but she doesn't break my gaze.

The hardest part about today is going to be not kissing her when she says things like that because it's all I want to do. But until she can enthusiastically tell me she wants that, I'm not going to try. Her feeling comfortable is the most important thing.

Instead, I channel that energy and take her hand, caressing my thumb over her skin. "Thank you."

Next to us, a throat clears.

Chelsea rolls her eyes. "This is Robbie."

"*Uncle* Robbie," he says.

"Oh, sure, *now* you want to use the word uncle," Chelsea mutters.

He pins her with a look. "Can you give us a minute, Chels?"

She sighs, but doesn't fight him, and walks over to my car. My eyes follow her round ass the whole way. I'll take things as slowly as she wants to go, but I'm still going to enjoy looking, whether I can touch or not.

A crisp snap draws my attention to Robbie.

"Enjoying yourself?"

Very much, actually.

"Is this the *I break her heart, you break my face* speech?"

"No." His face softens as he looks over at her. "It's not about you breaking her heart. It's about making sure she's safe and treated right. I would go to the ends of the earth to keep her safe. Her location is shared with me, and I won't hesitate to hunt you down if I think something is happening that shouldn't be."

Okay, I don't know what this is about, but his words tell me enough. It might've been an abusive relationship or something, but someone hurt her in far worse ways than heartbreak. It makes sense, especially since she told me she swore off guys.

I hold up my hands. "I don't fault you for that. I understand wanting to protect someone you care about. You don't know me, so my word doesn't mean much, but I have no intention of hurting her, and I'm also protective. If it makes you feel better, I can share my location with you too, so you always know where we are."

He stares hard at me for a moment, then his tough expression drops. "It's frustrating that you're so likable."

I crack a smile at that. "I can even have her text you every hour if you want. I'll set an alarm on my phone and everything."

He sighs and waves a hand. "No. Go on. Get out of here."

Chelsea laughs as we walk over to her. Robbie hugs her and whispers something I can't hear. She hugs him tighter, then they break apart. Robbie eyes me one last time, then walks away.

I open the passenger door for Chelsea and extend my hand to help her inside.

Her smile hasn't dimmed, and I'm soaking it in. This is how she was when we first met, but with how quickly that shift happened to her panicking, I'm not going to assume today will be all smooth sailing.

"So, are you ready to spend the day with me?" I ask once I'm seated.

"Excuse me? I believe I promised you brunch. If *you're* ready to spend the day with me, you have to earn it."

Challenge accepted.

"I'm all in," I tell her and let the words hang there. I'm in for brunch. I'm in for the day together. I'm in for anything she'll give me because somehow in less than a week I'm a goner for this girl.

"Guess we'll see."

I put the car in drive and get on the road, taking us past campus to the road that follows the far side of the lake.

"I haven't come out this way yet," Chelsea says, eyes on the lake view out her window. "It's beautiful."

"I like it because it's not as popular with the college kids. It's busier in the summer from what my friends have said, but once school starts up again, it's quieter. But don't worry, where I'm taking you always has a steady ebb and flow of people. Hope you're not expecting a fancy brunch, though. Because this is a much more low-key place, but the experience is worth it. Plus, there's great coffee."

"Darn, so you're saying I'll have to live without lobster Benedict?"

I quickly glance at her. "Lobster Benedict?"

"I'm a sucker for seafood and eggs Benedict, so combine them and you get my favorite brunch dish. Best sprinkled with chives."

"Okay, good to know you're bougie."

She fake gasps. "Rude. I prefer posh."

"My posh princess? Has a ring to it."

She snorts a laugh and looks out the window again. "That makes me sound way better than I am."

"Don't do that."

She turns back to me. "What?"

"Put yourself down."

"You don't know me well enough to know if I'm putting myself down or not."

"I don't have to know you well to know you're strong, smart, funny, and compassionate. In the short time I've known you, I've seen it all. I don't care about poise or any of that kind of bullshit.

A posh princess isn't what I want. I want you, and I'll tell you that as many times as you need to hear it."

I put my turn signal on and pull into the parking lot of a small wooden building. It has a covered front porch with Adirondack chairs on it, and above that, a sign that reads *The Lake Shack.*

I turn to Chelsea, who is still staring at me. After a moment, she sighs and shakes her head. "You might've just earned yourself a continuation of our date." My victorious smile makes her roll her eyes. She swings her door open, then looks back at me. "Don't let it go to your head. You still need to impress me with this brunch." Then she's out of the car and strolling toward the building.

I scramble out of the car and follow her, getting ahead of her just in time to open the door for her.

We walk inside the building, which is anything but a shack. It's a small but beautiful cabin-style building. Wood everywhere, with tasteful decorations and a homey feel. But the best part is out the back door. That's for after we order, though.

There are people at a couple of the tables, but no one waiting at the counter.

The swinging doors that remind me of a saloon fly open, as a woman in her late fifties appears with an inviting smile on her face.

"Can I help you two?"

I rest my hand on the small of Chelsea's back and guide her forward.

Chelsea's staring up at the menu, wide-eyed, so I order first. "This is her first time here," I whisper, and Chelsea elbows me. "I'll have the kitchen sink breakfast burrito and a raspberry cheesecake latte."

Chelsea blinks a couple of times, then finally looks at the woman behind the counter. "I'll have the Benedict sandwich." *Saw that coming.* "And a seven-layer wonder latte."

A younger girl at the end of the counter gets to work on our coffee orders as the older woman rings us out. I pay before Chelsea even has a chance to try to pay for hers.

"Those will be out in a few minutes."

"Thanks," I say.

Chelsea moves away from the counter, looking around the place.

"What do you think?"

She spins around and grabs my shirt, pulling me closer. "This place is really cute. There's something special here. How'd you find out about it?"

I chuckle at that. "Hyla and I were up visiting during freshman year, and Rae and Aaron were fighting, so Amanda and Mackie brought us. Mackie's dad is a total foodie and loves to find the best local places. He was the one who picked it when he was visiting one time. The rest of them come here pretty regularly. It's one of my favorite spots because it's quiet, but it still has personality. Plus, if you had any concerns about being alone with me, no worries here. I'm pretty sure the older lady would hit me with a frying pan if I misbehaved, and her husband would chase me out of here with a broom."

She laughs at that. "I appreciate you abiding by my rules. And this place is cool. Thanks for sharing it with me."

"Your coffees are ready."

We walk over and grab them, but stay close to the counter, waiting for our food. Plus, I don't want to spoil the surprise if she catches a glimpse of the back doors.

"Random and unrelated question... you said Rae and Aaron were fighting the day you first came here. Is that like a common thing? Because they seem crazy in love, and I don't want to get invested in shipping them if they're just going to break up."

I can't help but laugh at that. "There have never been two people more meant to be than Aaron Cooper and Rae McKinley.

They had a rough transition going from friends to more, mostly because they were both dealing with significant mental health stuff. They were broken up at that time, but since they got back together, their relationship has been strong and healthy. In a lot of ways, they set the example for all of us now. They communicate, prioritize each other, and focus on being the best versions of themselves. Long story short, you can ship it. The rest of us have been our whole lives."

She nods and takes a sip of her drink. "Wow. That's delicious." She clears her throat. "So, they set the example for the rest of you in terms of relationships. Does that mean something serious is what you're looking for?"

Before I can answer, the kitchen doors fly open again, and the woman walks out holding a tray with our orders on it. "Here you are."

"Thanks," I say quickly. It's not that I don't want to answer Chelsea's question, but I guess I wanted to settle in a little more first. I grab our tray, then nod toward the back. "Follow me. You haven't seen the best part yet."

She takes our coffees and follows me to the back of the restaurant, where heavy duty French doors open onto an expansive deck with a sweeping view of the lake.

"Oh my god..." Chelsea stands, mouth open, taking it all in. "This is stunningly beautiful."

I resist the urge to croon something cliché like *"so are you."*

"Like I said, one of my favorite spots. Come here." We set our stuff on one of the tables and walk over to the edge of the deck.

Wrapping my arm around her waist, I tug her closer, then fish my phone out of my pocket and hold it out, capturing a selfie of us in front of the gorgeous view. I quickly check how it came out and smile.

"And saving that as my background."

"Lock screen or home screen?"

"Lock screen."

She purses her lips. "Am I not home screen material?"

I shake my head. "I don't want a picture of myself on my home screen." I drop my voice and nod toward the view beyond us. "Look out at the lake again."

She stares at me for a beat, then does it. I snap a photo of her, standing there looking stunning as the wind blows through her hair.

I make a black and white copy of it. "Now that's home screen material."

Her eyes flit to mine, and I pull her close again.

"We only see our lock screen photos for seconds out of the day before our screens unlock. Those pictures aren't really for us. They're the ones we want to see for a second to smile or be reminded of something. Or to let other people see. But the home screen? Think about how much time we're on our phones daily. Whatever I set as my home screen photo is something I could look at all day, every day."

She huffs a sigh and looks up at me. "That is one of the most unexpectedly sweet things I've ever heard. You're making it impossible to want to do anything but continue this date all day."

I lean down and kiss her forehead. "And I wasn't even trying."

"Cocky little shit."

I laugh and grab her arm, leading her over to the table so we can dig into our food.

"So, now you know about my lock screen and home screen. What are yours?"

She pulls her phone from her pocket and sets it in front of me. The screen turns on when she touches it, and there's a picture of her smiling as she dances with a man I'm assuming is her father.

"Me and my dad at his wedding to my stepmom a couple of years ago. And you're right. It's a moment I like to be reminded of here and there, but not one I could stare at forever." She unlocks the screen, revealing a gorgeous shot of Birch Lake taken from her family's campground.

"That's beautiful. I'd love to go back sometime." I stop myself from saying anything else. If I think too hard about it, my throat will close up with emotion, and I want this morning to stay fun.

She elbows me. "Play your cards right and you might get an invitation."

Then she takes a bite of her sandwich and lets out a satisfied groan. "This is amazing. I'm going to be very poor since I'll need to drive here for breakfast every day now."

I chuckle at that. "No lobster, but I was hoping you'd still enjoy it."

She looks at her sandwich like she's going to take another bite, but then rests her hand over mine. "Thank you for bringing me here. It's a cute date spot, but more than that, it feels like you're showing me a little piece of you."

"Does that mean we're spending the rest of the day together? So I can show you more pieces of me?" I frown as soon as the words are out of my mouth. "That was more suggestive than I intended."

"Mhm. Sure." Her eyes dance, and she takes a big bite of her sandwich while staring out at the view. She's a breathtaking mixture of beautiful and adorable, but there's something about *her*. Her energy, her heart, I have no idea what... but it sucks me in more the longer I spend with her.

She wipes her mouth and turns back to me, her alluring eyes on me and her voice low when she speaks. "For the record, this date was never just going to be brunch. Unless you turned out to be an asshole. Then I would've let Robbie kick your ass."

"Already sure I'm not a jerk, huh?"

"No question. I haven't always been the best judge, but with you, it's obvious. Your character shines through. And the more

I see, the more I want to know. So give me the all-day date. I'm in. No complaints."

Chelsea

I'm not sure if our date is exactly what I was expecting or not what I was expecting at all, but it's been perfect. Sure, we've only made one stop, but it's the way Trevor cracks himself open with every little thing he does. He's so genuine that I have to constantly let my gut override my nagging brain. *No one is this perfect. It's an act.* But what does he have to gain by going through all this? Who would want to deal with all my baggage—even if he doesn't know it all yet?

I think he's just a good guy, and it's important to remind myself those still exist. My father is one. Robbie is one. Trevor is one too.

He's been understanding of every condition I set. He's not pushy. He wants to get to know me beyond the surface level. That alone is scary because it means harder conversations are coming. As much as I don't want to relive what I've been through, I also don't want it hanging over me. I carry enough shame about that day. I'm tired of holding on to it.

Since brunch, we've been taking a drive around the lake, stopping at the many pull-offs and enjoying the views. Our conversations have been light—mostly about music, movies, TV shows, or books.

Trevor pulls into the large park at the base of the lake, and since it's a Saturday and the weather is fantastic, it's already filled with people.

"So, you said no secluded picnics or hiking, but I figured a busy park right next to the police station"—he nods to the small strip of blacktop connecting the park to the sheriff's station—"would be okay."

"It's great. Thank you."

"Thank you for letting me steal you for an entire day. Ready for part two of our date?"

"How many parts are there?"

"Four to five depending on how strictly we define parts."

I can't help but smile. He's so ridiculous and sweet, and I kind of want to pinch myself to make sure this is real.

"We better get going, then."

I swing my door open and climb out, but he goes around the back of the car and pulls a bag and a blanket from the trunk.

When he gets to me, he grabs my hand, and my stomach whirls. There's something about him. He brings out a different side of me. I keep thinking it's the "old" me, but now I'm not so sure. This is something else. Something more. I'm lighter. Almost awestruck. The rest of the world slips away, and even if it's only for a moment, I see the world with childlike wonder.

Then he touches me or smiles at me and it's an electric jolt to my heart, jumpstarting parts of me I thought were dead.

He leads me to a shaded area that overlooks a pond with a fountain in the center. It's beautiful and serene, even with plenty of people sitting around it.

He sets out the blanket, and we both sit down. I'm still staring around at the expansive park while Trevor unloads snacks from the grocery bag he brought.

"Hopefully this isn't too much nature for you."

My gaze snaps to his. "Too much—" *Oh shit.* My cheeks heat, but he just laughs and keeps pulling snacks out of the bag. "I—I mean—"

"It's fine. I assumed that was a lie since you told me how much fun you had working at your family's campground every summer. For the record, you don't have to lie to me. If there's ever something you're not comfortable talking about or not ready to tell me, you can just say that. I'll respect any boundaries you give me."

"Thank you. And thank you for letting me get away with such a stupid lie. I'm not always great at thinking on my feet, and honestly, I wasn't expecting... this."

"A picnic?" His eyes are still dancing.

"No." I drag my finger between the two of us. "*This*. Us. You. I've spent the last year feeling the least like myself I ever have. Then I moved here, and I was surprised to feel like I was finding the old version of me—pieces of her, at least—then I met you and it both centered those pieces of me and knocked me on my ass. When I'm with you, things come so naturally that I forget the rest of the world. Then something forces me to remember it and it's like I don't know what I'm doing anymore. And I know none of this makes any sense—"

"It does. Believe me, I get it. I guess that's why..." He sighs and flips his hand through his hair, ruffling it up in the cutest way. "It's why I want to make you comfortable and I want you to know you're safe because the rest of the world isn't that way. But here, with me, it can be. I want to see that vibrant side of you because it's the part I can't stop falling for."

I stare at him for a moment, then shake my head and *laugh*. "You know we're ridiculous, right?"

He laughs too. "Absolutely. But that just makes me like it more. Life's too short to always be stuck in the hard or serious stuff."

"Agreed. Thank you for bringing that out in me." I look down for a second.

He pauses and looks at me with a childlike expression. "Anything to see that smile."

And, ugh. *Swoon*. He's so... dreamy. Which makes me feel like I'm in a '90s rom-com, but when I'm with him, I think I am.

He pulls two bright purple cans from the bag. They look like soda, but not one I recognize.

"What's that?"

His face lights up. "Oh, it's called Loganberry—which is an actual berry, a cross between a raspberry and a blackberry. I don't know if there are actual loganberries in it, but it's delicious." His face is all nostalgia as he looks at the cans. "Tastes like my childhood. It's fruity in a sort of indescribable way, and not carbonated."

"I'm always here for trying new things."

"Good to know," he says smoothly. He pops both cans open, then hands one to me. "Cheers."

God, he's like the sweetest little puppy right now. So genuinely excited to share this really special thing with me.

I take a sip, letting the fruity flavor dance on my taste buds.

"Holy shit. That's really good." I take another sip, surprised by how delicious it is. "Where is this from and how did I not know about it?"

I'm practically chugging it now, which makes him smile.

"It originated in Canada, I think, but it's popular in western New York. Especially Buffalo. You can find it scattered elsewhere, though. It's always been a special treat for me. It was my dad's favorite."

Was. That's the first time he's mentioned his dad. I kind of assumed his mom was a single parent by the way he talked about her, and maybe she is, but I'm guessing not in the way I thought.

"Was?"

He swallows thickly, a sad smile crossing his face. "Yeah. My dad died when I was eleven."

Without a thought, I reach over and take his hand. "I'm so sorry."

"Thanks. It sucks, but little moments like this, sharing something he loved with someone, helps keep his memory alive."

I move a little closer. "Thank you for sharing it with me. I can't believe I've been missing out the whole time."

Some brightness returns to his features. "I'm glad you like it. It's fun converting people."

"That makes it sound a little more cult-y, but fair enough."

"Hey, you've met my friends."

I snort at that. "They seem pretty great, though."

"Yeah. They are."

"How long have you been friends with them?"

"Pretty much my whole life. I met most of them in kindergarten or first grade. They're the kind of people who always show up for their friends, even outside of the six of them. Of course, everyone knows everyone in Ida. I'm sure you know how that goes."

"Oh yeah. Small towns. It's cool you've always had that, though. Close friends."

"Do you have anything like that?"

I shake my head. "Not exactly. I consider Robbie my best friend because I grew up stitched to his side. As adults, we love the same books and have similar tastes in most things, so we're naturally close. He's a big part of the reason I chose SUNY FL to transfer to. I do have a couple of friends back home, but we're not as close as we used to be. Growing up and stuff..."

I try to hide my cringe at how dumb that sounds.

"I have one of those too," he says. "It happens, and it sucks, but it also shows you the people who really matter."

"Yeah. It does."

"Did you make any friends at your previous school?"

I almost snort at that. "I thought I did." I grab a bag of cheddar and sour cream chips—the best flavor ever—and meticulously tug the seam apart as I talk. "I was there on a partial volleyball scholarship and spent a lot of time with my teammates, but I've since learned they were party friends, not real friends. I'm beginning to think that's all Syracuse was for me. One big—"

"Syracuse?"

It's not until I hear the word leave his mouth that I realize I told him where I used to go.

"Oh, uh, yeah. That's where I went before this." I stuff a chip into my mouth, savoring the flavor like it'll somehow calm the ache building in my gut at the direction of this conversation.

"That's where I went too." Disbelief drips from his words.

I drop the chip I'm holding and my mouth falls open. "Se—seriously?"

He nods slowly. "Yeah."

We stare at each other, confusion swirling around us. And tension.

Because his family camped at my family's campground for years.

And now... we went to the same college before this. For almost a year and a half, we were on the same campus every day and didn't even know it. How many times did we pass each other without ever realizing?

"Do you think we ever saw each other? Were ever in a class together? Knew any of the same people?" I ask.

He sucks in a breath, then slowly blows it out again. "Maybe. I mean, in terms of passing by or seeing each other, statistically I think we must have, but..."

"What?"

"If I'd seen you, we wouldn't be here right now because you'd already be mine. There's no way I would've let my dream girl walk past without doing something about it."

"Dream girl, huh?"

He shrugs and smiles. "Something like that."

That adorable smile grows as he reaches for a package of Dunkaroos.

"Well, as much as that inflates my ego, there's no way we didn't pass by each other, even if it was when we weren't paying attention and never noticed. Which is just... crazy." How do we have these built-in connections? How did we only find each other now?

I wish we would've found each other sooner. Maybe if we had met before, I wouldn't have—no. I'm not going to think like that. Those kinds of what-ifs will only hurt me in the long run.

"Maybe it means we were always meant to find each other, and we weren't paying close enough attention before," he says. And the calm certainty of his words almost makes me believe them too.

"Think we had a missed connection without either of us knowing it?"

He shrugs and dips one of the tiny cookies into the frosting before popping it into his mouth. "Possibly. I wasn't as social my sophomore year because I was more... focused, I guess. But freshman year, I was all about parties. Usually with my roommate or... friends."

He stumbles over the word friends. Maybe he means hookups? I guess that's not first date talk, but I already know about his ex. And I didn't know him then. It doesn't affect my life. But since he let me get away with lying to him, the least I can do is let that stumble slide.

"Well, we ended up here, anyway. Guess the universe is working hard to put us together."

He pulls his bottom lip between his teeth. "Or maybe we missed all the signs."

"Maybe." I grab one of his Dunkaroos and swirl it through the frosting.

He looks at me hesitantly, like he's not sure if he should say whatever he's thinking, but after a moment, he asks, "Why did you leave Syracuse?"

Panic claws at my chest for a moment, but I push it away. I refuse to let those types of feelings take over this date. This is an opening for a serious conversation, but I don't want to go there. Not yet. I'm not—I need to get to know him better. Especially knowing he has a connection to that place now. But also, I'm enjoying myself, and I want to keep today upbeat. I deserve to not be weighed down by emotion on my first date with a sweet, adorable, sexy, and genuinely kind guy.

"Can we just go with *it didn't work out* and leave it at that?"

He breathes out a sigh. "Only if you're okay with that being my answer too."

I also let out a breath of relief. "Yeah. Let's enjoy where we are right now."

"Here, surrounded by all this beautiful nature."

I groan. "I'm not going to live that down, am I?"

He laughs, and God, I love that sound. It's so rich and warm, like a blanket and some hot cocoa on a chilly day.

"Nope. Your family owns a campground and you're the marshmallow roasting queen. I want to know more about that, by the way. Do you teach classes? Wander around to campsites and critique people? Oh, is there a marshmallow roasting contest every summer?"

I playfully shove his shoulder. "You're hilarious. I'll have you know my grandfather was a stickler for how marshmallows should be roasted, and he taught all the kids in his family about roasting marshmallows. If anyone was going to walk around and critique things, it would've been him. But you're welcome. Because now you know how to flawlessly roast a marshmallow."

He dips his head. "I bow to the master. I take it he's not around anymore?"

I shake my head. "No. He died about five years ago, but he lived a long life. He was married four times, but his marriage to my grandmother was the only one that stuck. They were married for forty years. He was twenty years older than her. It was quite the scandal."

"Wow."

"Yep." I nudge his leg with mine. "So tell me something about you. Dirty family secrets or a random fact."

"I'll never admit this to any of my friends because they'd be annoying as fuck about it, but I'm a sucker for nostalgic things. Or I guess things that remind me of my childhood. It's why I love *Goonies* and *The Sandlot*. Loganberry and Dunkaroos. Things that remind me of the most carefree parts of life. One thing I really love to do is to lie in the grass and watch the clouds. Find shapes in them, whatever. It's relaxing and makes me feel like a kid again."

I don't know what I was expecting when I first met Trevor. Dudebro? Frat guy? I knew almost immediately I was wrong, but I didn't realize *how* wrong I was. Not only is he caring and thoughtful, but underneath his grumpy, grumbly exterior, he's a sweet, adorable puppy.

He sees the upbeat, playful side of me and wants to bring it out. I see this side of him, and it's now my goal to bring it out in him as much as possible.

"Then let's watch the clouds."

I lie back on the blanket and stare up at the blue sky with big fluffy clouds, partly blocked from view by the willow tree above us. He couldn't have picked a more picturesque spot for this little picnic. I'm glad he chose to do it despite my stupid lie.

The fluffy clouds float by on the gentle lake breeze as Trevor lies down beside me.

"What do you see?" I ask. Though I'm trying to find any clouds that look like shapes, they mostly look... like clouds.

He sighs and rolls onto his side, pushing up on his elbow. "This is going to sound cheesy and totally like a line, but I swear it's not. When I stare at the sky all I can think of is the blue of your eyes. They're captivating. I've never seen anything like them before. What are they? Blue hazel?"

I roll to face him, surprised by how close he is. Suddenly, what I notice is his eyes. The nuance in their dark color. From a distance they look almost black, but from here I can see flecks of gold and bronze, like little stars shining in his eyes.

Okay, I've been reading too many fantasy books.

"A lot of people call them blue hazel, but it's technically central heterochromia. One color near the pupil then it shifts to the other at the edge. There can be medical reasons for it, but mine are genetic, or so I've heard. Supposedly, my mother's eyes are similar."

He lies flat on his back again, but keeps his gaze fixed on me. "You don't know your mom?"

I shake my head. "Nope. I was a surprise. She and my dad were young and hadn't known each other long. She was on the fence about how to handle it, but her parents were pushy. They weren't okay with any option except her keeping me. My dad always wanted kids, so he promised to support her no matter what, but left the decision up to her. The way my dad put it, my mom tried, but only a few months after I was born, she didn't want that life. Didn't want to be a mom. She signed her rights away and left me with my dad. I've never seen or heard from her."

"Wow."

"Yeah. It's a wild story, but I have no ill will toward her. She didn't jump in and out of my life or confuse me—didn't let me be a casualty of her uncertainty. She did what was best for both of us, and I have a lot of respect for that. My dad's family is super close, so I grew up with a lot of love. She's part of the reason I'm an advocate for women's empowerment and freedom to make choices for themselves. No woman should be forced into a decision like that."

"That's so... well adjusted."

We both laugh at that.

"I had to have at least one area where I have my shit together."

"Have you ever wanted to see her again?"

I tilt my head back and forth. "Not in a sense of wanting her to be my mom, but because I'm curious about who she ended up becoming. I hope she found her place and is happy."

He looks back at the sky, and I find myself moving closer to him. I imagine it's strange for him to hear me talk about my mother in such a detached way, when I'm certain he'd give just about anything to have his dad back.

Slowly, I reach down and twine my fingers with his. "Is it hard for you to talk about your dad?"

He's quiet for a moment, then shakes his head. "Not exactly. I like talking about him—keeping his memory alive."

"Tell me about him."

"He was the best dad in the world. My literal hero. Wherever he was and whatever he was doing, I wanted to be there, doing it with him. He was funny and kind. He loved to see people smile and laugh. He loved sitting in his oversized chair and talking or reading with me—and Hyla too. She was his girl, and he considered her his daughter." His voice thickens with emotion. "And he loved my mom. Worshipped the ground she walked on. Truly, he'd have done anything for her. He set the example of what a man should be. Not just a provider. A caretaker."

"We haven't known each other long, but I can see the threads of that in you."

A hint of a smile ghosts his otherwise melancholy expression.

"I try really hard to be the sort of man he'd want me to be and make him proud. He valued his friends and family and the time he spent with them. I don't think anyone ever had a bad word to say about him. He died—" He clears his throat and shakes his head. "Sorry. Talking about how my dad died is probably too heavy for a first date."

I meet his gaze and give his hand a reassuring squeeze. "Do you want to tell me about it?"

He stares at me for a moment. "I want to be able to talk about it."

"Then tell me. This date is what we make it. We don't have to follow whatever stupid rules society sets."

This time I get a little more than a hint of a smile.

He nods and squeezes my hand back. "He was an electrician. He worked for the state, usually on construction of new projects. There was an accident on the job site—some kind of negligence, actually—and that was it. He was gone. And we ended up with a shit ton of money that was supposed to make up for the fact that someone made a mistake somewhere along the line and took my dad from me. Thing is, he wouldn't have wanted us to be mad at the other person. That wasn't him. I'm not sure where I got my temper or my grumpiness from, but I don't think they were from him."

"Your mom?" I ask.

He laughs. "No. She is a light. I wouldn't have made it through all that without her. She always says, 'Don't forget to smile.' I try to hold on to that. Not just the words, but her energy in them."

"I like that. I might need to remember it too."

He leans in and runs a hand through my hair, playing with the strands like he did the night we met. "She'll like you." His eyes drift to the sky again, then he smiles and with a playful tug of my hair, flops onto his back and points up at a cloud. "Saggy, baggy elephant."

And just like that, all the heaviness washes away.

We settle into a lighter conversation, and when we've had our fill of snacks, Loganberry, and watching the clouds, we walk through the weaving paths of the park, hands entwined.

"So, what do you want to be when you grow up?" he asks me, that sweet smile dancing on his lips.

"An empowerer of women."

"I like that. No idea what it means."

I laugh. "I don't know. I want to work as a counselor or therapist of some sort, but my biggest focus is wanting to champion women. To give them a safe space and help them grow and rise and be the biggest, best versions of themselves. We're told to make ourselves smaller all the time, in every way. I want every woman to take up the space she rightfully deserves."

"You picked a good first friend at SUNY FL."

"You?"

He laughs. "I am an excellent choice, but I meant Rae. All the girls. They're a tribe. They support each other and always want to empower each other. You fit right in."

I think I'd like that. I don't say that though. It sounds more insecure and maybe even pathetic than I want to come off on this date, so I blow past that sentiment and turn the focus back to him.

"So, what are *your* plans?"

"Something involved with athletics. I've always loved being active and as someone who isn't great with school or sitting still for long periods of time, I like the idea of working in that field. Maybe with kids. I'm not sure yet, but the idea of helping to develop athletic programs sounds interesting."

"And what about the rest of your future?"

He glances at me, then smiles. "I want a family. That's something I'm sure I got from my dad. The desire to find love and raise a family. Not to bring up an ex, but I was comfortable being serious with Sarah at a young age because I knew I wanted those things. After the breakup, I let go of it all for a while, but recently... life made me refocus on that again. I want an overall happy life with a partner and kids, and I'm not the guy who wants to wait fifteen more years for that to happen if I can avoid it."

"Cool. No pressure, then."

He bumps his elbow against mine. "What about you?" Though his voice is smooth, that same vulnerability from earlier shimmers in his eyes.

"I was the little girl carrying around my dollies and pretending to be pregnant or have babies for as long as I can remember. Which is funny since my biological mother didn't want any of those things. But for me? I've always wanted to be a mom. And if how much romance I read is any indication, I want to find love too."

"Ah, right. I forgot. But how will anyone ever live up to the book boyfriend standard?"

He's teasing me, but the truth is, he's more than living up to those standards.

"I don't know... maybe you should give a class or something. You're doing a pretty good job so far. Must be all those fantasy romance books you've read." I wiggle my eyebrows at him. He groans through a laugh, and I poke his cheek. "You're cute when you pretend to be grumpy."

"Who says I'm pretending?"

"Your smile."

He flashes it at me, and for a second, it's hard to breathe.

Tension swirls in and coils around us again, like it's binding us together.

Or maybe that's fate.

It seems like it's been trying to tie us together all this time and we keep slipping out of its grasp. No more.

I squeeze his hand and lean in. "You know, you never answered me this morning. What are your intentions with me?"

He stops, tugging on my hand and pulling me closer as he looks into my eyes.

"To be worthy of being the man at your side, holding your hand through everything."

Yep. Total book boyfriend material.

I push onto my toes and pop a kiss on his cheek. "I guess we'll see what happens."

"Does that mean you're interested in going to our next stop?"

"Hm. Depends where it is."

"Well, actually, you get to pick. I have two options for you."

"And you don't care?"

He shrugs, looking every bit the adorable puppy again.

"As long as we're going together, I'm up for anything."

I run my hand up his arm, looking into his captivating eyes. "What are my options?"

"There's an apple orchard not far from here. They don't have a ton of apples yet, but they have all the classic stuff. Hayride. Donuts. Cider. Option two is a longer drive. About forty-five minutes, but it's a small chocolatier. They do tours and live demonstrations of how they make their truffles, and then—"

"Chocolate."

He laughs. "Yeah?"

"When it's a choice between anything else and chocolate, chocolate is *always* the answer."

"Perfect. Let's go."

7
Ass Over Tits

Trevor

TODAY HASN'T BEEN WHAT I expected. Somehow, it's been better—more. It's been more than I thought it could be.

When I planned our all-day date, I was hoping we'd connect, but I wasn't expecting to tell her about my dad. I wasn't ruling it out because I never want to hide what he means to me or how his death shaped me, but getting that heavy on our first date wasn't part of my plan. But then she asked about him. Not only for herself, but for me. Because she knew I wanted to talk about it.

In the same way, I've gotten to see more sides of her than I was expecting. It's clear we're both holding back some things—like the reasons we left Syracuse. Talk about a mindfuck that we went to the same college and never knew each other.

Like I camped at her family's campground.

Growing up in Ida meant I knew all my friends from a young age. Now all of a sudden, my dream girl walks into my life like something out of an actual dream because I feel like there's some piece of me she found. Like it had been locked away and now that we've finally connected, I can touch it and feel it again... and that all sounds crazy.

But what's crazier than this tether between us? Years of missed connections leading us together now.

Were we supposed to find each other sooner?

I'm trying not to dwell on that because the answer doesn't do me any good.

We're here now, and I intend to enjoy every second, savor every smile, and memorize every laugh. And all the ways to her heart. Definitely adding chocolate right to the top of that list. She was bouncing with excitement from the second we walked inside the chocolatier, and she'd have bought the whole store if she could have. I spent double what I was planning to there, but it was totally worth it to watch her eyes light up as the cashier added chocolate after chocolate to her bag.

"Tell me one thing you couldn't live without."

We're on our way back to Old Lake Town now. Both on the drive to the chocolatier and now on the way back, we've been asking each other random questions to get to know each other better.

The first response that jumps into my brain is baseball, but I don't want to go there today. I don't want to bring up all the shit I went through. I'm having a good time, and if her response earlier is any indication, she doesn't want to talk about what she's been through yet, either.

The thing is, besides my mom and Hyla, which is kind of *duh* and not the point of the question, I don't know what else to say.

So when I open my mouth, what comes out?

"Sarcasm."

She laughs and turns to look at me. "Sarcasm. Seriously?"

I double down. "Yes. Why is that bad? Sarcasm is essential to my daily life."

"It's not bad. But it's either a copout answer—we all thrive on sarcasm. It's the curse of the chaos of this world. Or it's a serious answer, in which case I need to know more."

Her response gives me pause, mostly because I would've said it was the first, which is a little shitty of me. But when I think about it... why was that my response?

"Oh no. You've gone quiet. Did I break you?"

"No—maybe? I've never thought about it that seriously before. I said it as a copout answer, but I'm not sure it was. I use sarcasm to change the subject, shift the focus from anything that hurts me, keep a wall up. Fuck, am I just sad and broken? What have you done to me?"

She laughs. *Laughs*.

"You're dramatic. And no. I don't think you're sad and broken. Most people use humor or sarcasm or self-deprecation—hi, it's me—to avoid their feelings or deflect. The fact that you're self-aware enough to realize it means you're anything but broken. Plus, I see that vulnerability in you. It might protect you, but it also makes you smile—probably makes other people smile—and there's nothing wrong with that."

I glance at her, wishing there was a pull-off here so I could stop the car and really look at her. Am I that obvious or does she just *see* me? My heart flares, beating erratically.

I've never felt like this before.

I loved Sarah. It was real. Not puppy love or anything else. We cared deeply for each other and were a big part of each other's lives. When she broke up with me, I was crushed. But a part of me knew it was right. I didn't know how right until today. Until Chelsea smiled at me and laughed at my stupid jokes and saw me. Not the grumpy exterior. Not my sarcasm. Not the kid who's still mourning his dad after all this time. Me. Just me. The real me. Whoever that is. I'm not entirely sure I know anymore. But she does. And somehow, she hasn't run screaming yet.

I drag my hand back to the steering wheel and clear my throat. "Same question. What could you not live without?"

"Hmm..." She looks out the window, then she gets that stunning, vibrant smile that makes my heart feel all warm and gooey. "Can you roll down the windows?"

"Uh, sure."

I roll them all down a bit, but she grins at me and says, "All the way."

So I do it. Then she turns the radio on, messing with the buttons until she finds a station. Before I can even process what song it is, she cranks the volume up.

"Holy shit. What—why?"

"This is it. This is what I can't live without," she yells over the music.

"Party in the U.S.A?" I ask when my brain finally comprehends what song it is.

She laughs, all sweet and sultry. "No. Not the song. Blasting music with the windows down. I swear it heals a little piece of my soul every time."

She throws one arm out the window and sings along with the song, and damn if I don't fall a little harder watching her.

When the song is done, she pulls her arm back inside and turns down the music.

"We're almost to our next stop, so hit me with another question," I tell her.

She thinks for a moment, then a wicked smile crosses her face. "The other night, I called you adorable, and you said you had plenty of different words you'd use to describe me. What are they?"

Damn, she's good.

"Okay, for that, you're waiting until we get to the parking lot."

I navigate through downtown Old Lake Town until we get to the large parking lot on the main strip.

Once I'm parked, I turn to her.

"If we're being honest, I don't remember what all the words I was thinking that night were, but I've got plenty more words now. Better ones, because in only a day, I know you better. So let's start with adorable. That's what you asked me, and you are, but that's the tip of the iceberg. You're kind, thoughtful, funny, drop-dead sexy, hurting, strong, compassionate, and the kind of person I want to spend more time with and know in every way. You captivate me, Chelsea. I want more. So much more."

She stares at me for a long moment, exhaling a shuddery breath. "That was..." She clears her throat. "A really good answer. And I want to know you better too." She gazes at me, her eyes locking with mine for a moment, then she leans in and kisses my cheek. "Today hasn't been at all what I was expecting, but this is my best first date ever."

Good, because it's your last one.

It's on the tip of my tongue to say it, but I don't. There's no question I see an epic future with this girl. She sees me in a way I'm not sure anyone else ever has before. Besides maybe my mom or Hyla, but still, something about this is different.

It's right.

That's all I wanted from today, and so far, so good.

Chelsea

Trevor Matteny is the sexiest man alive.

I said what I said.

It's not the perfectly floppy curls or his star-flecked, raven-colored eyes. Not the grumpy exterior that's always betrayed by his gorgeous smile. It's *him*. His thoughtfulness, compassion, and big heart. He's the squishiest marshmallow on the inside, and I love whenever I see that side of him. Seeing the vulnerable, aching side of him—while hard because I hate knowing he's hurting—draws me to him even more. It's so earnest and a rare glimpse of the real him.

The voices in the back of my head saying it's too good to be true have been beaten to a bloody pulp. Because I've seen his nuances. He's not perfect, but he might be perfect for me.

It's hard to think anything but that when we're standing in the bookstore so we can pick a romantasy book series to read together.

When he told me he wanted to do this, I almost melted on the spot. Technically, we're just picking which series I already own but haven't read yet that we want to read together so he can buy them too, but the idea alone is so damn swoony.

As fun as it is to buddy read with Robbie, reading a series like this with Trevor might make me spontaneously combust.

It'd be totally worth it, though.

This is stop number three-point-five on our date, and I'm kind of hoping it never ends. I don't want my sparkly perfect date to turn back into a pumpkin.

Or something like that.

Maybe I should look for some fairytale retellings.

"You've got a wandering eye," Trevor says, voice way too husky for this small-town bookstore.

I turn to him with my sweetest smile. "You brought me to a bookstore. I don't know what else you'd expect."

He nods toward the books I was looking at. "Go pick one. And grab a copy for me too."

I pop a kiss on his cheek. "Keep treating me like this and you'll never get rid of me."

His smoldering eyes tell me that's the plan.

And if it is... I think I like it.

After buying all the books, he leads me back out onto Old Lake Town's main street.

It's not far from my apartment building, and there are views of the lake in the distance.

"So, what's next?"

He smiles and looks down the street. "Dinner, but it's not just one stop. On this strip, there are two food trucks and three restaurants with walk-up windows. We're doing a food tour and stopping at all of them."

"Books and street food? You know the way to my heart."

"Figuring it out, at least. C'mon."

He takes the bag of books in one hand and grabs my hand with the other. Something about the way he tugs on my arm makes me feel like a little kid running off to find the best ride at a carnival.

"Okay, so, we have a walk-up window at the Mexican restaurant, the noodle place, and the Italian restaurant with the grilled pizzas. Then there's a Korean food truck and Burgers and Sh!t, which is a food truck from Ida. Where are we going first?"

I laugh at that. "We're going to need our own truck to put all the food in."

"Nah, we'll take it slow."

"Okay, I'm thinking noodles first. Good appetizer. Then maybe tacos?"

"Perfect. Let's get started."

We don't take it slow. We order something from each place and try to balance it all in our hands. Burgers and Sh!t is our last stop, and when we get to the window to order, the man in the truck gets a huge smile on his face. "Trevor Matteny. How many of you kids are up here these days?"

"The whole friend group practically. How are you, Benny?"

"I'm doing well. Expanding out to some of the college towns has been great for our business. How about you? Since the accident?"

I almost laugh. Somehow, the small-town charm of Ida has landed here in the middle of Old Lake Town.

"I'm okay. By the way, this is Chelsea. Consider her an extension of the friend group."

Benny gives Trevor a knowing smile. "So always give her extra fries. Got it." He winks at us. "What'll you have?"

Gesturing to the rest of the food, Trevor orders the mixed sliders appetizer and some fries. Somehow, I don't think we were getting away without fries.

With all our food in hand, we find a picnic table in the small park and splay out all the food.

"This looks incredible. I have to say, you're pretty good at this whole date-planning thing."

He shrugs. "Sometimes getting dressed up for a fancy dinner is nice, but spending the day together seemed like a better way to get to know each other."

"It has been." I take a bite of the chicken tacos and almost groan in happiness. So good. "Is it weird that I already feel like I've known you forever?"

"I felt that way the second we met. It's stronger now, though." His thigh presses against mine. "Especially finding another connection between us. And talking. I know we didn't go too deep, but I liked learning more about you. The bigger things and the tiny ones."

"Me too. Especially the little things."

His eyes lock with mine and a blush creeps into my cheeks. I'm about to turn away, break the intense gaze, and focus on the food in front of me, but he catches my cheek, cupping it with his palm. The softest smile appears on his face, like he's in awe of me.

"Can we keep doing this? Talking, spending time together, dating? I don't want to push, but every second I spend with you makes me want another."

I'm nodding before he's even finished speaking, but it takes my mouth a second to catch up. "Yes. I know I've been cautious about this, but please don't take my hesitance for disinterest. I'm enjoying spending time with you too. That sounds stupid and too simple for what we've been doing, but—"

"Not stupid."

He stares at me for a moment longer, then his gaze drifts down to my lips. I hold my breath, lips tingling as I wait for him to kiss me, but true to how he's been all day, he holds off, sliding his hand down my cheek and into my hair, giving one of the strands a playful tug before turning back to his food.

I do the same, even though my heart is beating so hard, I'm struggling to catch my breath.

Shoving more taco into my mouth will help, obviously. And when I do, I groan out loud this time, and Trevor laughs.

"That good?"

"They remind me of taco nights growing up. My grandma has the best taco recipes. We'd do a whole taco bar. Her, my dad, and Robbie."

"Family recipe?" he asks.

I laugh. "Nope. As my grandma says, she's an English bastardess."

Trevor chokes on his taco. "What?"

"Her words. She's a mix of British, Welsh, Scottish, and Irish."

"She sounds like a character."

"Most definitely. She's where I got my love of spicy romance books from."

His eyebrows shoot up. "Seriously?"

"Yep. Don't act so surprised. Think about it. One day your mom is going to be the spicy romance reading grandma."

His face scrunches. "I don't ever want to think about it like that again." I can't help but laugh at his wounded puppy expression. "Subject change, please."

"Fine..." I take another bite of my taco, then ask, "Do you cook?"

He nods. "Yep. My parents were always in the kitchen together cooking. After my dad died, my mom had me in the kitchen with her to keep that tradition alive. Every year, we cook up a whole Thanksgiving feast, even though it's usually just us and sometimes Hyla."

"That's really cool. Special."

"Yeah. What about you? You cook?"

"I'm decent, but I get bored with anything longhand. I can do basic baked goods and one-pot meals, but beyond that, I lose interest and burn things."

"So, not a hobby then?"

I laugh. "Not quite. As you might've noticed, I'd rather be reading."

"Just not reading recipes."

"Hey, I'll read the recipe to you if you cook it for me."

"Sounds like a good plan for a future date."

"There you go assuming things again," I tease. But since I don't want him to think I'm not interested, I quickly add, "Although if there's food involved, I'd be hard pressed to say no."

He laughs and looks at the spread around him. "Glad I'm still a growing boy and need all kinds of calories."

"Thank God. It would've been horrible if you were one of those meatheads counting your grams of protein at every meal. Life is way too short to count calories. It sucks all the joy out of life, and being joyful and having fun is important to me right now."

He taps his taco against mine, nodding to the spread in front of us. "I think we're off to a good start."

"We are." But I'm not talking about food or even finding joy again. I'm talking about us, because no matter how slow we take this, I'm not delusional enough to believe this is anything but the beginning of *us*. As scary as it is, it's exciting, and I'm already dreaming about more.

We took our time eating, then wandered around town more. Both of us dragged our feet and tried to find any excuse not to walk back to his car. The drive back to my apartment has gone too quickly, and it takes everything inside me not to pout when I see its brick facade.

When Trevor pulls up to the curb by my building, it feels like another lifetime ago that I left it.

"Is it weird that I don't want this to end?" I turn to him. "I'd invite you in, but—"

"No buts. We're taking this slow. I'm good with that." Then he opens his door and climbs out, hustling around the front of his car to open my door for me.

He holds out his hand to help me out, and I take it, smiling like a schoolgirl with a crush.

Like the perfect gentleman he's proven himself to be, he walks me to the front porch of the building, stopping and turning to face me. He grabs my hands, holding them tightly as he looks into my eyes.

"Thanks for taking a chance on me today. This was the best day I've had in a long time."

"Same," I breathe. "Thank you for being patient with me. For still wanting to do this after the night we met. I had an amazing time with you."

He drags his teeth over his bottom lip. "Good. Does that mean we can see each other again? Maybe soon?"

I bite back my laugh. "Definitely. But I'm planning the next date."

His brows lift, but then he breaks into that gorgeous smile. "Sounds perfect."

I brush my thumbs over his as that breath-stealing tension seeps in again.

There's a tiny hitch in his breath as he unfurls our hands and cups my face, his fingers wrapping around the back of my neck as his thumbs brush my cheeks.

Kiss me.

I scream it internally. Even though I shouldn't because it'd be moving too fast again, I want to claw at him and drag him to my lips.

I don't, but I'm hanging on by a thread.

He rests his forehead against mine, his labored breaths tickling my lips until *finally* he closes the gap between us.

Sparks shoot everywhere as his lips touch mine, and I lean in, hands fisting the back of his shirt because I want him closer.

I leaped into our first kiss and was in over my head.

As much as I wanted him then, this is different.

It's chaste but still passionate. There's not even a whisper of his tongue against my lips and yet, I don't need more. This is perfect. Wild, but not unhinged.

My body hums with desire, and a contented moan slips out. His fingers curl into my hair at the sound. He drags the kiss out, lighting a fire inside me, and when he finally pulls away, it's like the burst of water that douses a fire, and I'm desperate for more flames—more warmth.

He smiles down at me. "Slow," he whispers.

Something else deep inside me relaxes. Some fear calmed by that one word. Even though I want to rush past where I'm comfortable, he keeps us in this safe space so I won't do something I'm not ready for.

I bite back the urge to thank him again and nod.

We stare at each other again, neither of us wanting to break the intensity of the moment, but slowly, his hands slide out of my hair and down my arms.

"Text or call me if you need anything." He gives me a sheepish smile. "Or you just want to talk."

I twine my fingers with his again. "I will." If anything, it'll be a feat not to text him as soon as I get inside. But I can wait until tomorrow. Let myself miss him a little. If I ever manage to let go of his hands.

I wait for him to let go, make a move to walk away, but he doesn't.

Then he leans in, that smooth voice sending a chill up my spine. "If you think I'm leaving before you're safely inside, you haven't been paying attention."

I laugh at that. He's right. After today, I should've been expecting that.

Since we can't stand here all night, I reluctantly pull my hands from his.

"Today was amazing." I press my lips against his cheek. "Get home safe."

"I will. Have a good night." I squeeze his hand and turn toward the door, only for his velvety voice to wash over me one last time. "Sweet dreams."

And then he smiles like he knows just how sweet they'll be.

I pause for half a second, smiling to myself, then go inside, hurrying up the stairs and into my apartment. Once I'm inside, I run to the window and watch him walk back to his car. Before he gets in, he looks up at my window and smiles.

I fall back onto the couch, kicking my feet and squealing.

Meeting Trevor wasn't on my bingo card. Neither was how easily I'm falling head over heels for him.

No, that's not right.

Head over heels is too smooth and delicate for the wild and chaotic chemistry flowing between us.

I need something that matches that. Something less graceful.

What's less graceful than head over heels?

Ass over tits.

Yep. That's right.

I'm falling ass over tits for Trevor Matteny.

Trevor

I'm on cloud nine when I get out of my car at the lake house.

I don't know who came up with that saying, but it's woefully inaccurate. After today I'm on cloud ninety-nine. One hundred. A thousand.

Chelsea is... everything. Looking at her, she's my dream girl. But in getting to know her, she's so much more than I ever knew I wanted. She single-handedly turned my world upside down and knocked me on my ass.

I'm loving every second.

I'm like Gene Kelly hanging off that streetlight in *Singing in the Rain.*

When I walk into the lake house, I'm *whistling*. I can't remember the last time I was this happy. Which must be why I walk straight upstairs, ignoring the stares from half of my housemates, and come to a stop outside of the master bedroom.

Sarah's inside, standing by the bed, folding clothes.

I quickly knock and her head snaps toward the doorway.

"Hey."

"Can I come in?"

"Of course. What's up?"

"Thank you," I blurt.

Her brows shoot up. "What?"

"Thank you. For breaking up with me."

"Oh." The surprise on her face morphs into a wicked, knowing smile that, despite not being genetically related, she got from her grandmother. "Today was your date with Chelsea."

"Yep."

"I take it things went well."

"Definitely." *Is calling it the best day of my life too dramatic?* "It was..." I'm struggling to find the words. Perfect still seems wrong. Right sounds too weak. "Everything."

Her smile grows. "That's adorable. I love it."

I run a hand through my hair. "So anyway, thank you for ending things when you did. I'm sure that sounds stupid, but I would've held on too tightly for too long, and even if I'd realized it felt wrong eventually, I would've tried to force it, and we both would've ended up unhappy. And missed out on something better. Because what I feel with Chelsea is—"

"Right."

She looks down at the clothes she's folding. Not just hers. Joel's too.

"Yeah."

"I'm glad you're happy."

"Are you happy?"

She looks around the room, a smile of wonder on her face. "Yeah. I am. I'm still scared to screw it up, but I feel like I'm right where I'm supposed to be."

Me too.

"Good. Well, I'll leave you to it. Have a good night."

"Yeah. You too." I turn to leave, but she calls after me. "Try to keep the *noise* down in there."

I laugh and throw my middle finger up as I walk away.

I'm too happy to even jerk off tonight.

When I get to my room, I strip down to my boxers, throw on an undershirt, and flop down on my bed. And despite how early it is, as I replay today like a rom-com in my mind, I fall asleep with a smile on my face.

8

Blossoming

Trevor

OBNOXIOUS BUZZING ON MY bedside table threatens to pull me from the last threads of sleep.

I close my eyes and pull the pillow over my head. My brain is lost in a hazy replay of yesterday's date and Chelsea's smile. My dick is half hard and I'm enjoying the fuzzy, peaceful feeling like I'm floating back to dreamland.

Until my phone goes off again.

With a groan, I throw my hand out, fumbling for it. When my hand connects with it, I drag it to my ear, barely swiping the right spot to answer the call.

"Who are you and what do you want with my life?"

"Do you like scary movies?" Hyla whispers in a creepy voice.

"No. Goodbye."

"You'd hang up on a serial killer? Really? Sounds dangerous."

"Almost as dangerous as hanging up on your mother." Mom's voice cuts in, and I groan again.

"I'm here. Say things. Can't promise not to fall back to sleep."

"You're very grumpy this morning," Hyla says. "Didn't your date go well?"

"Ugh. That's why you're calling? It's barely been twelve hours since it ended."

"Well, you didn't call either of us last night. Not even a text," Mom says dramatically.

"Yeah, for all we knew, she could've been some kind of succubus who stole your soul."

"Hy, quit with the scary movies. It's not even October yet."

"But they're the only things more horrifying than my life."

"Hyla."

"Ugh. Don't use that tone."

"He's right," Mom sings.

Good. Let them take on the conversation, and I'll go back to sleep.

"Nope. No topic changes," Hyla says.

So close.

"Come on, Mr. Grumpy Pants. Tell us what's wrong," she prods.

"The only thing that's wrong is that you're interrupting me reliving the date in my dreams—don't make a sex joke—and I'd like to get back to it."

"You really like her," Mom says, voice warm and comforting.

I finally throw the pillow off my face and let the sunlight wash the last bit of sleep away.

"Yeah, I do."

Hyla squeals. "Yes. I love it. Seriously, what's her last name? I need to know if it has ship name potential."

"And on that note, I love you crazy people. Bye."

"You're no fun," Hyla calls.

"Love you, honey. Bye," Mom says.

I hang up and toss my phone to the side, then flop against the mattress again, but I'm too awake now.

I sit up and stretch, then grab my phone again and check for any messages.

Any hint of the bad mood at having my dream ripped away vanishes when I see a text from Chelsea from late last night.

Chelsea: Thank you for today. I can't wait to do it again.

With a smile, I go to her contact information, and maybe stupidly, pathetically, change it to *Dream Girl*. Then I text her back.

Me: I'm already looking forward to it.

With that done, I climb out of bed and make my way downstairs, the same spring in my step as last night.

Unsurprisingly, most everyone is milling about the kitchen. From what I remember from visiting them over the years, weekend mornings are usually relaxed. Occasionally Rae will pick up a shift at Promise, Sarah will get caught up in nursing stuff, or Joel will go for a run, but otherwise, it's low-key.

Except right now. Because they're all staring at me like silent-as-the-grave pod people.

If I hadn't had the best date of my life yesterday, I'd have assumed Hyla put them up to this with her scary movie thing. But no. This is the calm before the meddling storm.

I wonder if I can get in, get my coffee, and get out before—

"You look happy this morning," Amanda says.

Here we go.

Aaron hands me a mug of coffee before I can get to the coffee maker, then Mackenzie appears in front of me with creamer.

"And you all seem preoccupied this morning." I take a seat at the kitchen counter.

"We're doing what we always do," Miles says, looking over his shoulder. He's at the stove cooking... something.

Then I notice him flip something. *Pancakes.*

"Standing around being creepy?" I ask, taking a sip of my coffee.

"Rude. I take offense to that. We're never creepy. We're just happy for you," Rae says.

I look around at all of them. "Wait, I know people joke about this being some kind of cult, but—"

"People joke about that?" Joel asks.

"Mostly people we like," Mackie says. "Nick and his friend group."

"Like they're any better!" Rae huffs. "Nicholas Asshole," she grumbles under her breath.

I choke on my coffee. I forgot she calls him that. Takes me right back to high school and the two of us annoying the shit out of her in every class we had together.

Miles flips the burner off, plates up pancakes, then slides one in front of me.

"Tell them something about the date or they will never stop being weird."

Truth.

"It was... good." I dip my head to hide my smile and dig into my pancake.

"Bullshit!" Sarah says, hoisting herself onto the counter. "He told me last night how *amazing* it was."

I look over at her with a big smile. "No idea what you're talking about."

"Aww, I love smiling Trevor," Amanda says.

Mackie pinches my cheek. "So cute."

"Enough," I grumble. I wish she and Hyla could figure their shit out because they really are a match made in heaven.

"On that note, I'm feeling a morning walk," Rae says, looking around at the girls.

"Oh, yes please," Amanda says.

Mackie hops off the stool next to me. "I'll come too."

Sarah slides off the counter to join them, her eyes lingering on Joel while he eye fucks her in return. They might as well just kiss in front of us and get it over with, but that's Sarah. She holds herself back from love because she doesn't think she deserves it.

Rae kisses Aaron, then, as the girls file out of the kitchen, she leans in and squeezes my arm. "For the record, it's good to see you smile like that. It's been too long since we've seen this side of you. Don't be afraid to enjoy it."

Then she heads upstairs to get ready with the rest of the girls.

The guys take spots around the kitchen counter, all focused on eating their pancakes, as that almost eerie silence settles in again.

"Really? You guys aren't going to annoy the shit out of me with questions?"

"We'll do that after breakfast," Joel says.

"Apparently we're going on a field trip," Miles adds.

"Where?"

"Baseball field." Aaron's smile is massive. "Since Miles is going to be playing with us again for the first time since high school, we figured we should start reconditioning him."

For the first time this morning, my good mood legitimately fades a little.

"Unless you don't want to come," Aaron says, voice softer.

"No. I'm—that's fine." I smile again, but it's forced.

Maybe I should tell them I haven't been on a baseball field since my accident. They'd understand. I knew I'd have to face it eventually, but I'm not sure I was ever going to be ready.

My love of baseball is intrinsically tied to my dad. It was something we did together and bonded over. My understanding and love of the game came from him. Losing it the way I did made me feel like I was losing a part of him too. Like I was letting him down.

Though I've been to a handful of baseball games since my accident—mostly here to support the guys—I haven't set foot on a baseball field. I haven't wanted to. Working with the team was going to be a way to push myself to get over the—not fear, exactly—discomfort or uncertainty of going out there again. I don't know how it will feel. I guess it might be better to do it with the guys than in front of the whole team—or worse, by myself. Because that's probably what I would've done. I'm good at isolating myself and dealing with my problems alone.

I'm a protector and caretaker by nature—the flip side of which is me not wanting to burden other people with my problems.

"Are you sure it's fine?" Joel asks.

I suck in a deep breath. "Yeah. It'll be good to get back out there again."

Or something like that.

Chelsea

Chelsea.
Hazy half-awake, half-asleep me closes my eyes tighter, trying to find the dream source of the voice.
Chelsea.
Mm. What's even happening right now? Am I dreaming?
"Chelsea!"

Fingers dig into my ribs and I jump up, nearly falling out of bed.

"Ah! What the fuck?" I'm panting as my eyes land on Robbie. "What are you doing here?"

He's sitting on the edge of the bed, a plate on his lap. He tosses a cheesy tater tot into his mouth and smiles at me.

"Had to make sure you were alive."

I press a hand to my chest. "Assuming you didn't give me a heart attack just now, then yes. I'm alive." I let out a huff. "That better be for me."

He passes the plate over.

I sigh with happiness as I inhale. Blueberry muffin, cheesy tater tots with scrambled eggs and chives, and fresh strawberries.

"Okay, you're almost forgiven."

"Almost? I made you all that for breakfast and all I get is yelled at and *almost* forgiven?"

"You forgot the coffee."

He throws his head back. "You're impossible."

"You started this. I was happily sleeping."

"Until 10:00 a.m."

My eyes flare. "Really?"

He shows me his phone. "Date must've worn you out."

I shove his shoulder. "That's not funny. It was a long, wonderful date. But if anything, I was so hyped, I kept replaying it and couldn't fall asleep."

"Wow. So you're saying I don't need to hate him?"

I roll my eyes. "I'd prefer if you didn't. I'm not going to get crazy and say he's *the one*, but no one else—even people I've dated longer—has ever made me feel like he does. Our connection runs deep and we have these little ties to each other from our past. Missed connections, kind of? I don't know. I don't want to jinx it or overthink it, but I'm really happy, and I'm looking forward to seeing him again."

Robbie lets out a dramatic sigh, then steals one of my strawberries. "He was great yesterday. I got a good feeling from him, and I'm not sure that's ever happened because I'm a naturally suspicious person. I won't tell you to be careful, but if you need anything, or if he fucks up, I'm here."

"Thanks."

He pops the strawberry into his mouth and climbs off the bed. "I'll leave you to eat."

"Thanks for breakfast," I say as he walks out of the room.

He waves as he goes, and I settle back on my bed. Grabbing my phone, I think about what audiobook I want to listen to—it's rare I don't have music or an audiobook playing—when I glimpse the book Trevor and I decided to read on the nightstand. I quickly check my library app to see if they have it. Score. And it's the one where I can instantly borrow without having to wait in line.

I start the book and enjoy my breakfast, lost in the carryover of fuzzy, warm feelings from last night. This is the fun part. Letting myself get swept up in romance and falling for him. There are heavier conversations ahead, but I'm going to enjoy where we are now and wait until I'm comfortable to get into that stuff.

My phone pings, and I dive for it like a feral animal.

It's a text from Rae, and while I'm initially bummed it's not Trevor, her text makes me smile and want to kick my feet.

Rae: Trevor is happy this morning, and I'm guessing we have you to thank for that. Seriously, I haven't seen him smile like this in a long time. Just thought you'd like to know.

My heart gets all flippy and fluttery at that.

It's exhilarating and a little terrifying all at once, but I like it.

As I'm closing out of the message, I see a text from Trevor from earlier this morning that I must've missed. It's a response to the one I sent him last night about our date and being excited for another.

Trevor: I'm already looking forward to it.

Another date. One I want to plan this time. Even if nothing can beat the epicness of our first date, I want to do something special for him. I think—way too long—about a reply, but decide not to send one. I don't want to force a conversation. If I'm going to text him, I want it to have some kind of substance, whether it's just fun or something more. But what I do is change his contact information to *Book Boyfriend*.

Cheesy.

So. Freaking. Cheesy.

But I don't care. I'm going to let myself be all dopey and ridiculous because I haven't felt this carefree in a long time.

I'm about to set my phone aside when another text comes through.

Unknown number: Hey, Chelsea. It's Amanda. I got your number from Rae. I was wondering if maybe you wanted to meet up for coffee today? Get to know each other better? Let me know.

I quickly add her as a contact, then reread the text. Amazing date yesterday and now a new friend date today?

I glance at my plate of food. Robbie conveniently didn't make coffee. It would be perfect. And I'd like to get to know Amanda better. Even if she might be asking only to get the details about my date with Trevor. Maybe she wants to know if I'll stick around. It should still be fun, though. And I'll never turn down coffee.

Me: Sure. Sounds fun. Want to meet at Buzzing Brews in like an hour?

Amanda: Sounds great! See you then!

One week. I've been in Old Lake Town for a week and more good things than I could've expected have come my way.

Maybe, just maybe, karma really is on my side, and she's finally getting the universe to pay up.

The bell above the door chimes as I walk into Buzzing Brews and smile like a fool at the heavenly scent of coffee. So much coffee. They roast their own beans here, and it makes it taste that much better.

I'm debating whether to grab a table or order at the counter when the door chimes again, and I turn to see Amanda walking toward me, a bright smile on her face, and her long, strawberry blonde hair swaying behind her.

"Hey, it's good to see you." She gives me a quick hug.

"You too. Thanks for suggesting this."

We move toward the counter.

"Of course. I know Rae will just walk up to people and decide they're friends—and I love her for it—but it's never come as easily to me. I'm glad you said yes."

"I'm looking forward to creating new friendships too."

We order our drinks and small talk for a few minutes. Like the rest of their crew, Amanda seems genuine, but the timing still has me thinking she asked me here for the gossip about my date. Not that I'm against gushing about Trevor. His friends would probably appreciate it more than Robbie would.

We take a table by the window that looks out over the edge of town and toward the lake in the distance, Amanda telling me about how she met Rae and the girls—and everyone else by extension—and how it's been living at the lake house with them so far.

Once a waitress brings our drinks, she's quiet for a moment, inhaling the scent of her coffee and gazing out the window.

Should I start another conversation? Or maybe get the one she's interested in out of the way?

I clear my throat and take a deep breath. "So aren't you going to ask?"

Her gaze drifts back to me. "Ask what?"

"How my date with Trevor went. Isn't that why you asked me here?"

She scrunches her face. "I didn't ask you here because you went out with Trevor. Well, okay, that's why I thought of texting you. Not the date exactly, but how you reacted the other night... it had the mama bear part of me concerned. Trevor talking about the date again made me think of that and I wondered if you're okay. I'm not here to get information from you. I'm here to build a friendship with you."

My cheeks blaze. *Shit.* I need to stop that gut instinct of not trusting people. Or assuming the worst. My stomach goes cold. Or stop believing I don't deserve better than that.

Amanda puts her hand on the table and leans in. "Okay, who hurt you? I'm going to need names and preferably phone numbers so I can call them up and tell them what feckless idiots they are."

"Feckless?" I choke on a surprised laugh.

She shrugs. "I was listening to an audiobook with a Welsh character. He kept saying that. Anyway, no avoiding my question."

I sit with that for a moment, debating what to tell her. It's not one clear answer. What I went through with my assault and dealing with Bridget and Lex both have played a part. I haven't told anyone here what I went through yet, though Rae obviously has some idea. Do I want to tell her before I tell Trevor?

"Sorry. I... you're right that I've been hurt, and I'm sorry I put that on you. I appreciate you asking me here, and I want to get to know you. As for who hurt me, that's complicated, but friendship-wise, it has to do with my friends back home. Who I'm starting to think aren't my friends at all. Not in the real sense. I spent the last year struggling, and all they did was nag me about how I wasn't fun anymore."

"Again, I'll take phone numbers. Always happy to tell off some asshole friends."

I don't know whether to laugh or cry because she's serious. She's not just here to build a friendship. She's giving me her instant loyalty.

"I appreciate that, but it's not just them. I went through something... well, you know where I work. With Rae. There's a reason for that."

She leans forward and grabs my hand. "I'm so sorry."

"I'm doing better now, but still healing, and trust doesn't come easily to me."

"What happened with Trevor makes a lot more sense now."

"He doesn't know," I say quickly. "Rae knows about as much as you do, and I—"

"Breathe, Chels. I'm not going to tell him—or anyone—anything. I know it's probably weird or strange because there's this big group of us who are close, but we all have unique friendships. My friendship with Rae is different from my friendship with Sarah, which is different from my friendship with Mackie. And all of that is different from my relationship with any of the guys. Or Hyla." She laughs. "Who, funny enough, I didn't even like at first."

"Wait, you don't like Hyla?" I ask in surprise. Especially since Amanda and Trevor seem to be good friends.

"I *love* Hyla. But when we first met, I didn't trust her. I just hadn't realized how much the world had hurt her or how badly she needed love and protection." Amanda squeezes my arm. "Now I get the feeling you need that too. And you've got it. Anything you tell me stays with me."

With a sigh, I drop my head and run my hand through my hair. "I kind of feel like an asshole now."

"Hey, part of my friendship is not letting anyone talk badly about you. Including yourself. You're not an asshole. You're healing. And I'm here for any part of that journey you want to share with me."

"Even if it's messy?"

She laughs. "In time you'll learn, messy is what we do best. Not only are the girls amazing friends, they're an amazing tribe of women who come together and support each other. I was really lonely and pretty insecure before I found them. They made me feel accepted and wanted. I hope in time you'll feel that way too. Not just with the group, but with me."

Fuck. I'm not used to this easy vulnerability. But I want to be. I've craved strong female friendships for a long time, and I'm not going to let that untrusting negative voice inside me ruin this.

"I'm already feeling that way with you."

"Good. Now. No more about Trevor or emotional things—unless you have something you want to share—otherwise, I want to know about you. Tell me something about you. What you do for fun. What you enjoy."

"Reading is my number one hobby. I'm deep in a fantasy romance hole right now."

"Ooh, I'm here for that."

"And I love volleyball."

"Ah! See, friendship goals already. I played all through middle and high school."

"Seriously?" My face lights up. "Wait. We must've played each other. You're from Woods Junction, right?"

She nods. "Yep. I remember playing against Birch Lake in high school. That's crazy."

Wow. Apparently, this invisible string vibe I have going on extends beyond Trevor.

"I played in college too, but after leaving my old school, I kind of gave up on it. I've been getting the itch to play again, though."

"I don't know if there's anything around here, but there's a three-on-three rec league back home over the summer. I usually sign up to be assigned to a team, but we could sign up together as a team if we found a third. If you're interested."

She smiles a little sheepishly, and it doesn't suit her. She seems too confident for that.

"I'd love to. Maybe we could convince one of the girls to join us."

"Mackie or Hyla might be interested. Or maybe my best friend back home."

"Well, however it works out, I'm in." I take a sip of coffee, then we settle into a relaxed conversation.

Mostly, she asks questions about my life, but I try to sneak some in about her life too, and find out she has two older brothers, one who is the bane of her existence and the other who she's pretty close with.

Once our coffees are gone, we decide to go for a walk and do some window shopping.

Amanda is naturally energetic and her brain is always going. She has another topic to ask about as soon as I've finished one, and she has plenty of funny, quippy responses. Conversation flows naturally. She's surprisingly easy to talk to, but I'm starting to feel like that's all I've done. When I finish saying something about Robbie and our close relationship, I stop her before she can ask something else.

"I feel like all I've done is talk about me and my chaotic life. I want to hear about yours."

She smiles and loops an arm through mine as we stroll down the block.

"Hm, let's see. I'm twenty. I'll be twenty-one in January, which tracks because I'm a total type A Capricorn. In case you didn't catch on earlier, I'm loyal to the bitter end and would cut a bitch for the people I love. Bring me sushi, coffee, or chocolate and I'll love you forever. I always wanted to be the girl with the huge found family of friends, and when I met Rae and the girls, I felt like I was coming home. I'm bi and have only had two serious relationships. A girlfriend in high school who I thought loved me but decided she didn't want to be with another girl, and my boyfriend, who is amazing and kind and who I hate doing distance with, but it's worth it for our love."

"Wow. You're like a total badass when it comes to vulnerability."

She shrugs one shoulder. "I figure if I open up to other people, maybe they'll open up to me—or at least know I'm a safe space."

I let that settle for a moment. That's what meeting up today has been about.

"Thank you for asking me to hang out today."

"Thanks for saying yes."

Something deep inside me awakens. Everything with Amanda has been simple, yet not simple at all. It's the blossoming of a friendship that goes deeper than hanging out. And it makes me feel stronger. Like I have someone to stand by my side, to catch me when I'm falling. Someone outside my family. Someone who's choosing me. Maybe I'm reading too much into it, but I don't think I am. I think this is exactly what we both need. And it's a reminder for me—or maybe a lesson—of the importance of female friendships.

That's what I want. Strong female friendships. Not toxic ones. Friendships rooted in vulnerability and support. Where we uplift each other and rely on each other and get each other through the hard times. That's where our power begins, within our tribe. When we learn to stand together, empower each other, and fight back, that's how we create change and lead the next generation of women who will do the same.

I'm honored that Amanda and Rae have seen that in me—and in that brief meeting Sarah and Mackenzie did too. I can't wait for our friendships to grow deeper and take roots, and I'm determined to put in the energy—and the vulnerability—to make that happen.

Trevor

The mixing scents of grass, chalk, and dirt wash over me as I hover at the fence, staring at the field in front of me. The baseball stadium at SUNY FL is about the same size as an exhibition league stadium, but still bigger than usual for a D3 school. However, baseball is big in this area, and with no other teams locally, there's a surprisingly big local fan base.

I've sat in the seats here, watching Joel play and Aaron coach plenty of times over the last couple of years. Why is stepping onto the field so damn hard?

Probably for the same reason I've avoided it.

The way it all ties into my memories of my dad. The dreams we dreamed together. My plans, and how it felt to have them ripped away. Aaron encouraged me to explore my options, and I'm glad I decided to be involved with the team. I could never truly let baseball go. I hope one day, I'll coach my kids' teams.

But stepping out here today is as much a fresh start as a reminder of what I lost.

And I'm so fucking scared it won't feel the same.

That I'll feel that overwhelming grief again. I don't want that.

I've lost enough. Grieved enough.

The guys, who were horsing around on the field, now come to a stop in front of me.

"Okay?" Joel asks.

"I, uh... haven't been on a field since my accident. What if it doesn't feel the same?"

Aaron smiles. "What if it feels better?"

"Or what if it feels like having fun with your friends and remembering why you loved the game in the first place?" Miles asks.

Fuck it.

I step onto the grass.

And...

I start laughing.

"What's happening?" Miles asks.

"I think he's broken," Joel says.

I stop laughing suddenly. "No. Sorry. I just—wow. I really built that up in my head, all to feel... nothing." And then I'm laughing again. "This isn't *Field of Dreams* or *Angels in the Outfield*. Why did I think this was going to be some massive moment?" I'm an idiot.

Aaron claps me on the shoulder. "Good to know we haven't lost you."

My laughter finally fades, and I look around the stadium.

Good to know I haven't lost this.

It's still the same. Same comfortable feeling of coming home. Like I know my place out here, and right now, I'm realizing that has nothing to do with third base or the batter's box and everything to do with this place being a part of me.

Because of my dad. He's the reason for all of it. Baseball has a piece of my soul because of him. It grounds me because he taught me to let my pain and my fears drift away on the field. It brings me comfort because of every game of catch he played with me, every time he cheered me on, and every game we watched together where he taught me about the skill, mechanics, and camaraderie of the game. It's a safe place because of the friendships he taught me to build here. I look over at the guys. The friendships still standing today.

I blink back tears.

I'm going to be okay.

The words sound in my head, but not in my voice. In my father's.

Maybe that's why this is the first time since my accident that I've believed them.

Miles steps closer and rests a hand on my shoulder. "Let's enjoy this. It's been too long since we've been together out here. Let's have some fun."

Aaron pitches. Miles catches. Joel and I take turns batting, then we switch it up again. Miles bats. Joel does a terrible job as catcher. Aaron lets me pitch.

They tease me about being crushed out on Chelsea—it's not like they're wrong.

And when I hit a ball way into left field and run the bases, I reconnect with the part of me that loves the game for what it is, and I let go of the loss.

Playing professional ball could've been amazing, but it would never have been what made baseball special. Knowing I haven't lost that gives me peace I've been craving for months.

The guys surround me when I get to home plate, and Miles asks, "How did that feel?"

"Awesome." I glance between them, and Aaron's bright smile makes me realize something. "Coming here wasn't just for Miles, was it?"

Aaron shrugs, smile growing. "Sometimes we all need a reminder of why the game's important to us. But this is also a reminder that if you're struggling, we've got you."

"Thank you. I'm lucky to have you guys." I clear my throat. "And I've hit my deep emotional quota for the day. Wanna grab lunch before we head back to the lake house?"

"Yeah. We can pick up stuff for the girls too," Joel says.

As we leave the field, I'm reminded again of my father's lesson—to leave it all on the field. Today I left some of the weight in my chest behind, no doubt.

I love a lazy Sunday.

Even though playing ball with the guys was anything but lazy.

After that, though, I spent most of the afternoon on the back deck, hanging out with my friends and relaxing. Then I called my mom and let her ask me a million questions about Chelsea.

As I walk back into my room after dinner, my phone goes off.

And I'm thrilled when I see it's a text from Chelsea.

Dream Girl: Have you started the book yet?

Dream Girl: I'm hooked. I'm on chapter 3. You better catch up so we can talk about it.

I flop on my bed and grab the book. Guess I'll be up late reading. I'll take any excuse to talk to her.

Me: I'm starting right now.

Dream Girl: Can't wait to hear your thoughts.

Me: Should I live text you?

Dream Girl: Then how would you read? Send me your thoughts when you hit the end of the first chapter.

Me: Will do.

Me: Hey, Chels?

Dream Girl: Yeah?

Me: Can I see you tomorrow? Maybe eat lunch together?

Dream Girl: Like a date?

Me: Like more getting to know each other before our next date.

Dream Girl: Always thinking so highly of yourself.

Me: Or I'm just obsessed with you.

Dream Girl: Duh. Who wouldn't be?

Dream Girl: I guess I could agree to lunch. Keep reading and we can discuss tomorrow. I'll stop after chapter five.

Me: I'm in. See you tomorrow.

With that, I set my phone down and get lost in the book, excited to text her more, get to know her better, and hopefully let whatever is happening between us keep growing into something bigger.

9

Pinch me

Chelsea

I LAUGH INTO MY coffee cup as I read my most recent text from Trevor.

Book Boyfriend: Just got to the first spicy scene. And the whole cafe got to hear a snippet because my headphone cord popped out.

Nope, I can't stop laughing.

Me: This is why they make wireless headphones. But at least it was a good scene?

Book Boyfriend: I'm glad you can laugh at my pain.

Me: You don't strike me as someone who embarrasses easily. Or gives a fuck what people who don't know you think.

Book Boyfriend: I love that you've already got me figured out. Lunch today? I'm free at noon.

Me: Sounds good. Are we continuing our quest to see which dining hall is best?

Book Boyfriend: Obviously. I'll meet you after your 11 to 12 class.

Me: Already learning my schedule?

Book Boyfriend: Is it cool or not cool to say yes?

Me: I don't know if it's cool, but it's kind of adorable.

Book Boyfriend: Might be destroying my reputation, but okay. I'll see you later.

Me: Later.

Robbie clears his throat and stares at me from across the table.

"Anyone ever tell you it's rude to be on your phone when you're at the table eating breakfast with someone?"

"Says the guy who has had me run interference to kick your hookups out of here or made me endure breakfast with them. If having my nose in my phone is the worst thing I've done, I'm doing better than you."

He grimaces. "It sounds worse when you say it like that."

"Like what? Like how you let them think I'm your girlfriend so they'll leave without question? That's not just *worse*, it's gross."

He flips me off. "See if I cook you breakfast ever again."

I give him my sweetest smile. "But I'm your favorite niece."

I get his signature eye roll at that. "Thorn in my side is more like it. I assume you were talking to the boyfriend."

"He's not my boyfriend," I say quickly. Because we haven't had that talk yet, and I'm still easing into this.

"Mhm."

"Robbie."

"I'm just saying, if you text nonstop like a couple and spend time together like a couple... you might just be a couple."

"Rude."

"Delusional," he sings.

"And on that note, I should get to class." I push out of my chair and take my plate to the sink.

"Or to your boyfriend."

I shove his shoulder as I walk past. "You're the worst. Why'd I move here again?"

He puts his hands under his chin like he's an angel. "Because your life would be boring without me."

"You might be right about that." I sling my bag over my shoulder. "But who says boring is a bad thing?"

I smile at his perturbed look and wave as I leave.

The second I'm out the door, I put in my wireless earbuds and start up the audio of the book Trevor and I have been reading. We went for the fairytale retelling first, and even though it's only been a few days and we've both been busy, we're making progress. I like it because it gives us a reason to text without feeling like it's too much too soon.

The connection between us has been intense from the start, but that's a big reason I want to take things slow. My past aside, I don't want to rush into this. I want to let it build slowly—both so I can get comfortable in it and so we build a strong foundation. Chemistry and connection are amazing, but they aren't what make relationships last. We've had mini-dates at lunch each day this week to get to know each other better, and then we'll have another actual date on Saturday—one I'm planning. I know nothing will compare to the all day first date, but I'm still excited to do something special for Trevor after how thoughtful he was planning it.

My morning goes by quickly. It's nice because I have a class with Rae and another with Mackenzie. I didn't think about how much better classes are with built-in friends, but I'm glad I have people I know with me. It's helping me feel more settled here.

Though, if I'm honest, from the beginning, I've felt more settled here than I ever did in Syracuse. Going there made me feel special because it was a big D1 school with a sports team who wanted me, but I never fit in there. I stayed busy, hung out with people, and went to parties because they made me feel like I fit when I didn't.

Here it's easy.

Maybe that's why it's easier for me to feel like myself.

"Hutchins Hall," Trevor says, holding the door open for me. There are four dining halls, three cafés, and one sandwich shop on campus. We're trying them all to see which is best. This will be our fourth one this week.

As we make our way to the dining area of Hutchins Hall, I'm surprised to find it's open and well-lit with a wall of glass doors leading to a courtyard.

"Based on aesthetics, this one is already my favorite."

"Yeah, it's nice. Want to eat outside?"

"Sounds good."

We both grab food—a steak burrito bowl for Trevor and broccoli cheddar soup with fresh bread and a chicken Caesar salad for me—then find a table outside. The gorgeous late summer weather makes me want to skip classes the rest of the day. Seventy-five and sunny with the lake breeze is the best weather ever.

"How's your day been?" Trevor asks.

"Good. I think I'm... happy."

He laughs. "You sound so unsure."

"I'm not. I'm surprised, I guess. I wasn't sure I'd be *happy* here. Or at least not this soon. I figured I'd be indifferent for a while until I got used to it."

He gets a big, cheesy grin on his face. "It's because of me, right? I get it. I totally make your days better."

I snort and roll my eyes. "Has anyone ever told you that you're incredibly humble?"

He pretends to think about it. "Nope."

"There's a reason for that."

He clutches a hand to his chest. "Always trying to hurt me with your words. I'm starting to think you don't like me at all."

Even though the massive pout he gives me is pretend, I can't help but want to fix it.

I kiss his nose. "Yep. Totally hate you."

He laughs and runs a hand down my back, playing with my hair.

I smile to myself because it seems almost involuntary. I love that he does it, so I don't pick on him about it—I'm worried he'd stop or think it was too much for me. Instead, I enjoy the sensation and lean into the touch.

"How's your day been?"

He nods. "Fine. Classes bore the shit out of me, but I'm told I still have to go to them. Lame, if you ask me."

"The worst."

"Our lunch dates are a bright spot in my day."

"I knew it. You're totally obsessed with me." I flip my hair and give him a sultry smile.

He kisses my cheek. "Totally obsessed."

"Well, unfortunately for you, you're going to have to get by without me tomorrow. Friday mornings I'm at Promise."

"Damn. Well, I'll have to get by dreaming of our date this weekend. Any chance you want to tell me where we're going?"

"And spoil the fun? No chance."

"Fine. I guess I can wait."

I nudge him with my elbow. "It'll be worth it. I promise."

He glances down at me, smiling, but doesn't say anything.

We settle into a comfortable silence, until I get an idea.

"Want to read together?"

A smile splits his face. "Fuck yes. I've been wanting to do that since we picked out the books. Reading separately and texting each other is fun, but I've been wanting to actually read together."

"Got your book?"

"Yep."

With that, we both pull our books out and continue eating as we read.

Reading the same book as someone when you're in the same space is underrated. Even if you're not at the same part, you get to see the moments they pause and reflect, when a line hits just right, little gasps at unexpected moments. It's a unique look into something that is normally a solitary activity.

Out of the corner of my eye, I steal glances at Trevor, but I'm the one to draw his attention when I let out a little *mm* noise.

"Get to something good?" he purrs in my ear.

"The second sex scene," I whisper.

"I better read faster."

He looks back at his book, and I continue on, but a page later, I snap the book shut.

Trevor stops reading and turns to me.

"You okay? Did someone die? Do we need to put the book in the freezer?"

I laugh out loud. "Like Joey on *Friends*? And who would be getting killed during a sex scene? This isn't a dark Mafia romance."

He shrugs. "What's up?"

"Eh, there was a line in there that..." How do I say this without dragging it into a conversation I don't want to have right now? "It just made me feel a little icky. Nothing bad. It's a me thing, not a book thing. I just need to take a break for a second."

It's a romance book. I should be expecting these kinds of lines. But the male main character slipping his fingers between the female main character's legs and saying, "Is this all for me?" hits differently now. Sure that can happen when you're turned on. But it can also happen from hormones or increased white blood cells when we're sick. It's not cut and dry.

That night is hazy and I can't recall exact words, but I remember the implication that I must've wanted it or should've stopped fighting it because my body clearly wanted it.

It makes me want to puke now, thinking about it.

It's such a small inconsequential line, and that fucker took away my ability to read it and not have any reaction to it. Yet another part of my peace he's tried to destroy.

I was so broken after what happened that I didn't fight. Didn't push the police investigation. But there's a fire growing in me every day, wondering if I *can* push now. Or if they've already tossed my case aside because who gives a fuck about a drugged-up woman who can't remember the fuckhead who raped her?

I clench and release my fist, and that's when Trevor shuts his book.

"Do you want to tell me what it is? I can read ahead and look out for it."

I suck in a deep breath, then turn toward him. The expression on his face is so... earnest. I seriously don't know what to do with him. Cupping his cheek, I lean in closer.

"No. I'm okay. I'll be okay."

He pushes his book away, then stretches and looks around.

"Up for a walk before your next class?"

"Sounds perfect."

I don't tell him that whatever we're doing, I'll enjoy myself because I'm with him, but it's the truth.

Robbie's words come back to me.

Are we boyfriend and girlfriend?

Trevor hasn't asked me, and I still think it might be too soon for that. *I don't want to rush.* But as Trevor's fingers twine with mine and that sense of peace washes over me, I'm starting to wonder if I'm kidding myself.

Trevor

I hate school.

I hate it at an irrational level, and it's only getting worse.

Maybe focusing so much on baseball before helped. Maybe I need to be exercising more to relax my brain. I don't know. But it's like I can't focus on any task for any of my classes. I like some of what I'm studying, but I don't know if I'm not engaged enough or if I have some kind of undiagnosed learning disorder because I can't keep my focus where it's meant to be.

As much as I'd like to blame Chelsea for that, I've struggled with this on and off before I met her. It's just worse now.

Which is why I spent most of the day studying before our date, trying to get things done, only to flit between three projects and not make much progress on any of them. Whatever. I'll get it done. Eventually.

For now, I'm putting it all on the back burner and focusing on Chelsea.

I have no idea where we're going on our date, but I'm excited to find out.

When I pull up to her apartment building, I find her sitting on a picnic table in the front yard, wearing a smile that could end me. Her hair is tousled and extra sexy, looking redder in the autumn sun, and it sways behind her as she hops off the table and walks over to me.

"Waiting for me?"

I want to sweep her into my arms, spin her around, and kiss her.

But I'm still not sure where we stand on that.

I know how I feel and what I want, but she gets to call the shots on this.

She shrugs, her two-tone eyes dancing in the late afternoon sun. "I was excited to see you."

Then she throws her arms around my neck and presses onto her toes to kiss my cheek.

Kill me dead.

My heart beats in the most over-the-top erratic way, and I don't give a fuck. I hope she can feel it, so she knows just how crazy she makes me.

I wrap my arms around her back and hold her close, burying my face in her neck, and hoping it's not too much for her. Not only does she not pull away, she slips her fingers into my hair, and I'm a goner.

Such little time we've known each other, and yet, I crave her.

"Missed you," I whisper.

She clears her throat and steps back. "I missed you too." She pulls her bottom lip between her teeth and fuuuck. I wish I was the one doing that to that pouty bottom lip.

I card my fingers through her hair, twisting one of the strands around my finger.

"How was your day?" she asks.

"Boring. I hate school stuff. The only bright spot was texting you. How was your day?"

She lights up. "It was good. Texting you is always a bright spot in my day. And looking forward to tonight. I missed our lunch date yesterday, and I kept thinking I wanted to see you, even though I knew I'd be seeing you today. Actually, you're kind of infiltrating my brain."

"Uh oh."

She smacks my chest. "It's not bad. It's just..."

"What?"

"Are we boyfriend and girlfriend?" she asks in a rush.

As much as I'd love to say yes to that, it's not my call to make. Not totally.

"Do you want us to be?"

She's chewing on her lip again, but this time it's out of nervousness.

"Yes? No. I don't know. I want that *eventually*, but—"

"Okay, here's the deal. Until you can look at me and enthusiastically tell me you're ready for that, then we're not going to use labels. This is new, and we agreed to take it slow, so the ball is in your court. Whenever you feel ready for that, just let me know."

"But—do you want to be my boyfriend?"

"Of course I do. I already see myself that way. I'm going to treat you the same regardless. I'll eat lunch with you, walk you to your classes, take you on dates, be there whenever you need me. But I don't need a label that will only add pressure and expectations to what we're doing. I'm yours, Chels, in whatever way you want me. You tell me when you want to add the label."

She stares at me, lips parted, an adorable look of surprise on her face.

Then, out of nowhere, she pinches me hard on the arm.

"Ow. What was that for?"

"I needed to make sure you were real."

I laugh and cup her face in my hands. "If you're questioning that, I must be living up to the fantasy book boyfriend reputation."

She rubs her mouth, trying to hide a smile. "Something like that." A moment of comfortable silence passes between us, then she takes a deep breath. "Ready for our date?"

"Absolutely."

The sound of air bubbling through a straw makes me laugh, especially when Chelsea makes a satisfied "ah" and looks down at the now-empty cup in her hand.

"That was delicious." She bounces over to the nearby trashcan and puts it in before returning to my side and grabbing my hand so we can continue our walk through the zoo.

There's an event here tonight. Some kind of fundraiser for a local women's shelter. There are food trucks and even a mobile tattoo shop. Chelsea was tempted by that but ultimately couldn't pick which design she wanted, so we continued on.

We sampled several food trucks, but then Chelsea saw a sign for milkshakes, so we got some before enjoying a walk around the zoo.

"I'm learning food is the way to your heart."

She grins up at me. "Took you this long? You haven't even fed me garlic bread yet."

I chuckle. "Italian for our next date night?"

"I won't complain."

I pull her closer and wrap my arm around her back, enjoying the heat of her body pressed against mine. As September goes on, the nights have gotten cooler. She leans into the touch, wrapping her arm around my back as well. The wind ripples across the lake, adding an extra chill to the air.

"So, food is one thing. What are the other ways to your heart? I need to take some notes if I'm going to stay on your good side."

She tilts her head and looks up at me. "Hm. Let's see. Puppies. And kittens. I always think I want one, even though I know they're a lot of work. Really, I want to go play with some or steal someone else's for a day. Well, puppies at least. I might get a kitten eventually."

"Okay, volunteering for an animal shelter is now a date option. What else?"

"Psychics."

"What?" I ask with a laugh.

"It's a weird thing, but I'm a sucker for psychics—the hokier the better. I won't book an appointment at a place for the heck of it, but if I'm at some event or carnival with a psychic, I always stop into the tent. I've never had an accurate reading, and they've always been ridiculous, but it's so much fun. I'm also obsessed with psychic reality shows."

"A date to a psychic. We can try and confuse them and see if they figure it out."

She laughs. "Brilliant."

I brush my lips over her cheek. "Tell me more."

"I love road trips. Especially in the late summer. Something about it makes me want to jump in the car and just go, destination unknown. Makes me feel whimsical, like I'm living in an Eagles song."

My grip on her tightens, and I feel the familiar tug of that tether between us. The one I still don't fully understand, but want more of nonetheless.

"My dad loved the Eagles. He always had music on in the car, but if we were going on a road trip, vacation, whatever, we always ended up going through his collection of Eagles albums."

"Sounds like the perfect summer plan."

I glance at her out of the corner of my eye, but she's smiling, taking in the view of the lake in the distance.

Is she thinking about summer... together?

Fuck, I love the thought of that.

If I'm honest, it kind of scares the shit out of me too. I didn't realize until she said it, but I've been picturing her in my future. Christmas, summer break, next year.

When did I get this lost in her and us? It's not a bad thing, but... if things don't work out between us, I already know I'll be crushed.

So, I'm going to manifest the shit out of it. Anything to help make sure it happens.

I want so much more with her, and at this point, I can't imagine a time when I won't.

That's almost unsettling, so I quickly push it away and focus on the sprawling tiger enclosure in front of us.

"What about you?" Chelsea asks.

"Huh?"

"You want to know all the ways to my heart. What are some of yours?"

It's on the tip of my tongue to mention baseball, but I don't want to. For now, I like that it's separate from my relationship with her.

Before she can say anything else, she adds, "Besides lazy days looking at the clouds, Loganberry, Dunkaroos, and generally anything nostalgic."

Damn. I've been making notes of all the things she loves, but I wasn't expecting her to do the same.

"Been paying attention, huh?"

She shrugs one shoulder, giving me a mischievous smile.

"Okay, uh, Mint-Ting-A-Ling. It's a flavor of Perry's ice cream. One of my mom's favorites and my dad always made sure we had some in the freezer. It's so comforting and nostalgic. It's one of my favorite ice creams. And going along with that, I'm a sucker for little gestures. My parents were never big gift givers—at least not between each other—they showed their love through small thoughtful acts. Like the Mint-Ting-A-Ling in the freezer or how my mom would leave little notes in my dad's lunchbox."

Oh, shit. Move away from this topic before I start crying.

"And *Terminator* movies. Some of them are legitimately terrible, but I can't help it. I love them. I'll watch them anytime I see they're on TV, and if I'm sick, they're my go-to movies."

She squeezes my hand a little tighter. "Good to know."

A smile tugs at the corners of my mouth. "Are you making a list?"

"Maybeeee. Oh look, penguins!" She tugs on my hand and leads me down the path, eyes already on the penguins, but I'm watching her, trying to memorize everything about her. The way she's smiling. The brightness in her eyes. She's so beautiful it makes my chest ache.

She's so giddy when we get to the enclosure and she starts cooing at them.

"Fan of penguins?"

"Yes. I love them. They're so cute, but they're also spicy. They're known to be incredibly loyal, but they also don't take shit from other penguins or zookeepers. And they'll fight a bitch for food. So basically, they're a cute, waddling, little version of me."

I move closer, wrapping my arms around her from behind. "You're so much cuter than them."

She leans back into me. "Did you know they can also be grumpy sometimes? Like this *adorable* guy I know. They also tend to mate for life."

Her words hang in the air, and my lips ache to kiss her. I have to physically hold myself back, because we haven't talked any further about what she's comfortable with, and I don't want to ruin tonight by taking things too far.

She turns her head and looks up at me, her eyes flitting to my lips. It takes all my willpower to hold back. If she wants to start this, it's up to her. But after a moment, she tilts her head back and brushes her lips over my cheek instead before looking back at the penguins. I hold her a little tighter, loving the feel of her body so close to mine.

"This was a perfect date idea."

"And for a great cause too."

Slowly, she steps away from me and takes my hand, giving the penguins one last look before we continue down the path.

"How did you hear about this? I don't remember seeing anything about it on campus."

"Promise. We had signs and little handouts about it. I figured what better way to spend a date night? Delicious food, cute animals, supporting women? All my favorite things."

I feign disappointment. "Should I be upset that you didn't include me in that list?"

She stops and spins to face me, tugging on my shirt to pull me closer. "You're the best part about tonight. Getting to share my favorite things with you only makes them better."

Her eyes sparkle in the setting sun as she stares up at me. It's impossible to keep my eyes from drifting down her face to her lips. I want to brush my lips over hers, dive in, and get lost in her, but she's been trepidatious from the start. She ran away after we kissed that night at the lake house, and the panic in her eyes was unmistakable.

So I lift my gaze, pull her close, and press my lips to her forehead.

When we pull apart, she wraps her hand tightly around mine, and we continue our adventure around the zoo.

My girl still has the most vibrant smile on her face as we walk through the parking lot to my car.

My girl.

Maybe I don't get to call her that yet, but in my mind, that's what she is.

She lets go of my hand and skips toward the car. God, I'm a sucker for her.

She leans against my driver's side door. Waiting for me?

The mischievous gleam in her eyes sets me on fire.

"You asked if you're living up to the fantasy book boyfriend reputation. You're almost nailing it."

"Almost? You have some complaints?"

"Only one." She sucks in a sharp breath. "I need you to kiss me. I know I've wanted to take things slowly, but I love the feel of your lips on mine, and I'm kind of... desperate for more."

Well, fuck me.

"You don't have to ask me twice." My fingers tangle in her hair as my mouth lands on hers.

The contented sigh she lets out goes straight to my dick. As much as my brain knows we're taking it slow, my dick hasn't gotten the message, so I keep my hips back.

Or at least I try.

But then she fists my shirt and pulls me closer. Her lips part, then her tongue brushes my lips, encouraging me, giving me permission.

The second my tongue brushes hers, I know there's no going back. Sure, our tongues danced when we kissed that first night, but it's different this time. There's so much more to it now, and despite the way she ran away, I'm glad it didn't go any further then. Every delicious touch means so much more now.

She pulls me closer, and I try to shift my hips away, but she doesn't let me. She drags my body until it's against her, pressing her into the car door.

I wait for her to panic, to push me away and look terrified, but she doesn't.

She takes what I give her and begs for more. Her throaty moans have me a second away from coming unglued.

I run my hands down her ribs, soaking in the spark I feel with every tiny touch.

Her swollen lips are soft against mine and her tongue delicately teases mine. With every movement, she's in control, and my mind goes blank. All I feel is her. Not the breeze on my skin or the evening sun shining down on us.

A rave could be happening all around us and I wouldn't know.

It's only her. Me. Us. The beautiful, unlabeled, simply complex *us*.

I've never wanted anything more.

She finally breaks our kiss with a hand to my chest. The first thing I do is search her eyes for any sign of that fear, but all I find is hazy contentedness—and a heavy dose of lust.

"God, I've been wanting to do that."

"And you're okay?"

"I had to push myself through the first ten seconds—not because I didn't want to do it, but because I needed to quiet the nagging voices in the back of my head. Once I did..." She sighs dreamily. "I could do that all night."

I drop another kiss on her lips. "I'll keep that in mind."

"Mm, I don't want this date to be over."

"Want me to take the long way back to your apartment?" I don't know what that is, but I'm sure I could find one.

"Anything to make it last a few minutes longer." She kisses my cheek and lingers with her lips there for a moment, her breath tickling my ear.

I'm going to need a long drive with the windows down to cool off after that.

I'm pretty sure I drove around in circles, but I made the drive back to Chelsea's apartment take forty-five minutes instead of fifteen.

We laughed and talked and enjoyed each other's company.

I still don't know the exact reason Chelsea wants to go slow, but I'm grateful for it. Having this no-pressure time to date and get to know each other has let us have fun. And after everything that's happened in the last year, I didn't realize how much I needed that.

"You're going to turn into a popsicle," I mumble against Chelsea's lips.

Her hands are frigid as I wrap my hands around hers.

"I didn't think it would be this cold in September."

She moves closer, making no effort to stop kissing me as we stand on the front porch of her apartment building.

But then a chill rolls through her, and I break our kiss.

"Babe…"

She pouts in the most adorable way, but then her gaze shifts to the door.

As much as I'd love to go inside with her to do something as simple as relax on the couch together, this is all about what she's ready for. I don't want her to feel pressured or rushed. She rushed herself the first night we met, and it took a toll on her. I don't want that to happen again. I take her hesitance into consideration with everything we do, and if she's not one hundred percent sure, then I'll be the one to put a stop to it.

"I, um..."

I lean in and kiss her cheek. "It's fine. When you're ready to ask me in, you'll know."

She stares at me for a moment, then she sighs and looks down.

I lift her chin and give her another soft kiss. "Now, get your sexy butt inside before it freezes off."

Again she pouts, but slowly slips her hand from mine. "See you Monday?"

"Of course. Can't wait for our lunch date."

"Good," she whispers, then with a lingering look, she walks inside.

I watch until she's out of sight, then turn and head for my car, hoping one day soon she'll be ready to hold the door open for me to follow her.

10
I'll Take A Bear

Chelsea

Friday mornings at Promise are quickly becoming one of my favorite things. It's quiet to start, and I'm getting to know the team better, but as things pick up throughout the day, I get to shadow the counselors and even the nurse practitioner. Kristen says spending time with the nurse practitioner helps understand a different side of helping women after sexual assault.

I'm in the midst of working on some potential campus outreach options when the locked front door buzzes, then the interior glass door swings open, and Rae flies into the room like the devil's on her heels.

"Hey," I say with a laugh.

She sighs heavily. "Hi. I got stuck behind someone going thirty the entire way here. My soul temporarily left my body while I rage-screamed behind the wheel. But it's fine. I'm fine."

"You seem it."

She sets her purse on the counter and sighs. "Everything's crazy right now. But that reminds me, I have something for you." She fishes through her bag until she finds what she's looking for, then hands me a creamy pink envelope.

I pull it open to find an invitation to her wedding. October twenty-third. Only a month-and-a-half away.

"What—you didn't have to put one together for me."

She shrugs. "We haven't known each other that long, but I consider you a friend and I'd love to have you at the wedding, regardless if you go with Trevor or not."

"I'd love to come. But I thought when we talked about your bachelorette party earlier this week that you knew I'd be coming to the wedding too."

"I wanted you to know it wasn't something I just threw out there. I really want you there."

"Well, I appreciate the invitation, and I'll definitely be there."

And to prove that I mean it, I grab the response card and start filling it out.

"Good. A bunch of the girls will be getting ready with me, so I'd love to have you for that too."

"Text me all the details." I hand her the response card with a smile. "So, is wedding stuff why you're stressed?"

"Part of it. As great as it sounded to have my wedding on my grandparents' property in the fall with the leaves changing and everything, it's been a lot to organize mid-semester. We're taking our honeymoon the week after, so it's been a lot to work out with professors and plan ahead. So far, they've all been great, but then Aaron's having surgery in early November, so we're trying to figure all that out too."

"What's the surgery for?"

"His hand. He broke it—" She takes a deep breath. "He ended up with a bunch of microfractures in his fingers from punching the guy who assaulted me."

My heart aches for her. Were they together at the time? That all sounds awful.

"He didn't realize there were breaks—and didn't initially go to the doctor—so he's dealt with the pain for a long time. I'm hopeful the surgery will help. And trying not to get my hopes up too high that he'll finally be able to pitch again."

"Pitch?" I ask, my heartbeat ticking up.

"Yeah. I must not have mentioned that. He was an amazing pitcher, and he misses it. He coaches for the college team because it's a part of him. Like it is with all the boys."

"All the boys?" I squeak.

Oh no. Oh no, no.

Her brows pinch together. "Yeah. Aaron, Joel, Miles, Trevor and a few of our other friends have played together for years. I'm surprised Trevor didn't mention it." Then she winces. "Shit. Of course he didn't. I—Chelsea, are you okay?"

That's a great question.

But if my nausea, clammy palms, sweating, and the pain in my chest are any indication... no. I'm not okay. Because Trevor... Trevor plays baseball? And we—I—fuck.

"Come with me." Rae grabs my hand and drags me down the hall toward the break room, only stopping long enough to stick her head into the door of the counseling area. "Hey, Levi, can you cover the front for us for a few minutes?"

"Sure thing." The younger intern makes her way out to the front, and Rae's still dragging me.

Am I breathing?

My chest is heavy.

It's been months since I've had a panic attack. But this?

Rae guides me into a chair, gets me a cup of water, then sits down opposite me and wraps her hands around mine.

"Breathe with me. In through your nose. Nice and slow."

I try, but my breath hitches halfway through.

"Hey, you're safe here. You're surrounded by caring women, two armed security guards, and locked doors. Look at me. You're safe. Let's try another breath."

I nod, and this one comes easier.

We take a few more before the slightest touch of calm settles in. I grab the water and take a long sip, the cool liquid calming me a little more.

"Do you want to tell me what's going on? What just triggered you?"

I open my mouth, but then close it again. Take another breath. I won't feel shame for this. It wasn't my fault. I want to learn to be more open about it—to talk about and use my story to help others. My story itself isn't where this reaction is coming from, but I want to get it out to Rae. I want to let her in.

"The guy who raped me was—said he was a baseball player."

"Oh wow. Your reaction makes sense—"

"No. You don't understand." Tears crest in my eyes. "The school I went to before this—where it happened—was Syracuse."

"Oh my god. Does Trevor—wait, you don't think it was him, do you? Because he'd never—"

I shake my head. "I know it wasn't him. I have a hazy memory of that night because I was drugged, but the guy looked nothing like Trevor. Shaggy blond hair and hazel eyes. He was bigger, too. I think? Either way, I'd trust it wasn't Trevor, even if I didn't remember at all." At least I hope I would. This is all a mindfuck.

"That's a lot."

I nod. "It's... too much. I don't know what to do with this. Or how to process it."

"Do you want to leave early? I can let Kristen know."

That snaps me back to the moment. "No." Even though I'm barely functioning, I want to be here. "In moments like this, I want to be here more than ever. It gives me back some of my power. Or gives me control."

She nods, eyes shimmering with tears. "I totally understand."

"Trevor doesn't know about any of this yet, so could you please not tell him?"

"This stays between us. I promise. Anything you tell me always will. But the same goes the other way too. If Trevor didn't tell you about his past with baseball, I shouldn't say anything more."

Sarah's words from the day we met come back to me.

He's been hurt too.

"I understand."

I just wish this wasn't triggering me so much. The idea that Trevor might know the person who assaulted me. I don't know if I can handle that. It makes me sick to my stomach.

"Whenever you do tell him, he'll be... I'm not sure what the right word is. He'll care. He..." She blows out a long breath. "I think he blames himself a little for what happened to me. We were on the dance floor together beforehand, and even though he went to find Hyla and I went to talk to Aaron, he felt responsible when he finally found out."

I grab her hand this time, and that leads to us pouring out our stories to each other. Both raging for the other. Rae's story is almost as horrifying as mine, but in a different way. A football player dragged her off the dance floor at a party in high school and forced her to a bedroom guarded by other football players. Men are trash.

Sure, not all men.

But enough men.

More than enough to consider them the problem.

Man vs. bear? I'll take a bear any day of the week.

Of course, on the flip side of that, there are good ones. My dad and Robbie. From what I've seen so far... Trevor. And Rae's friends, who saved her from the guy who assaulted her. If they hadn't—if she'd been alone like I was—her story would've been too close to mine.

I know there are good guys out there, but there are way too many bad ones.

Which is all the more reason I want to support and empower women. The stronger we are individually, the stronger we are together. And the stronger we are together, the better we can fight back.

But that doesn't come easily, especially when we have wounds to heal, when we have to bear the consequences of selfish man-children who think they're entitled to our bodies.

And today, when I have to try to wrap my mind around this new ugly connection Trevor and I have. My stomach roils with nausea thinking of it, and I start to feel panicky again.

I don't want Trevor tied to this moment in my life, and I don't know if I can handle it if he somehow is.

Rae heads back out front, giving me a few minutes to myself, and the first thing I do is text my therapist and ask if we can schedule a video session for today. She texts back right away.

Now I just need to make it through several hours of work and two classes.

With all my strength, I push everything down and do what all women have been trained to do since we were young. Plaster on a perfect smile and pretend I'm fine.

I wasn't fine. I'm *not* fine.

I don't have to be fine.

Work was okay. It's healing being there. But my classes? I could hardly focus, and walking across campus had me on edge.

I've been triggered with a capital T all day. Hell, might as well capitalize the whole word at this point.

Which is why I'm sitting on my couch, clutching a cup of tea, waiting for my therapist to connect to our video call.

It's my first therapy session since I started school. My last one was in person, shortly before I left. I was lucky to find my therapist, Carina, in Birch Lake. Finding the right therapist is a challenge, and I went through two—one in person and one online—before I found her. I've only stuck with therapy as long as I have because Carina understands me and my needs.

She's young, only in her early thirties, and maybe that's why she's the perfect match for me. She's relaxed, and I often feel like I'm talking to a friend or older sister rather than a therapist. But one who is extremely direct and doesn't let me get lost in my bullshit. She's helped me a lot in reframing what I've been through and helping me orient myself to what I want going forward. She's careful never to *tell* me anything, but to ask the right insightful questions and let me do the bulk of the work.

When the call connects and she appears on the screen, she's instantly a calming, if slightly concerned, presence.

She also gets right to the point.

"Hey, Chelsea. What's going on?"

I open my mouth, but nothing comes out. My mind spins like tires trying to gain traction, but everything inundates me at once and I can't get any grip. Can't make the spinning stop or words make sense.

"It's too much. I don't know—I..."

"Chelsea, look at me. I'm going to count down from five, and I want you to take deep breaths while I do. Can you do that?"

I nod and she starts counting backward.

I close my eyes and breathe, not trying to clear my head, not trying to do anything, just focusing on breathing. It's not until several deep breaths later when I realize she's finished counting and I snap my eyes open.

"Tell me one thing. One sentence. It doesn't have to make sense to me. We can fill in the context later."

"I met a guy," I blurt out.

"What else?"

"I'm really falling for him."

"What else?"

"He plays baseball. Or something with baseball. I haven't told him about—"

"One sentence at a time."

I take another breath. "He doesn't know about my past yet."

"Okay."

"I'm scared." I let out another long breath. "I need more than a sentence now." She gives me an encouraging smile. "He's kind. Caring. A little bit of a tortured soul like me. He loves his mom and his sister and he'd do anything for the people he cares about. I think that includes me. We hadn't fully discussed our pasts yet, and I didn't know he had any connection to baseball. A mutual friend is how we connected and she mentioned it today, not realizing he hadn't yet. Now I'm curled up in a ball on my couch feeling so... triggered."

"Because he's a baseball player."

I force another deep breath because these words are almost painful to get out. My chest gets tight again, and it's like I've forgotten how to breathe correctly.

"Because he also went to Syracuse."

Her eyes widen and her mouth slips open. "Oh."

"Yeah."

A stilted laugh slips from her. "I'll admit, I wasn't expecting that."

"Me either."

"But you don't think—"

"I know it wasn't him. But... we've had these cool little connections to each other. His family camped multiple summers at my family's campground. We both went to Syracuse, and we talked about whether we passed each other on campus or ever saw each other. It was a surprisingly warm, fuzzy feeling given the negative memories I have there. But now this? Knowing he might know the person who assaulted me? Be friends with them? I'm not sure I can handle it."

"What is it that scares you the most?"

I pull my knees up to my chest and close my eyes for a moment, tears filling them. When I finally look back at the screen, my stomach churns with nausea.

"That he might be connected to the worst moment of my life. I don't want to even vaguely associate him with that."

"That's fair. But let's take a step back. It may not have been a baseball player who assaulted you, right?"

"Right. I know that. He drugged and raped me. Why should I believe he was telling the truth about that?"

A bit of the tension in my chest uncoils.

"But if it was someone he knew, are you worried he'd take their side? Continue to be friends with them? Stand up for them?"

"No." Because I may not have known Trevor long, but his character is evident. And Rae's words about her assault back that up. "I'm fairly certain he'd cut that person out of his life entirely. Not because of me, but because he wouldn't want to be friends with someone like that."

"And if he did know them and it could help convict that person?"

A rush of air falls from my mouth. I hadn't even thought of that.

"I think he'd help however he could."

"And how would you feel about it?"

"It scares me, but I'd want to pursue it. No one should get away with rape."

"So, now that we've gone through all those things... what's really upsetting you the most about this?"

"That I finally found something good. Some*one* good. He makes me happy. And it was so nice not to live under the umbrella of what I've been through. I don't want this connection to taint that."

"Then don't let it. Yes, you know this connection exists, but it doesn't have to color your relationship with him differently. There are still unknowns here, but from what you've said, he sounds like a good person. There's every chance that once you tell him, if you let this color your relationship with him differently, those colors will only be more vibrant if he chooses you, stands up for you, fights for you."

She's right. God, she's so right it hurts. Letting *him* affect my relationship with Trevor is the last thing I want. Letting him affect me at all anymore is not okay. He took enough from me. He's not getting anymore.

"I kinda feel like you just punched my soul."

She gives a soft smile and a shrug. "Therapy will do that."

"Is it okay that I'm not quite ready to tell him yet?"

"Whatever you're ready for is okay, but don't let it slip into hiding this from him. If you're going to have a true relationship with him, you will have to tell him."

"I know. I was looking forward to just enjoying falling for him."

"And you still can. You set the timeline on this."

I nod slowly. "Our friend said something that makes me think he's been through something traumatic regarding baseball. I'm not sure if I should talk to him about it."

"Do you want to?"

I ruffle my hair and stretch my legs, anxious energy kicking in now that my mind is a bit more settled.

"I want him to know he can talk to me about it."

"Then you can bring it up and let him decide what he's comfortable with."

"And if he pours his heart out and asks me to do the same?"

She purses her lips, holding back a smile. "Then you're still in control of your own journey. You can decide in the moment what, if anything, you want to share."

I lean back against the couch and let out a breath. "Thank you."

"All I did was help you clear your mind and recenter yourself. You did the rest. Show yourself some gratitude too."

I scrunch up my nose. "But I'm not good at that."

"And this is why you're in therapy."

We both laugh at that.

"Was there anything else you wanted to talk about today?"

I shake my head. "No. I'm feeling a lot better now."

"Good. Feel free to send me a text if anything else pops up. Have a good rest of your day."

"Thanks. You too."

I close my laptop and sink into the couch. I'm soaked through with stress sweat and feel gross. Talking to Trevor about what I've been through isn't something I'm ready for yet. Once I do, there will be a *serious* cloud in our sunshiney sky. I want to enjoy the cozy warmth for a bit longer first. That said, if he wants or needs to talk to me, I want him to know I'm here.

After a shower.

A long, hot shower to wash off the sweat and emotion of the day.

Trevor

"All right. Cooper, you'll be working with the pitchers as usual. With the newbies, technique is going to be important."

We're in Coach M's office in the midst of a coaching planning meeting ahead of our first practice and team building day next Sunday.

"Matteny, what's your strong suit?"

"Third base?"

Coach rolls his eyes because *obviously*. I played third base.

"Infield," Aaron says. "You know how infield dynamics work and how important good teamwork is."

Coach glances at me like he's asking if that's true.

"Yeah. Sorry. Still transitioning out of thinking like a player. But if you want someone working on how the infield is gelling together, which players need more work on building trust—or skill—I've got that. We had a seamless infield in high school, and I carried what I learned from that with me."

"Good," Coach M says. "Now, we still need a good option for team building. We've done ropes courses and escape rooms. They encourage team building but remove the baseball aspect. I want to tie it all together."

"What if we put a twist on baseball? Make it fun, but not as practice-y. But we can still get a read on what's working and what's not?"

"You have a suggestion on how to do that?" Coach asks.

Aaron lets out a silent laugh, knowing where I'm going with this. God knows we played it enough in Joel's backyard.

"Wiffle ball. Divide the roster—and maybe the coaching staff too—into two teams and make a five-inning game out of it. It takes the pressure off and lets everyone have fun, but they're still in the baseball spirit."

The other coaches in the room nod in agreement.

"You sure you aren't interested in coaching? You've got a good sense for it."

I laugh at that. "Nah. I'm just still five years old inside and want to play wiffle ball with my friends."

"Those were the days," Aaron says with a laugh.

"I'll get to work on the full plan and send out emails on Monday. For now, get out of here. Enjoy your weekend."

"Thanks, Coach."

I'm energized leaving the meeting. I like feeling helpful and like I might actually be on the right path. I'm in a good mood. Until I check my phone. And there are still no texts from Chelsea.

I don't want to seem like some needy psychopath, but it's weird. Normally, we text all day. Some flirty, some silly, some sweet—but it's always something. I've only sent a few at random times, but it sets off something inside me. So, I quickly send one more.

Me: Are you okay?

I hit the send button and that's when I notice it only says sent. Not received like usual. Which only makes me worry more. *What if something's wrong?* What if her phone died, and I need to chill out?

Aaron claps me on the shoulder. "You okay?"

I turn to look at him. I didn't even realize he was still there.

"Yeah, just debating if I'm being stupid."

"Obviously, you are. So let's move on from that existential crisis to whatever's bothering you."

He's got that warm, disarming counselor smile on. He hasn't even graduated yet, and he's already got the therapist vibes down. I hate it. Especially when he sees right through my bullshit.

"Chelsea and I usually talk throughout the day, but she hasn't answered me at all today. And I just realized my texts aren't going through."

"And you're worried?"

"Wouldn't you be if it was Rae?"

Maybe an over-the-top comparison since they've been in love since they were like five years old, but the way I care about Chelsea...

"Of course I'd be worried. Have you tried calling her? Sometimes messaging apps get weird."

"No. I guess I can do that. I don't want to come off as too pushy if she purposely hasn't answered."

He squints at me in question.

"We're going slow. She's been hurt—or something—before. I haven't even been inside her apartment yet. So I don't want to scare her if she just doesn't want to talk."

"Well, from experience, that might be when she needs you the most—needs you to reach out. Sometimes people need space. Ideally, they should tell the people they care about if they're going to stop communicating, but let's face it, good communication is rarely born. It's something you have to work at. It's impossible to know exactly what she needs, so all you can do is try to figure it out without seeming like a psycho stalker. Don't try to break her door down, but check in."

I snort. "Brilliant."

"I know. I'm so smart. That's what happens when you fuck up your relationship for years. I know I'm super awesome, but try not to be too much like me."

He winks at me, then smacks me on the shoulder before continuing down the path toward the parking lot.

I give him a lame-ass wave while staring at my phone.

Just call.

Worst case, she doesn't answer.

Because something's wrong?

She doesn't want to talk?

Which makes me worried all the same.

I hit the call button next to her name, but it goes directly to voicemail. Which means she didn't deny my call. Her phone is off.

Or dead.

Am I reading too much into this?

Fuck.

And then my feet are moving, and I don't realize what the fuck I'm doing until I'm in my car, leaving campus from the opposite exit as usual.

I guess I'm going to see Chelsea.

She said her apartment is on the third floor, so when I get there, I go inside and take the stairs two at a time, heart beating in my ears.

What am I doing?

What if she thinks I'm crazy?

What if something's wrong?

That's the one that keeps my feet moving.

Not at all the idea of losing her before I've even had a chance to fully fall for her.

When I get to her apartment door, I pause, only for a moment.

You're here because you care, not because you're a psycho stalker.

Fuck.

I run a hand through my hair, then knock.

It takes a second, but then I hear footsteps.

My stomach churns, and I brace myself. I'm not sure for what.

God, I'm pathetic.

The door swings open, and the second Chelsea sees me, her eyes fly wide.

At least she's physically okay.

"Trevor. What are you..." She trails off and looks over her shoulder, then winces. "Shit."

"Sorry. I should go. You weren't answering my texts, and I was worried about you, but you're clearly okay, and if you need space—"

"Whoa, slow down." Again, she looks over her shoulder. "How many times have you texted me today?"

"Only a few," I sputter. "And I called once."

"I'm sorry. I had a moment earlier and turned my phone off, then forgot about it. I was going to call you once I was done making some hot cocoa." Her teeth sink into her bottom lip, and fuck, now I want to kiss her. Maybe I should've left that roller coaster emoji next to her name in my phone. "Do you want to come in?"

I stare at her for a moment. So far, that's one thing she hasn't been comfortable with.

"I want to, but are you sure? I don't want to push your boundaries."

She lets out a weak laugh, and for a second, she looks like she might cry.

"I want you to come in." Her voice is a little raw, and now I'm on edge again. What happened today? Something that upset her? Someone? Because I'd be happy to put the fear of God into whoever it was. She shakes off the emotion and smiles at me. "Come on. We should talk—and I don't mean that in a bad way."

When I walk inside, I'm still worried but also feeling like an idiot. Maybe I should've waited for her to reach out to me. I don't want her to think I came here just to get her to let me in.

But she seems okay? She's smiling softly as she gestures to the living area.

"Well, this is it... not huge, but it's home." She spins around the small living room that gives off all the cozy vibes I'd expect from her. There's a fully loaded bookcase in the corner next to a window. Under the window is a table full of plants. There's also a small couch, a chair, a coffee table, and a TV stand with a TV that's nearly too big for it.

"It's perfectly you."

She smiles brightly at that. "Thanks." She throws her thumb over her shoulder toward the kitchen—which butts up against the living room. "I was just going to make some hot chocolate. Want some?"

"Yeah, sounds great. Can I help?"

"Hm. I don't know. Can I trust you with my super secret recipe?"

I follow her into the small kitchen area and lift the package of hot cocoa off the counter. "Boxed hot cocoa mix?"

She opens the fridge, then peers over her shoulder at me. "That's just the beginning."

"Well, I promise if you share your super secret recipe, it'll stay safe with me."

She sets milk, canned whipped cream, and chocolate syrup on the counter, before spinning around and returning with chocolate chips, vanilla extract, and sprinkles.

"Getting fancy," I say.

"And this is just my base recipe. Wait till you try the caramel version. Or peanut butter. Ooh and one time I added raspberry jam. So good. You like raspberry stuff, right?"

"Uh, yeah." Did I tell her that? "How did you know?"

"You ordered a raspberry cheesecake latte on our date."

Something mushy and romantic swells in my stomach. She was paying attention. And now I feel like an asshole for thinking she was ghosting me. Maybe she's not the only one who has to learn to trust.

"Yeah. Raspberry and chocolate go great together."

"Agreed. I don't have any raspberry jam right now, but I'll put it on the list."

She bops around the kitchen, warming milk and then assembling the fancy—and delicious smelling—hot chocolate.

With a mug in each hand, she nods toward the living room. "Let's sit."

We take seats at opposite ends of the couch, and Chels hands me my mug. She opens her mouth, but then grabs her phone and turns it on.

"I'm sorry," I say, but her voice sounds over mine, saying the same words.

Then we both laugh.

"Why are you sorry?" she asks.

"I know you said it's okay, but I don't want you to feel obligated to have me here. Respecting your boundaries is important to me."

Again, she smiles, but this time there's something brighter with more mischief in it.

"You don't need to apologize. Despite what happened the night we met, I am capable of knowing what I need and making my own decisions. I didn't mean to scare you that first night, but I didn't really know you then. Now that I do, I see all the ways you respect me and my boundaries, and I'm grateful. So I need you to trust that if I say I'm okay with something, I am."

I nod. "Got it."

"Anyway, I'm sorry I turned my phone off and worried you. I appreciate that you were worried. That you came to check on me."

"I'll always come check on you, and if you need me, don't ever hesitate to call me. I'm happy to be here for you, even if it's just to sit in the silence."

She takes a sip of her drink. "I did a lot of that today."

"Are you okay?"

"I'm doing better now. I had a moment today where something triggered me, and it hit me so hard I was overwhelmed, almost had a panic attack, went a little catatonic, and it took a call with my therapist to get me out of that space. Then I desperately needed a shower, and... here we are."

"Can I help? Do you want to talk about... whatever it is?"

Slowly, she shakes her head. "Not yet. It's heavy, and while I don't doubt you'd listen and handle it well, I don't want that heaviness hanging over us yet. I want us to enjoy getting to know each other better and letting this grow."

"I understand that."

She takes a deep breath, then looks at me, eyes serious. "That said, I'm grateful that you're always open to me talking about anything, and I want you to know it goes both ways."

"I appreciate that. And... fuck, I got a little scared when you didn't respond to any of my texts. I could say that it's just because I was worried about you, but there's more to it than that. You've become an important part of my life, and I'm scared to lose that. Lose you. And it's terrifying to admit just how crushed I'd be if this ends."

She's trying and failing to bite back a smile. "Good to know. I don't want this to end either. As usual, you're adorable. And your vulnerability means a lot to me. It makes me feel safer to be open with you. But I actually said all that for a different reason."

Oh.

"Rae and I were talking today," she continues. "And she mentioned Aaron having surgery, and then the huge impact baseball had on his life, and the rest of the guys too—including you. She didn't tell me anything more, but she alluded to something happening with baseball for you. Anyway, you don't have to tell me about any of it right now if you don't want to, but it's important to me that you know I'm here if you do."

Fuuuuck.

That's so not where I saw this conversation going.

"Like I said, you don't have to talk about it," she says, when I don't answer.

"No, I... I'm ready to talk about it. Ready for you to know. Part of me wanted to tell you sooner. It was actually hard not telling you about baseball sometimes, but..." I blow out a breath.

"It's okay," she says gently, but I shake my head.

"The only reason I didn't tell you sooner—well, I guess there are kind of two reasons, but they go together—is that I liked getting to know you without you knowing about that part of me. Baseball has always been a part of my life—a big part—but lately it's been a sad part too, and it's been something I've struggled with. It wasn't until a couple of weeks ago when I played with the guys that I felt okay about it again. And I realize I'm telling you all this backward."

"You can tell me in whatever order you want." Her voice is gentle and encouraging.

"My dad is why I love baseball. He instilled that love in me. It was something we did together and shared. Like every little kid who loved a sport, I dreamed of going pro, but for a while thought it was a pipe dream. But I had a great coach in high school, and I was recruited by a couple of schools, but Syracuse was by far the biggest. I still wasn't sure where it would lead me, but my coach there saw something in me, and he was working with me to get me on track for the draft this year. Until winter break last year when I went snowboarding with my best friend Nick, bounced off a few trees, and ended my baseball career—at least as a player."

She sets her mug down and moves closer. "Oh my gosh. Wow. That must've been terrifying. And awful. I'm so sorry."

"It was."

She rests her hand over mine, lazily running her finger in circles over the top.

"Anyway, it sucked, and I had a long recovery. You should probably know that I still struggle physically sometimes. If I do too much, I end up in a lot of pain, particularly in my leg, hip, and lower back. Which is why I can't play at any serious level anymore. It's been hard feeling like I left the game behind, and maybe a piece of my dad too. But then I spent a few hours playing with the guys at the stadium, and it made a big difference for me. I realized I haven't lost it. I'm just gaining a new perspective as I transition to more of a coaching and behind-the-scenes role."

There's intensity in her gaze as she looks at me. "I'm glad you found another way to hold on to it. I admit, I don't fully understand that kind of connection. I loved volleyball, but not at that level."

"I'm sure there's something similar for you. Like your family's campground. If you could never go there again, it would suck, right?"

She takes a deep breath. "Yeah. It's part of me—like going home."

"That's exactly how I feel about baseball. But knowing I can still honor that without playing has helped me."

"I love that for you. Seriously. It's healing for you, right?"

"Yeah. It is."

"I'm glad you're on that path. And I'm glad you're here with me." Something heavy settles over her like clouds on a stormy day.

So I squeeze her hand and drag her attention back to me. "I'm glad I'm here too. Thank you for letting me in." I mean that in more than just the literal sense. Whether she realizes it or not, opening the door for me today was more than physical. It was handing over a fraction of her trust. I'll keep doing whatever is needed to earn it.

Again, she moves closer, this time until she's right next to me, and I can wrap my arm around her.

After a beat, she looks up at me. "Now I feel like I should tell you—"

"You don't need to," I say quickly. "If you want to, I'm listening, but don't do it unless you're absolutely ready. I was ready to say all that. But I want you to know that vulnerability doesn't need to be an exchange. Being vulnerable was a choice of mine. Whenever you're vulnerable with me, even in the smallest ways, I want it to be because you want to, not because you feel like you owe me."

She stares at me for a moment, blinking like she can't believe I just said that.

Then her fingers skate over my arms and—

"Ow. Why did you just..."

I trail off when I see her smiling up at me, more than a hint of mischief dancing in her beautiful eyes.

She pinched me. *Again.*

My little hellion.

"You have to stop pinching me every time I do something you deem book boyfriend worthy. I'll have welts all over me."

She laughs, and it's so vibrant and free, it's hard to believe she was struggling a couple of hours ago.

She grabs her mug and nestles into my side with a contented sigh.

"Thank you for letting your guard down." Her voice is soft, like the lull of cascading waves. "Is it okay if I say I'm getting there?"

"It's perfect."

We sit together in a silence that's mostly comfortable, if tinged by the weight of things we've talked about—or haven't yet.

After a few minutes, I finally say, "Maybe I should go."

But Chelsea instantly grabs my arm, then turns to face me. "No. Stay. The reason I was hesitant to ask you to come in is because I'm not ready for anything sexual to happen yet, and I don't know when I will be. But you've shown me over and over that you're trustworthy. Letting you in today was me actively trusting you. And now that you're here, I realize how silly it was to wait. Because somehow you make it cozier. More comfortable. And I want you..." She swallows and meets my gaze, eyes shimmering. "Today's still a bit raw, and I'd love to snuggle on the couch with you. You always make me feel safe—cared for. I want to feel that."

"I'm all yours."

With that, I settle in again, truly relaxing for the first time tonight. She wants me here. I could get used to this feeling.

She grabs the remote control.

"Any preference on what we watch?"

"Nope. Put on whatever you were going to watch."

"I hadn't decided yet, but definitely a comfort show. Oh, I was thinking of starting my rewatch of *Haven*. Have you ever seen it?"

"No. I've heard of it, though. Something supernatural-ish right?"

"Yeah. Plus, there's a great love story at the center."

"Let's do it. But the deal is, if I get hooked, you're not allowed to watch it without me."

She glances up at me. "Guess that means you'll have to come over more often."

I couldn't hold back my smile if I wanted to. "Guess so."

She starts the episode, and we watch for a few minutes. Then, she points to the screen.

"The meet cute."

And it's a dramatic one. Car teetering on the edge of the cliff.

She points at the police officer on the screen. "That's Nathan. He is the ultimate love interest. Would sacrifice himself for Audrey. But we'll get to that."

I groan dramatically. "Great. More fictional men for me to live up to."

She pauses the show and spins so she's sitting on her knees next to me. "I thought I already told you, you're living up to the expectation. The only difference is, you're real. Which makes it even better." She presses her lips to mine and my mind goes fuzzy. I let her take the lead, and she goes for it. Kissing me hard, teasing my lips with her tongue until I part for her, then owning my mouth. My body. Probably other parts I don't want to think about right now.

Then she climbs onto my lap, and for a moment, I freeze.

We've been here before, and it didn't go well for me.

Hands in the air, I pull back. "Chels..."

But unlike last time, where her eyes were wild with fear, this time they're hazy. Her body is relaxed. And the smile on her face could kill me.

"Trev..."

My heart stutters in my chest. That's the first time she's called me that. I'll happily let her call me anything she likes, but hearing her say the shortened version of my name is further proof of how much more comfortable she is around me now.

"Are you sure?" I whisper.

"I ran away from you once. I'm not doing it again. This is where I want to be. This is what I want to be doing." She takes my face in her hands. "Let me kiss you."

"I'm yours," I breathe. And then her lips are on mine again. This time I wrap my hands around her back, playing with the strands of her hair and letting her take the lead, giving in to every twist of her tongue, every playful flick, every nip at my lips.

Would saying I'm a goner for her be too dramatic? Because I am. So gone for her. Out in the deep end, lost in the waves. Lost in her.

She kisses me like she never wants to stop, and I hope it's because she feels safe now. She knows I'll always be her safe place. It's clear she's been through something difficult. Whatever it is broke her ability to trust. The fact that she's letting me in at all means everything to me, and I'll keep doing whatever I can to make her feel at ease and care for her. I don't need labels or anything else. I just need her, and while she's deciding what she's ready for, I'll still be taking care of her in any way she'll let me.

11
Trust Fall

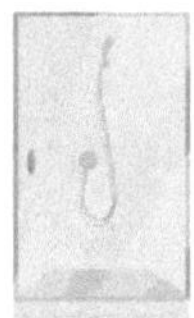

Chelsea

I THINK I'M FALLING in *trust* with Trevor Matteny.

I wasn't expecting it to be so easy with him, and at first, that made my guard go up. I wondered if I was slipping back into old habits and trusting too easily, but then I realized I wasn't just handing over my trust. He earned it.

And while I'm incredibly grateful he continues to be respectful, I can also sense him holding back.

Like right now, as we stand in the middle of my kitchen, kissing. We came in here to get hot cocoa, but then he smiled at me and ruffled his hair... and here we are.

But as usual, he's being tentative about it. While I appreciate him being respectful, the more he shows me his vulnerability, the more he shows me the way he respects my boundaries, the more I know I'm safe with him.

So when his hands slide down my back until they're almost brushing my ass, then he yanks them away, I groan and pull back in frustration.

"Sorry. Was that too much—"

"You have to stop doing that." I put my hands on his shoulders and stare into his eyes.

"Stop doing what?" he asks.

"Deciding what I want."

His eyes go wide. "I'm not trying to decide what you want. I'm trying to respect you."

"You are." I sigh and take his hands. "Look, I know everything about this is colored by how I reacted that first night and what I've told you I'm ready for, and while I appreciate your concern and I value your respect, you not giving me the chance to tell you or show you what I want takes my decisions from me. I don't need you to guess or assume what I want. All I need you to do is respect what I say or the clear signs I give."

He stares at me for a moment, his face going through a range of expressions, each one too fast for me to read.

Finally, he purses his lips. "Have I been doing that a lot?"

He's so genuinely concerned it's adorable. "Not a lot. Here and there. But I don't want you holding back or acting like I'm fragile. I'm trusting you to respect any boundary I set up. I need you to trust me to know what they are. Can you do that?"

He dips his head. "Yes."

"Good. Because you wanted to grab my ass when we were kissing, didn't you?"

His cheeks tinge pink and a crooked smile appears. "Maybe."

I grab his shirt and tug him closer. "I was waiting for you to do it. I *wanted* you to. Yes, I plan to take things slow when it comes to... sexual stuff. But kissing and getting a little handsy, maybe even grinding... I'm okay with that. If, for some reason, I'm not, I'll tell you. So, can you please do whatever feels natural—what you want to do—and trust I'll be clear if it's too much?"

"Yes." His voice is thick and gravelly.

"Good boy."

He groans a little, making me smile, but he steals the laugh trying to bubble out when he captures my lips in a rough kiss, and *fuck*. I like this side of him. I can feel it lurking beneath the surface—the rough bossiness and possessiveness. And I want more.

I lean into him and flick my tongue against his lips, begging him to play with me. But he takes it a step farther by shoving his tongue into my mouth and owning it. Then his hands are on my waist again and slipping lower, but just when I think he's going to squeeze my ass, he grabs it and lifts me up, setting me on the kitchen counter as he rocks into me.

"This good?" he breathes against my lips.

"Perfect."

I wrap my arms around his neck as he kisses me again. He's perfectly nestled between my thighs, and that buzzing awareness hits—the underlying current of desire. I want more. In the past, I'd already be going for his shirt or brushing my hand over the bulge in his jeans, but I actively don't allow myself to do that.

I always used to rush, but with Trevor, I don't want to do that. Instead I focus on the pressure of his lips against mine, the way he'll occasionally drag his teeth over my bottom lip, giving me the slightest hint of pain. I savor the little hums of pleasure he makes and how warm his hand is on my thigh. As I let my hands roam, I explore the defined muscles of his back, then lean into him when I feel a different muscle press against my thigh.

Kissing when I know it won't lead anywhere else is different from anything I've done before. I like it. I like the safety of getting lost in him while knowing we won't cross any lines. His tongue twists around mine, and I almost moan. He feels so good. His chest presses into mine giving my hard nipples the slightest friction, and I let one hand slip down and grab his butt.

He groans against my lips, then breaks the kiss and leans back, panting.

"Sorry. This time I'm stopping for me. Otherwise..." He looks down at his crotch. "I might've made a mess, and I'd like to save *that* happening until a time when we get to do it together."

My body flushes at his words.

"I like that idea. And trust me, you weren't the only one turned on by that."

My stomach whirls... with excitement. It's still a new feeling. I haven't been excited about the possibility of anything sexual since before I was assaulted. Trevor is rapidly changing that, which sets off that voice inside me, telling me I need to be honest about my past. I can't try to cross any sexual lines with him until I do. I'd be lying if I said fear of crossing those lines is what's holding me back. I know it'll be a process for me whenever we step over those lines. It may not be easy, or I could be building it up more in my head. But I know it'll create a mix of emotions in me, so he has to know.

Falling in trust.

The thing holding me back is how cozy and comforting our relationship is right now. I don't want to lose that by adding the heaviness of my past to it. But as my therapist said before, I control how that factors in.

Tonight?

I don't want to.

There's something else I want to tell him tonight. I'll do that first. And then sometime over the next few days, we'll set aside a time to sit down and talk. I'll tell him everything.

I make a mental note to put it on my calendar later. If it's on my calendar, it has to happen. That's the rule.

Now his eyes drift to my chest where my nipples are no doubt poking through my bra and T-shirt. He smiles, then kisses my neck.

"Trev..." I groan.

He steps back and puts his hands up. "Nope. You saying my name like that? Fuck, Chels. It's so hot."

I laugh and hop off the counter. "Sorry. I'll get back to making hot chocolate. Don't want to give you blue balls." I run my finger under his shirt along the top of his waistband. "Even if teasing you is my favorite kind of fun."

"Mean," he grumbles, but he's smiling. "Need any help?"

"Nope. Go set up the next episode of *Haven*. I'll bring the hot cocoa over when it's done."

He grabs my arm and pulls me to him for a chaste kiss, then as I walk toward the fridge, he smacks my butt.

I look over my shoulder at him, giving him my biggest smile, because I like settling into this space in our relationship. Something more open.

Relationship.

Yeah, it's time to tell him.

I pull out all the hot chocolate ingredients, including the raspberry syrup I didn't tell him I made, and make up a batch of raspberry vanilla hot chocolate. Once it's all done, I top the mugs with whipped cream, raspberry sauce, and then a vanilla sandwich cookie for good measure.

Trevor's eyes get big and he gets that childlike smile on his face when he sees me walking over to him.

"What's this?" he asks as I hand him his mug.

I set my mug on the coffee table, then sit down.

"The boyfriend special."

He slowly turns to me, eyes even bigger. "Boyfriend? Really?" And then that childlike smile appears again, and I almost melt on the spot.

"Let's not pretend that isn't what you've been this whole time."

He sets his mug down, then wraps his arms around me, kissing me deeply. It's not the wild kissing we were doing in the kitchen. It's slower, gentler, but all-consuming.

He rests his head against mine and cups my cheek as he pulls away.

"Get ready for me to become the ultimate fantasy book boyfriend. Now that I have the official title needed."

I bite back a laugh, smiling up at him. "Guess we'll see."

Then I lean forward and grab my mug, heart beating hard with all the swirly, gooey, emotional things.

Making this official and telling him about my past is giving him a new level of trust and feels like cutting myself open and bleeding out all my pain. But if anyone is worth seeing everything I've kept locked inside—every painful, heartbreaking moment—it's Trevor. Especially since I can see a future with him, and I've never felt that way about anyone before. *Ever.*

I get a twisty sensation in my gut that's starting to feel familiar. How can I be thinking about a future with him after such a short time?

Because it feels right.

It feels right in a way very few things in my life have.

Every summer spent working at the campground with my family feels right.

The first time I played volleyball felt right.

Choosing counseling as my major in college felt right.

Moving to Old Lake Town and taking the internship with Promise felt right.

And now my relationship with Trevor.

I curl into his side, and he plays with my hair, and I know I have to face it all, tell him my past, because the last thing I want is to keep holding back from the man I'm falling for.

I loathe night classes. As I walk out of my ethics class, I promise myself for the third time I will never sign up for a five o'clock class ever again. It's only once a week, so it's two full hours—when the professor doesn't run over.

Most people make a beeline for the door, complaining about the professor as we go. She's nice enough, but goes on and on and *on*. About ethics of all things. I didn't want to take the class in the first place because I hate ethical debates—we live in a world of gray, not black and white—but it filled a credit I needed while not taking away from internship time at Promise. I figured a two-hour class once a week was manageable. I was wrong, and I'm going to hate myself every Monday—of course it's on a freaking Monday—for the rest of the semester because of it.

I stop by the bathroom because I didn't feel like waiting in line during our break in the class, and then head downstairs. There are a handful of people in the lounge by the door where there are vending machines, and I consider grabbing a cup of crappy vending machine coffee, but don't.

Home is only five minutes away. I can make coffee—or better yet, hot cocoa—when I get there.

I pull the strap to my messenger bag over my head and tuck it slightly behind me, then aim for the doors to the building, where two girls are entering.

They're close to each other, talking and looking over their shoulders.

When they catch sight of me and a couple other girls ready to walk outside, they stop in front of us.

"You might want to wait or go out a different door. There's a guy outside acting creepy. He was staring at us, following us, and yelling things, asking if we'd sleep with him or if we were sleeping with each other. Be careful."

My stomach drops, and my gaze snaps to the doors. I see the guy milling around out there, and instinctively back away. There are a few guys in the lounge, but not one of them makes a move to help any of us.

Shouldn't be surprised by that.

Or the panic that's settling in.

My limbs feel like jelly, and my heart's beating way too fast.

Breathe.

There's another exit on the far end of the building on the next floor up, since the building is built into the hill. It's farther from my car, but I could loop around the building if I needed to. And hope the guy doesn't see me or follow me.

Fuck.

I lean against the wall and close my eyes.

I hate this feeling.

The fear and weakness this awakens in me.

I force myself to take a deep breath. I can handle this. I'm a strong, badass woman.

Who is feeling triggered right now.

So triggered, I almost yelp when my phone goes off while I'm holding it.

After another breath, I turn my screen on and find a text from Trevor.

Trevor: Miss you.

Without thinking, I push the phone icon next to his name and put the phone to my ear as I walk up the hallway.

He answers on the first ring. "Hey, babe."

"Hi. Um, are you busy right now?"

"No, I'm just leaving the library and about to head to my car."

Okay, this can work. He can talk to me the whole time, and he'll know where I am in case of emergency. Hopefully it's nothing.

"Good. Could you stay on the phone with me for a bit?" I'm walking toward the other door now, my heart still pounding.

"Why? What's wrong?" His voice fills with concern.

"I'm just leaving my night class, and these girls said there's a guy outside who was following them—"

"Where are you?" His voice is rough and a little murdery.

"Carlan Hall."

"Stay there. Stay inside the building. I'll be there soon."

"You don't have to—"

"Chelsea." His voice is firm and insistent. "Are there other people inside the building?"

"Yeah, in the lounge."

"Good. Stay near other people. I'm going to hang up now, but call me if he comes inside, okay?"

A rush of air leaves my lungs. "Okay. Thank you."

"Don't ever thank me for stuff like this, Chels. Stay safe. I'll see you in a couple of minutes."

"Bye."

He hangs up, and I walk back to the lounge, still in shock. Yep. I'm definitely falling in trust with him. But I might be falling in something else with him too.

It's barely been five minutes when Trevor comes through the doors of the building. His eyes land on me before he's even through the second set of glass doors, and I get up to meet him. The tight hug he wraps me in seems as much for him as for me. I melt against him, basking in the peace I feel. Because when I'm in his arms, I'm just... safe.

"Okay?" he murmurs into my hair.

"I will be. I just want to go home."

"I've got you. Let's go."

"Out this door?" I choke out.

He leans back and looks into my eyes. "I can handle him. If he's bothering us, he won't be bothering someone else. Trust me?"

I do. The absolute certainty of those words shouldn't surprise me. He's shown me over and over again, and when I crave safety, I want him.

"Yes."

He takes my bag and slings it over his shoulder, then wraps his other arm around me, pulling me tight to his side. Kissing the side of my head, he whispers, "I've got you."

I wrap my arm around his back, fingers curling into his sweatshirt, and try to remind myself I'm safe, even if all I can think is that I want to be anywhere but here. Especially when the front door opens and the cool air hits my face.

When we step outside, the guy is a bit farther up the path, looking toward the entrance at the top of the stairs. We'll have to go right past him.

Breathe, I remind myself. I can't be catatonic right now. I have to face this.

I'm safe. I'm not alone.

Trevor holds me tighter as we get closer, and the guy's eyes fix on us. They're hazy like he's drugged up.

He tilts his head and then gets this almost predatory smile on his face. "Mm, you're real pretty."

I swear to the goddess, Trevor *growls*.

"She belong to you?" the guy asks as we move past him.

"You need to back off, man," Trevor says.

"Aw, come on. We could share her."

Trevor stops, his body going rigid. He spins, blocking me with his body while still keeping one hand on me.

"You need to back the fuck up."

The guy raises his hands. "I was just asking."

"Well, don't. You need to walk away and stop harassing people."

But Trevor doesn't wait to see if he does. He turns back around, tugs me close again, and hurries toward the stairs. Thankfully, the guy doesn't make a move to follow us.

I'm a little shaken, but it's clear the guy needs some help.

That's when I notice the flashing light at the top of the stairs. When we get up there, two campus police officers are waiting there.

"Hey, I'm Trevor Matteny. I'm the one who called. It's that guy down there. He looks drugged out of his mind and he's saying inappropriate sexual stuff to women."

"We'll take care of it," the first officer says, then they head down the stairs.

"You—you called the police?" I ask in surprise as he guides me to the parking lot.

"Yes. It needed to be done. The fact that none of the people in that lounge did anything..." He shakes his head in frustration. "Everyone should feel safe to walk across campus—leave their classes—and that guy clearly needed help."

He helps me into the car, and I'm still so stunned, trying to make sense of everything.

Of course he called the cops. Trevor cares. He's one of the good ones. I think Rae told me something like that. Or maybe it was Sarah. It doesn't matter who. It's the truth, and I know it in my bones.

Trevor sits down in the driver's seat and heads for my apartment, as I sit here, fidgeting, overwhelmed with feelings. My fear is rapidly fading and my anger is seeping in.

Anger that the baseline for men is to feel comfortable sexualizing and going after women. I don't care if he was high or drunk or anything else. Plenty of guys do it without. Maybe that guy wouldn't have hurt me. Maybe some other guy who I wouldn't have thought twice about would've been the dangerous one.

When we get back to my apartment, I fling the car door open, desperate for that cool air to wash over me, maybe give me a hint of calm, but nothing does.

"Chels?" Trevor appears at my side.

"Come on."

I'm in a spiral of anger and frustration at men, at our society that accepts treating women like trash, at myself.

When we get to the third floor, I shove my apartment door open and chuck my bag on the floor.

Trevor follows me in, watching me like he did the night we first met, when I ran away. I might be just as jumpy, but that was a very different emotion. That was pure panic. I'm not panicking anymore.

"This is going to sound stupid, but I don't know how else to ask... are you okay?"

I spin to face him, swallowing hard, and shake my head. The words start flying out of my mouth.

"No. No, I'm not okay. I'm mad. I'm mad that men ever make women feel unsafe or like objects for their sexual pleasure. Get a fucking sex toy, you pathetic pieces of shit. Hey, a sex doll won't talk back, either. They won't *fight* back. Not that I can say much. I didn't exactly fight tonight. I fell apart. I mean, what if you hadn't been there to save me? I should be stronger than this by now! I've healed. Or I'm healing. And I want to be able to fight back, not cower in fear. Why is my first response to panic? How do I stop that? How do I stop being catatonic and learn to fight past my fear—my trauma? I—I want to be strong enough..."

I drop onto the couch, my head in my hands, crying. Tears that make me feel even weaker.

The couch shifts next to me.

"So, I never want to pressure you to talk, but you just said a bunch of things that I don't know what to do with."

My head snaps up, and I meet his gaze. *Shit*. That's not how I wanted to tell him this. We were going to cook dinner together tomorrow night, and I was going to tell him, but... no point in waiting now.

"Do you want me to get Robbie?" he asks.

I rest my hand on his thigh and shake my head.

"No. I need to tell you something."

"You don't have to."

"I do. I'm ready for you to know."

As soon as I say the words, that ugly *shame* hits me all over again.

Why does rape have to be such a dirty word?

Why am I the one who has to face the consequences?

Why am I the one who has to deal with people's opinions and judgment?

Why am I the one who has to deal with the scars of this for the rest of my life?

I can't change any of that.

But I can say *fuck shame*. I can own what I've been through and do my damndest to hold the world accountable so there will be one less girl like me out there one day.

I turn to Trevor and take his hands, focusing on him. This isn't about me pouring out my soul. This is about trusting him. Letting out the final part of myself that I've been hiding. Because this is official now, and as our relationship moves forward, he deserves to know. And I deserve to have unwavering support as I continue to heal from this.

I bite my lip as I breathe deeply through my nose. His eyes are so gentle, and his expressive features are filled with concern *for me*.

"I've held back telling you why I left Syracuse because I know what I'm about to say will change things—add a weight to our relationship—but it's important to me that you know. Before our relationship goes any further, I need you to know because it ties into why I have to ease into any kind of sexual relationship and my ability to trust. But you've shown me how deeply I can trust you, so..." I take another breath, then force out the words. "I was drugged and raped at a party sophomore year of college."

Trevor

This must be what having a stroke feels like.

My girl...

My beautiful, strong, incredible *woman* was raped?

The raw, primal anger burning inside me is too much. I want to rip my clothes off. I feel like I'm about to Hulk out. But then she keeps talking.

"I didn't tell you last week, but the reason for my panic attack and turning off my phone was because I found out you play baseball—played at Syracuse—and the guy... he said he did too. My memory is so hazy, but I remember him being almost too proud about it, and—"

I fly off the couch.

"Who was it?" The words are a barely contained scream. Not at her. *For* her. Because if I know the person who laid his hands on her, forced himself inside her, I will cut off every part of his body that touched her, then dump him in a shallow grave. I've never wondered if I'm capable of murder before, but fun fact, I am. I'm not sure I've ever experienced visceral rage like this. I've wanted to rain hell on Hyla's parents before, but this is next level.

Knowing that anyone has endured such a deep violation is horrific. But Chelsea? She's mine. And even though she wasn't when it happened, I'm still ready to go scorched earth, hunt this fucker down, and make him pay.

Kill my way across a continent? That's cute. I'll chase this guy to the ends of the earth, and when I get my hands on him, I'll make him sorry he ever looked at her.

Chelsea blinks at me. "I don't know. We had one drink together while playing pool, and he flirted with me. He must've spiked my second drink. The whole night and next few days after that are hazy. I don't remember how I got back to my dorm that night, I only remember stumbling through the door and collapsing on my bed. For two days, I barely moved. Drank some water. Went to the bathroom. That was it. My roommate panicked and called our RA, who called my dad. He and Robbie showed up, and when I mustered a few words to tell them what happened, they took me to the hospital. I was swabbed and poked with all the tests they could do. My bloodwork showed trace evidence of me being drugged. And supposedly they got some DNA from my kit that didn't match mine, but it didn't match anyone else on file, either. It's technically still an open case because I couldn't remember his name or give a stronger description than hazel eyes and shaggy blond hair. On a campus that big... they weren't going to find him."

"But you said he played baseball."

She shakes her head. "That's what he told me. But who knows if that was true. I have no idea how much the police looked into that because I dissociated from life." Her shimmering eyes drop to the floor. "I moved home and spent the next few months lying in my dark bedroom and refusing to talk to anyone. Not a shining moment for me. Eventually I clawed my way out, but—"

I drop to my knees in front of her, cutting off her words, and run my hands up her legs.

"I'm so sorry you had to endure that. No one should ever have to feel like you felt, and if I could take it away for you, I'd give anything to do it. But don't be hard on yourself for feeling every feeling you needed to after or for how things went tonight. It takes an incredible amount of strength to climb out of the darkness, and it takes time to face even the smallest pieces of your trauma again without shattering. You should be proud of your strength and your grace and the way you've risen. I am honored to be the man you share your pain with, and I promise to protect it and you always."

She cups my cheek and rests her forehead against mine.

"Thank you."

I wrap one hand around her arm, and we sit like this for a moment, the weight of it all swirling around us.

I don't blame her for being surprised by my actions or being cautious with her trust and her heart. A guy with no care for anyone but himself stole a part of her and broke the person she used to be. It takes time to recover from that kind of trauma. While I've loved the little ways we've found that we're connected, I'd cut this particular string if I could. If it would somehow erase that past for her.

And yet, here she is. Still struggling, but I've seen her vibrance—the way her eyes dance with mischief and that joyful smile that sends me to my knees.

"What do you need?" I whisper.

"Hot cocoa. Food. And you. My safe place."

I brush my lips over hers. "You've got it."

No matter what she asks for, what she needs, I'll find a way to give it to her. I'd do anything for her. Support her, uplift her, fall to my knees and worship her. That's what she deserves and more, and I have every intention of giving her everything I can. It might not be that guy's head on a platter, but if I can help her find him and make sure he pays for what he did, I will. Most importantly, I'll protect her and her beautiful heart with my life, so no one can ever hurt her like that again.

We talked through half of our first episode of *Haven*. Chelsea gave me more details that sent my blood pressure skyrocketing. Knowing that it happened in the baseball house—not where I lived, but where I regularly was—made me want to puke.

It also made me discreetly text one of the few guys on the Syracuse team I trust when she went to the bathroom. I didn't give him any big details, but asked him to poke around and see if any investigations might've happened. From what she said, it's been almost a year since it happened, so I would've still been there, and I figure I probably would've known if any investigations happened—but if there was a stronger suspect maybe it would've been kept quiet. I'd like to think my old coach—asshole that he might've been to me after my accident—wouldn't push aside sexual assault allegations, but I've learned people aren't always who you expect them to be.

Damn straight I'll be going through my old team photos to find anyone who might match the description she gave.

My anger is still roiling beneath the surface, but I'm keeping it calm for her. She's had to deal with enough. I can rage about it later to one of my friends. I assume Rae knows. I'm a dumbass for not putting that together. She works at Promise. I just took it as her wanting to empower women, but that's only a piece of it.

When our second episode of *Haven* ends, Chelsea switches the TV off and turns to me.

"I want to talk about sex. Sexual stuff. I don't know. It feels like a massive elephant in the room right now, and I feel better when I can talk things through with you."

A surprised laugh slips out. "Uh, yeah. Of course. We can talk about anything you want to talk about. But before you say anything, I want you to know I will never push you. You give me whatever you're comfortable with, and whenever we take those steps, I'll do whatever I can to make sure you feel comfortable and safe."

She runs her hand over my cheek. "I know you will because you already do. And that's part of the reason we're having this conversation. You're the only person who has brought out sexual desire—specifically sexual desire with another person—since it happened. I've been turned on by book scenes and things like that, and before that, when I was trying to feel comfortable in my body again, I focused on enjoying my body and turning myself on... if that makes sense? But the first time I imagined doing something with another person was the night we met. I felt so free for a moment—"

"And that's why you were upset and panicky. I'm so sorry. I understand why you wouldn't have randomly told me that, though. It makes a lot more sense now."

"I still feel bad about how I handled it."

"You shouldn't. You had no idea who I am or anything about me—not the things that mattered. I understand more now why you were adamant that I let you tell me what you're comfortable with rather than assume and hold back. The last thing I want is to take any autonomy from you."

She lets out a heavy sigh. "I appreciate that. And with where we are now, I have complete trust that you'll respect my boundaries. That's why I'm not afraid. Even if you move a little faster, I know you'll stop the second I ask. That's what really matters to me."

"So, where are you at now? Just so I understand. You said getting handsy and grinding might be okay last week. Is that still where your mind—or body—is?"

She throws her head back. "This is the hardest part. I *want* more. I've been starting to really imagine—and maybe touch myself to the thought of—being with you." Her cheeks go bright red, but she continues. "Not sex. Not yet. But maybe touching each other—or even touching ourselves while laying together. But that would require getting naked, and I don't even know if I'm comfortable with that yet." She sighs. "I want to be, but I don't know how to get there."

I rub my thumb over her shoulder, thinking.

"What if we took the sex out of getting naked together?" I ask.

Her eyebrows go up. "What do you mean?"

"Well, if you're considering getting naked as the first step to something sexual happening, what if we just be naked together in a nonsexual way? It can help you build trust that being naked doesn't have to lead to anything sexual. Then whenever you're ready for something else, you'll already feel safe being naked together."

She climbs onto my lap and gives me a soft, slow kiss. "That is a very sweet suggestion. Should we just become nudists around my apartment?"

Finally, I see a hint of that amusement in her eyes again.

"Maybe we should start slow. Watching more TV together? Eating a meal might get messy. We could take a shower—"

"Yes. I like that. There's intimacy to that. It might... help build the trust. Not that I don't trust you—"

"I understand. And I'm good with that. Tell me whenever you want to do that."

She climbs off my lap and grabs my hand. "How about now?"

"After everything today? Are you sure?"

She nods. "I think that's why I want to do it now. I want to wash away—accidental pun—everything else that happened tonight, and focus on you and us."

I let her pull me up, then I look into her eyes. "If that's what you want, I'm in."

She intertwines our fingers and leads me to the bathroom.

Once she has the water running and towels set out, she turns to me.

"Will you start?"

I strip my shirt off and drop it on the floor. "Are we doing tit for tat or do you want me fully naked so you can get the whole show first?"

She smiles, and the remaining wisps of uncertainty vanish from her eyes, replaced by playfulness. "Get down to your boxers. Then I'll give you some tit."

"Is this a preview of the dirty talk I have to look forward to in the future?"

Now I get a full laugh out of her. "Oh yeah, baby. Take off those socks. Let me see your hairy ankles."

"You can blame my genetics for my yeti-like state. Sorry." I shrug and drop my pants before toeing off my socks.

She tilts her head. "Legs maybe. Your chest isn't too bad." She runs her hand over my pec. "Just the right amount of hair."

She tugs on one and smiles, then pulls her shirt over her head.

I have no issues with doing this tonight, other than I wish I could've beaten off first. Because not getting hard at some point is going to be a challenge. And while I'm not some asshole who is worried about blue balls, I don't want to make her uncomfortable.

It doesn't help that she's my absolute dream. All soft curves with the slightest hint of muscle beneath them. Her creamy skin is dotted with freckles. I can't wait until I get to kiss every single one. But that's not the point tonight, so I force a deep breath, think of non-boner-inducing things, and watch as my dream girl gets almost naked in front of me.

"How are you feeling so far?" I ask.

"Better than I thought. Trying to turn my sex brain off."

I chuckle at that. "I think it's understandable that we'd be at least a little turned on. We're dating and obviously find each other attractive. It's bound to happen. Maybe that even helps. This will prove to you that even with those feelings, there can be intimacy—and safety—while naked without anything sexual happening."

"You're so smart," she breathes, then takes her bra off.

One day. One day I will get to play with her beautiful, full breasts. And I can't wait. But today isn't about that.

"Same time?" I ask.

She nods and a few seconds later, we're both naked. Thankfully, I'm keeping my dick to barely a semi.

"I know it's not about that, but you're stunning," I say.

"Funny, I was going to say you're hot as fuck. Potayto-potahto."

We both laugh, then she opens the shower curtain and we climb in, switching out for space under the showerhead.

Once her hair is wet, I trail my fingers through it, then grab her shampoo. "Can I?"

She looks at me over her shoulder with big eyes. "Yes."

I squirt some into my hand, then work it into a lather and slowly work it into her hair, making sure to get everywhere, then I spend a little extra time at the roots and massage her scalp.

She lets out a happy noise, and I keep working my fingers.

"You're safe," I whisper. "You can be naked with me anytime and I will never touch you in any way you don't want. If you let me, though, I'll take care of you. Naked. Clothed. However you want me. However you'll let me, I'll make sure you're cared for in every way."

She lets out a shuddery breath, and when my hands drop, she spins around, eyes closed, like she doesn't want to break the spell yet, and rinses her hair. Then she turns back around.

"There's conditioner too. Use plenty."

With those words, she's given me another sliver of trust.

I work the conditioner in, making sure I get every strand, and when I'm finished and she's rinsed it all out, her gaze finds mine, eyes rimmed with tears. I almost worry until she leans into me, resting her head on my chest.

"Thank you."

I wrap my arms around her. "You don't ever need to thank me for caring about you, and I hope one day you'll know deep in your bones that you never need to thank me for anything like this."

She leans up and presses her lips to mine. "Stay with me tonight?" She looks down at our naked bodies and laughs. "Fully clothed?"

"I'd love to."

We both still have wet hair and shower-warm skin when we settle into her bed. I always keep an extra set of clothes in my car—a habit my mother drilled into me after our car broke down out of town once—so I'm comfortable in sweats and a T-shirt. I might sweat my balls off tonight, but I'll do anything that makes her feel safe.

"Still good?" I ask as Chelsea pulls the sheets up. She's wearing pink pajama bottoms with pictures of iconic women—Rosie the Riveter, RBG, Frida Kahlo, and some others—and a black tank top.

"Yep. The only weird thing is... I can't remember ever really sharing a bed with anyone. So sorry if you catch an elbow in the middle of the night."

"Violent sleeper?"

She shrugs, smiling. "Guess we'll find out."

"Guess so."

She flicks her lamp off and slides down in bed, turning toward me.

"When was the last time you... *shared a bed* with someone?"

My brows flick up.

"Sorry. It's the only thing we didn't talk about tonight, and I'd rather get it out of the way before we're in a heated moment."

"You don't need to apologize. Last time I only shared a bed with someone was probably after my accident. Hyla slept in bed with me for a couple of nights when I first came home and was struggling to move. So, not exactly anything fun. As for the sexual stuff... it's been a while."

"Yeah?"

"Before my accident."

"Wow. Really?"

I turn to face her. "Yes. Why is that surprising?"

"Because you're hot as fuck."

That gets a laugh out of me. I lean over and kiss her. "While I appreciate that, so are you..."

She scrunches up her face. "You weren't damaged the way I was."

Fuck that. "Damaged? How about we pick a new word? I don't like that one. There's nothing damaged or broken about you."

She shakes her head. "You didn't see me at my worst."

"If I had, all I would've seen was your strength. The ability to keep going through the darkness, even when you have no idea when it will end is strength."

"Even when you feel like all you're doing is floating?"

I brush my thumb over her cheek. "Floating's better than drowning."

She stares at me for a moment, then shakes her head. "Okay, *that* is why I'm shocked you haven't been with anyone in that long. You're not just hot, you're kind. And sure, some girls like dickhead guys, but most of us want one who gives a shit."

I wrap my arms around her and pull her close. "Maybe *I've* been looking for someone who gives a shit. After everything I went through, meaningless hookups were the last thing I wanted. I wanted something more."

"That makes sense. I'm sorry for assuming."

"Don't be. I'd rather you ask than sit around and wonder. I can't read your mind, but I'll answer any question you ask me."

"Back at you."

I hold her tighter, playing with her. To my surprise and stupid delight, she reaches up and does the same, resting her hand in my curls.

After a few minutes, she whispers. "I like this."

"Me too. Just promise you won't run away in the morning if you feel anything poking you. My morning wood thinks you're hot as fuck, and he has no chill."

She bites her lip as she laughs. "Then I'll smother him with a pillow."

"Fair enough."

She rests her head on my chest and the comforting feeling of home washes over me. I'm not sure I've ever been this happy before. Not in this way. There's a feeling of total peace when I hold her like this. And my heart goes wild feeling like I finally have something I've wanted for so long. There's no doubt I'm falling hard for her, so I hold her tighter, savoring every second, and hoping that we're headed for something deeper because I already know I'll be crushed if I lose her.

12
Wild and Free

Chelsea

"I CAN'T BELIEVE YOU didn't tell me," I huff.

"Didn't we already have this conversation an hour ago?" Trevor asks, folding his arms over his chest in amusement. Which just pisses me off.

His birthday is in six days, and he didn't tell me until an hour ago. Actually, he didn't tell me anything until after Amanda started asking me questions about whether I was planning to do a party for his birthday. When she realized I didn't know, she grumbled something under her breath and immediately sent a strongly worded text to Trevor.

He was apologetic when we met up after my night class, but I don't think he fully understands why I'm upset.

"Yes, but I'm still annoyed. Now I'm rushing to plan a special date and get you a present."

"I told you I don't care about those things."

"Well, I do," I snap.

His eyebrows shoot up, and I take his hand, leading him from the kitchen.

Since our sweet shower moment a week ago and then him staying the night, we've been spending more time together. He's spent the night a couple more times—still fully clothed—and we showered together both mornings after that. It's helped me grow even more comfortable with him.

Comfortable enough to yell at him right now.

The dinner we were cooking together is in the oven, and I need him to understand *why* this is bothering me.

I shove him onto the couch and climb on his lap, jamming my finger into his chest. "How would you feel if I didn't tell you when my birthday was?"

The cocky little half smile appears. "Technically you haven't."

"We'll get to that in a minute. But seriously. How would you feel if you found out from my friends a week before my birthday and I just hadn't told you?"

He drops his head back against the couch. "Crappy."

"Exactly." I run my fingers through his hair, drawing his attention back to me. I'm not really mad at him, just frustrated. "I know you say it's not that important to you, but it's important to me because *you* are important to me. You would bend over backward to do anything for me. You're patient, and the way you care for me is unparalleled. But I want to take care of you too." He opens his mouth, but I hold up one finger. "Not because I feel like I have to or to pay you back. Because I want to. I'm your girl. That's why you want to take care of me. It's why I'm sure you'll want to spoil me on my birthday. You're my person,

Trev." I suck in a breath to keep my voice from breaking. "I want to take care of you and spoil you. It's my right as your girlfriend."

He stares at me, his hands running up and down my back. "I'm sorry. For the record, just being with you on my birthday is more than enough for me, but I get your point. I'm yours to spoil."

"And take care of," I say pointedly because I see the ways he holds back. He might not even realize he's doing it, but in his desire to take care of others, he hides his own pain. I see it, though, and I'm not letting him get away with that shit.

"I guess I could agree to that."

I lean in and brush my lips over his. "You better."

"Sounds like a threat."

"Could be."

Pressing my lips to his, I rake my fingers through his hair. Thankfully, he's learned to stop holding back and to give in when I kiss him like this, and soon our tongues are tangled, and we're getting lost in each other.

Suddenly, he pulls back. "You're supposed to be telling me when your birthday is."

I lean back a little, but he keeps his hands on my back, holding me in place on his lap.

"Mm. I think you should guess." I give him my sweetest smile.

He groans. "What am I supposed to do? Go through every day of the year?"

"You could guess based on my star sign."

"Yeah, because astrology is one of my favorite things."

I shrug. "I could see Hyla making you learn it."

He cocks a brow. "Have you been talking to Hyla?"

No, but that makes me want to. Plus, she sounds like a lot of fun.

"No. But from the way you and the girls have described her, it seems like something she'd be into and force you to learn about."

"She's tried," he grumbles under his breath.

"Fine. I'll give you a hint. It's right around my favorite holiday."

He tilts his head. "Okay, I'm guessing either Thanksgiving, Christmas, or Valentine's Day?"

"One of those." I smile sweetly.

"I'm ruling out Christmas. I feel like it would've come up if your birthday was near there. But then... maybe that's true of Thanksgiving too. Okay, Valentine's Day?"

"Ding ding, we have a winner. Now you have to figure out the day."

"Valentine's Day is your favorite holiday?"

"Have you not figured out how I feel about romance?"

"True. I should've seen that coming. Okay, fine. Is it..." He trails off, eyes narrowing. "Is it the thirteenth?"

For some reason, his words have a heaviness to them.

"Yeah, it is."

He swallows and shakes his head. "That's my dad's birthday."

My eyes go to his, emotion rippling through me.

Tug. There's another string, tying us together. Pulling me to this kind, compassionate man, who I'm certain I was meant to find.

"Guess I have a new special reason to celebrate it now," Trevor whispers, voice gravelly.

"We should still honor him too."

He stares at me for a long moment, then pulls me tight to him, and that warm fuzzy feeling blooms in my heart. I know what it is. I know what's growing there. I'm not ready to say it yet. It's still taking root, but I know once it grows, it'll be stronger than anything I've ever felt before.

"My mom's going to love it."

"Yeah?"

He nods. "She loves celebrating birthdays—it's her way of honoring people. It took some convincing to keep her from coming up for mine."

"Oh, so it really isn't just me. You don't want *anyone* to celebrate your birthday. Got it."

"I didn't say that," he sighs. "Just would rather see her when I'm back there in a couple of weeks anyway. I'd rather her stay back home with Hyla. I know how much my mom loves me. Hyla needs more of that love right now."

"That's sweet."

He shrugs. "There's no getting out of celebrating it anyway, she'll do it when I'm home next. So, no, I'm not trying to avoid celebrating. I just don't need anything special."

"Mhm. And that's why there's a party at the lake house on Saturday."

"Have you met Amanda? We should talk about that, though. Are you going to be okay at a party?"

Ah yes, one of the lovely things we've discussed over the past week, how I haven't been comfortable with parties or drinking since my assault. Though I want to get comfortable being able to have a drink here or there—especially as I get closer to twenty-one—I don't have much desire for parties.

"With most other parties, I'd say no, but Rae told me the first time I ever went to the lake house that it's a safe space."

"She doesn't like parties much either. But I think for her it's different with our friends."

"That's how I feel too, though you said some guys from the baseball team will be there?"

"The SUNY FL one, yes. But only a couple. Otherwise, it should be small. Though I'm sure Amanda is trying everything possible to get some friends from back home here. Hyla has to work, but we'll see if Amanda gets anyone else here. No matter what, though, if you feel uncomfortable at any time, my room will be a safe place. And if you need me to go up there with you for any reason and make you feel safe..."

"Now who's threatening who?" I tease.

He grazes his lips over mine. "I just want you to know you're safe with me. Especially when you're in my arms. And when your lips are on mine... nothing safer than that."

"Hm. I guess we better test that out."

"We better." He leans back against the couch and pulls me to him again, and I happily get lost in the warmth of his arms, the peace in my heart, and yes, the safety I always feel with him.

My lips press firmly to Trevor's, my tongue teasing his as I straddle him on the couch, completely unhinged as I kiss him.

Fire burns in my gut, all desperation for him. I love making out with him, and I'm starting to think I might be ready—or inching toward ready—to take things further. Even if it's only half a step.

Every curve of my body is pressed against his hard muscles, my lips fused to his like I need them more than my next breath. And I might. I really fucking might.

I swear, kissing him breaks my brain, and needing more air is irrelevant. All I need is more of Trevor.

Slowly I roll my hips over him, breath hitching in my throat at the friction. I'm horny all the time these days with how badly I want him. I can't even give him a chaste kiss without feeling a little hot and bothered. My toy collection has been getting a workout, and I'm all too aware of how many times he's left my apartment with a boner. It's hard not to feel bad, but he's insistent that it's not my responsibility to take care of his needs—even if he and his hand are getting friendlier than ever.

Then my mind conjures up that image. Him lying in bed, stroking himself.

My stomach whirls—not because it makes me uncomfortable, because it makes me hot. And because suddenly, I really, *really* want to see how that image plays out. The noises he makes. The expression as he...

Whoa.

Do I want to do that with him right now?

Do I want to be the one to touch him like that?

I'm not sure. Which means no.

But I want to see it. I want to...

I roll my hips over him again, that delicious bulge hitting all the right spots. I'm not ready to do that in front of him yet. But maybe...

I roll my hips again, and again, then his hands land on my hips.

"Chels." His voice is raspy with barely restrained need. "You need to stop or I'm going to—"

I kiss him hard again, then barely lift my lips off his. "What if I want you to?"

His eyebrows lift like he's about to argue, but then he really looks at me. He sees the vulnerability on my face, and that I'm still in control, and he understands what I'm asking. For him to go first.

In answer, he leans in and sucks on my neck.

More exchanged trust.

With his lips next to my ear, he rumbles, "You want to take care of me, gorgeous? Want to hear how I say your name when I come?"

Holy dirty talk.

"Yes." My voice is so breathy it's almost a whine.

"Then I'm all yours."

I stare at him for a second, then take his lips in a rough, possessive kiss. He wraps his arms around my back, holding me steady as I take control and grind against him.

He gives in to our kisses, groans spilling out as I drag him toward the edge. The warmth of intoxicating power floods me as I watch him, the twist of pleasure on his face, his hazy, hooded eyes. Because of me.

Not only am I safe, not only am I in charge, but I get to take care of him.

I fist his hair as I move faster, and I know the moment he's getting close. His muscles tighten and he breathes out my name again.

I rip my mouth from his and stare down at him, at his swollen lips and begging eyes. Then I move my hips again, harder, faster, until his hands come to my hips and he holds me in place.

"Oh, fuck..."

His eyes slip closed, his lips parting as his orgasm tears through him.

And as I continue to grind, I feel the warmth of him pulsing under me.

He pulls me closer and buries his face in my neck. "Holy fuck, baby."

Heat rushes through me, and my clit tingles, and that's when I jump off his lap. *Whew*. Too close. Not that I have any regrets. Seeing him come was so fucking hot, but I didn't realize how close I was to coming, and even though I could probably handle that, I can't confidently say I'm ready for that yet. For the weight of his eyes on me when I fall apart.

I flush more at that thought.

Sanity seems to return to him all at once, and he jumps off the couch too, clearly concerned that was too much for me. But I bite my lip as I smile, quickly reassuring him.

"Okay?" he asks.

I fist his shirt and pull him to me. "Amazing. Watching you..." A shiver runs through me. "That was sexy. So sexy I needed to climb off your lap before I—"

"Got it."

"Still working on being ready for that."

He curls his fingers through my hair. "There's no rush."

As if on cue, the alarm on his phone goes off. After the third night of not realizing it was almost one in the morning, he started setting an alarm for ten-forty-five, hoping he'd be in his car by eleven, then back to the lake house and in bed before midnight.

He shuts off his alarm and turns back to me, cheeks still flushed and still breathing a bit heavily. "Guess that's my cue. Sorry to come and run." He flashes me that cheeky smile.

"Missed opportunity for a come and go pun, but fine. Go home, get some sleep. Dream of me."

"No chance I won't."

He gives me a steamy kiss that only stokes the fire raging inside me.

"Happy birthday week."

"Was this part of my birthday gift?"

"Mm. With how little notice you gave me, it might be your only one."

"Then I would have zero complaints." He gives me one last kiss, then a firm squeeze to my ass before walking out the door with a lazy smile on his lips.

Once I hear his footsteps on the stairs, I dash over and lock the door, then run to my bedroom and throw open the drawer on my bedside table. Which toy do I want tonight?

I'm so keyed up, but I kind of want to play around.

I want to imagine Trevor is here with me.

Which catches me. Because that made me nervous a little while ago. The thought of him seeing me come, but now... I don't know. I wish there was something in between.

I look over at my phone. Maybe there is.

I quickly pick it up and send a text.

Me: Call me when you get to your room.

Then I pick out some toys and entertain myself for the next twenty minutes while I wait for him to get home. I bring myself to the edge and pull back, enjoying my body in a way that was so foreign for many months. Pleasure that isn't just related to me, but Trevor, too.

When my phone rings, I barely pull the vibrator from my clit in time to answer.

"Hi."

"Babe, what's up? Are you okay?"

I bite my lip, trying and failing to hold back my moan, and put the call on speaker.

Suddenly, his raspy voice fills the room. "What are you doing?"

"Take a guess," I pant.

He curses under his breath. "How long have you been doing that?"

"Since you left." I moan again, so tantalizingly close.

"Are you using your fingers or a toy?"

I look down at the vibrator I'm swirling around my clit and my fingers, still moving in and out of my pussy. "Both."

"Are you close?"

My breath trembles. "So close. I want you to hear it. I want you to know"—I stop holding back and moan loudly—"I want you to know when I come, I'm thinking of you. I'm thinking of the look on your face and the noises you made, and the way you pulsed under me." My toes curl into the sheets as I cry out. "Trev. I'm so close."

"Keep going, baby. Work your sweet clit until you shatter."

Fuck, I can't wait until we can talk like that in the same room. Getting ourselves off or each other.

"Trevor. Ohh..."

"That's it, baby. You're doing so good. Let me hear you come."

The vibrator hits the perfect spot as his words ring in my ear and an earth-shattering, unholy orgasm rips through me. My ass flies off the sheets as every muscle contracts. I don't know if I'm moaning or screaming or making any coherent words, I only know it feels so damn good, and he's listening to every second, and that turns me on more, making it last even longer.

"Trev..." I pant as I finally start sliding down from that high.

My heartbeat is pounding in my ears, but his smooth, sultry voice cuts through it all.

"So good, baby. Perfect."

"Mhm." I pull my fingers out and look down at them, wondering if he'd lick them off if he were here. I'm definitely inching toward wanting more. Or leaping. And after this...?

"Thanks for listening," I say playfully.

"I will listen to *that* anytime."

I almost ask, *and what about watching?* But I think I know the answer to that, and I trust that we'll get there when the time is right. For now, this unlocks a whole new way to play together.

"I'll keep that in mind. See you tomorrow?"

"I'll meet you after your 10:00 a.m. class."

"Perfect. Goodnight, birthday boy."

"Night, Chels. Sleep well."

I hang up, then stumble around on my shaky legs, barely managing to clean myself and my toys before collapsing back into bed and drifting off into absolute bliss.

Trevor

Twenty-one.

For some people, this is the birthday of drunken shenanigans and getting so shit-faced you don't actually remember anything about your birthday.

That's never been me. Maybe in another life it could have been, but being thoughtful and responsible was ingrained in me from a young age. Not just with my parents' expectations, but with the examples they set for me. Dicking around and goofing off with my friends is all well and good, but I've never been the type to get blackout drunk or even much past tipsy.

Maybe it's because I like to be in control—keep the people I care about safe—or maybe it's because of that nagging voice in the back of my mind that it wouldn't make my dad proud.

Ah, the baggage of idolizing your parent, then losing them at a young age. Do I have my dad on a pedestal? Yeah. But he fucking earned it by being one of the greatest humans ever. And that's not a *me* thing. Everyone I've met who knew him always tells me the same.

Of course, my dad was also my personal hero, and if he were still alive, he'd be my best friend, my closest confidant. I love my mom, but I was obsessed with my dad. I wanted to spend all my time with him, and he was never ever annoyed by that. He thought I was cool too, and wanted to spend his time with me. And Mom. And Hyla too. He wore his love for his family like a badge of honor, and he made every moment with us extra special.

That's part of why I don't put much emphasis on my birthday. Before my dad died, it was the day I looked forward to every year. I knew it would be incredible because he always made it that way. My mom has gone above and beyond since he died, trying to make it feel just as special, and I love her for it, but what I miss isn't something replaceable. It's my dad's joyful energy. The massive smile on his face when whatever surprise he concocted was finally revealed. And even though this is my tenth birthday without him, I still don't feel a big desire to celebrate.

Does any of that excuse me not telling Chelsea? No. But I truly wasn't thinking about it. I wasn't keeping it from her. If it hadn't been for Amanda planning a party, I wouldn't have thought of it until two days beforehand. I understand why she was upset, and maybe I should've told her the reason I don't want to make it a big deal, but if she wants to celebrate me, I want to let her do that. Because I know how that feels. To want to make the person you care about happy and bring them joy. It's all I think about with her. It'd be hypocritical of me to stop her from doing that for me.

So, we're going on a date she planned, and I'm going to focus on having fun.

Not that the party last night wasn't fun. I appreciated that too. Chelsea did great, and once she realized how small and relaxed it was, she was completely comfortable. Amanda got Nick and his wife, Leigh, to come up for a few hours, and that was awesome. Chelsea fit in with them seamlessly, bantering with Nick and probably scheming with Leigh. It was all great, and I had fun.

Fuck, I wish I could stop being such a sad sack about this, but losing my dad colored things differently, and my accident brought a lot of those things up again. I hadn't realized how much I had compartmentalized until after that.

Maybe I should go back to therapy.

I went right after my dad died, but... whatever.

I don't want to get on this train of thought today. I'm determined to have a great time with my girl.

There we go. That's the train of thought I can jump on.

My dick too.

Unfortunately, he gets a little jumpy at even the mention of Chelsea these days. That might have something to do with that hot as fuck grinding session followed by listening to her get off over the phone.

I swear I memorized every sound she made, and fuck if I'm not desperate for more. Not that I'll push. Just the memory of her breathy moans or the feel of her body grinding against mine is enough to get me close to coming.

Speaking of which... I glance down at the obvious bulge in my pants.

Just what I need while I'm driving to pick up Chelsea.

I don't even have time to beat one off, unless I want to find some back road, but that sounds pervy.

Maybe I need to start jerking off before our dates.

Is that more creepy or less?

And now I'm thinking about jerking off. Not what I need right now, brain.

I take a deep breath, trying to think of anything that will get the blood from my dick, only for the noise of loud ringing to scare the shit out of me.

I jump and glance at the screen in my car. Then I cringe hard at the name I see.

My mother.

Well, at least my boner is dead now.

I click the button to answer the call and try to sound normal. "Hey, Mom."

"Happy birthday!" The mixture of my mom's and Hyla's voices reverberate around the car as if they were right next to me.

I grunt but smile.

"Thank you."

"How's your birthday weekend been so far?" Mom asks.

"Yeah. I'm sorry I had to miss your party," Hyla says.

"It's all good. It was low-key. Well, as low-key as Amanda knows how to be. I know you'll celebrate me when I'm home next." There's a noise like my mom is going to start worrying, so I quickly add, "And don't worry about today, Chelsea has a whole plan to spoil me."

"Ooh Chelsea," Hyla sings.

"And how is *Chelsea?*" my mom asks with the same lilt in her voice.

"You guys are annoying."

"I'm still working on your ship name. Now that I know her last name is Winters—"

"How do you know her last name?"

"Uh..."

"Hyla Aria."

"Trevor Mitchell."

"Hy."

She inhales deeply and forcefully lets it out. "Fine. We follow each other on Instagram."

Mom laughs loudly at that.

"You're stalking my girlfriend?"

"Not stalking. But she's very pretty," Mom says.

"Wait. Chelsea is following you back?" I ask Hyla.

"Yep." She pops the P.

"Have you talked to her?"

"Not yet. Just learning everything I can about my future sister-in-law."

"She won't be that if I disown you first."

I pull up outside Chelsea's building to a chorus of laughter from my mom and Hyla. They get into too much trouble when left to their own devices. I wouldn't be surprised if they're both social media stalking us on every platform, waiting to see pictures of the two of us together.

"As fun as this phone call has been, I have to—"

"Wow, only a few weeks in and you're already making me walk to your car? Is chivalry dead?" Chelsea's playful voice dances through the car as she swings the door open and climbs in, putting a cooler in the backseat as she does.

A squeal rings out, and I groan.

"Is that her?" Mom asks.

I turn to Chelsea. "There was a reason I didn't get out of my car yet. Do we need to come up with a signal so you know when it's not safe?"

My voice gets rumblier than it should when I'm still on the phone with my mom and sister, but I stop functioning normally when Chelsea is around.

"What could be unsafe about this?" Chelsea teases.

"Trevor Matteny," my mother says.

"Fine. Chelsea, you're on with my mom and Hyla. Good luck."

But Chelsea just smiles brightly. "Hi. It's nice to, uh, talk with you both."

"You too. Is my son behaving himself and being a good boy?"

"Uh..."

"Mom!"

"Seriously, we might not want to know the answer to that," Hyla says.

"Well, this has been fun, but Chelsea and I have a date to get to. I'll see you both in a couple of weeks."

"Are you bringing Chelsea with you?" Mom asks.

Chelsea's eyes widen and she looks at me questioningly.

"We haven't talked about that yet, so thanks for throwing me under the bus."

"Anytime!" Mom says cheerily.

"Yeah. It's our job. Our *right*."

"And it's my right to hang up the phone now. Love you, bye."

"Bye, honey. Nice talking to you, Chelsea."

"You too."

There's another round of happy birthdays and goodbyes, then I finally hang up the phone.

Chelsea is staring at me, amusement dancing in her eyes. "Well, that was fun."

"Maybe for you."

She pokes my cheek. "Aw, you're so cute when you do the grumpy thing. Don't act like you don't love your mom and sister."

I sigh because she's right. They're the most important people in my life. Only now Chelsea is on that list too.

"I love them, but they give me headaches."

She buckles her seatbelt, then looks over at me, eyes dancing. "So, what were they talking about you bringing me to in a couple of weeks?"

"You know about Rae and Aaron's bachelorette and bachelor party shenanigans?"

"Amanda and Sarah have mentioned some things."

"I'll be home for the night beforehand, and that's what Mom was talking about. I'd love for you to come meet her, but I don't know exactly where we are on things like that. But if you want to, you can come for a couple of hours or stay the night, or whatever—"

"Trev. Breathe."

"Sorry."

"I'd love to meet your mom and Hyla. And I'm getting kind of used to snuggling in bed with you, so I wouldn't mind staying overnight."

I lean in and kiss her. "Good answer."

She brushes her thumb over my cheek and smiles at me. "Happy birthday."

"Thanks, baby."

"Ready for your super special birthday date?"

"I can't wait to see what mischief you have up your sleeve. Just tell me where we're going."

She doesn't. She leads me on a wild goose chase of random side streets until we end up on campus and she has me park in some side lot that's away from most buildings.

"Still not going to tell me where we're going?" I ask.

She pops a kiss on my cheek. "See if you can figure it out."

I grab the cooler before she can, then meet her at the back of the car. "Lead the way."

She takes a random path off the edge of the parking lot I didn't know existed. We pass a sign that reads "college camp" and I stare at the trail as we pass.

"We have a college camp?"

Her brows shoot up. "Wow, you really said, *eh, my friends have a lake house, I guess I'll go there*, didn't you?"

I shrug. "Pretty much. It was more about the friends than the lake house, though."

"Well, the college camp can be a date for another day. There are hiking trails there along with a field station with all kinds of biology and meteorology things."

I blink at her.

She sighs and rolls her eyes. "I actually checked this place out before I decided to come here. Plus, Robbie went here. Anyway, come on. We're almost there."

I follow her and don't realize where we are or where we're going until we're there.

Chelsea smiles at me as we look at the baseball stadium in front of us.

"Are you sure?" I ask her.

She sighs dramatically. "It didn't happen in a baseball stadium."

"But a baseball player..." After hearing she had a panic attack when she found out I played baseball, I've been cautious about bringing it up in front of her.

"Maybe he was or maybe he wasn't. Either way, it doesn't matter. I refuse to let what he did affect our relationship—affect something that's a part of you. A part I want to know. So take me inside and let me see it—and love it—through your eyes."

I stare at her for a beat longer, making sure there's no true hesitance in her eyes. When she shoves my shoulder, I finally relent and grab her hand, leading her into the stadium.

When we get inside, I take her to the field, because that's the best part. Watching a game is amazing, but there's nothing like being on the field.

We stand at home plate, and I get a little lost staring out at the field.

"Sure you're okay?" I whisper.

"Yeah. I can handle this. Syracuse, not so much. I haven't been back since I left school, and the thought of going back makes me want to vomit. But this? I don't know. Being here with you makes it feel like an extension of you."

I sigh, the rush of peace and the pang of nostalgia washing over me. "To some degree it is. They might not have happened on this field, but some of the best moments of my life happened on the ball field."

"What position did you play?"

"Third base."

Then I'm running down the line, pulling her after me, until I'm standing at third, and looking over the place from my favorite point of view.

"What's your favorite baseball memory?"

I smile at that, emotion washing over me. If I close my eyes, I could be there again.

"Easy. We won the state championship game in eleventh grade. It was the dream team. I was on third, Nick was shortstop, Joel was on second, Rae's shitty ex Davey was on first—but we'll pretend he didn't exist—Miles was catching, and Aaron was serving a masterclass in pitching. We had some killer plays that night, but really being out on the field with some of my best friends was the best part. I'll never forget the feeling when Aaron struck out the last guy to win us the game. That night was one of the best of my life."

When I turn to her, she has a massive smile on her face. "That sounds amazing. I wish I could've seen it." She brushes her thumb over my cheek. "The joy on your face right now is indescribable. I have lots of happy memories, but I'm not sure I have one that stands out like that. That's special."

I squeeze her hand. "It is. Most of my other favorite baseball memories involve my dad."

"He played too, right? What position?"

My eyes drift to the outfield. "Right field. He tried and tried to get me to play outfield. He told me how underrated of a position it was, but I hated waiting to track down a fly ball or hope for a double to get out there. I loved the intensity of the infield, and third base called to me. Once he saw how well I took to it, he never pushed me toward the outfield again. He helped coach my little league teams, and loved being a part of the game, even when he wasn't playing anymore. I understand why now. He just loved it. He knew so many baseball stats and that translated into a deeper love of the sport for me. And I think that's the difference in players. Some people play because the sport is fun and they enjoy it. But then there are those of us who have a piece of baseball inside us. We know years and years worth of stats, analyze games, and will keep baseball in our lives any way we can have it." I blow out a breath. "Sorry. I jumped on my soapbox."

But then I glance at her and find her staring at me with a giant smile on her face.

"That's what I wanted. You light up at the mere mention of baseball, and I don't want you to hold that back. That fire inside you—the passion for the game you love—I want to see more of that. I know you were worried about how I would feel, and maybe I was a bit too, but after seeing this through your eyes, I can't imagine not feeling the same happiness I do now."

"Even if I'm not playing?"

"Whether you're helping with the team or sitting next to me watching, I know it'll bring you joy, and when you smile, it's impossible for me not to smile too."

"Baby..." I pull her into my arms, holding her tightly and playing with her long, wild hair. "Thank you for bringing me here."

There's a heavy pause, then she whispers, "Happy birthday, Trevor."

And even though I probably shouldn't, what I hear in her voice and the emotion behind those words is *I love you*. Or maybe I'm projecting because with every passing day, I'm becoming more and more certain. She's not just my dream girl. She's the love of my life.

We're laughing and chatting as we sit on a picnic blanket behind third base. Chelsea brought Loganberry and sandwiches from The Lake Shack, the place I took her on our first date. Which is when it hits me...

"It's been a month since our first date."

"You've put up with my crazy for four whole weeks. You must *really* like me," she teases.

"Didn't I tell you something that day about not being self-deprecating?"

She shakes her head. "Not self-deprecating if it's true. I'm not saying it in a bad way. You've seen most sides of me now—except for my wildest one. Then you'll learn how *crazy* I can be."

"I prefer the other word you just said. *Wild*. Everything about you has a wildness to it. Your eyes, your hair, your smile, your mouth." She laughs at that. "You're wild and free. I love that about you."

She leans in, those *wild* eyes dancing, and kisses me. It's surprisingly soft and sweet, and when she pulls away, she looks out at the field.

"So, we covered baseball. Tell me about your best birthday ever... though at this point I'm expecting baseball to be a part of it."

I laugh at that because it's true. "You called it."

That same wistful feeling sweeps over me. My eyes go to right field again, and as I stare beyond the wall, warmth surrounds me for a moment, and I feel like my dad is here with me. It might be all internal mind-games, but it's comforting to feel that connection to him today.

I clear my throat and look at Chelsea. "It was my ninth birthday, and the minor league team in Binghamton was playing in the minor league championship down in Pennsylvania. So my dad organized a trip for us to go down there—I had no idea where they were playing, so I thought we were just going to Hershey Park. Which we did. We spent a day there, him, my mom, me, and Hyla. We did the chocolate tour and went on rides for hours. The next morning, we had this fancy breakfast, then left early and drove to Allentown, where the game was being held. I was so excited when we got there, but then my dad pulled out the showstopper. A meet and greet with the team. To this day, I have no idea how he pulled that off, but he laughed with the GM like they were old friends, while the players signed jerseys for Hyla and me. Binghamton won, and we celebrated with dinner at Waffle House—and I had candles in my waffles. It was amazing, and I will never forget the unending joy on my dad's face for all of it. Never a complaint. When we got stuck in traffic, he turned up the radio. He made every birthday special, but that was one for the books."

Chelsea leans against me and looks up at me, eyes rimmed with tears. "That's why you don't like to make a big deal about your birthday." Her voice is hushed, as if in awe of the story I just told.

I let out a sigh.

I shouldn't be surprised she figured it out.

She sees me. Even when I try to hide and say I'm all good, she sees right through me. I kind of love that.

I rub my hand down her back, twirling her hair around my finger. "Yeah. But today has reminded me why celebrating it is important." I brush my lips over her cheek. "Thank you."

"I still have one last thing for you. It's not big or fancy because I know you can get yourself whatever you want, but I hope you like it."

She pulls a small box from her purse and hands it to me.

I lift the top off the black box and pull out a keychain. It's shaped like a baseball jersey and is gray and red—Ida's colors. When I look closer, I see my last name and high school number on it—twelve.

"Flip it over," she whispers.

And when I do, I see my last name again, but this jersey is white with red pinstripes, and the number is my dad's—number six.

"How did you—"

"I called your mom. She even found a photo of your dad in an Ida jersey—what they looked like when he was in high school. Then I made the designs online and took it to a local shop to have it made."

"It's perfect." I pull her to me and kiss her hard, telling her with my body what I'm not quite ready to say with my words. "You're perfect," I breathe.

"Agree to disagree," she says against my lips. "But I'm glad you like it. Thank you for letting me in and showing me this side of you."

I break our kiss and rest my forehead against hers. "Thank you for wanting to see it."

One more kiss, then I tug her over and widen my legs so she can sit between them, peace washing over me when she does.

She grabs the cooler and gets the cupcakes from the local bakery out, handing one to me and quietly singing *Happy Birthday*.

Today has been so much more than I thought it could be. Mostly because of Chelsea and partly because of my mindset. I stopped thinking my birthdays could be as special without my dad. While nothing will ever beat my ninth birthday, everything about this quiet, heartfelt celebration with the girl who has stolen my heart makes me think this might be the best birthday since then, and I wouldn't mind a whole lot more spent like this.

13

Have Fun

Chelsea

YOU'D THINK I'D NEVER been in a car before.

Or been to Ida.

It's only forty-five minutes from Birch Lake, and on more than one occasion, we came here to shop in the cute stores downtown—especially at Christmas time. Birch Lake has some cute stores too, but everything is touristy or wilderness focused. Ida is all small-town charm and coziness.

I've been here before. It's not shiny and new.

Yet here I am, staring out the window and vibrating with excitement as Trevor pulls off the highway exit for Ida. Across the river, all the backs of the little shops downtown are visible, and a river walk runs behind them. It's so idyllic it hurts.

I can't wait to experience it in a new way.

Forget being a dog looking out a window. I'm Princess Jasmine on a magical carpet ride.

As we head toward the bridge that leads into town, I look to my left at the hillside.

"Wait, are you a country boy or a townie? Rae mentioned they all lived on the same block growing up, right? What about you?"

He laughs at the pep in my voice and shakes his head. "Yes, their whole friend group started because her backyard butts up to Joel's. As does Aaron's. Mackenzie's family owns the bakery on the corner. Miles lives across the street from Rae and Sarah. And before the McKinleys adopted her, Sarah lived around the corner with her shitty biological mother."

My eyebrows fly up at that.

He continues, voice a little gruff. "Sorry. That's her story to tell, but I know the scars it left her with." He clears his throat. "Anyway, yes. They were the townies, and I spent my fair share of time down there with them, especially in high school. But..." He nods to the road in front of us that leads up into the hills. "I grew up in the country. First in a tiny two-bedroom house with hardly any land, and then... well, you'll see."

He flips on his turn signal to cross the bridge into town.

"Wait, if you live over that way, why are we heading into town?"

He glances at me and sucks in a breath. "There's somewhere else I want to take you first. Someone else I want you to meet."

He drives across town, turning down a couple of side streets until the houses start fading into a sea of evergreen trees. It's not until we pass through the iron gates that I understand where we're going.

To see his dad.

The cemetery is set into the rolling hillside. I've never seen another like it. It feels almost like it's one with nature. Like it's truly a place of peace.

He follows one of the winding roads up toward the top of the cemetery. There's a monument and a lookout around a curve from where he pulls over.

When he shuts off the car, he turns to me, emotion heavy on his face.

"This is the first time I've ever brought someone here."

My brows tick up. "Really?"

"I mean, Nick's been here with me before, but that's because..." He lowers his voice. "His mom's buried here too."

My mouth slips open, but I suddenly understand their friendship even more. Two outwardly sarcastic and troublemaking boys with soft hearts who have experienced a loss no one should have to at a young age.

I reach over and take his hand. "You can share as much or as little as you want with me."

"I know you don't get to meet him, but I wish you could. This is as close as I'll get, so..."

I swing my door open. "I'll be right by your side."

The gratitude in his eyes makes my heart squeeze. I wish I could take this hurt from him, but if all I can do is lessen it, I will.

When he meets me by my door, I'm still taking everything in.

"This is surprisingly beautiful. Most cemeteries feel stuffy and manicured. As strange as it sounds, it's like this one grew here."

"Yeah. It's why my mom picked this one. My dad wanted to be cremated, but since that wasn't in writing, and she didn't feel like fighting with his family about it, this was the compromise. A place that feels real, connected to nature, and more inviting than a lot of others."

He takes my hand and leads me through the maze of headstones.

"Do you come here a lot?"

"When I'm at home, maybe once every month or two. Whenever I want to center myself and try to feel connected to him. When I'm away at school, I usually stop either before I leave or when I get back. Last time I was here was the day I left for SUNY FL." He sucks in a sharp breath. "Here we are."

The headstone is large, with a picture of his dad's face etched into it. Even in the stone, I see the similarities between him and Trevor. The face shape, the dimples, the hair.

The stone still looks brand new, and there are flowers planted at the base.

"My grandmother plants those."

I squeeze his hand as I read the headstone.

In loving memory of Mitchell Osborne Matteny. Devoted father, cherished husband, and beloved son.

"Hey, Dad." Trevor's voice catches, and I can't imagine that kind of ache.

My dad has always been my number one supporter. Losing him—or Robbie—would crush me.

Then my gaze drifts back to Trevor.

Losing him?

Nope.

No matter how short a time it's been, I'd be heartbroken.

He runs a hand over the stone.

"I brought someone with me today." He rolls his lips and clears his throat. "I get how you looked at Mom now. Anyway, this is Chelsea. I'm not going to ask her to talk to your headstone, because that's kind of weird, but I just wanted you to know she's here with me, and she means a lot to me. You'd like her. She keeps me in line and doesn't put up with my shit. Like Mom was with you."

Tears spill down my cheeks, and I walk over to Trevor, taking his hand again.

"I don't care if it's weird." I rest my other hand on the stone. "It's nice to meet you, Mr. Matteny. Your son is a pain in the butt, but I kind of like him."

Trevor laughs, though his eyes are glassy.

"He'd insist you call him Mitch."

"Mitch. Well, even though he pretends to be a curmudgeon and can be a little full of himself sometimes, he's pretty awesome. You did a good job with him."

I meet Trevor's eyes as I say the words because I want him to know they're the truth. I don't have to know his dad to know Mitch would've been proud of him. He's an unfailingly good man, and that's why I fell for him.

He pulls me close and kisses my forehead. "Give me a few minutes?"

"No problem." I kiss his cheek. "I might go check out the view."

"I'll meet you over there."

The clearing overlooking the town is more beautiful than I thought it would be. All of downtown is visible with patchy views of the houses outside the center of town. I look at all the ones I can see, wondering if any of them belong to Rae and Sarah or their friends. Then my gaze drifts to the rolling hills beyond and I get a familiar sense of home. The same one I get when I'm looking out at Birch Lake from the campground.

Trevor sits down next to me, emotion still swirling around him.

He silently wraps an arm around my back.

We're quiet for a moment, taking in the view as the early autumn breeze dances around us.

Finally, I look at Trevor. "Is it always this emotional for you when you come here?"

He shrugs. "It depends. Sometimes it barely hits me. Today was heavier." I reach down and squeeze his hand. "He would've loved you."

"I meant what I said back there, and I'll come here with you anytime you want."

"Thank you," he breathes.

"Don't thank me."

Our eyes meet, and then his hand slides up my back and into my hair.

His lips land on mine in a raw, sloppy kiss. Not meant to lead anywhere, but it's an expression of everything he's feeling right now.

With a sigh, he pulls back and looks at the view again.

"Ready for the chaos?"

I laugh at that. "Let's do it."

"Holy crap." I look up at the iron gate in front of us. A very different iron gate from the one at the cemetery. "When were you going to tell me you lived on a fancy estate? I believe on the way here, you described it to me as *quaint*. I think we have very different definitions of that word."

I can't even see the house from here.

He laughs as he keys in the code and the gates swing open.

"I guess I meant quaint not in size, but in vibe?"

"Ah, like an old English country home?"

"That's pretty on-brand, actually. Except it's not old. And no murders take place here. When I think English country home, I think murder mystery."

"Good to know."

As he drives up the winding gravel drive, the house comes into view, and his description was dead-on.

"Wow. This is beautiful."

"It is. It was my dad's dream house. They'd been saving for years, and it wasn't going to be on this big of a piece of property, but they'd already had plans drawn up. They'd been dreaming of it together since before I was even born. My dad wanted enough room so my grandparents could live here after they retired if they wanted, or so I could live here with my family one day. He loved the idea of multi-generational living and that kind of family structure. My mom liked it too and wanted something private and safe. When he died and we got all the money that was somehow supposed to take his place, she built his dream house."

My heart shatters for him—for his mom.

I know Trevor would rather live in a shack if he could still have his dad with him.

I run my hand up his arm. "Well, I'm excited to get to know more about him from his dream house."

Trevor lets out a soft sigh as he parks the car. "Thank you."

I don't bother to ask what for. I know why he's thanking me—for understanding that as much as he loves his home, there's a part of him that hurts because of it. "Don't thank me for being here for you."

He leans in to kiss me, but sighs and hangs his head before he gets there.

"What?"

"You might regret being here for me in a couple of minutes."

"Why?" I ask, biting back a laugh.

"Because we've already got a stalker."

He flings his door open, and as I open mine, I look over at the house in time to see someone moving away from the window.

Trev grabs our bags, then leads the way up to the front porch and swings the front door open.

"Having fun, creeper?" he says.

"I'm not trying to be creepy. I'm just excited to meet—"

He cuts Hyla off as I walk through the door. "Chelsea. This is Hyla, the reason for most of my insanity." I laugh when she sticks her tongue out at him. "Hyla, this is Chelsea. The reason I sound less like a grumpy asshole these days."

"You only pretend to be grumpy." Then I turn to Hyla, nerves swimming in my gut. She's a little taller than me and thin with long blond hair, a bright smile, and mischievous eyes. I want her to like me. So I say the truth. "Hi. I'm not sure exactly what to say. This feels like it could be weird, but I don't want it to be."

She sighs in relief. "Me either. So I'm just going to decide we're best friends now, okay?"

I laugh as relief washes over me. "I'm down."

Then Hyla wraps me in a massive hug before looping an arm through mine and guiding me farther into the living room.

"Is Trevor behaving himself while he's away at school?" she asks.

I smile and say, "Define behaving."

Behind us, Trevor groans, making Hyla and me laugh more.

"She's here!" Hyla yells.

"We. *We* are here," Trevor mutters.

Hyla waves a hand. "We've had you for twenty-one years. We're over you now. You're washed up. Old and stinky."

"I'm not stinky." He pokes her in the ribs.

She sticks her tongue out as footsteps sound, then a woman dashes from a hallway leading to the other side of the house.

"Where? Gimme!"

Hyla shakes her head and laughs as Trevor's mom runs over to us. She's wearing leggings and a sweater and has medium-length dark blond hair. And a smile just like Trevor's.

"Mom, this is—"

She comes to a stop in front of me, then throws her arms around me. "Chelsea. It's so good to meet you."

"It's good to meet you too, Mrs. Matteny."

"No way. Call me Liz. Please." She lets me go and grabs my hands. "I'm so excited to meet the girl who makes my son smile like that."

I turn in time to see Trevor looking down and rubbing the back of his neck. "Mom..."

"Don't give me that tone. I like seeing you happy."

He sighs. "Yeah, I know."

Then he walks over and throws his arms around his mom, and it's so... touching.

It makes me feel all swoony and mushy and...

As he steps out of his mom's embrace, I reach for his arm, but when he feels my fingertips on his skin, he yanks his arm away.

"Don't pinch me."

I give him my most innocent smile. "I don't know what you're talking about."

"Pinching?" Hyla asks.

Now it's Trevor's turn to smile, but his is more evil. "Yeah, whenever she thinks I'm being too much like a fantasy book boyfriend, she pinches me to make sure I'm real."

Liz blinks, then breaks into a smile. "You're just like your dad."

"Fantasy book boyfriend? Does that mean you'll read books with us?" Hyla asks.

"Definitely. Trev and I have been reading together."

"That's so cute," Hyla says, making Trevor groan again. I love the dynamic here. They outnumber him, but he's so soft for them. It's adorable.

"Who else is hungry? I'm starving. Mom, need help with dinner?"

"I'll never say no to your help."

"I'm happy to help too," I say, but Hyla shakes her head.

"Don't bother. Cooking together is their thing. Unless she's making cookies and needs all hands on deck, she won't ask for our help. Which is fine, because it means *I* get to steal your attention. I'm going to give Chelsea a mini tour!" she calls.

There are muttered affirmations, but they're already halfway into the expansive kitchen.

She slips her arm around mine. "Don't worry. I'll let Trevor show you all the spots that are important to him, but I can at least show you around the downstairs... drag you through the library."

"There's a library?" I squeak.

She laughs. "Don't get too excited. It's not quite a *Beauty and the Beast* kind of library, but it'll do."

She leads me down the hall Liz came from until we get to a large room lined with bookshelves—except for one wall where Liz's desk is.

I stand in the middle and spin around, looking at the floor-to-ceiling shelves. There's even a rolling ladder like in *Beauty and the Beast*.

"This is incredible."

"Liz loves for anyone who's here to borrow books, read, and enjoy."

I find myself in front of a fantasy section, which includes collector's editions of several popular series.

"I'll definitely be taking her up on that."

"Come on, let me show you my favorite little reading nook."

She leads me up a set of stairs at the back of the house—apparently there are two stairwells—and around the corner, where there's a small open space by a large window that looks out over the backyard and woods beyond. There's a loveseat and two extremely comfortable looking chairs.

Hyla plops down in one and sighs. "So cozy."

I sit down too. "Wow. It is. Do you spend a lot of time here?"

She shrugs. "Liz likes having company, and it's better than visiting my actual parents. I have my own apartment, but Liz lures me over for girls' nights, and when I don't have to work, I'll stay the night or weekend sometimes."

"She sounds awesome."

Hyla nods. "She is."

I laugh a little at the awkwardness trying to creep in again. "You seem awesome too."

She scoffs at that.

"No way. Trevor never lets me get away with being self-deprecating. Somehow, I doubt he lets you do it, either."

She barks a laugh. "No, he doesn't. Even though he says that stuff to himself all the time. Such a double standard."

"I'm doing my best to remind him how awesome he is."

"Good. He needs that. This last year... it's the roughest I've seen him since his dad died. Liz is right. His smile is brighter again. Thanks to you."

"He's doing the same for me."

"Good. I know we've only just become besties, but I already know you deserve to be treated like a princess."

I can't help but laugh at that.

"Well, since we're best friends now, I should probably have your phone number. I need to be able to text you if Trevor does anything annoying... or just because I want to get to know you."

"I want to get to know you too."

We exchange numbers, then head back downstairs and take seats around the kitchen counter, chatting as Hyla makes some tea and puts cookies on plates for us. I laugh at her retelling of how Amanda 'hated' her, even though there's still a flash of pain in Hyla's eyes. Trevor has mentioned before that he worries about Hyla, especially with her parents being so crappy. I get it now. I'm not sure exactly what I'm picking up on, but there's deep pain beneath her bubbly exterior.

"So you teach yoga?" I ask. I've always thought a job like that might be fun. And an entirely different avenue through which to uplift women.

"Yep. Big, exciting job."

So, not exciting, then. "It doesn't have to be exciting, as long as you enjoy it."

"I do. It's not a career, but it's something for now. I'm still figuring out what I want to do. And who I am. How not to be a mess."

There's that self-deprecation again, but I get it. Wound yourself before someone else can wound you. Call out your flaws, so no one can use them against you. It's something that's been ingrained in us—especially women—for a long time.

I know for me—and I assume for her—it comes from somewhere deeper, though.

I put my hand over hers and lean in closer. "For the record, I'm a mess too. Still figuring out how to heal from my own trauma. Just know I'll never judge you. I know Trevor is a safe place for you. I want you to still feel that same safety and know you're safe with me too."

She lunges forward and pulls me into her arms. "And you're safe with me."

"Thank you."

"Hey," Trevor calls from the other side of the kitchen. "No stealing my girl."

We pull apart, laughing, then Hyla wraps her arm around my back. "Sorry, she's mine now."

He smiles contentedly. "Good. I need my two favorite people to get along." Liz clears her throat, and Trev kisses her head. "I don't have to worry about you getting along with anyone, Mom. And you're always number one in my heart."

She laughs and swats him with a towel. "You're a kiss-up just like your dad was."

His smile grows. "I learned from the best."

Then that smoldering look is turned on me, only it's not just a smolder. It's laced with something so much deeper. Something that tugs on my heartstrings the same way watching him with his family does. It deepens that feeling growing inside me. The one I'm too afraid to name because I keep telling myself it's too soon or I don't want to jinx it.

But it's there all the same, growing quietly in the background.

I have a feeling it won't be long until it grows so big, I'll have no choice but to let it burst out of me.

I'm cozy and close to sleep nestled in Trevor's insanely comfortable bed when he climbs in with me, hair still damp from a shower.

He leans over and kisses me, but doesn't settle in. Which makes me flick my eyes open and look at him.

"Are you okay?"

He lets out a little grunt. "I don't know."

"Talk to me."

"I'm worried about Hyla."

"How so?"

"She's lost weight since I saw her last. She was picking at her food tonight. And underneath everything, I can just see the pain..." He sighs and runs a hand through his hair. "It reminds me of—"

"What?"

He swallows, that weight in his voice growing heavier. "Senior year of high school, she went through some hard shit with her parents, and... she took a handful of her mom's sleeping pills."

A gasp slips out of me, but Trevor continues.

"When my mom told me... it was the second-worst moment of my life behind losing my dad. Even hitting all those fucking trees on my snowboard and my recovery, it was nothing compared to thinking I could lose the girl I consider my sister."

I throw my arms around him, sliding closer and holding him tightly. He settles in my arms and then tells me the whole story. Everything Hyla's been through. How horrible her parents are. How they manipulated her and her relationship with Mackenzie. It sounds truly awful.

"And she's still holding out hope they'll come around," he grumbles. "I've been trying to get her to cut them out of her life for years, but she won't do it."

I sweep my hand over his cheek. "You can't force her to do that. Another person trying to control her decisions isn't what she needs. She needs your support." He opens his mouth, but I keep going. "I know it's hard. We both know that, right? But at the end of the day, she's the only one who can make those hard decisions. All you can do is support her and show her you love her. I know you want to fix it for her, but it's not up to you. She'll only face her trauma when *she's* ready."

His sigh is rough and painful as he looks at me, but he runs his fingers through my hair, some of the weight finally lifting off him.

He brushes his lips over mine. "You make me better."

"You do the same for me."

A moment of silence stretches between us, and I feel that word rumbling in the depths of my soul, pulling at me, making me question if I should say it.

Then his eyes meet mine, and I swear I see the same thing mirrored in them.

But we're both chickens and don't say anything. After a moment, he pulls me close, kissing me deeply.

"Thank you for being here with me."

"Thank you for wanting me here."

"Night, baby."

I press a kiss to his cheek. "Goodnight."

And then, like every time we've slept in the same bed, I easily fall into a peaceful sleep wrapped in Trevor's arms.

Trevor

Holy fuck.

Every so often in life, you know while something's happening that you'll remember every detail for the rest of your life.

That's right now. Because I'm standing in the clubhouse of the New York Metros' stadium for Aaron's bachelor party. I'm wearing a Metros jersey with my last name on the back. And I'm about to play a game against the fucking New York Metros.

If I looked up surreal in the dictionary, I'd see a picture of this. No doubt.

I don't care if it's all technically for Aaron. I get to spend a few innings living a dream I thought I'd lost.

Back when our friend—and Amanda's boyfriend—Jamie was preparing for the draft and had scouts coming to see him, Aaron connected with the Metros' pitching coach, Marc Demoda. Marc and Aaron bonded over being pitchers who'd suffered hand injuries and became friends.

Because of course they did.

Aaron could become friends with anyone after talking with them for twenty minutes. That's just who he is.

With some coordination from Jamie, who plays for the Metros minor league affiliate back home, Marc helped set this up for Aaron.

Not only do I get to live this tiny piece of my dream and play in a major league stadium against members from a major league team, I get to do it all with my best friends.

A couple of guys from the SUNY FL team are here, but otherwise, it's our high school friends, including the dream team infield. Miles catching, Joel on second, Nick at shortstop, me at third, and Aaron pitching—for a bit of the game, at least. Like me, he won't be able to play through the whole thing. I already know I'll only last a couple of innings, but Nick's older brother Vince played third on our high school team ahead of me, and he'll be taking over when I'm done. Aaron will be bouncing around playing different positions before he pitches the final inning or two.

"You boys all ready?" Marc asks.

Aaron looks at him and smiles. "Give us a second."

Marc nods and talks with Jamie as they head to the dugout where the rest of the guys are, but Nick, Miles, Joel, Aaron, and I hang back.

"Somehow a lifetime of playing ball together ends up here," Aaron says. "I know Jamie and Marc pulled out a lot of stops to make it happen, but part of the reason I'm here at all is because of this—our team. The one we built and refused to break up. Do you remember when we were eight, and they tried to put Nick and Miles on a different little league team than us?"

Nick claps his hands and laughs. "Oh man, my dad was ready to lose his shit over how many tantrums I threw about that."

Joel laughs. "Luckily, my dad threw money at the situation and fixed it."

"I know we've had our own friend groups over the years, but this little team is the reason we won the state championship in high school. No one plays like we do. No one knows their teammates like we do. Fifteen years of playing together... they've got nothing on us."

"So what you're saying is... we're about to go kick some major league ball players' asses?" Miles says.

"Sounds just delusional enough to be right," I say.

We all laugh.

"Thank you all for being here. I know this moment isn't just for me. It's for all of us. Let's go kick some ass." Aaron sticks his hand out. "Warriors."

We all put our hands on top of his and yell, "Warriors!" in honor of our high school team.

Then we make our way out to the dugout to live our fever dream.

It's the bottom of the third, and I'm savoring every moment of this game, ignoring the pain in my leg and lower back. Today is a dream, even if three innings is my limit. Vince batted for me in the top half of the inning and will take over for me after this.

If this is the last few minutes of baseball I'll ever play—at least like this—I want to soak in every moment.

Despite playing against major league players, we're holding our own. It comes down to teamwork. I know and trust every person on this field. We'll all be right where we need to be and the way we play is second nature, even after all these years.

"Let's do this. Get these outs and close out the inning," Marc Demoda yells from the dugout. He's serving as our coach for the game, while Metros' pitcher and Marc's honorary brother-in-law Corey Matthews is serving as coach for the Metros' players.

Jamie's been killing it pitching, proving he can hold his own against the pros—not that it's a surprise. His talent has always been on another level from everyone else.

Between fouls and balls, it's a full count, but Jamie stays cool. There's no one on base right now, but any hit is a risk.

I'm on high alert as he throws the next pitch. I know before it hits the box that it'll be a hit, so I wait, ready for what might come my way.

The crack of the bat sends the ball flying in Nick's direction, a few feet above his head, but nothing fazes him, and perfectly timed, he jumps and snags the ball out of the air. Out number one.

We bump fists as the next batter takes the box. After a few pitches, he hits a line drive that's quickly fielded, but gets him on base.

Next up is Declan Lowery. My rival third baseman.

After a strike and a couple of fouls, he's hungry for the ball, but I'm hungry for the play. I hope he hits it. If this is my last play on the field, I want it to be a good one. I want to remember why I love this damn game so much. The thrill of the moment. How one perfectly executed play can change the course of a game. How a well-oiled infield can control the outcome of a game or an entire season. It's in the littlest movements and the big things like teamwork. Baseball shines in the nuance.

Another strike, and as much as I want to win, I want the action more.

Come on, Declan. Give me something to play with.

Next pitch is a ball, and I'm crawling out of my skin.

Jamie's jaw is set as he throws the next ball, and this time, Declan's bat connects with it.

A grounder flies down the third base line and instinct kicks in. One second. Two seconds. Then the ball is in my glove. I turn and whip the ball to Joel, who's waiting effortlessly at second. The second the ball hits his glove, he turns and fires it off to his brother Jesse at first. My heart is in my throat as I watch Declan running. It'll be a split-second difference, but then I hear the magical sound of the ball landing in Jesse's glove right before Declan crosses the base.

My eyes shift to the stands, where all the girls are watching and cheering—including *my* girl. And fuck, I wish I could've had this for years. Wish Chelsea could've seen me play before I was injured.

The high of the play crescendos as Nick throws an arm around me, but it fades instantly when I realize I'm done.

It'll always be hard walking off the field with both a pain in my chest and in my leg, but getting to do it at all—it's the stuff of dreams.

"Awesome play," Aaron says, jogging over to Nick and me. He extends his fist, and I bump it, then Joel, Miles, and Jamie are walking with us too.

We pause outside the dugout, looking out at the field.

"I was struggling so much senior year, it didn't hit me that it was our last game together. I'm glad we got to do this," Aaron says.

Everyone murmurs their agreement, but I'm at a loss for words. The emotion of the moment sweeps over me, and all I can do is enjoy it. Cherish it. For half a second, I swear I hear my dad's laugh. He would've loved seeing this.

He always told me that the most important part of baseball wasn't winning, it was having fun. There were plenty of times when I didn't agree with that, but today I do. Win or lose, it's been the best game of my life.

I thought I'd be bummed to be out of the game... until Marc Demoda shoved a microphone in my hand. Apparently, he felt my sarcastic dugout commentary deserved to be heard by everyone in the stadium. Now cheering on my boys and heckling the Metros' players is my new favorite pastime.

"The count is two and two. Runners on second and third. Two outs. Pitching legend Aaron Cooper is on the mound, and the Ida Warriors alumni lead the Metros by one run here in the bottom of the fifth." My voice rings out across the stadium.

"Who gave him a microphone?"

"My third base rival, Declan Lowery, is annoyed that I'm here to give you all the play-by-play, but personally, I think he's just jealous of my youth, charm, and good looks."

"I'm annoyed that this sounds more like a comedy roast than a baseball game!"

"I think he's more annoyed about that strikeout at the hands of Aaron Cooper, but he's not the first and he won't be the last. Over the course of his high school career, Aaron set the record for most shutouts ever pitched—both in a season and in his high school career. Neither record has been broken, even by his protégé and current pitcher for the Binghamton Knights, Jamie Henderson. So, don't feel too bad, Declan."

He shouts something else I don't hear, but I'm enjoying myself way too much to care.

It's the bottom of the fifth, and Aaron's finally pitching. Despite his injury, he's pitching well, even though I know it wouldn't last for him much more than an inning at this point.

The batter up right now, Tim Tillerson, is giving Aaron some trouble, but it's clear Aaron's also feeling the pressure. There are two outs, and as much as none of us want this game to be over, we all want to win. All it'll take is one strikeout, and the game is over.

"Aaron with the fastball, but Tillerson gets a piece and... another foul. The count is two and two with two outs. The Metros are clawing for the win, not wanting to be shown up by this ragtag bunch of players, but that ragtag group of players has a secret weapon—the chemistry built by years of playing together."

Aaron throws the next pitch, but it drops and is called a ball. I watch from the edge of the dugout as Miles gives a signal that I know all too well. They had a special sign for it in high school. Our high school coach would get so mad when they'd go rogue and do this, but it almost always worked. Will it against a major league team? Who knows. But we've made it this far.

"It's the payoff pitch, and after a brief communication with his catcher, Cooper makes a decision. Is this the end of the game? When we all win lifetime bragging rights over beating a major league team? Here we go, and the throw is... a screwball! Unbelievable!" At least for anyone who doesn't know that's Aaron's and Miles's hail Mary. "And it's good. Tillerson connects with the pitch for a line drive right between first and second." My heartbeat ticks up as I watch, my voice rising as I watch what I knew would play out. "But Joel Wilkinson is there, and he snatches it out of the air! You know what that means! We've all officially won bragging rights over this fine team of players for a long time."

With that, I set the microphone down and go join my team congratulating Aaron and Joel. Even the Metros' players surround us, and I know with certainty, I'll be telling this story to my grandkids.

Did I ever tell you about the time I beat the New York Metros?
Sure, Grandpa. Whatever you say.

"Seriously, were you the one who gave him a microphone?" Declan asks Marc.

Marc just shrugs innocently as Corey rolls his eyes.

"Hey, that was some good commentating," Ryan Daily, the Metros pitcher, says.

"Thanks. I guess that's the benefit of me having a big mouth." And all the years I spent watching games and talking about them with my dad.

"Speaking of that," Jesse says, pointing at me in amusement. "I'm planning a winter carnival at the Knights' stadium, and I need someone to emcee a couple of contests and the baseball trivia. Any chance you'd be interested?"

Jesse works as the media and marketing manager for the Knights.

"Hell, yeah. Sign me up."

"Sweet. I'll send you more info. And hey, if you enjoy that, we might have a commentating gig open up over the summer. I'll keep you posted."

"Thanks, man."

He claps my shoulder and walks off, but I'm staring after him, surprised. I'm enjoying working with Coach M behind the scenes, and I'm looking forward to our first real practice in January, but that doesn't compare to centering myself in the game like I did while I was commentating. Watching Joel make that play, I felt like I was right there on the field.

It hits me for the first time that maybe this was always a fever dream. Did I really have what it takes to go pro? Maybe minor league. But even then, would I have enjoyed it? All the travel. The stress on my body. You have to really want it, and as much as I love the game, I'm not sure I would've enjoyed it long term. The joy I get watching a game is almost the same as the joy I have when I'm playing it, but I have to admit, playing today was the most joy I've felt for the game in a long time. Playing with my friends was one of the best things about today.

That and beating the Metros.

And my girl getting to see me play. Even if it's the only time she gets to see it—until we all inevitably get bored in our day jobs in our thirties and create some sort of rec league.

When the girls make it down to the field, they come barreling toward us, and in the time it takes Chelsea to run to me, I soak it in. Then she jumps into my arms and kisses me as I hold her tight.

When I set her down, she smiles up at me. "You were amazing. I saw it all in a new way today. Your passion was indescribable. And it came through when you were announcing too. Watching you play and hearing your sexy voice bouncing around the stadium has officially turned me into a baseball fan."

I chuckle at that. "Good. Because I want you at every home game this season. I don't care that I'm not playing, I want to be able to look into the stands and see your smiling face."

She lets out a soft sigh and kisses my cheek. "You're on."

I take her hand and look around, my eyes drifting to right field. I hope my dad was watching and loving it all the way I did.

I turn to Chelsea. "Walk the field with me?"

"I'd love to."

With my arm wrapped around Chels, we wander the field together before ending up back at third base to close out what has been one of the best days of my life.

14
Heals Something

Trevor

THIS IS GOING TO drive me insane.

I swear, I'm *thisclose* to hiring a private investigator to figure who the fuck it was who... raped Chelsea.

The word makes me want to vomit, but if Chelsea has learned to stomach it, I will too.

I reread the texts from my buddy BK—Blake Klein—one of the few on the team I trusted, mostly because he was like me. Down to earth. Cares about his family. And he had the same girlfriend all through college. They met at freshman orientation and fell for each other. There were a couple of other guys on the team who were similar, and they were the ones I gravitated toward. Sure, I was friendly with most of the guys because that's how you make a team work. Being fuckheads to each other only destroys the team morale and ability to trust each other and play well together. I let shit slide—playing girls or talking about them in the locker room—when maybe I shouldn't have for the supposed wellbeing of the team.

Look where it got me. Most of them stopped speaking to me after my accident. Like I never existed. Poof. Ghosted. Not that I cared—about most of them at least. The only one that actually hurt was my roommate freshman and sophomore year—until I left—DJ. I thought we were good friends, but he was the first to fuck off out of my life after my accident. But maybe these texts from Klein explain why.

BK: I've been poking around the team, trying to find out any dirt I can, but I've come up empty. I've even discreetly mentioned it to a few of the gossipy ball bunnies, but no one has heard anything.

BK: I guess it could've been a senior from last year and it get swept under the rug or pushed to the side. Which would be extremely fucked, but D1 sports have done worse in the past. Aside from asking Coach, I don't have any ideas. I won't do that, though. It might push things too far.

BK: Unless you want me to.

Me: No. If it was swept under the rug, he'd have to have known, which makes me sick to think about. A grown man protecting a rapist. Fuck that. I appreciate you looking into this for me, though. There's every chance the police never looked into it. You should see the statistics on how frequently cases like this are blown off by police departments.

BK: That's some serious fuckery. If someone had done that to Sasha... nah. I can't even think about it.

Me: Believe me, I understand. Again, I appreciate you checking it out.

BK: No prob. I'll keep my ears open in case I hear anything.

Me: Thanks. So... how's the team this year?

I've purposely stayed away from any info about it. Not that there are any games yet, but I don't keep up on social media with any of the guys on the team. If we don't text, I don't know about it.

BK: Shitshow. So many newbies who need to be broken in. Oh, and get this shit. Guess who tried out for your spot on the team?

Me: Who?

BK: None other than your former roommate.

Me: DJ? Seriously? Did he get it?

BK: LMAO no. Coach offered him a second-string center field position. Dude couldn't play well on the team if he tried. He declined the offer, then bitched about it for a month. I don't even know why he still hangs out with all of us. I thought it was because of you, but he's held on like a stage 4 clinger.

Me: Wow. And really? You're going to hate on clingers? Isn't that how you got your girl?

BK: Shots fired. Damn. And we're both clingy, thank you. Maybe a little co-dependent, but whatever. We're happy. I'm actually starting to think about proposing.

Me: That's awesome, man. Wish you the best.

BK: Back at you. Let me know if you're around Cuse and we can get together.

Me: Sounds good. Later.

BK: Later.

With a sigh, I flick my phone screen off and stare up at Chelsea's building. I wish I could solve this for her. Fix it. I know I can't retroactively protect her, but I want to. My mind wanders, and I wonder what could've been if Chels and I had met at freshman orientation like BK and his girl. Maybe neither of us would've ended up here. Maybe neither of us would have gone through hell over the last year.

I snap myself out of that useless train of thought.

I wish I could've been with her longer, protected her from everything she went through, but I'm grateful to have her now. She's stolen my heart in a way I never could've expected, and it's forcing me to face some of the trauma and hurt I've buried deep inside for years, but if that's the price of falling for a goddess of a woman like her, I'll pay it over and over again.

With my frustration fading, I get out of my car, ready to see my girl. She's done nothing but text me flirty things since last night, and I get the sense she might want to play a little today. I don't know what to expect, but I'm here for whatever she wants to give me.

I sling my bag over my shoulder and head up to her apartment. I walk in without knocking because we're officially at that place now, but the first thing I hear is Chelsea grumbling. I find her pacing the small kitchen, tapping furiously on her phone before dropping it roughly on the counter while muttering something under her breath.

I set my bag down, then walk over and wrap my arms around her. "Okay, who hurt you, and where can I find them?"

She laughs and loops her arms around my neck. "I love when you say sexy things like that."

I quickly kiss her, then reach over and tap her phone with my pointer. "Seriously, what's wrong?"

She sighs and unlocks the phone, then slides it into my hand.

"Had a lovely conversation with my supposed friends back home, and I'm just... mad. I'm mad at them. I'm mad at myself." She waves a hand. "Just read it."

Apparently, it's a bad night for texting.

I scan the texts and my blood pressure immediately rises.

Bridget: Tell me you're coming to my EPIC 21st birthday party. I just saw you RSVP'd as maybe. Maybe you'll come to the hottest party of our lives?

Chelsea: I'm sorry. I have a friend's wedding to go to this weekend.

Bridget: Since when do you have other friends?

Lex: I think you mean why does she NEED other friends?

Chelsea: There's no such thing as too many friends. I've made some great ones here, and I already agreed to go to their wedding.

Bridget: Ugh. Are these your boyfriend's friends?

Chelsea: They're my friends. Anyway, I'm sorry I can't be there, but I hope it's amazing.

Bridget: Well, duh. All my parties are. You're the one missing out on all the fun.

Lex: Chelsea doesn't like to have fun anymore, remember?

When I set the phone down, Chelsea throws her hands up and starts pacing again.

"I responded maybe because I was going to see how the timing worked out with the wedding, in case I'd have time to stop by, but after all that, I don't even want to. I want to respond no, I don't like having their kind of fun anymore, since their kind of fun involves getting shit-faced. Like I want to drink and party after a guy drugged my drink at a fucking party. Which they have never been able to understand! And that just makes me mad at myself because I shouldn't care. I shouldn't freaking care."

She yells in the direction of the phone, and again, I pull her into my arms.

"How long have you been friends with them?"

She snorts at that. "Most of my life."

"So you have a lot of memories with them?"

She nods against my shoulder. "Yeah. Some really great ones."

"It's okay to have mixed feelings about that. I've been through similar stuff with my childhood best friend, and I haven't cut him out. I've distanced myself, but he hasn't even noticed we're not as close anymore. Some people struggle to see outside of their own selfish wants and needs. That's no excuse, but it's understandable why it's hard for us to shut down a lifetime of memories. It's okay for you to take your time and figure it out. It's also okay to yell at them if you want to. Or be honest about your feelings."

She laughs weakly. "Here I was expecting you to tell me to cut them out or tell them to fuck off because they're not really my friends."

That makes me laugh. "I get how complicated it is. But for the record, no, they don't seem worthy of your friendship or seem like good friends to you. You were the one to remind me I can't make anyone else's decisions for them. I'm not always great at that, but I'm trying to do better. That said, if I meet them at any point, I will be pleasant, but I won't be patient. If they say that shit in front of me, I won't hold my tongue. Because seeing you hurt sets off the irrationally angry and ferally protective side of me. I'll cut a bitch—with words, unless you're physically threatened."

Her smile is bright as she presses onto her toes to kiss me. "There you go, saying sexy things again." She shakes her head and shoves her phone away. "Enough of all that. It's taking away from the surprise I have for you."

"You have my attention."

"Good," she purrs, grabbing my hand. "Come with me." She leads me down the hall to the bedroom.

"Bedroom surprises?"

She shuts the door behind us, then leads me over to the bed and pushes me onto it.

"Consider it a late birthday gift." She pulls a box from the bottom of her nightstand and sets it on my lap. "Open."

My brows lift, but I don't say anything. I have no idea what to expect. She climbs onto the bed next to me and watches as I lift the top and lift some tissue paper out of the way.

Oh. Oh, damn.

Staring back at me is a Fleshlight.

"Chels, what..."

"So, when we were down in New York City, a few of us stopped by an adult store and picked things out. I have plenty of toys, but I bought this for you." Her lips press into my neck, her breath tickling my skin when she speaks again. "You have been so patient with me, and I want you to have something special to take care of yourself with. I hate how many times you've walked out of here with a hard-on."

"While I appreciate this, and it looks fun, my cock is not your responsibility. I'm a big boy. I can take care of myself."

"And this will help you do it."

She kisses up my neck and across my cheek, turning my head so my lips meet hers.

My cock presses against the zipper of my jeans, way too excited by this turn of events.

"What do you want me to do with it?"

"Use it." She leans over and pulls something from the drawer. "While I use this."

She holds up a vibrator, and I pull her onto my lap, my hands skating up her back as our lips collide in rough kisses.

She pushes me back, so I'm lying flat, and meets my eyes. "I'm ready to be naked with you. Like this. And maybe for you to touch me a little."

I push past the urge to ask if she's sure. Only she can decide that. I don't want it to seem like I'm trying to undermine her.

"Then I'm yours."

She gives me another hard kiss. Then it's a frantic race to get our clothes off. Get naked.

We've seen each other—held each other—like this before. But it's never been moving toward sex.

There's a flash in her eyes, the briefest hint of hesitance, but she quickly pushes it away, her eyes drifting over my body. Then there's a different flare in her eyes. Lust. But instead of flitting away, it burns deeper, until we're side by side on the bed.

She adds some lube to the toy for me, then hands it and the lube to me.

She watches raptly as I squirt some into my hand and stroke my cock a few times.

"Mm. It's hard not to touch."

"You can if you want."

She shakes her head. "Not yet."

But as if in consolation, she leans over and kisses me, then drags her lips across my neck as I line up the toy.

She flicks her tongue against my earlobe, then rolls back, lying half on her side as she watches me slowly push the toy down my length.

It holds my cock so tightly, I almost come when I'm halfway in. Plus, Chelsea put so much lube in. Once I'm fully seated in it, I have to hold it in place for a minute, letting myself adjust.

"Holy shit. That is so hot." Chelsea bites her lip and slips her hand between her legs.

"Back at you." My voice is gravelly and thick, and the haze is already settling in. I turn to her and watch, then slowly slide the Fleshlight up before pulling it back down.

Oh fuck, oh fuck, oh fuck.

My abs tighten and I break out in a sweat.

What the fuck is this thing?

It doesn't feel as good as a pussy. Nothing feels like that, especially when an emotional connection is added in. But this is a damn good replacement for a hand job.

Even better when I'm watching Chelsea pinch her nipples and fuck herself with her fingers.

"Are you okay, baby?" I whisper, cautiously moving the toy faster.

"I'm perfect. Keep going. Watching you keeps me out of my head."

Her words snap the tether of my control, and I buck into the toy, working it hard and fast over my cock.

It's so good. So tight.

I keep my eyes on her, gripping the sheet with my other hand.

Even though I'm getting myself off—with some help from a toy—I feel completely out of control.

"Faster," Chelsea whispers.

So, I move faster. I'm not used to it. Normally, I'm the one in control. The one giving orders. The one with my hand twisted in a girl's hair and owning her body. But right now, I'm at Chelsea's mercy, and that... is a turn-on I wasn't expecting.

"Keep going, Trev. You're doing so good. I want to see you come again, then I want you to watch while I come, screaming your name."

Fuck.

"Chels... I'm—" I can't get the words out before pure pleasure ripples through me. I claw at the sheets, my orgasm ripping me to shreds. Black clouds my vision as I collapse against the bed, slowly pulling the toy off as my cock pulses one last time.

Chelsea's whine and the low hum of a vibrator are the only things that pull me back to the moment.

I set the toy on the bed, rolling onto my side as I watch her. Her beautiful face is already slack with pleasure. She reaches to pinch her nipples with her free hand, but I grab her hand before she gets there.

"Can I do that?"

Her gaze snaps to mine, then she relaxes and smiles.

"Yes."

"Fingers or mouth?"

A groan.

"Both."

I don't wait for any further invitation. Diving forward, I capture one of her nipples in my mouth, while stroking my hand over her neck, down her chest, then cupping her heavy breast and massaging it. With my other hand, I tweak her other nipple, rolling it between my thumb and forefinger while I palm her breast.

"Yes. Just like that," she hisses.

When I casually graze her nipple with my teeth, she arches off the bed and her free hand tangles in my curls, holding them tightly as she rides the vibrator.

"Trevor... fuck..."

I lift my eyes to her gorgeous face, just in time to see her lips part and her head drop back.

Her body spasms as she moans, going higher and higher, her breaths growing shallow as she comes undone.

Slowly, her body melts into the bed and she pulls the vibrator away, one last aftershock pulsing through her.

"Oh my god. That was amazing."

I run my lips up her chest and over her neck. "You're beautiful like this. Skin flushed. Splayed out and completely comfortable in your body. Fucking stunning."

Her hand, still tangled in my hair, drags me to her lips again.

"As usual, you're more eloquent than me. I just wanted to say you were hot as fuck."

I laugh at that, but she bites down on my lip, then I'm halfway on top of her, kissing her like I'll never get enough. Because I don't think I will. I'm a complete goner for this girl.

"Mm, I'm already looking forward to doing that again. And again." She peppers kisses across my cheek. "You might want to leave the toy here."

Arching a brow, I flash her my most troublemaking smile. "Liked it that much?"

"Every second. Plus, I have a high sex drive." She pats my cheek as she moves to sit up. "I hope you can keep up with me."

"Sounds like a challenge I'm definitely up for."

"We'll see just how *up* you are."

We both laugh at that. Seeing her playful side come out more and more is one of my favorite things.

I was worried she'd be uncomfortable with dirty talk, but she likes to play as much as I do. And while it may take time for her to be ready to try different things in the bedroom, the trust we build with each new experience makes it even hotter. Going slow like this is totally underrated, but I'm loving it. Our relationship is deepening in time with our sex lives, and there's something to be said for how the connection grows in both ways at once.

"Shower?" Chelsea asks.

I smile as I sit up. "Definitely."

I'll never say no to more intimacy with my girl. More building of the trust—safety—between us.

I can't take away what she's been through, but I can make sure she never feels anything but safe, worshipped, respected, and... that other word. The one neither of us has mustered yet, but that we both seem to be feeling.

I'll give her all that and more for as long as she lets me.

Then a thought trickles through my brain that almost makes me stop moving.

Forever would be fine.

It's scary as fuck, but it would be.
Forever would be fine with me.

Chelsea

Mornings at Promise are one of my favorite things. Sunday mornings tend to have that calm, soulful quiet about them that brings me peace. Of course, at some point someone will come in—not a guarantee, but a likelihood.

It's barely been two months of working here, but I've learned a lot. Rae has been an incredible leader, and my boss, Kristen, is warm and supportive. She seems to see the same things in me that she sees in Rae, because she's put me on somewhat of an accelerated track as well.

Rae and I have been talking about creating a Promise support group on campus, and Kristen contacted the campus counseling center about working with them to host it. They said they'd be happy to have a counselor available or we could just use their space to run it. Kristen essentially put Rae and me in charge of it all.

I'm not complaining because any way we can reach more women is a good thing. The more women we reach, the more we can help find their way out of the darkness. And that's only part of what the support groups do. They also help women feel less alone and heal, while building strong friendships and support systems. Empowered women empower other women.

I wish Bridget and Lex understood that.

The only response I managed to their texts last night was to reiterate that I'm sorry to miss the party, and tell Bridget I wish her the best birthday. Neither of them responded.

Fine by me. Amanda, Rae, Hyla, and the rest of the girls have shown me what true friendship means, and I refuse to settle for less. I don't intend to cut Bridget and Lex out of my life, but I won't keep trying to maintain a friendship with them that only hurts me.

Especially not when I have so much good in my life.

I'm enjoying school, I love Old Lake Town, I'm making great friends, and of course, there's Trevor.

Trevor, who has spent every night at my apartment since Thursday, when I gave him that toy. The orgasms since then have been countless, and with each one, I let him explore a little more. I haven't let him touch between my legs yet, but I'll get there. I've gotten more comfortable touching him, too.

I'm just... happy. I like the direction my life is headed in, and I'm hopeful in a way I'd forgotten how to be for a while.

After grabbing myself a cup of coffee, I finish working on some social media graphics and then go to the document of outreach ideas and start reading through it. I only have about an hour left here, then—for once—I plan to spend most of the day alone. I'll probably have dinner with Robbie, but Trevor and I agreed it's best for him to not spend *every* night at my apartment. As fun as it is, we want this to keep growing naturally and not lose important pieces of ourselves along the way.

Out of the corner of my eye, I see someone on the camera—a girl around my age—at the front door. She pushes the button that goes to our security office, then the front door buzzes open. The outside door is locked for safety, and the security guards are the ones who unlock the door after someone pushes the doorbell outside.

Once they come in, there's a small entrance area before the glass door that opens into the reception area of Promise. I glance at the other screen and watch the girl hover by the door for a minute.

There's a swish of nerves in my stomach. This is my first time being out front alone when someone has come in, and even though I've done this with Rae or Kristen or one of the counselors by my side, I'm still nervous. I want to get this right.

I suck in a breath and look back at the screen. She's still standing there, uncertain. I debate getting up and going over to the door, but as someone who has been through it, I know it's a decision she has to make for herself. If she's not ready yet, that's okay. We'll be here when she is.

She looks back at the outer door again, then finally pushes herself forward and opens the glass door. My stomach twists with anticipation and anxiousness.

When she finally steps all the way inside, I stand.

Her eyes dart to me and she swallows hard.

"Hi. I'm Chelsea."

She looks around the space, and I slowly make my way around the counter.

"Do you want to tell me why you came in here today?" I ask, my voice calm despite my insides roiling. But there's something inside me propelling me forward. An innate protective instinct. I want to help. I want her to know she's safe.

She bites her lip and tears well in her eyes.

"Let's sit." I gesture toward a small table in the corner, and she follows me over to it.

I grab a cup of water from the nearby cooler and set it on the table, which already has a box of tissues on it.

"Do you want to tell me your name?"

"Chloe."

"I'm glad you're here, Chloe. If you want to talk, we can, or we can just sit. Either way, I want you to know you're safe." My voice almost breaks, but I keep it together.

There's a phone on the table in case I need to call one of the counselors out, though I'm sure one is monitoring the camera feed for this room. It's how they know if someone else needs to come out here, and if no one else is, it's how they keep an eye on the interns. We go through some online training before we start here, but overall, we're tossed in the deep end. I think that's mostly because we've been there and we're all studying counseling, so we have a frame of reference. A lot of this job is learning as we go, and as our counseling coursework picks up, we'll sit in with the counselors more.

Out front, the job is to calm, diffuse, make sure they know it's a safe space, and offer options.

"I need help," she finally says.

"Then you're in the right place. If you want to tell me more, I can direct you to the right help."

Tears slip down her cheeks.

"I—I—my tutor..." That's all she gets out before choking back a sob.

Watching for her reaction, I rest my hand on her arm. When she doesn't flinch, I let the weight of my palm settle there.

"Take your time. There's no rush. This is a safe space."

She takes in a shuddery breath, then starts again, relaying her story through choppy breaths and broken sobs. Her tutor decided he needed something in return for helping her, and when she didn't want to give him what he wanted, he held her down and took it.

Hearing her say the words sends a wave of nausea through my stomach and chills up my spine. And anger. I'm coursing with violent, reckless anger.

Then she starts to do what every rape or assault victim does and blame herself.

Under the table, I curl my hand into a fist, my fingernails digging into the skin.

"It wasn't your fault. None of it was your fault."

She looks at me with big eyes. "I—"

And then the words I needed to hear for so long—the ones I still have to repeat to myself every day—pour out.

"You feel ashamed right now, but you shouldn't. You didn't do anything wrong. I know the weight of that shame is heavy, but it isn't yours to carry. Only one person deserves that. Him. You deserve love and support and peace." I slide my chair over and wrap an arm around her back. "We can help. If you want to talk to someone, we have counselors available right now, and we have a nurse practitioner available to give you an exam. We can also contact law enforcement if you want us to, but we don't have to. Just know you're not alone. You've already done something amazing for yourself by coming here. We'll help."

She sniffs and lifts her head, her puffy, red eyes meeting mine. And realization hits her. Ugly, horrible realization.

"Were you—"

"My story shares some similarities with yours. That's why I can tell you you're in the right place. I wish I would've had somewhere like this. You did the right thing coming here."

"When did it happen to you?"

"Almost a year ago."

She stares at me for a moment. "And you're okay now?"

"Still healing, but I've come a long way. You will too."

The relief and hope shimmering in her eyes heals one of the cracks in my soul.

"Th—thank you. I think I want an exam."

One of the counselor's voices floats from the other side of the room. "I can take you back to the nurse practitioner whenever you're ready. Is there anyone we can call for you? A family member or a friend?"

"My aunt," she whispers, pushing out of her chair. "I didn't know how to tell her."

The counselor extends an arm. "We can take care of it if you give us her phone number."

Chloe nods and lets the counselor lead her down the hall, but then she stops and turns back, taking a few steps toward me again.

"Thank you." Her words hold so much weight they nearly crush me, but I keep my emotions back.

"You're welcome. I'm here if you need anything else."

"Thanks," she whispers, then follows the counselor down the hall to where the nurse practitioner is waiting.

I stand there for a moment, a thousand emotions rolling through me.

Then a thought catches me off guard.

I want to call Trevor. I want to tell him everything that just happened.

But as I turn back to the desk, I'm surprised to see Rae standing here.

"If I hadn't been to that swanky lake house, I'd ask if you live here."

She laughs and sets her bag down. "I'm picking up extra shifts since I'll be out for my honeymoon."

"Makes sense."

"How are you feeling? I caught the end of that. I waited in the entryway so I wouldn't disturb you."

"I was nervous," I admit. "I didn't want to screw it up. I was hoping someone was watching on the camera just in case."

"From what I saw, you handled it well. Most of the time, no one wants to interrupt. We all know how important the first time solo is."

"More important than I realized. I thought most of my heavy emotions would be tapered since I've assisted you and Kristen before, but today... I felt like I made a difference." I blow out a shaky breath. "I wish I would've had that after what I went through. It almost felt like I was talking to myself. Then seeing the recognition and relief on her face that she wasn't alone…" I blink back tears and watch Rae wipe her eyes.

"It's the best and worst thing," she murmurs. "You hate that anyone else has been through it, but it's a relief to know someone else understands." Rae grabs my hand. "You okay?"

I nod and sniff. "Yeah. As hard as it was, it reaffirmed for me that I'm exactly where I want to be. I want to make a difference, and I know I just did."

"I had that moment too. The very first time when you know you helped change something for someone. It doesn't take away what we've been through, but—"

"It heals something."

"Exactly."

She pulls me into a hug.

After a long squeeze, we separate, both wiping our eyes. It's crazy how this can both hurt and heal. The healing is so much stronger.

"You should get out of here," Rae says. "You've only got a few minutes left. Grab your stuff and head home. You deserve it."

I give her a big smile. "Thanks."

With that, I head to the back room and collect my stuff, but when I leave, it's not with any intention of going home.

I get in my car and head straight for the lake house.

When I get there, I'm halfway to the front door before I realize what I'm actually doing. I've never just shown up here. They don't seem like the type to be uncomfortable with me stopping by, but… do I knock? Text Trevor?

There are a bunch of cars in the driveway, so I go for a knock while opening the door approach.

"Hello?"

"Hey!" Amanda says, face lighting up when she sees me. She's in workout clothes with her hair pulled back, and she looks absolutely radiant.

She hurries over and gives me a quick hug.

"I didn't know you were coming over today."

I shrug. "Just wanted to stop and say hi to Trevor quick if he's around."

She nods. "In his room. You two are adorable. Okay, I'm off to work out. If I don't see you before you leave, then I'll catch you tomorrow."

She blows me a kiss as she walks out of the room.

Feeling a bit more at ease, I head upstairs to Trevor's room, then knock on the door.

"It's open," he calls.

When I open the door and he sees me, he jumps off his bed wearing a massive smile. "Hey, baby. What are you doing here? I thought you had Promise today."

"I do—did. But... that's why I'm here."

"Everything okay?"

I throw my arms around his neck and look up at him. "Yeah. I had a kind of amazing morning. When I started at Promise, I didn't know exactly how it would feel to work there. To help others when my own stuff is still healing, but this girl who came in today... she needed to know she wasn't alone, and I think I needed it too. Logically, I've known that. But saying it to someone who has lived a story way too close to mine made it hit in a different way." Tears well in my eyes. "The relief on her face when she realized she wasn't alone and she was safe—that there was still a light for her to walk toward—I think it healed a part of my soul."

He pulls me tight to him. "Babe, that's amazing."

"It is. It meant so much more to me than I could've anticipated. When I was finished helping her, my first thought was that I wanted to tell you. I know I've said it before, in passing, at least, but you're my person. You're the one I want to run to when I'm struggling and the person I can't wait to celebrate with when something good happens. I know we said we'd make sure we still took time away from each other—didn't get too caught up—but I had to come here and tell you all that."

He leans back, then kisses my forehead, running his fingers through my hair.

"I'll never complain about that. We both have separate interests, and we'll make a point not to spend every night together, but I wouldn't mind seeing you every day. Stay for lunch? We always have sandwich stuff in the fridge, and I make a heck of a turkey club."

"That sounds perfect. I—"

Oh. Holy crap. What was I—I almost just told him. Holy freaking fudge balls. I've been feeling the thrum of it somewhere deep inside me. But it was all shrouded in uncertainty. In me not being sure if it was true. Now, it's irrefutable. I'm in love with Trevor Matteny.

"I'd love to spend the afternoon with you," I choke out.

Trevor smiles at me so big it almost hurts, and I see it in his eyes. This isn't one-sided. We're falling into something wild and beautiful, and I can't wait to see where it takes us.

He wraps his hand around the side of my neck and presses his lips to mine. In a second, I'm lost to him and all those swirly, twirly, butterflies-in-my-stomach feelings. Things I'd been too broken over the last year to even hope for again, but standing in his arms now, I know this is where I'm meant to be. After all I've been through, I'm stupidly happy. Thanks for showing up for me now, karma. It's about time I get to enter my happiness era.

15
It's Love

Chelsea

"Good morning," I call as I fly through the door of Robbie's apartment.

He wanders out from the bedroom. "Oh my god. Are you okay?"

My stomach clenches with worry. "Why wouldn't I be?"

"Because you're here, and Trevor isn't attached to your face."

I mock laugh. "You're soooo funny."

"I am. Hilarious."

"Well you can feast on your jokes for breakfast then, instead of the very fancy breakfast sandwich and home fries I brought for you."

"I mean, I love you. And you're sooo pretty."

"Much better."

We sit down at the table, and I slide his container over to him.

As he opens his, he says, "Not making fun, but genuinely curious... what has you up so early?"

"I took an early shift at Promise this morning. Since it's close ish to the best little breakfast spot in Old Lake Town, I figured I'd be nice and bring you something."

"Ah the first date spot you won't stop raving about?" He takes a bite of his sandwich and groans. "Nevermind. It's all true. Holy shit, this is delicious."

"Told you."

"Well, it's impossible to believe anything actually is as good as you make it sound if you experienced it with Trevor. He makes your brain all mushy."

I sigh dreamily. "He does."

Robbie snorts at that. "Oof. If I have to listen to love-drunk ramblings, I need coffee. Want any?"

"No thanks. I'm meeting up with the girls at the coffee place downtown after this."

He stops halfway to the coffeemaker and smiles at me.

"What?"

"Nothing. Just happy for you. I like seeing you find your people."

I smile too. Over the last few weeks, my friendship with the girls has only deepened. I spent more time with them at Rae and Aaron's wedding. Including getting ready with the girls—and Rae and Sarah's mom and other female family members. It was beautiful. The whole day was absolutely perfect, and I'll remember dancing in Trevor's arms like that forever.

I've also spent a little more time with the girls in smaller groups, including hanging out alone with Sarah and then with Mackie and Amanda, all while Rae was on her honeymoon. They all make it a point to include me in their lives and seek me out. Until I had friends doing that for me, I didn't realize I'd been missing it before from my high school and college friends.

"I'm happy too."

"Good." He returns with his cup of coffee. "I know how important that is. That reminds me, I talked to Nadine today, and she's planning something that might interest you."

I perk up at that. Part of the reason Robbie moved here—and away from the family campground—is because he went to college here and found his tribe. We may be the closest people to each other, but he has the queeries—his group of besties, all of whom fall on the LGBTQIA spectrum and met as students at SUNY FL. They're called the queeries because one of the guys in the group—who is now a full-time author—was querying a manuscript, and one night when a few of them were high, another person said, 'Whoa. Queries sounds like queer-ies. Like us. We should totally call ourselves the queeries.' And since they were high, it sounded like a brilliant idea. The rest of the group will never let them live it down and kept the name as a punishment for their ridiculousness. The whole group is all snarky and hilarious and give each other shit—a lot like Rae and everyone else in the hive mind.

Nadine is the hippie free spirit of the group, but she's also a badass feminist and considers herself a witch.

"You have my attention. What did Nadine say?"

"She's organizing a women's festival. It's part hippie stuff but mostly feminist driven and she's looking for help with planning and organizing it all. I mentioned you might be interested."

"Might be? Uh, that sounds amazing. Plus, Nadine is the perfect person to do something like that. She's both brilliant and so out of the box that I'm sure it'll be amazing. How do I sign up?"

He laughs at my bouncy puppy energy, but I'm so in. It sounds like the kind of festival Gran would have taken me to as a kid. Helping to plan it? I'm so in.

He grabs his phone and fires off a text. "There's her number. Just send her a text and she'll give you all the info."

"Perfect. Thank you."

"Nadine will be lucky to have you and all your feminist passion. If only she knew she was getting Gran's energy wrapped in a spicy, slightly feral, bat-boy-loving package." He gives me a shit-eating grin.

"Wow. Just rude to me like that?" I glare at him, then casually reach for the container in front of him, but he swats at my hand.

"You're really pretty. That's all I said."

"Mhm. See if I ever bring you breakfast again."

He makes a heart with his hands. "You're the best."

"Yeah, yeah. Eat up."

But as he dives back into his breakfast sandwich with a happy groan, I can't help but smile.

I finally feel like I've emerged from the darkness.

Who knew sunlight was kinda great?

The bell above the door chimes as I hurry inside Buzzing Brews and toward the table where the girls are sitting.

"Sorry I'm late." I slide into the empty chair at the end of the table. "I got caught up talking with one of Robbie's friends who's organizing a women's festival at the college camp in the spring."

"Ooh, that sounds awesome," Amanda says. "Are you helping plan it? Because that's totally your jam. Love your shirt, by the way."

I look down because I don't even remember which one I put on this morning. It has silhouettes of women of all body shapes and sizes, and says, *all bodies are beautiful.*

A gift from Gran. She will always be my feminist idol.

"Thank you. Oh my gosh. I hope you all get to meet my grandmother at some point. She's the one who got this for me, and whatever energy of that type you see in me, I definitely got it from her. She's a true feminist badass. She has a framed picture of her being hauled away from a protest by police... *topless*. It's iconic."

Sarah and Rae glance at each other.

"She and Gram would get along," Sarah says with a smile.

"Definitely," Rae agrees.

A waitress appears next to me. "Can I get you something?"

"I'll have a butter pecan latte and a chocolate croissant." Because life is far too short to not eat chocolate croissants.

As the waitress walks away, Mackie looks at me. "So a women's festival?"

"Yeah. It's all in the early stages, but the plan is to have workshops and speakers and just general vibes that are all about women. Oh, and promoting local businesses that are women centered too."

"You should talk to Kristen," Rae says. "She loves to get Promise involved with local things."

"Oh, that's a good idea. I'll mention it to Nadine—the person organizing it. Promise having some kind of booth there might help women who need support to find it. I didn't know where to look, but God knows I needed it after—"

I stop, glancing between Rae and Amanda. Rae knows my whole story. Amanda knows something happened. I'm guessing Sarah and Mackie have assumed.

My gaze drops to the table. I hate the immediate feeling of shame as I think about telling someone new. Someday, I want to get to a place where that's not my gut reaction. I guess I have something specific to work on with my therapist now.

Rae rests her hand on my arm. "You okay?"

I take a deep breath and look around at the girls. "Just working up the nerve to... tell my truth."

"You know you don't have to," Sarah says.

That's exactly why I want to.

"This is what real friends do. They rely on each other. Or so I'm learning. I don't want to get into all the details right now, but I guess I want you to know what I've been through."

Sarah's eyes find mine, filled with understanding. This is me offering up vulnerability. Giving them a piece of my trust. I never thought twice about it with Bridget and Lex, and yet they didn't give me the support I needed. These girls—women—are different. I see it in the way they act and I feel it in my heart when I look at them.

"So, I'm just going to say this, and then we're going to move forward like you've known the whole time, okay?"

They all nod.

"I was raped at a party in college. It's why I left school. I went through all the testing and stuff after, but they never caught the guy. Not sure if they ever will. Oh, and Trevor might have known him since we went to the same college and the guy maybe played baseball. I went through a whole dark period, then I moved here because my uncle, who is more like my older brother, went to college here and lives here now. So that's it. Now you all know."

For a beat, no one says anything, but finally Amanda looks at me.

"Just know, if they ever find out who did it, it'll be a *No Body, No Crime* situation. We'll handle it all, including alibis."

For some reason, that makes me laugh. A wicked, unhinged laugh. Because I could see them doing it.

If one—or multiple of them—committed a crime like that, no one would ever be able to catch them because their alibis would be foolproof.

"You might have to fight Trevor for that."

Sarah gives me a knowing smile, like she'd expect nothing less, but it's Mackie who speaks.

"He'd *want* to. But if it came to it, we wouldn't let him. He'd be the obvious suspect. That's where we come in."

Laughing, I look around the table. "I love you ladies." The words slip out before I realize what they are, but the moment of panic I'm expecting doesn't come. I'm completely calm. Because despite the short time, I do love them. They've shown me what deep female friendships can be, and I'm never going back to being treated like crap by supposed friends again.

"We love you too," Rae says. "In fact, since we're all here—minus Hyla, but she's already claimed you, anyway—I think it's time to officially indoctrinate you." She grabs her phone and types something out. "We're adding you to the Girl Gang group chat."

"Yes!" Amanda agrees.

My phone chimes, but Rae continues.

"Fun fact: before our parents adopted Sarah, I was an only child. I didn't want to be, so I made it my mission to start collecting friends. It started with Joel, then Mackenzie, then Aaron." She looks at Sarah, emotion brimming in her eyes. "Then my sister. Then Miles. Along the way, there were lots of others—Hyla, Trevor, Nick—then Amanda. I love the friend group we've formed, but nothing means more than this. This sisterhood, the tribe of incredible women who I can trust with my heart and my life. We'd be honored to have you be a part of it. If you're willing to drink the... coffee."

I can't help but laugh. "I'm in." I hold my cup out and they all touch theirs to it, then we drink.

It's sweet and silly and fills me with joy.

My phone chimes again, and I grab it, checking the group text.

Chelsea Winters has been added to the group.

Rae: Time to make Chelsea one of us!

The next message is from Hyla.

Hyla: Woohoo! It's about time. Love you all.

Me: Back at you.

After I type out my reply, I change the name of the group chat to Girl Gang.

The ache of my past friendships hurts, but this is separate. This is joyful. This is my future. And I want to let the roots of these friendships grow deeper.

"Feel any different?" Amanda asks.

I nod slowly. "I can already feel the chaos creeping in... and the tug of the hive mind."

"Yes, she's officially one of us," Mackie says, throwing a hand up in celebration.

I lean back in my chair and allow myself a moment to soak in this... *love*. I've never experienced this kind of platonic love before, but I want to be a part of this tribe as much as they all want me here. Even though it means dealing with my complicated feelings about my friends back home, the only people I want in my life now are the ones who want to be here and who truly support me. There's no doubt I have it with this little group, and I get the sense that wherever I end up, I always will.

I go to turn my phone screen off, but then something catches my attention. The text I sent to Trevor hours ago. He usually responds to me faster than I respond to him.

I must make a face because Amanda asks, "What's wrong? Tired of us already?"

I muster a little smile. "No. But... did any of you talk to Trevor this morning? We weren't planning to meet up today, but he usually texts me back quickly. It's weird that he hasn't. I just want to make sure he's okay."

"Crap. I was going to mention that to you," Amanda says. "It slipped my mind, but no, he wasn't around this morning. I went to check on him before I left, and he didn't answer his door. But then I told him it was a wellness check, and he told me he was still alive."

"That's weird," Mackie says.

Then Sarah's eyes go wide, and she grabs her purse. "What's the date today?" She rummages through her bag, trying to find her phone, but I flick my screen on first.

"November thirteenth."

"Today's the anniversary of his dad's death."

"Shit," I mutter. "Why didn't he tell me?" It's only after the words are out that I realize I said them aloud.

"Because he does the caretaking. He doesn't ask for it in return," Sarah says. "Which I'm guessing you've figured out based on the look on your face. The first year we were together, he didn't mention it until the day after. I felt like crap for not realizing—because I knew him when it happened—but my dad helped me understand I didn't do anything wrong. Still, I made it a point to mark it on my calendar so I'd know. And then I just started conveniently showing up."

I stand suddenly and grab my coffee and croissant. "I need to go. Sorry to bail."

"No, don't be. We all get it," Rae says. The way her eyes shimmer tells me she'd do the same for Aaron—likely has plenty of times.

"He's lucky to have you," Sarah says.

"We'll bring pizza for dinner," Amanda says.

"Thank you! Bye!"

They call goodbyes after me, but I barely hear them. As much as it drives me crazy he didn't tell me, I'm learning Trevor has to be bullied into support. He loves being a caretaker and protector, and that's fine, but he needs to learn I'm as fiercely loving and protective as he is, and I will always be there when he needs me, whether he asks for it or not.

Trevor

I don't think I'm okay.

I said I would be okay.

That's what I told myself. That's what I told Hyla when she texted yesterday. It's what I told my mom when I convinced her she didn't need to come up here today.

But I don't think I'm okay.

Maybe it's because this is the ten-year anniversary of my dad's death, but I think it's more about how the last year of my life has been. Throughout high school, and especially early college, I took on this playful, shit-giving, sometimes grumpy role. Usually with an air of I don't give a fuck. When it comes to people who don't know me... I don't. I don't care what they think of me. But I played all of those things in trying to find myself again after losing my dad, and I never realized how much they became a coping mechanism. Something I latched onto.

Are those things still me? Yes. But they've hidden the broken bits well enough that I forgot how many there were.

This morning I woke up and immediately, everything felt wrong. Dark.

I hate that darkness. I will always hate it. It's like an extra thief, robbing me of my father's joy.

In an attempt to tune that out, I thought I'd go through pictures of him, remind myself of his smile and how happy he'd be to see where I am now.

But then I started thinking of specific memories and looking for those pictures. Now I'm sitting on my bedroom floor, surrounded by every photo I brought with me—and there are a lot—looking for one I can't seem to find. It's from my ninth birthday. I'm standing with my parents, Hyla, and the mascot from the Binghamton team at the time. A giant bee. My dad's smile was massive. My mom was looking at him instead of the camera. Hyla was vibrant and happy because she was surrounded by love. And I'd never been so damn happy in my life.

But I can't fucking find it. Now my brain is trying to gaslight me into thinking it doesn't exist. That I made the picture up. The logical side of me knows I didn't, but I also can't stop looking for it. I don't know what time it is or how long I've been doing this. I only know I have to find it. Have to figure it out.

I pull my knees up to my chest. It's all too much.

Ten years since my dad died.

Almost half my life without him now. It makes me sick. In a few years, I'll have spent more of my life without him than with him. And that's not fucking fair.

Where's the picture?

I just want to remember. Feel it again. Live that moment for a few seconds. Feel the weight of his arm around my shoulders and the unending happiness I always had with him.

My breaths get sharp and heavy.

I hate this.

A picture catches my eye. One of him and my mom. She's making a silly face, and he's looking at her like she's the entire world.

I should call Mom and see how she's doing. This is harder for her than me.

I need to check in with Hyla too.

She's not okay for a whole list of other reasons.

I lost my dad, but she never really had parents. Not ones who count anyway. If you can't do the bare minimum and love your kid, can you even be called a parent?

Hyla's not okay. Mom's not okay.

I need to take care of them.

I need to get myself together.

My eyes roll over the mess in front of me again.

I need to find the picture.

"Trevor?"

I jump and spin, only to find Chelsea standing there, wide-eyed.

She sets whatever she's holding down and walks toward me.

"I knocked, but you didn't answer. I thought you might be sleeping. I wanted to see if you were okay."

I look down at all the photos, unsure how to answer that.

Part of me says I'm fine. Because I have to be. I have people to take care of.

But the array of photos and the absolute need to find the one I can't says I'm not fine at all. The weight sitting in my chest and making it hard to breathe says I'm far from okay.

Chelsea delicately steps around photos before sitting down next to me.

"Why didn't you tell me?" Her voice is soft and even. There's no judgment, only concern.

I grab a handful of my curls and tug them through my fingers in frustration. Or resignation. I'm not sure.

"I didn't think I'd struggle this much."

"I'm still here to support you."

I let out a breath and say the truth. "I didn't want you to see me like this."

She loops her arm around mine and rests her head on my shoulder. "Lucky for you, the girls told me anyway. You don't need to hide your hurt from me. I'm here for you, and I want to see every version of you. Even the hurting ones. The broken ones." She gestures to all the pictures. "What's going on here?"

"I'm looking for a picture, but I can't find it."

She rubs her hand over my back in soft, soothing circles. "What's the picture of?"

"Me with my family on my ninth birthday—the one I told you about."

"And why do you need to find it?"

"I don't know." My voice catches. "I just need to see it. Maybe my skin will stop crawling if I do."

"Okay. I'm assuming you've been through all of these multiple times."

I nod.

"Do you have any other pictures here?"

I shake my head.

"Come here." She wraps an arm around my back, guiding me off the floor, but all I can do is look back at the pictures. "Trust me?" she whispers.

My eyes lift to hers, and all I see are those intoxicating eyes full of vulnerability and something else I've known for a while and have been afraid to say.

With a heavy inhale, I stand up. After all the trust she's given me, I can at least give her enough to get off this damn floor.

She leads me over to the bed and pulls me onto the mattress with her. I lie flat on my back and she wraps her body around mine, like a weighted blanket. Her head rests on my shoulder, and she lets me settle for a moment before speaking again.

"Why is this picture so important?"

I can't answer for a second because my emotions have gone crazy and I can't rein them in.

"Because I want to see it. Stare at it. Remember every detail. Pretend for a minute that if I open my eyes, he won't be gone. Sometimes... fuck, it doesn't make sense after ten years, but sometimes it still feels like yesterday that I saw him, and if I close my eyes and breathe, I'll wake up from a bad dream and he'll be here. I want to see it and live in that fantasy for a while."

"Okay." That's it. A simple *okay*. She doesn't even question me. "Would your mom have a copy?"

"Maybe."

"Why don't you call and ask her?"

"I don't want to put that on her. Make her go through all those photos. It's not easy for her."

She nestles in closer. Her body is pressed so tightly to mine we might as well be one. Then she mindlessly twirls a finger around one of my curls, and it calms me in a surprising way.

"I'm sorry you have to relive this pain. But if this picture will bring you peace, it's okay to ask your mom. She's an adult, and if going through those photos is too much, she can say that."

"She won't though. If I ask, she'll do it. And it's my job to take care of her."

"As the child, it's never your job to be emotionally responsible for your parent."

"Not just emotionally. I—" I blow out a breath. "It became my job the second my dad died. Not because anyone forced me into it, but because he always took care of her—and everyone. That void needed to be filled, so I filled it. My mom never asked. She doesn't rely on me in ways she shouldn't, but it's important to me to be there for her."

"But if you're always trying to be there for her or take care of her or take the perceived burden of your needs off her, who's taking care of you?"

Her words land with every bit of force intended.

"You can't carry the weight of the world or even the responsibility of caretaker for everyone in your world. I love that you're protective. I love how much you care for the people in your life. But you're doing all of them a disservice if you don't take care of yourself—let yourself be taken care of—too."

Her words shatter something deep inside me, and I roll over, burying my head in her neck.

And then tears come. Tears of grief. Tears of anger. Tears of relief. Because as she holds me, I don't feel like I have to be on. I don't feel guilty or hyper aware of the fact that I'm crying. I just let go. This is safety. She's my safe space. I don't know when it happened, but I love that it has. Even if this level of vulnerability doesn't come easily for me.

Chelsea runs her fingers through my hair, playing with the strands.

In time, my chest aches less, and though the desire to find that picture is still there in the back of my mind, it's not clawing at me.

When I'm finally breathing normally again, I force myself to look at her, only to find her resting against my pillow with her eyes closed, still soothingly running her fingers through my hair.

"Chels," I whisper, and her eyes flash open.

She runs her hand over my cheek, a soft smile appearing. "Hey, baby. You look a little better."

I nod, even though everything inside me is still twisted up.

"I think I'm broken."

Her voice is soft when she speaks. "Why? Men are allowed to have feelings."

Slowly, I push myself up to sitting and wipe my face. "It's not that. But I felt like I was drowning when you walked in. I was stuck and couldn't figure out how to break out of that thought process."

She tilts her head. "Has that happened before?"

"Not really. Not like that."

"Sometimes people experience hyperfixation in response to anxiety or depression. What this day triggers for you is probably a messy mix of those things."

I blow out a breath and try to root myself in reality again. That's when I notice the achy pain in my stomach.

"I haven't eaten," I say numbly.

Chelsea smiles and climbs off the bed, bringing over a bag and then grabbing my water bottle. Inside the bag I find a croissant.

"It's a chocolate one," she says with a smile.

"Thank you."

She kisses my cheek. "No problem."

While I eat, she taps away on her phone, like she's on a mission.

Once I've finished and moved on to chugging water, she turns to look at me with a serious expression.

"Does your mom know that you do that? Try to be the man of the house or whatever you want to call it?"

The cool water soothes my scratchy throat. "Yeah. She's called me on it before, but I can't help it. She deserves to be taken care of too."

"She does. And I know you feel the same way about Hyla, but there has to be a line. You can let them rely on you, but you need to rely on them too—and trust them to take care of themselves."

I know she's right, but it's my natural instinct to want to protect the people I care about—all of them. My mom, Hyla, and now Chelsea are at the top of that list.

Chelsea leans in and brushes her lips over my cheek. "Don't worry. I won't think you're any less of a sexy, fantasy book boyfriend if you do."

That gets a rough laugh out of me. I turn and press my lips to hers. "Thank you. For being here. Taking care of me."

"You don't need to thank me. I mean it. I'm happy to do it. I *want* to do it. But you have to let me. I told you that you're my person. The one I want to run to in my best moments and my worst. Am I that for you?"

"Yes."

"Then stop shutting me out. I know you want to take care of me and protect me, but I don't need you to be my protector. I need you to be my partner. Which means it's not one-sided. You take care of me, but I get to take care of you too. Let me take care of you."

Fuck. I can't even explain what those words do to me. They crack something open deep inside me. A lock I didn't know was there.

I lean in to kiss her, overwhelmed by her desire to care for me, by how much it means to me—but then her phone vibrates on the bed between us, and I almost laugh, until she quickly pulls away and grabs it, a smile growing on her face as she looks at it.

"What?" I ask.

She turns the phone sideways and hands it to me, and there on her screen is the picture I was so desperate for.

Tears rim my eyes again, but I blink them back, wanting to see the picture with clear eyes.

Chelsea curls against me again, looking at the picture too.

"Where did you—"

"I texted your mom and asked. Turns out she had a copy on her desk."

I almost facepalm. I can see it so clearly now. That's why I thought of the picture. Every time I'd go to her office, I'd always see it there.

"I'm an idiot."

Chels shrugs. "You were spiraling. We all have our moments. Some people kiss a really cute guy, run away like their pants are on fire, and think they'll never see him again."

I grab her chin between my thumb and forefinger. "Good thing I found you."

She rests her head on my shoulder and sighs softly. "Yeah. It is. I kinda like you."

I lean in and kiss her forehead. "Back at you."

"Now, a chocolate croissant is tasty, but nothing close to a meal. Can I go make you something to eat? I'm not a sandwich connoisseur like you, but I do all right."

"Yeah." I grab her hand as she climbs off the bed. "Thank you."

"It's nothing."

"No. I mean thank you for coming here. For caring for me even when I tried to stop you. For not taking offense to me not telling you. For seeing me. You always see me."

She smiles, though her eyes are glassy, and leans down to place a gentle kiss on my lips.

"You always see me too."

Chelsea made me the best sandwich I'd ever eaten, then I passed the fuck out. Apparently, emotional turmoil is exhausting. When I woke up, Chelsea was sitting next to me, all my pictures neatly stacked in piles at the end of my bed.

Now we're going through them all together, and it's awakening a whole other part of me to share these pieces of my life with her.

The last couple have made her bristle, though, because they're pictures of me in my Syracuse baseball uniform with some of my teammates. Have I been watching her extra closely to see if there are any signs she recognizes any of them? Of course. She's right that we should be partners—taking care of and protecting each other—but my protective heart will always lead with her. Especially when it comes to this.

Still, she hasn't reacted like she's recognized anyone, and I'm happy to move on to different memories.

My smile almost splits my face when she picks up the next one. It's a picture of me with Aaron, Joel, and Miles, arms slung around each other, sweaty and covered in dirt.

"After we won our last game before the state championship. It was the farthest our high school team had made it in like twenty years or something. I think Miles's mother orchestrated that photo. She's tiny and terrifying and runs everything with a sugary sweet voice and a deadly glare."

She laughs at that, and I grab the next picture, my smile only growing when I see it.

"Huh, look at that."

It's a picture of me with my parents under the sign for her family campground.

She smiles big too, then drags her finger over the blurry figures in the background, standing near a golf cart with the campground logo on it.

"That's me."

I turn to look at her, mouth hanging open. "Seriously? You're sure?"

She nods. "It's obvious to me. My hair was redder back then, and I'm standing next to Robbie, who had shaggy hair at the time—actually, he pretty much had an entire Shaggy vibe, like from *Scooby Doo*. I spent a lot of my summers riding around in that old golf cart with Robbie. We named her Bertha. Bouncing Bertha."

"There's that tether again. I can't believe all this time I've had a picture of you. I guess that answers whether we ever saw each other. We must have."

"Sometimes I wish I'd have felt that pull sooner. Looked up and locked eyes with you. There's no way I wouldn't have known."

"Known what?"

"That you're my person."

I set the photos down and turn to her, my palm resting on her cheek.

"Sometimes I let myself imagine what would've happened if I'd met you at any of the previous points when our paths crossed."

"And?"

I shrug. "It always would've ended up the same. You here next to me."

She grabs my shirt and pulls me closer. "Always such a sweet talker." Then she kisses me, quick and spicy, finishing with a nip of my bottom lip.

I laugh and kiss her nose, then she cuddles in close, and we get back to looking through the stories of my life.

After Chelsea and I spent the afternoon relaxing in my room and looking through pictures, she coaxed me out of my room for pizza at dinner time, where my friends gave me shit and reminded me they are also here for me. I know I should get better at letting everyone in, but I like being the one they can count on, either to talk to about hard shit or to make them laugh with my stupidity.

My day was better because Chelsea came over. Because she encouraged me to let myself be supported. She probably would've stayed the night if I hadn't said I wanted to check in with Hyla and my mom.

I had a quick video chat with Hyla, who still looks exhausted and like she's not taking care of herself, but I can't fix that, so I'm trying not to stress about it. After that, I called my mom. I didn't mention how much I was struggling earlier today, but I told her I was having a hard time. No surprise she was too. That's why I want to be strong for her. I lost my dad, but she lost the love of her life. They'd been together for over fifteen years when he died, and they were still madly in love. She's never even considered wanting to date again.

I pick up the picture Chelsea left sitting on my nightstand. The one of my parents, smiling and laughing.

I can't imagine how painful losing him was for my mom.

But then a thought clangs through me.

I can.

Because if I lost Chelsea...

It hasn't been fifteen years. Not even a whole year. But it doesn't matter. What I feel for Chelsea is the same thing reflected in that picture. It's the way my dad felt about my mom. The way he loved her. And while that's terrifying, it makes my chest warm and my head feel light.

I'm stupidly in love with Chelsea Winters. I love her more deeply than I knew I could love someone. And I haven't told her yet. If I lost her today, that would be the biggest regret of my life.

I need her to know how I feel, and I don't think I can wait another day to do it.

Chelsea

I'm cozy in bed, reading about a brand new set of bat boys. I love discovering a new fantasy series. Maybe I should mention it to Trevor so we can read it together, but I get the feeling this is going to be a binge read for me.

The crisp sound of a knock at my door makes my brow furrow. It's almost ten o'clock, which makes me wary. But Robbie also locks the downstairs door at sundown, so he would've had to let whoever it is in. Which means it's probably him wanting to talk randomly about something or he finished a great book and is about to throw his copy at me and tell me to read it. Either way, not the worst way to spend my night.

I climb out of bed, wearing leggings and an oversize tee, and walk down the hall to my front door. But when I swing it open, it's not Robbie, but Trevor.

"Hey, what—"

He grabs me and pulls me into a passionate kiss, kicking the door shut behind him.

His tongue sweeps my mouth possessively, and I melt into him. I'm confused, but I'm not complaining. He's cradling my face in his big hands, his warm body pressed against mine. This is heaven. I wrap my arms around his back and let him deepen the kiss. I barely move, just melting further into the kiss, twisting my tongue around his and taking all the rough, wild passion he's giving me and throwing more back at him.

But then, out of nowhere, he pulls back, panting, eyes wild.

"I love you."

My brows shoot up, my eyes flaring as his words hit.

"I love you. And I think I've known for a while, but I've been too scared to say it. Scared to let it be real. To admit how much

I have to lose if that's the truth, but it is. There's no denying it, and I don't want to. I was looking at the picture of my parents, and it hit me hard because I understand now. I understand how they loved each other, and I realized if I lost you without you ever knowing—"

This time, I leap into his arms, attacking him with kisses. He braces a hand against the couch to steady himself, and the other he wraps around me. We're both wild and untethered. Two souls that have been unleashed and are dancing around each other, twisting together, trying to become one.

I kiss him and kiss him until I can't stop the words from bubbling out of me.

"I love you too. It's terrifying how much I love you, but I do, and I need you to know it. Never question it. I'm yours."

He stares at me for a moment, then kisses me again. Wrapping both hands under my ass, he holds me in place as he carries me down the hall. Damn, those arm muscles do more than just look good.

I drag my lips across his cheek and down his neck. "I need you," I whisper against his skin.

He sets me down and meets my gaze, his voice thick and raspy. "Tell me what you want."

"You. I want you to touch me. Take care of me." I run my hands up his chest. "And I want to take care of you."

We kiss again, then we're messily stripping off clothes, desperate to feel our bodies touch. Warm skin against warm skin.

Once we're naked, I climb on top of him.

Trevor's gotten better about not questioning me if I'm sure, and I'm grateful, because I'm not questioning a thing about this. It's been so long since I've done this, but I love it. I love taking control and owning a man's body. *My* man.

His hands are all over me as I kiss down his neck and then his chest, but they freeze in place when I hit his stomach and keep going lower.

I look up to see him biting his bottom lip as he watches me.

I add an extra flair of confidence to my smile.

In understanding, he nods, then runs his fingers through my hair as my mouth dips lower and I stroke his thick cock.

Am I nervous?

Just a smidge.

But I'm giving those nerves a big middle finger and focusing on my man.

My stomach whirls with anticipation as I settle between his legs and run my hands up his thighs. Then I pause to look at him and memorize his face. His pupils blown out with lust. The dusting of pink on his cheeks. The way his lips are parted like he can't get enough of seeing me like this.

Then I lean down and run my tongue up the bottom of his shaft. I lick the salty precum off his tip and my stomach warms. Everything else floats away. I'd forgotten what it's like to connect with someone like this. I've missed it. The power of controlling someone else's pleasure—making them feel good. And the head rush of doing it with the guy I love? It's unlike anything else I've experienced.

His scent surrounds me as I lick and tease him, making his already thick cock even harder. His gasps and groans make me wild, and I can't hold back.

I breathe in through my nose, relax my throat, then take him as deep as I can.

"Oh, fuck. Chels. God, baby. You feel so good. I can't—ah. Can't handle how good you look swallowing my cock like that."

I wrap one hand around the base, and with my other, I massage his balls.

His groan is immediate and so rough and gravelly it takes everything in me not to hump the mattress.

But this is for him. I want to show him how special he makes me feel by giving him a mind-blowing orgasm.

After teasing him a bit more, I hollow my cheeks, sucking and slurping on his cock like it's my last meal. More of his precum dribbles into my mouth, and it sets me on fire. I want to taste all of him.

He gently plays with my hair, and I know he's holding back for my comfort, and I appreciate it. I hope I can get back to a place of being a little more rough, but since I went for this without much discussion first, I'm grateful he's not pushing those boundaries. Not that I'm surprised.

I squeeze his balls a little harder, and when they grow tighter in my hand, I know he's close.

I take him as deep as I can, almost gagging in the process, and his raspy moan sends me too close to the edge. I don't know if I can come without being touched, but I might find out.

Picking up my pace, I take him as deep as I can, working the rest of him with my hand.

"Holy shit. Chels. I'm close."

I keep going. Suck a little harder. Move a little faster.

"Babe, if you don't want to choke on my cum, pull off."

But I don't. I look up at him from under my lashes just in time to see his face twist with pleasure. His eyes roll back, his mouth falls open, and the groan he lets out as he comes is sinful.

I swallow every drop and pull off him, licking my lips.

Sitting back on my heels, I take him in. He's limp against the bed, arm thrown over his face as he breathes heavily.

I lie down next to him, and bury my face in his neck, still riding the high of making him feel that good.

Trevor's hand curls into my hair, and then his face is next to mine. He stares at me a moment, then his lips find mine for a toe-curling kiss. My whole body is flushed and warm, and I am... desperate. I'm desperate for him. For his touch. Anything he'll give me.

But then he pulls back and I almost pout.

"Are you good?" he asks, that low-level concern on his face.

I rest my palm on his cheek, ready to ease his mind. But my mouth must be feeling cheeky because it goes rogue.

"I'll be better when you're touching me."

A predatory smile appears on his face and he runs a hand down my side. "How do you want me to take care of you?"

"With your hand."

He kisses across my chest. "Can I still use my lips here?"

"Ye-es," I hiss, then his tongue flicks over one of my nipples.

"Good. Because these are my new favorite toys, and I really want to play with them." Then his mouth and hands are all over my breasts. Squeezing them, licking and tweaking my nipples. Not surprising. Since we first got off together, he's been obsessed with my boobs, and he's right—he plays with them like they're his toys any chance he gets.

I bite back a moan. Damn, he's good at it. He drives me crazy in the best way, and I'm practically riding the mattress. The throbbing spot between my legs is in desperate need of attention, and when Trevor catches the way I shift, he pulls back, his gaze sweeping over me.

"Open those legs for me, baby. I want to see that pretty pussy."

I almost shudder at the words. I was raised to see all bodies as beautiful, and my grandmother actively worked to undo all the toxic diet culture shit society puts on women. Because of that, I grew up confident in my body. Still, you always want the person you're with to see you as attractive too. Trevor looking at me hungrily, like I'm the most beautiful thing he's ever seen makes me feel wanted. Worshipped.

Then he sucks in a sharp breath and bites his bottom lip.

"Goddamn, baby. I've never seen anything more beautiful than you splayed out on this bed for me. Except maybe seeing you come." He lies down next to me and runs his hand down my stomach. "Now I'll get to see both." His lips graze mine. "Tell me if you get uncomfortable, want me to stop, or want me to change anything, okay?"

I nod so quickly it's almost frantic. "I will."

Then I bite my lip to keep from begging. *Please touch me.*

"What are you comfortable with? You want me to just rub your clit?" One finger barely grazes that swollen, sensitive spot, and I hiss in response. "Or do you want my fingers inside you?" Two fingers trail lower, but he waits for my answer.

I throw my head back, overwhelmed and needy. "Both. Please. Just touch me. I need you."

His lips close around one of my nipples, then he circles those two fingers around my opening. When he finally pushes inside, I gasp, but then his thumb lands on my clit, and I fist the sheets, already coming apart at the seams for him.

"Yes. More. Fuck me with your fingers."

He flicks his tongue over my nipple, then moves to the other one, before pulling his fingers almost all the way out and pushing them back in. He picks up the pace achingly slowly, teasing and flicking at my clit as he does.

I'm going insane, skin prickling, absolutely fucking desperate for this man. He touches me like I'm an extension of him. Like he knows exactly what I want without me saying it.

My skin heats as desire builds inside me. I'm overwhelmed, but I need more.

A moan falls from my lips, and though I try and make words to tell him what I want, my brain is too swamped with lust. But he knows anyway. He curves his fingers inside me and I cry out.

"Yes," I whine. "More."

My mind goes blank. I'm burning up, a volcano ready to erupt.

"So close."

He looks up at me in awe.

"Come for me, baby. I want to see your beautiful body writhing."

My stomach tightens, and I clench the sheets.

"Trevor..."

The intense burst of pleasure shocks me. My body contracts with wave after powerful wave.

"Oh, yeah." He groans as he watches my orgasm rip through me.

I'd forgotten how good it feels when someone else controls my orgasm.

Toys are great, but they're no substitute for the connection during sex.

And this was just his hand.

I'm in so much trouble. *Just his hand.*

He lies down next to me and licks his fingers, looking as smug as I felt after the blow job I gave him.

I roll on top of him and kiss that smirk right off his face.

When I finally lift my lips off his, he's all dazed and relaxed, but clearly still thinking of me. He runs his fingers through my hair and meets my gaze.

"Feeling okay?"

"Perfect," I breathe. But then it really hits me. This was my first orgasm from someone else in over a year. "I thought it would be more difficult. When I imagined taking this step, I mean. I assumed I'd struggle, but it barely crossed my mind tonight. Only briefly when I was about to take care of you. Not when you were taking care of me. But maybe it's not all that surprising. It's not like there was any foreplay when—" I cut off, not wanting to go to that place right now. "More importantly, I was lost in you and us. Our love."

I rub my nose against his, and he tugs on my hair, pressing a kiss to the corner of my mouth.

We hold each other tightly. Warm naked bodies melting together like one.

"Stay with me tonight?" I whisper.

He gives me a smile that's somehow both lazy and cocky. "I'll stay with you forever if you want."

My heart leaps at that. Maybe I shouldn't want it yet, but falling for Trevor meant leaping into the deep end. Instead of learning to swim, I had to learn to breathe underwater. That's how lost in his love I am.

My heavy eyes try to close, but as romantic as it sounds, falling asleep without cleaning up after is a great way to get a UTI. So I force myself up and head for the bathroom. He stands up too, so I glance at him over my shoulder.

"Don't get dressed."

His answering smile is cheeky, then he stretches, purposely showing off as many of those muscles as he can.

Troublemaker.

My troublemaker.

When we've both finished using the bathroom, we collapse in bed together, both ready to crash.

In the quiet dark, I curl my naked body around his and whisper, "I love you."

My spine tingles as he brushes his lips over mine and whispers back, "I love you too."

With those words dancing around in my head, I drift off to sleep, sated and wrapped in a warm embrace of love.

16
Invincible Goddess

Trevor

CHELSEA LETS OUT A long groan and buries her face in my shoulder.

Unfortunately, it's not in a sexy way.

I rub my hand over her back in soft circles.

"I'm sorry," she groans again. "I wanted this weekend to be fun. To show you around Birch Lake. Not for me to be in the fetal position in bed with evil cramps and my worst period in months."

I press a kiss to her forehead. "Don't apologize. I'm happy to be with you, no matter the circumstances. Of course, I wish you felt better because I hate seeing you in pain, but you don't have to be any certain way for me." Sweeping some hair off her face,

I look into those two-tone eyes. "I wish I could help you feel better."

"You being here helps. Other than my family, I've never had someone who would just lie here with me."

"Whenever you need me, I'll be there. I'd wade through the darkness to find you."

Her glassy eyes meet mine. "I wish I would've had you in my life in my most broken moments. Instead, I had friends *supporting* me by saying 'bitch, stop moping and have fun.' I would've shown up for them whenever they needed me, but they never took care of me. I'm not sure if they didn't know how or they didn't want to. Or our ideas of friendship are just totally different. Probably that one. They're face-value friends. That's not who I am or who I ever want to be."

It blows my mind how they've treated her in the past. It also makes me realize I've consistently had examples of strong female bonds in my life. My mom with Hyla, the girls with their friends. Sarah and Rae are fiercely protective of each other, but also the first to jump in and take care of each other. When Sarah was having a rough day, I usually found her snuggled up in Rae's bed. When Rae was really sick and needed surgery, Sarah was the first to realize something was wrong. That extended to their entire friend group. They never trash talk each other. They only support each other. I wish Chelsea could've had that.

"Just know that even if for some reason I couldn't be here, all you'd have to do is mention to the girls how you were feeling, and they'd storm the place. Rae would bring brownies—her grandmother's recipe. Amanda would for sure bring wine. There'd probably also be coffee, sushi, and the best comfort movies around. Honestly, you're kind of settling picking me over them."

That gets a laugh out of her. But then she strokes her hand over my cheek.

"There's nothing *settling* about this."

"I love you."

"Love you too," she says weakly.

I run my hand over her stomach, then notice the heat wrap is barely lukewarm now.

Grabbing it, I lean down and press a kiss to her head. "I'm going to warm this up. Want anything to eat?"

She grunts like it's too much effort to think about that, but then says, "Mashed potatoes."

"On it." I set the remote next to her. "Find something to watch."

Her eyes flick toward the TV on her dresser. "Cheesy Christmas movie?"

"I'm in. Be back soon."

I head down the stairs of Chelsea's childhood home. It's large, with a small house out back. Apparently Chelsea's grandparents lived in this house and Chelsea and her dad lived in the small one until Chelsea was seven or eight, then they moved into this house with her grandparents while Robbie took the small house out back. Now her dad and stepmom live here, and her grandmother lives in the small house.

When I get down to the kitchen, I'm surprised to find no one is around. Chelsea spent the first couple of days of Thanksgiving break at my house, then we spent Thanksgiving apart—until late last night when I decided I didn't want to wait until today to see her and drove over. It's only a forty-five-minute drive, so we could've stayed at our own places and still seen each other every day, but I wanted to really experience her world.

And boy, has it been an experience.

Within a half hour of walking through the door last night, Chelsea's grandmother had already asked for my stance on abortion and my thoughts on whether men should have vasectomies as a form of birth control, then have them reversed when ready. My answer to the first was that every woman deserves the freedom to make choices about her body, and men need to fuck off about trying to control those decisions. My answer to the second was mostly sputtering while Chelsea and everyone else laughed. Except her grandmother. Eventually I got out my response—I think it's an option for anyone who is looking at not having kids for a while or who knows for sure they don't want kids. I personally wouldn't want to do it until I was done having kids because I know I'd like to have kids young. Her grandmother only nodded in some kind of approval. Then the topic of conversation turned, and Robbie started poking fun at Chelsea getting me to read books with her favorite bat boys and shadow daddies. I then informed him my mom and sister had already corrupted me on that front.

Overall, they seem like a fairly relaxed group, even if they're passionate about certain topics ranging from politics to whether Josh Allen or Patrick Mahomes was a better QB. I wisely kept my mouth shut. Baseball is my sport.

I stick the heat wrap in the microwave, then pull the refrigerator open. There are plenty of Thanksgiving leftovers, so I pull out the mashed potatoes and gravy and dish up a big bowl for Chels, since she's barely eaten today.

The back door opens and shuts, then Chelsea's grandmother appears.

"Finding everything okay?"

"Yeah, I think so."

"How's my girl?"

"In pain."

She nods. Then slides something wrapped in tin foil over to me. "This is for her too."

I open it and find... garlic bread. Chelsea's favorite.

"Thank you. Maybe that'll lift her spirits a bit. Oh, do you have any tea? I remember there was this tea my mom used to drink..."

I trail off. It's been close to five years since she started going through menopause, so I don't remember what the hell it was called.

But Chelsea's grandmother—Matilda, but goes by Mattie—walks across the kitchen and pulls open the cupboard.

"I know what you're talking about. She hates the taste of that one, but this..." She holds one out to me. "Is milder and should still help. Brew it lightly and add some honey."

"Thanks."

Before I find a mug, I grab my phone and snap a picture of the box so I can grab some for her when we get back to Old Lake Town.

"I like how you take care of her," Mattie says.

My eyes lift to hers. "I'm happy to do it. Anything to help her feel better. I'd take on all that pain if I could."

She looks at me, assessing. "Good. I'm sorry if we came on strong when you got here last night."

I laugh as I move to the sink to fill the kettle with water. "No, you're not. I know why you do it. Put it all out there. Be a little over the top. Scare off the wrong ones right away before anyone gets too attached. I'd do the same. If they can't handle it, it means they're not the right fit." I flick the burner on, then turn back to her. "Not much scares me. The only thing that drives me away is people treating someone I love poorly—or being assholes in general. That's far from the case here. I can take a little family wildness."

"I had a good feeling about you. Glad to know I was right. Keep taking care of my girl. Let me know if you need anything."

"Will do."

"Oh, and there are trays under the island to help you carry all that upstairs."

"Thanks."

She smiles, then walks out the back door.

When I get back to Chelsea's room, she's propped up on some pillows, watching some Netflix Christmas movie.

She perks up at the sight of the tray. "What's all that?"

I set the tea on her bedside table and hand her the heat wrap before putting the tray on her lap.

"Tea and sustenance. Your gran made garlic bread."

"Mm. Yes. I'm starving."

I sit down next to her, and she leans over to kiss me, her hand skating up my arm as she does. Then she pinches me.

"The fantasy book boyfriend thing again?" I sigh.

She bites her lip and smiles. "Nope. My real-life book boyfriend."

"I'm moving up in the world."

"I'm finally starting to believe you're real."

I wrap my arm around her back, then press a kiss to her head. "Believe it, babe. I'm here, and I'm not going anywhere."

"No way. The Metros are the best baseball team in New York," I say adamantly.

"You're just saying that because you got to play against them, and have friends who work and play for them," Robbie says.

"Technically, my friends work for their affiliate team, the Binghamton Knights." I stare at them for a beat. "Because they're the best team in New York... if not the whole East Coast," I add, making Chelsea's dad—Gene—and Robbie yell.

"Better than the Boston Revs?" Gene demands.

I shrug, then look at Chelsea. "You didn't tell me your family are baseball people."

"They're sports people." Chelsea waves a hand. "I only paid attention to the ones I was interested in." I gape at her and she pats my cheek. "Sorry, babe. I promise, I'm interested in baseball *now*."

Which I'm grateful for. With her past, I could understand why she wouldn't be. I love that she enjoys it because she sees how happy it makes me.

"All right, if we're going to get into a serious debate, let's head to the living room. It's more comfortable and there's more room for pacing," Mattie says.

"Agreed," Hilary, Chelsea's stepmom, says.

"Actually, Trevor, could I borrow you for a few minutes?" Gene asks.

I glance at Chelsea, but she gives me an encouraging smile. "Sure."

He leads me down the hall to an office, then sits down at the desk. I take one of the comfortable armchairs in front of it.

"You're not going to give me a *what are your intentions* speech, are you?"

He laughs. "No. Robbie did his part when you first met Chelsea, and with how you treat my daughter, your intentions are obvious. No, actually, I have something for you."

He pulls an envelope from a drawer and hands it to me.

I take it, still confused, and pull it open to find a picture of my family staring back at me. We're in front of a canoe, my dad holding the paddle. I pull the small pile of pictures out, emotion gripping my chest.

"This is..."

"Chelsea texted me a few weeks back, asking me to look for any pictures of your family we might have. We regularly took pictures for marketing, but also to remember returning guests. She mentioned your father passed away and thought you'd like to see these."

Oh, fuck.

I'm not against crying, but I usually don't do it with someone I don't know well.

I bite my cheek and look through the pictures, barely keeping my emotions in check. When I get to the last one, I'm shocked at what I see. It's my dad, holding a wiffle bat, with his arm around Chelsea's dad.

My gaze snaps to his. "You knew my dad?"

"Got to know him a bit. We always had silly competitions and events. The second year you stayed with us, he overheard me talking with one of my cousins about ideas for a competition, and he suggested wiffle ball. When we decided to do it, I emailed him and let him know. He conveniently booked your summer trip for when the competition was taking place and told me he'd better be on my team. We kept in touch here and there. I don't know if I'd call us true friends, but he was a good man. Kind. But then we lost contact. Now I know why. When Chelsea said your last name, I thought it sounded familiar, but it wasn't until she asked me to look for the pictures that I figured it out."

I press my fingers to the bridge of my nose. "You don't know what this means to me."

He reaches across the desk and squeezes my arm. "From one man who has lost his father to another, I do."

Tears blur my vision as I look at him. "Thank you."

To my surprise, he gets up and comes around the desk, then pulls me into a hug. "No problem. If you ever need someone to give you a bit of that dad energy, I'm here."

Fuck.

I sniff back my tears. "Thank you."

He pats my back and steps away. "If I know my daughter, she's making some hot cocoa right now. Go find her, maybe enjoy the hot cocoa on the back porch."

I nod, at a loss for words, and follow him out to the kitchen.

As Gene predicted, Chelsea is standing by the counter where two mugs of hot cocoa sit. I toss the pictures on the counter and wrap Chelsea in the tightest hug I can.

"I take it you liked the pictures?"

"I loved them. But I love you more. Thank you."

I let her go, and she looks up at me, vibrant eyes filled with warmth. "Anything to see that smile. Come on."

She nods to the mugs, then grabs one. I grab the other and the pictures and follow her toward the back door. She stops and gets two blankets from a basket near the door, then leads me onto the screened-in back porch.

Once we're comfortable on the outdoor loveseat, I show her the pictures, saving the one of our dads for last.

Her mouth drops when she sees it.

"They—they—"

"Were friends. Or friendly."

She brushes her thumb over the photo. "Another tether between us."

I put the photo back in the envelope and pull her close. "Further proof that we were always supposed to find each other. End up here."

She leans against me, resting her head on my chest.

"Here is pretty great."

And as I hold my girl, nestled under blankets on this beautiful night, feeling more in love with her than ever, all I can do is agree.

Chelsea

I feel fantastic.

It's a marked change from a week ago when I was lying in bed and wanted to roll into an early grave. I haven't had a period like that in a while, and it almost makes me want to try birth control again, but somehow every birth control I tried made things worse for me. They either made me sick or gave me migraines or made my periods worse somehow. Apparently, my body doesn't like additional hormones added to the mix.

Speaking of hormones, mine are on fire.

My period finally fucked off two days ago, and now I'm frisky and want nothing more than to turn that wild hormonal energy on Trevor. Not that I think he'll mind. I've been amping up my flirty texts all day, but I didn't want to tease him too much before I see him.

I just finished up a meeting with the planning committee for the women's festival. It's so much fun. A little more hippie than I'm used to, but the powerful female energy is strong. While drum circles aren't my thing, learning more about women's health and wellness and channeling my inner power—yes, that's one of the festival events—is one hundred percent my thing. And I can't wait. It's not until May, but there's already been some ticket sales, and I'm hopeful it'll be a great event.

I wave to one of the other women on the committee as I open my car door. Trevor should be waiting for me at my apartment, reading the fantasy series that I've already halfway binged. Thankfully, Trevor doesn't complain about me being ahead, he just tries to get me to give him spoilers, which I don't do because *sacrilege!*

I lock my car, then turn it on before pulling my phone out to text Trevor one more deliciously dirty thing—and let him know I'm ready to kick things up a notch. I've had my mouth on him—more than once since that first time. Now I'm ready for him to have his mouth on me. Below my chest. A shiver of anticipation rolls through me when I think about it. But it dies almost immediately when I see new texts in my group chat with Bridget and Lex.

Preparing for my blood pressure to rise, I open the conversation.

Bridget: So, I'm bummed we didn't get to see you over Thanksgiving break. Any chance we can plan something for winter break?

Lex: Yeah, we miss you! And we want to meet the boyfriend.

I blink in surprise. Not the typical passive aggression I'm used to. It still has the feel of them ganging up on me, which it hurts to admit they've always done, but I'm used to that. I go to type out a response, but stop myself. Because I was going to apologize that I wasn't feeling well, but what Trevor said last week has stuck with me. That if the girls had known I didn't feel well, they'd all have shown up for me. I don't need to apologize to Bridget and Lex. If they'd wanted to see me, they would've made the effort.

Instead, I take a deep breath and respond in a way that doesn't give them room to blame me.

Me: It would be nice to see you. Trevor will be there with me before Christmas, so maybe sometime in there?

Bridget: Yes! Finally.

Lex: We'll make it happen.

Me: Throw some dates at me and we'll figure something out.

Bridget: Hooray!

With a sigh, I close my texts and toss my phone onto my seat. It's not that I don't want to see them, but it makes me sad it doesn't excite me like it once did. Then again, there's a reason for that. People talk about moving on from a relationship after a breakup, but no one talks about how hard it is to let go of a friendship, even when it's hurting you.

Whatever.

I tuck those feelings into a box for another day and take the short drive back to my apartment. My mood is still a little funky when I get home, but then I walk into my bedroom and find Trevor splayed out on my bed, reading a book.

I stop just inside the doorway and enjoy the view.

"I could get used to coming home to this."

He pulls the book down enough so he can see me.

"Should I flex a little?"

"No. You're perfect."

So perfect. Perfectly delicious. Which must be why I'm licking my lips.

I drop all my shit on the floor and cross the room to him. Tossing his book to the side, I climb on top of him and kiss him like a wild woman.

"Someone's feeling frisky," Trevor murmurs against my lips.

I pull back slightly and meet his eyes as I roll my hips. "I told you I have a high sex drive. Are you ready to keep up?"

He wraps his arms around me and does some crazy spin move that leads to me lying on the bed. He stretches out beside me and kisses my neck, running his fingers along the edge of my waistband.

"What do you want today? A toy or my fingers?"

I swallow down the nerves that are always there when we try something new and say, "Your mouth."

When it occurred to me the other day, I was surprised by how right it felt. But thinking about it, I guess it makes sense that oral sex might be easier. That wasn't a part of my assault. He only used one part of his body. That's why I'm still not ready for sex. I want Trevor every way I can get him, but there's no rush for me to be ready for that step, so I'm taking my time.

But this feels right.

He sits up. "Chels..."

"Trevor," I whine, knowing where this is going.

"I thought we agreed you'd make decisions like this outside of the moment."

"I was going to text you with the gist of that, but then I saw a text from Bridget and Lex, and it left my brain."

"Time out. What was their text about? Did they say something else shitty?"

"No. They asked if we could get together with them over winter break."

"We?"

"They want to meet you."

He lets out a little laugh. "They might regret that."

"Trevor! Stop changing the subject."

"Fine." He strips his shirt off, then undoes the button of his jeans. "But I still want to be sure you're ready for this. That you won't regret it later."

I stand up and meet his gaze, staring him down as I pull my shirt off, then shove down my pants. "I thought we agreed you'd trust that I know what I'm ready for and can tell you if something doesn't feel right." I raise my eyebrows, but he doesn't say anything. Just smiles, all charming and sincere. Irritating as fuck. So I pull off my bra, then glide my underwear down my legs until I'm standing in front of him, stark naked. "I don't need protection from myself. Now eat my pussy."

He sucks in a sharp breath, eyes gleaming with trouble.

"Only if you ride my face."

Um, what?

Did that just happen?

I think my brain broke. I heard a definite pop. Or sizzle.

"Chels..." His voice is pure sex.

All I get out is a ridiculous squeak.

Come on, get it together.

This is book boyfriend shit.

"Come here."

He grabs me and pulls me onto the bed with him, so I'm sitting on top of him again.

I look down at the position, and... there's no way this is going to work.

He palms my ass and looks up at me. "This way, baby."

"Are—are you sure? My thighs... might smother you."

He smirks like the devil. "Sounds like a good way to go."

I smack him hard on the chest.

"Ow. Why are you always trying to hurt me?"

"I don't want to hurt you. That's the whole point."

"If you say some ridiculous shit about being too big for this, I'll have to spank your perfect ass."

I'm not self-conscious about my size. I love my body. But I'm also aware that I'm not tiny like all the heroines in my books, and I'm suddenly wondering if this whole idea is an act of fiction.

"We're practicing trust. I'm trusting that you'll tell me or stop if anything feels uncomfortable for you. You're trusting me to tell you if I can't breathe, but I don't see that being a problem when all I want to breathe is you."

He inches me forward again, and this time I go willingly, hovering over him until I'm angled over his stupidly gorgeous face. His dark eyes are wild with excitement as he takes me in.

"Now what should I do?" I ask.

"Grab the headboard."

I almost whimper at the words, but I do it.

"Good girl. Now drop your hips. My hands are on your thighs, so I'll keep you from going too far. You set the angle and the pace, just make sure it's comfortable for you."

I close my eyes and breathe in, slowly lowering my hips, until... he groans.

I snap my eyes open and look down at him, but before I can take in what's happening, his tongue brushes my clit.

Oh.

Well, okay. I'm sold on it now.

He flicks his tongue around, then holds it steady. Gripping the headboard, I slowly roll my hips.

"Oh, fuck."

I settle into a rhythm, lost in pure bliss. The little flicks of his tongue are sinful and the way he occasionally brings his lips together to suck on my clit... oh my god.

My body is chanting, *yes, more.*

My brain has mostly melted at this point, but the awareness of crossing this line is there. Every time I take a step forward, I'm worried it'll trigger me and I'll freak out, but there's nothing about this that's triggering. I'm in control. I'm riding his face. I'm taking what I want. It makes me feel powerful. Like a goddess stealing the life of mere mortal men.

Not that Trevor is a mere mortal. He's a god among men.

The god of pussy eating, possibly.

Yeah, my brain has definitely melted, but I don't care.

It feels too good.

My body is awash with pleasure. Goosebumps prickle on my skin. My arm muscles burn from holding onto the headboard, but I don't care.

I'm a screaming, whining mess, barreling toward the edge, chasing the high I know is only a few strokes of his tongue away.

Fire blooms inside me, and all at once, explodes out of me.

"Yes," I cry as my body goes taut.

My sweaty hands slide on the headboard as my body convulses and I struggle to stay upright.

Trevor's arm snakes up around my waist, holding me steady as my legs tremble around his head.

Holy shit.

I'm not sure if I think the words or say them.

My eyes slip closed as I come back down, a shaking, panting mess. Then I hear Trevor groaning.

"Fuck, fuck…"

I open my eyes halfway, trying to figure out what happened. It takes me a second, but then I see his pants shoved down and his hand around his now softening cock. Apparently, that was hot as fuck for him too.

I don't know how Trevor does it, but we end up side by side on my bed as I melt into a pile of pillows.

For a few moments, the only sound is the blood rushing through my ears, but then Trevor's fingers graze my navel.

"God, you're beautiful." His words are a reverent sigh that force my heavy eyelids open.

He's staring at my naked, flushed, wrung-out body in awe.

"So beautiful. I can't believe you're mine."

"I know. I'm pretty amazing."

He laughs and kisses my neck. "And so humble."

"It's hard to be humble when you worship my body like I'm a goddess."

"You are. My strong, invincible goddess."

I snort at that. "Invincible?"

"You've survived everything that's tried to break you. I'd call that invincible."

"Well then, I guess you are too."

"Perfectly matched."

His lips find mine again, and even though I'm starving and need to pee, I barely notice. Nothing has ever felt this right. No one has ever made me feel so desired… so cherished before. And I get the feeling no one else ever will. Maybe it's too soon to know for sure, but I already know he's my person. I already know I'm in love with him. Now, blooming deep in my gut, is the piercing certainty that he's more than that. He's it for me. He's everything.

17
Lifeline

Chelsea

WINTER BREAK HAS BEEN a whirlwind. It's already mid-January, and I don't know how we got here so quickly—except I do. Trevor and I have done all the things. First there was the winter carnival Joel's brother Jesse organized at the Binghamton Knights stadium. Trevor acted as emcee for the baseball trivia and a few other games. Of course, he had a great time, and watching him full of charisma and sarcastic quips was hot as fuck.

Did I give him a blow job on the way home from there? Maybe.

Every day I feel a little more free with my sexuality, and the big S—sex, or is it the big I for intercourse?—has been on my mind. I'm getting closer to being ready, but that's going to be a whole conversation and not something I'm ready to get into while we're staying with either my family or his mom.

After the winter carnival, it was straight into Christmas things. All the Christmas things as we tried to balance his family and mine. Not to mention taking time for ourselves. The day after Christmas, there was the annual friend group party, which apparently Rae and everyone have at Joel's house. It's grown since they were in high school to include lots of other friends. It was a good time. Mostly. Hyla and Mackenzie had a heartbreaking confrontation. I still don't know all the details there, but it's clear they still love each other, but there are things holding them back from being together. A part of Hyla has been utterly broken since then, even if she's trying to play it off otherwise.

Trevor is, unsurprisingly, concerned about it all and wants to fix it. He can't, so supporting her is all he's got left. Apparently, that includes going to some dinner with her family in a couple of days. I offered to go if only to be a buffer. They don't know me and I don't give a fuck about them, but Trevor said it's something Hyla wants and needs to do. He doesn't sound thrilled, but if they're as awful as he's said, that's not surprising.

In the midst of all that, though, we made time for a cozy New Year's Eve celebration, just the two of us in a little cabin at my family's campground. It was absolutely freaking perfect and the best New Year's of my life.

Now, since we didn't have time to do it at the start of winter break, we're finally meeting up with Bridget and Lex. At the best bar in Birch Lake, apparently. They still haven't gotten the message that I don't like to drink much.

I'm finally comfortable having a little here and there. I had a glass of champagne at Rae and Aaron's wedding, and Trevor and I split a small bottle of champagne on New Year's Eve. But other than that, drinking is minimal, and not a social activity I enjoy.

But whatever. I've decided to meet them where they are, offer whatever friendship I can, and work on being okay with that.

Trevor pulls into a space down the street from the bar and rests a hand on my thigh.

"Are you ready? Because if not, we can go. Run away to Mexico."

I laugh at that. "Sounds like something someone would say right before the bride walks into a wedding."

He shrugs. "It's multi-use."

"I'm ready. Ish. I just want it to be low-key. I want no drama. But I'm also not willing to let them hurt me anymore, even if it is unknowingly."

He grunts in that very Trevor way. "I doubt it's unknowing. But I will go in there with my supportive face on. I'll be nice. I won't flip my shit on them. Unless you ask me to."

I grab his chin between my thumb and fingers. "You're so cute when you're respectful of my boundaries while still somehow being all growly and protective."

"Cute." He hmphs.

"Sorry. I meant *adorable*."

He shakes his head, but can't keep his smile in. "You're lucky you're sexy, gorgeous, smart, kind, and put up with my annoying ass."

I shrug and fling my door open. "Five out five. Not bad."

With a wink, I climb out, channeling that inner strength I haven't needed to rely on in a while. I've healed more than I realized in these last few months, and maybe that's what I'm most afraid of walking into the bar. I don't want to feel like that broken shell of a person I was before.

Then Trevor steps up beside me and wraps his arm around my back, and I know I won't feel that way. I'm stronger now, and when I'm not, I have his strength to bolster me.

I'm wearing a shimmery gray sweater dress and heeled boots that make me feel sexy as fuck and give me an extra boost of confidence. Trevor likes it too. At least if the hand resting on my ass is any indication.

When we walk in, I quickly spot Bridget and Lex. They're at a table at the far side of the bar near a row of windows.

"Hey, bitch!" Lex yells, throwing her hand up in an over-the-top wave.

The subtle grumble under Trevor's breath is everything. I have to bite my lip to keep from laughing.

Bridget and Lex both stand up when I get to the table, throwing their arms out for me to hug them.

I step away from Trevor and into their arms, but when I do, I notice something I never have before. How hollow it is. When Amanda hugs me, she throws her arms around me and holds me like a mama bear would. Rae's hugs are soothing and comforting. Hyla hugs like she might never let me go. But this? It's empty. There's space between our bodies. It's more like one of those bro-hug, pat on the back things. Oh my god. Is there such a thing as a cliché girl hug? Because I think I might've found it.

"Yay! I'm so glad you're here," Bridget says.

"And we get to meet the boyfriend," Lex claps.

"Yes. This is Trevor. Trevor, meet Bridget and Lex."

"Best friends since first grade!" Bridget says.

"It's nice to meet you ladies."

He pulls out a chair and sits down, then drags the other chair right next to him and pulls me into it, protectively wrapping his arm around me.

Lex notices and giggles about that. "So romantic."

But that mood is quickly broken when Bridget loudly calls to the nearby bartender, "Shots!"

I hold up my hand. "I'm not drinking."

Bridget rolls her eyes. "Of course you're not."

"Mm, but maybe your boyfriend will. If we get him drunk enough, maybe he won't notice if one of us steals him."

Oh my god.

It comes rushing back to me, all the times they've said things like this. Things I wrote off as innocent jokes, but when I look between them, there's something cold in my stomach as I realize they might actually do something like that. I don't know.

"Yeah, that's not cool," I say clearly.

"You know we're just kidding," Lex says.

"Plus, it's clear he only has eyes for you. And hands," Bridget adds, tracking the movement of his fingers over my shoulder. A calm reassurance.

"Anyway, we want to hear all about the new college!" Lex exclaims, giving me a genuine smile. And finally, I relax.

We settle into a conversation about school and what we've all been up to, and it's easy to remember why I'm still friends with them. There's a lot of shared history, and I really do believe they care. But I'm not sure they've ever learned what a strong female friendship looks like. Who knows if they ever had it modeled for them. Or maybe they have it with each other in a way they don't with me. Whatever the answer, it's okay. No one is perfect. My issues are less about them and more about me. What I want from my friendships and what I'm willing to tolerate.

In my last session with my therapist, she reminded me that boundaries are essential for building the lives we want. They're there to help us structure our lives the way we want. They don't shut anyone else out. People shut themselves out if they refuse to respect those boundaries.

So, that's my plan. Set boundaries as needed with Bridget and Lex—or anyone else—and if they want to be in my life, they'll learn to respect them.

Overall though, tonight has been good. We've talked and laughed, told some old stories that even had Trevor laughing, and ate a shit ton of appetizers.

When I've yawned three times in a row, Trevor says, "Babe, maybe we should head out."

Another yawn stops me from answering. "Probably should. I didn't sleep much last night."

"I'll bet you didn't," Bridget says.

And even though it's said playfully, it makes me feel a bit icky. Assumptions that we were up all night having sex. When we haven't even done that yet. Not that I have any intention of telling them that. The only reason I didn't sleep last night is because my mattress is so freaking old and uncomfortable that I couldn't find a position that didn't make my neck or back ache. Trevor sleeps like the dead and can fall asleep anywhere.

"Wait," Lex says. "Come on. Do one round of shots with us before you go!"

"I told you, I'm not interested in drinking."

"It's just one shot," Bridget protests.

"It doesn't matter. I'm telling you I don't want to. Why you still can't get it through your heads is beyond me."

"Maybe because it's been over a year of this," Lex says. "When are you going to stop letting that night destroy your life?"

Trevor's hand tenses on my thigh, but I go stock still.

Only my eyes move, dancing between Bridget and Lex.

"First of all, not drinking is not destroying my life. I drink here and there when I feel like it, but most of the time, I don't. It's not fun for me anymore." I hold up my hand. "And no, you don't need to crack yet another joke about me not being fun. I get it."

"We just want you to stop letting what happened define you," Bridget says, a hint of snark or maybe condescension in her tone.

I brace my hands on the table and stand, making sure I catch both their eyes before I say this.

"There is a difference between letting something define me and staring into the darkest storm and finding my way through it to the other side. I don't let what happened define me. But I continue to let how I heal from it shape me into a new, better, healthier version of myself. My work isn't done. Some days, I feel like I've barely healed at all. Some days, the memory still suffocates me, but I keep putting one foot in front of the other and trying to move forward. I won't apologize for that. Or for not being the fun person you remember. But that you can say those words to me at all shows how little you understand of what I've been through. Every experience changes a part of us, no matter how small. To reduce anyone to being defined by their trauma while they work to heal from it is one of the most disrespectful and ignorant things someone can do."

They both gape at me, both a little pissed, a little hurt, a little drunk. Not a good combination.

"But you have let it change you," Lex insists. "Doesn't he win if you let it change you?"

"All you did was lay around and wallow, and even when you stopped, you turned into this sad, small version of yourself. How is that healing?"

I wish I'd worn my *sleigh the patriarchy* shirt—which has a cute picture of Mrs. Claus driving the sleigh on it. Because that is them spewing back the internalized bullshit our society has pushed for years.

Instead of helping and protecting women who have been raped or assaulted, we shame them. Then on top of that, there are horrible stigmas surrounding getting help of any kind—especially mental health help—so many women never get the help they need and fight through it alone. Or they pretend they're okay, when really, it's destroying them on the inside.

I haven't done anything wrong, but because I didn't plaster that pretty smile on while I was dying inside, because I let myself grow and change from who I once was in the face of something terrible, somehow society looks at me like I'm in the wrong.

I get it. That's the messaging women receive from the time we're young.

Stand up. Dust yourself off. Smile pretty. Move on. If someone tries to break you, they only succeed if you let them. It's all bullshit.

We are allowed to break. Every single person in this world is allowed to feel the very real fractures that life and other people inflict on them. We're allowed to process and grieve and cry and scream however we need to. And we're allowed to grow into something better in spite of it all.

I won't be sorry. And if Bridget and Lex don't get that, then they've just collided with one of my boundaries.

So I grab my coat off the back of the chair and offer what little smile I can muster.

"This isn't working for me."

Lex scoffs. "What are you doing? Breaking up with us?"

"I'm saying I need space. If you can't understand that I have grown and changed for the better and all I need is your support, then this friendship isn't what I need."

"You're serious? After all these years? You get a new boyfriend and new friends and just drop us?" Bridget demands, hands on her hips.

"I'm not dropping you. I'm telling you what I need. If you can't give it to me, then maybe this is where our lives diverge. No matter what, I will always wish the absolute best for both of you, and if you really need me, I'll always be around. Take care of yourselves." I look up at Trevor. "Ready?"

He nods, pride shimmering in his eyes. Then he pulls out his wallet and puts down two fifties. "That should cover everything. Goodnight."

Of course. Of freaking course he'd do that. Because he's a good man. A damn good man.

He wraps his hand around mine as we walk for the door, and I give him the slightest pinch.

Forever my sweet, kind, protective, real-life book boyfriend.

We got back to my family's house to find a new gel mattress topper on the bed. Apparently, Trevor ordered it a few days ago.

Sigh. He's truly the swooniest guy ever.

As we lie in bed—far more comfortable tonight—he lazily strokes his fingers through my hair. "How are you feeling?"

I swallow and shrug. "Okay, I guess. Hearing them say all that again tonight was hard."

"You handled it really well. With dignity and grace. You should be proud of that."

"Thanks. And I am. But..." I bite my lip. "It all kind of hit me at once. They're right. I am different now. Not in a bad way, necessarily, but not so carefree. In some ways, I miss that girl. Sometimes I wish I could let loose and completely forget about everything I went through, but I can't. I miss that freedom sometimes—no matter how careless or naive it might've been."

He throws his leg over mine, using it to pull me closer as he tugs at a strand of my hair. "I think it's natural to grieve who you once were, but it's also important to remember the things that are more beautiful about who you are now. You are amazing. You inspire me with your strength. You awe me with your grace.

And you crack me open with your love. I love this version of you, and I'm so glad I get to be the one by your side."

Tears trickle down my cheeks.

"I love you."

"I love you too. In case that wasn't clear."

We share a gentle kiss, then I rest my head on his shoulder.

"What are you thinking about?" I whisper.

He sighs. "About what you did tonight. Setting boundaries. Being compassionate but firm. Wishing Hyla could do that. She *needs* to do that. I'm worried about how things will go with her parents."

I graze my knuckles over his cheek. "I know you are. But all you can do is stand by her and help where you can. She has to be internally ready to make those decisions. If she's not, they won't stick."

He kisses my forehead. "As usual, you're right."

"Duh."

We share another quick kiss.

"Night, baby."

"Goodnight."

His arms close around me, and that warm feeling of safety surrounds me.

Standing up for myself tonight was important, and it felt good. The weight is off me.

I hope Hyla can find the strength to do that too, if for no other reason than she deserves to let go of the mountains she's trying to carry.

Trevor

Life is unfair.

People are disgustingly cruel.

Hyla has been struggling. I've known that. But I didn't realize how bad things were until after that moment with Mackie at the Christmas party. Until she suddenly had a chaotic need to put everything on the line with her parents and essentially beg them to still love her. That's what happened tonight. It didn't go well.

Hyla's parents pulled out all the shitty stops, and while I'm not surprised by much with them anymore, they even surprised me with their manipulative bullshit. And then I had to watch it break Hyla. It took everything in my power—and the reminder that her father is a state senator—not to beat the shit out of her dad. Hell, not to scream at them about what vile, despicable humans they are.

I made my feelings clear in only a few words and then got Hyla out of their house.

But the damage has been done. And I don't know what to do now. We're back at Hyla's apartment. She doesn't want me to call my mom. I haven't even dared touch my phone because I don't want her to get angry. I'm her last lifeline, and I can't risk severing that when she's at the edge. But I can't stop questioning if I'm doing the right thing.

Maybe we should've gone to the mental health unit, but she said she wanted to go home.

I'm scared, and I have no idea how to help her, so I'm just staring at her, and that's all I'll be doing tonight, at least until she finally falls asleep too.

She's sitting numbly on her bed now, watching some sitcom rerun, and I don't know what else to do. I want to text Chelsea.

Want to call in a lifeline. But everything feels like the wrong decision now, and I'm panicking. But I don't want her to see that.

So I check to make sure she has water. Try to get her to eat something, even though she refuses. Then sit back down next to her, everything inside me screaming that I have to fix it, but I don't know how. Fuck, I have no idea how.

I should've done something more. I fucking failed her.

"Can you try to take a deep breath for me?" a paramedic says, but I'm looking past her, into the bathroom where I found Hyla on the floor, blood seeping from her wrists.

I don't say the words I want to. That I'm not important now, and they should be taking care of her. But my face must say it anyway.

The paramedic rests a hand on my arm. "They're taking good care of her. She was still breathing on her own. That's a good sign. Is there anything you need? A glass of water? Is there someone you can call?"

I already called my mom. I called 911 from Hyla's phone, then called my mom from mine afterward. She's on her way over, but at this point, it might be better for her to meet us at the hospital.

And... even if she got here, she's not the person who can make it better. Not better, but I need... I need Chelsea.

I look down at my phone, then back at the bathroom.

"Make the call," the paramedic says. "She's in good hands."

Good is relative, but I reluctantly step away, sink down onto Hyla's couch and dial Chelsea.

She answers on the first ring.

"Hey, baby. How was last night? I've been thinking of you, but didn't want to go crazy texting."

Fuck. How do I say this?

"Babe?" Her voice rises with concern, and the fragile threads holding me together threaten to snap.

"Chels..."

"What happened?"

"It went really bad. I stayed at Hyla's with her. Then this morning, I woke up to noise in the bathroom, and"—my voice breaks—"she slit her wrists. She's alive, but—"

"I'm on my way. When you know what hospital, tell me. I'll be there the second I can."

"Drive safe. Please, please drive safe."

Because I can't lose her. I can't. I fucking can't. It will destroy me.

"I will. I love you. This wasn't your fault."

It sure fucking feels like it was. Like I should've seen it coming, been able to stop it.

When I don't respond, her voice comes through loud and strong.

"It was not your fault. Don't take that on. Breathe. Take everything as it comes today, and I'll be there soon."

"I love you, baby."

"Do you want me to stay on the phone with you? Or call anyone else?"

"No. That's okay. Focus on driving. I... fuck, I should call someone. Maybe Mackenzie." Though the thought of telling her makes me want to vomit.

The paramedics come out of the bathroom with Hyla unconscious on a stretcher.

"I've got to go. I'll see you soon."

"Soon. Keep breathing."

"Do my best. Bye."

She hangs up, and I follow the paramedics out of the apartment. My mom is pulling up to the curb, which is good since they won't let me ride in the ambulance with Hyla.

I fucking hate that. But it's probably for the best. They don't need me glaring at them the whole way. Or having a panic attack from staring at her body. Wondering if she's going to die.

Mom pulls me into her arms, and I hold her tightly, fighting back my emotion. I know she's scared and pissed and probably wants to rip Hyla's parents' heads off.

The nagging *what if* in the back of my mind is ugly.

What if she dies?

She seems like she'll be okay—whatever the fuck okay is after all this—but what if I hadn't found her? What if it still wasn't fast enough? I'm not—I can't lose her. I call Hyla my sister because she is. She's my best friend. Aside from Chelsea, no one knows me like her. No one sees me like her. She came to our house as often as she could after my dad died, just to try to bring us light and joy and make us smile. We always did. Because that's Hy. Bringing joy to the world when her own is shattering.

I failed her.

When she needed me the most, I let her down, and I don't know how to forgive myself for that.

The rhythmic beep of hospital monitors threatens to drive me insane as I sit by Hyla's bed, waiting for her to wake up.

Mom's on the other side, intently reading something on her phone. Thankfully, Mom has taken over and made the executive decision to keep all of this from Hyla's parents. Which is doable since Hyla is twenty-one and on her own insurance.

Mom sighs and pinches the bridge of her nose.

"What's wrong?" I ask. Besides the obvious.

"I'm trying to figure out what her insurance will actually cover. Too many insurances pretend mental health isn't important. Clearly it fucking is."

She sets the phone to the side and lets out a shuddery breath.

"Mom," I whisper, reaching over the hospital bed for her hand.

She takes it, but it doesn't stop the tears from streaming down her cheeks.

"I should've done more to help her," she breathes. "All these years I stuck it out, putting up with all of her parents' bullshit just to be there for her, but I should've done more. I—"

"It wasn't your fault," I tell her, even as I feel the weight of that blame on my own shoulders.

Maybe I didn't get all my protectiveness from my dad. My mom is just more subtle about it.

There's a sharp breath and Mom and I pull apart and stand, both of us staring at the bed. My eyes are tired and itchy from crying, but I stare, refusing to blink until...

Hyla mutters something as her eyes slowly open.

She looks around in a haze, but I see the moment realization hits her all at once.

Then she's crying, and Mom leans forward, gently sweeping some hair off Hyla's face.

"Shh, baby. It's okay. You're here with us. You're here."

Hyla clamps a hand over her mouth as she sobs, but I can't move. I'm still standing here, staring at her.

All I manage is to whisper, "Don't fucking do that again."

"Trevor," Mom says, voice gentle but firm.

Probably not the best words, but I can't stop them.

"Don't ever fucking do that again!" I sink back into my chair as my emotions overwhelm me. I'm still so on edge that it happened and now it's mixing with relief. I can barely breathe.

But then I hear her crying too.

"I'm sorry. I'm so sorry. I'm so—"

I lunge forward and throw my arms around her, hugging her as tightly as I can. *She's still here.*

"I love you. Do you hear me? I fucking love you. Do not—do not ever do that again because I need you. I have lost enough. I've lost enough, and I cannot do this without you. I can't. I don't care what I have to do to get it through your thick skull that my life will be a much shittier place without you, so don't you fucking leave me. Do you understand?" My voice breaks. "Don't leave me."

"I won't. I promise I won't. I'm sorry. I fucked up. Everything is so broken. I need—I need help," she says into my shoulder. "I need so much help. I don't know where to go from here, but I need help because I can't do it alone."

Thank fuck.

I slowly stand and wipe my eyes as Mom sits down on the edge of the bed with fierce determination in her eyes.

"That's exactly what you're going to get."

The doctor is talking with Hyla and Mom, plans are being made, and Hyla seems better. Better than she was last night, at least.

But I'm not better.

I'm not okay.

I called Sarah as soon as we got to the hospital, and she rallied the troops. Nick got here first, but everyone else has been filing in. I've just finished explaining the gist of what happened—as best I can when I want to cry and throw up—when the elevator at the edge of the waiting room opens.

The first thing I see is her auburn hair, then Chelsea is pushing her way through our friends, and the dam inside me breaks. She throws her arms around me, and I bury my head in her neck, holding her tight, her body molding to mine. Everything inside me shatters as I melt into her. Finally, I have her in my arms. I'm safe. Like the world can't get me as long as I have her.

Somehow, she guides me over to one of the double chairs and pulls me onto it with her. She curls up against me, still holding me close.

"This has been the worst day of my life," I mutter.

All Chelsea does is run her fingers through my hair.

"I thought she was dead. I really thought—I should've taken her to the mental health unit last night, but I thought me being there would be enough. I was wrong. I—"

"Breathe," Chelsea whispers. "She's here. She's going to get the help she needs. And she's going to have a lot of support while she does." Chelsea looks around the room. "So will you."

"I don't need it."

"Of course you do."

"I just need you." I drop my head against her shoulder again, her hands soothingly rubbing my back or playing with my curls.

"You've got me. Always."

She moves closer, like she's trying to wrap herself around me, protect me.

There's no protecting anyone today.

Chelsea

When Trevor called me this morning, my heart nearly stopped. Then I jumped into action. I packed a bag so fast I realize now I forgot underwear, and ran out of my house in my slippers, shouting fragmented sentences at my dad, stepmom, and gran. Gran chased me out of the house and threw some money and a pair of sneakers in the back of my car before I drove off.

Trevor is rightfully a mess, but I don't think I've seen the worst of it yet. I can feel him holding it in. While he let out some of it when I first got here, I see him actively pushing it all down. As usual, he's trying to hold it together for his mom and for Hyla. Though he did tell me he broke down a little with her, I'm guessing he was still restrained.

I finally got him to eat a little something. Now he's with his mom, talking with Rae's grandparents, who brought some food. I take the opportunity to sneak down to Hyla's room. I saw her briefly earlier when I went in with Trevor and Liz, but a doctor came in so quickly we didn't have time to talk.

Rae and Aaron are leaving her room when I get there.

"Is she awake?"

Rae nods. "Yep. I was just going to find someone else to keep her company. She needs that."

So I'd assume.

I've never dealt with anything like this before. Somehow, I made it through middle and high school without any of my friends attempting suicide. I remember hearing about a couple of kids at school who had, but I didn't know them, so even though it was sad, there was no personal connection.

When I push the door open, I'm greeted with more light than I was expecting. Gray, late afternoon, winter light streams into the room, mixing with the bright white hospital lights. Every single one in the room is on.

"Hi," I say when I get around the curtain.

Hyla looks at me with big eyes. "Hi."

I'm not familiar with someone attempting suicide, but I'm familiar with feeling lost in the darkness. I know what I needed when I was struggling, even if I didn't recognize it at the time. Someone to crawl into the darkness and sit there with me. So, I make my way over to her bed and sit down beside her, resting my head against hers.

"I love you."

She sniffs and takes my hand. "I love you too. I'm—"

"Don't. Do not apologize to me. The darkness has a way of whispering things that we somehow believe as the truth. Don't let the darkness win."

"I'm ready to fight," she whispers, wiping away tears.

"Good. Because you've got an army at your back."

She turns her head, and I meet her gaze. I see the strength in her eyes along with the broken shards that got her here.

"I was worried you might hate me."

"What?" A surprised laugh slips out. "Why would I hate you?"

"Because I hurt Trevor. And I'd hate anyone who hurt him."

I arch a brow. "Do you hate Sarah?"

"Of course not."

"But she hurt him once."

"She wasn't trying to."

I look right into her eyes as I speak. "Neither were you."

Her lips tremble for a second, then she sucks in a deep breath, a ghost of a smile appearing. "I'm so glad you're going to be my sister-in-law one day."

That gets an actual laugh out of me. "You're confident."

"Confident in the love I see between you two. For the record, I saw him with Sarah. What you two have is different. It's stronger. It's more. He adores you. And I'm taking partial credit because I've been manifesting this ever since he first told me about you."

I eye her suspiciously. "Which was when?"

"The morning after you met... and freaked out."

I run a hand down my face. "And you were rooting for us based on that?"

"I could hear it in his voice. It's like he already knew what you were going to mean to him."

I slowly shake my head, but I can't deny I felt it too.

The door swings open, then Liz strolls in, a bright smile gracing her face when she sees us.

"There are my girls."

Something inside me cracks when she says that. That she thinks of me as a daughter. Crap. Tears well in my eyes and Hyla laughs.

"Yeah, she's good at getting that reaction."

"I'm sorry my love makes people cry," Liz says playfully.

As much as I loved being raised with Gran as my maternal role model, I find myself wondering what it would've been like to be raised by Liz. She's strong, fierce, deeply loving, but also so vibrant and playful.

"Well, if it isn't my favorite girls," Trevor says, strolling into the room. He's got that casual calm mask on. There's even a hint of playfulness there, but I know beneath it all, there's a storm brewing.

"Suck up," Liz teases.

Trevor kisses my forehead, then Hyla's.

Then he gives Liz his sweetest smile.

He sits down in the chair beside the bed and an unimportant conversation picks up, but as I sit here, Trevor's knee brushing my leg and Hyla's hand wrapped around mine, it hits me that this is my family. A new one. One I wasn't expecting to have, but one I love nonetheless.

I'm grateful I can be here, not just for Trevor or Hyla or Liz individually, but as a whole. To be their support and walk through this with them.

I'm so thankful Trevor found me, that I didn't push him away, and we ended up here.

I'm glad Hyla was manifesting it.

But I think fate was manifesting it for longer.

It's close to 7:00 p.m. when we finally leave the hospital. Liz is staying with Hyla overnight, so it's just Trevor and me, and the second we walk out the doors and into the brisk cold of mid-January, the mask he was wearing slips off, and he looks like he did when I first got to the hospital. Empty. Broken. Numb.

Twining my fingers with his, I lead him down the street to my car, then drive us back to his house. He's silent the whole way. We get back to the house, and while he takes a shower, I make ramen noodles. Everything is steeped in silence.

It's not until he climbs into bed with me that he finally lets go.

His chest shudders with a sob, and I curl my body around his, holding him tightly, letting him cry like he did at the hospital. Except this is worse. The noise he makes with every gut-wrenching sob tears my heart apart. I wish I could take his pain. He's holding on to too much.

I stroke my hand over his cheek, fingertips brushing his soft curls.

"I failed her," he chokes out. "I shouldn't have tried to handle it alone. I should've—should've—"

"You did the best you could."

"It wasn't enough. It's never enough. I should've protected her. Shouldn't have let things go as far as they did with her parents."

"It's not your fault," I say firmly. "She's where she needs to be to get help now."

He shakes his head. "All I can think about is those horror stories of people killing themselves inside the mental health units. What if she just put on that happy face? What if—" He coughs on a sob, and I hold him tighter. I don't know what else to do.

"We both saw her before we left. There was genuine light in her eyes. Plus, your mom is there. I know it's scary, but she's safe. It will take time to heal, but she will."

"But I could have lost her. I thought I did. I thought she was dead. And now, every time I close my eyes, all I can see is her lying on the floor, bleeding. I can't lose her. I can't lose anything—anyone—else."

He lost his dad. He lost his ability to play baseball. And as I've slowly begun to realize, when he had that accident, he lost parts of his humor and his happiness. He's damn good at making it look like he's fine, but he's not. I'm the only one he shows that to.

I lace my fingers through his curls, tugging at them, playing with them. Anything to comfort him.

"At least my mom didn't have to see it. Didn't have to see her like that. I'd do it all over again as long as my mom wouldn't have to. She's lost more than me."

She lost her husband and the father of her child along with any future she thought they'd have. But still, I think Liz would say the same of Trevor. She would've taken it on, so he didn't have to.

"I know you would, but you don't have to martyr yourself to take care of everyone else. You deserve that protection and safety too. Stop trying to face the world alone."

"I'm not alone."

His swollen eyes find mine.

"No, you're not." I kiss his forehead. "Never."

He buries his face in my neck again. "Please don't leave me. Don't ever leave me."

Tears stream down my face as I kiss his head. "I'm not going anywhere. I'm yours and you're mine. I'm here."

He nods against my chest, arms still wrapped tightly around me.

"I love you," I whisper into his hair.

He's quiet, then the last words I hear him say before his sobs subside and he drifts off to sleep are, "I love you too."

Trevor

I wake up with a headache from hell and my body aching like I got hit by a bus.

I stretch and sit up, finding the bed next to me empty. On my bedside table is a glass of water, ibuprofen, and a note.

Take the ibuprofen. Drink ALL that water.
Then come downstairs and find me.
-Chels

No surprise, my amazing girl is taking care of me.

Letting my guard down and my vulnerability out so she can care for me was hard, but I'm so glad I did it. So glad I let myself have that safe space.

I needed it last night. I'm going to continue needing it.

Running a hand through my hair, I grab the water, then the meds. I swallow them down, then chug the whole glass.

I hit some kind of bottom yesterday. Whether it was when I saw Hyla on her bathroom floor, at the hospital, or once I was in bed with Chelsea last night, I'm not sure. But it happened. The last time I felt that emotionally fucked up?

After my dad died. I was close after my accident, but I had so much physical healing to do that I set my focus on that. Which might have done me a disservice in the long run.

I love that I can rely on Chelsea—that she'll hold me while I break. But the way I broke down twice yesterday—or even a couple of months ago on the anniversary of my dad's death—was extreme. And maybe a sign that I need to take care of my mental health.

Hyla didn't. I don't ever want to end up feeling that hopeless or broken.

With a deep breath, I climb out of bed and grab my phone. There's a text from my mom that reads: *Starting the next step off the right way.* There's also a picture of her and Hyla drinking coffee from a local coffee place and eating cinnamon rolls. Of course. That's Rae and Sarah's mom's specialty. I bet they delivered them early this morning.

I blink at the clock, which tells me it's past ten, which seems impossible, but a good night's sleep was also needed.

I stretch my back, rubbing at my sore muscles, then head downstairs, where I find Chelsea in the kitchen, cooking.

"Hi." My voice comes out like I've smoked a pack a day for the last forty years.

She spins and smiles, a spatula in her hand. "Morning, babe."

I stroll over and wrap my arms around her waist. "Pancakes?"

"It seemed like a pancake morning. I've made blueberry, chocolate chip, some with extra vanilla and sprinkles, and classic ones."

"Comfort food."

"The best kind." She turns her head slightly, brushing her lips over mine. Then she flips both pancakes on the griddle in front of her, sets the spatula down and spins in my arms. "How are you doing?"

I hold her close, breathing in her sugary, coconut scent. "A little better."

"You seem it. A little less weight on you, at least."

"I think I need to go to therapy."

Her brows lift and she smiles softly. "Yeah?"

"There's a lot I haven't processed. And maybe trying to take on the world doesn't help with that."

She shakes her head. "Not so much. It's okay to have trauma, but it's better when you work through it. I told Hyla yesterday not to let the darkness win. We shouldn't either. I keep up on therapy because it helps me with that. If it's something you're ready to do, I think it'll help you too. Just make sure you're doing it for you, not for anyone else."

"It's for me. I want to feel better. You say my grumpiness is all an act, but it's not always. Not inside, at least. Sometimes I feel like Eeyore on the inside."

She runs her hand over my cheek. "You are kind of like Eeyore sometimes. That's fine. I can be your silly Winnie the Pooh and make you smile."

"I don't think Eeyore and Winnie the Pooh were sexually involved."

She laughs, big and beautiful. "I'm sure there's a fanfic for that."

"Two cartoon characters having sex?"

She pats my cheek. "Oh, my sweet summer child."

"I take it back. Those are the people who need therapy."

"Hey, bookish rules here. We don't yuck someone else's yum."

"This conversation has taken a turn."

She shrugs. "Add it to things to unpack in therapy."

In a quick motion, she balances both pancakes on her spatula, opens the oven door, and sticks them inside, then turns the burners off.

"I found maple syrup, chocolate syrup, jam, whipped cream, and Rainbow Chip frosting. Think that's enough pancake fixings?"

"I think that's enough for a sugar coma."

"You need lots of sugary sweet energy for today. I'm going to drop you off at the hospital, then head home to grab some more clothes. Currently not wearing underwear because I forgot to pack some—"

"Not a problem for me." I wiggle my brows at her, feeling lighter and a little more like myself.

"You're trouble."

"Always." I lift her onto the counter and step between her legs. "I love you, and I'm insanely grateful to have you. You're the reason I got through yesterday. Thank you for being here."

"There's nowhere else I'd be. You must know that by now. I'm kind of obsessed with you, book boyfriend."

Even though it's our running joke, I'm too lost in gratitude to laugh. Instead, I lean in closer, capturing her lips in a raw, passionate kiss. Not one meant to lead anywhere, but to show her the depth of my feelings—my gratitude and love for her.

And as she kisses me back, fingers curling in my hair, a sense of home sweeps over me. Not because of this house, but because of her. I lose myself in kissing her and my shoulders relax. Everything tight inside me eases, and for this moment at least, I let myself believe everything will be okay.

<h1 style="text-align:center">18
Need You to Hold Me</h1>

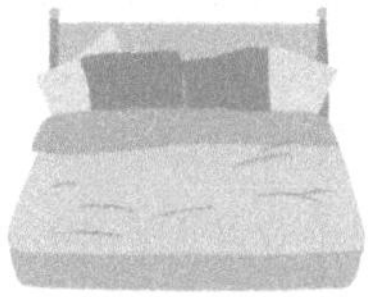

Chelsea

THINGS ARE LOOKING BRIGHTER.

If I have a one-word mantra for this year, it's gratitude.

After everything that happened over winter break, it's the key thing I want to focus on. Gratitude for where I am, how far I've come, for Trevor and my friends, that Hyla's doing better. Thank God, she's doing better and getting healthier by the day.

She's living with Liz now and getting the help she needs. I swear, the other night on the phone, I heard her genuine laugh for the first time. I didn't realize how good she was at putting on that happy mask until she finally stripped it off. For two people who aren't biologically related, she and Trevor sure have a lot in common.

He's also starting therapy this week, and I hope it'll be good for him. I want him to be the best version of himself. He deserves that. And he deserves to let go of the weight of the world that he's constantly trying to shoulder. He deserves peace.

Which I've been surprised to find has settled over me despite all the craziness over break.

Bridget and Lex haven't reached out—not that I'm expecting them to—and I'm okay with that. Having the courage to finally speak my truth came with an overwhelming sense of freedom. I don't have to cling to those relationships because of what we once had. I can still love my memories with them, while acknowledging they might not be an active part of my future. That's okay. I'll always care for them and silently cheer them on from a distance.

I glance across the room at Rae and make my way over to her. We're hosting the Promise support group meeting on campus tonight.

"Good turnout," she whispers.

"It is," I agree. "I love it, and I hate it."

"I know. I hate that so many women have endured anything like this, but I love that they feel safe enough to come here."

"Agreed."

It's a complicated feeling, but one I embrace. It sucks that we've all been through it, but it's what we do now that matters, and supporting each other as we heal is big.

Rae kicks off the meeting and we both introduce ourselves. As usual, we don't force anyone to talk. We simply open the floor to anyone who wants to tell their story or discuss something.

A few people who are new give a little information about themselves, meanwhile I make it a point to look around the room at who isn't talking. Who's the most withdrawn or looks in need of the most help. Many of the women I recognize—it's one of the things I love, the community of support we're building—but a few I don't. Then one girl catches my eye. She's got her hood pulled up and isn't making eye contact with anyone. I make a mental note to check in with her later.

One of the women who has been coming to the Promise support groups since at least the first one I attended back in September holds up her hand when there's a lull. Rae nods to her to go ahead.

"I wanted to talk and maybe ask advice about... having sex again. I haven't since... and I don't know. I guess I'm wondering what anyone else's experiences have been, if they'd be willing to share."

The tiniest bit of pink splashes across my cheeks and I force a breath, trying to keep my breathing even. I don't want it to be obvious how intently I'm listening. Hoping for an answer. Because it's been on my mind too. I *want* to have sex with Trevor. I've known that for weeks now. But I chicken out every time I try to bring it up because thoughts of that night infiltrate my mind, and I don't want any of that mixed in with Trevor.

Rae starts by sharing her story, how she took it in stages and it helped for her that it was someone she trusted, but she also acknowledged that she wasn't raped, so it's very different.

One girl speaks up saying she forced herself to have sex within a few weeks. She cried and even threw up after the first few times, but she did it because it was her way of taking control back.

Another says she still isn't ready, but that's partially because in healing, she learned a lot about herself and has discovered she's demisexual—which in the loosest terms means she needs to establish a strong emotional connection before sexual attraction forms.

A third woman, who Rae says has been going to the support group at Promise for almost two years now and also volunteers as a peer counselor, talks next.

"I tried a lot of things. Meaningful sex. Meaningless sex. It wasn't until I got together with my now-fiancé that I started enjoying sex again. He made it really safe for me. That's going to be key with anyone. You have to feel completely safe. After that, it'll really depend on you. Go slow. Try different things." She huffs out a breath. "What I'm about to say won't work for everyone, but it worked—still works—for me. My fiancé taking charge and being dominant helped me a lot. It took my mind off things. We don't do the Dom/sub thing, but there can be kinks within the BDSM realm that may be healing for some. I'm actually doing my thesis on some of this stuff right now. Sex and sexuality are not one size fits all. The absolute best advice I can give is to focus on reconnecting with your body and figuring out your desires first, and then exploring them. You can do that through research, with a partner, reading romance books... however it feels right to you. The more you understand your own needs, the easier you can find what you enjoy."

Wow. That was a lot. And also very useful.

Rae thanks her and someone else starts talking, but I'm replaying what she said. About her fiancé being dominant and it taking her mind off things. That might be exactly what I need. Trevor talking dirty to me always helps get me out of my head. Maybe the more immersive sex is, the easier it'll be for me.

I need to talk to Trevor about it. My stomach both lightens and knots at the thought. At least I've already done some of the work of reconnecting with my body, and I know without a doubt I'm completely safe with Trevor and can explore this with him.

The topic of conversation shifts and we continue on until everyone who wants to talk has a chance, then we disband and people can grab refreshments—cookies and brownies that Rae and I had a blast making before this—talk amongst themselves, or head out.

As I'm walking toward the refreshments table, I spot the girl in the hoodie, and surprisingly, she makes eye contact with me and aims for me.

"Hi," she says quickly. She doesn't look as withdrawn as she did earlier, and her expression is calm.

"Hi, I'm Chelsea. Did you want to talk? Can I help you with something?"

"I'm Maura, and I hope so. I was nervous coming here tonight, but not for the reason you're probably thinking. I haven't been through anything like this. That's why I probably looked uncomfortable earlier. I felt like a fraud. But I wanted to check this out because I think... I don't know for sure, but I think one of my friends may have been sexually assaulted or raped. I don't know the right words. I don't even know for sure, but... I want to help her."

Melt my freaking heart.

That is real friendship.

And it hits me so hard I have to bite the inside of my cheek to keep from crying.

"First, I just want to say your friend is really lucky to have you. I know because I would've killed to have a friend like that when I was struggling. Second, is there something specific that makes you concerned?"

"She went to a party with a few friends from one of her classes. I usually go with her even though parties aren't really my scene, but I had a paper due the next day that I'd slacked on. When it hit midnight and I hadn't heard from her or seen her, I started texting her, but she didn't respond and I stupidly forgot to ask where the party was. She didn't get home until almost five in the morning, and when she walked through the door, she looked broken. When I asked if she was okay, she laid down next to me and cried. Then she refused to say anything about it. She's trying to pretend she's okay, but I can tell she isn't. Should I just ask her?"

"You might need to. But let me grab Rae. She kept it all to herself for much longer than I did, so it might be more helpful to get her thoughts."

Maura nods.

I get Rae's attention and after talking with Maura for a bit, we both agree she should create a safe space for her friend and gently ask her without being pushy. Maura leaves looking relieved and I let out a heavy breath.

"I wish I'd had a friend like that."

Rae gives me a soft smile and squeezes my hand. "You do now. It's not the same, but if you're ever struggling with anything, all it'll take is a text and we'll all be there for you."

I squeeze her hand back. "Back at you."

My life hasn't gone like I planned it would, but *gratitude.*

I'm unbelievably grateful for how far I've come and the direction my life is headed in now.

Trevor

Life never stops moving.

It feels both like mere days ago and another lifetime ago since Chelsea swayed into my life like a russet-haired goddess and stole my heart in one glance.

It feels like hours since I saw Hyla lying on that bathroom floor, but also like somehow months have passed. Especially when I talk to her. Her healing is evident in everything from her voice, to the weight she's slowly gaining back, to the brightness that has returned to her eyes.

And now I'm on the track to healing more too.

I shouldn't have let my mental health slip for so long. But the protective coping mechanisms I used started seeming too real, even to me.

My first meeting with my therapist earlier today proved that. Aaron recommended checking into the college counseling center as they usually have availability sooner than some private practices around here. There was a new therapist who just started this month. She's around my mom's age, and from her profile was neutral, kind, and not too pushy. At first I thought I'd want a male therapist, but the more I thought about it, the more I knew getting any kind of dad energy from one would mess with me more.

I made the right choice. My therapist—Colleen—was great at letting me talk but also helping to suss out my problem areas. In case it was unclear that I try to handle all my burdens alone and haven't dealt with some of my past trauma. She also reframed my dad's loss and pointed out that even though I went to therapy shortly after he died, that only helped me work through what losing my dad meant back then, not what losing him means to me now as a grown man. A mostly grown man. I still feel like a child some days, and I'm starting to think no one ever completely stops feeling that way. Which is why she encouraged me to tell my mom how I've held back, and make it a point to ask for her support. I'm still hesitant to do that—tell her how I've held back—because I don't want her to think she did anything to cause that. But I will try harder to move past that protector mode and ask for more support from her.

I'm not expecting it to be easy, but I don't think therapy is supposed to be easy or everyone would be doing it.

Although, a good chunk of my friends are doing it and I didn't realize it. Apparently, therapy is good for you or something. Who knew?

It was a good session, and it left me feeling a little lighter, which I think means I'm heading in the right direction.

For the moment, I'm in the exact right place. The feeling of weight slipping away continues the second I set foot on the baseball field. The ground is frozen, and it's cold as shit, but there's no snow, so here we are, having our first practice outside. There's nowhere I'd rather be.

A guy I don't recognize but who also looks strangely familiar sets a few bags of gear near home plate as Aaron, Joel, Miles, and first baseman, Ricky, wander over.

"Who's that?" I ask Aaron, but Ricky is the one who answers.

"He's our ball bitch."

I throw my hand out. "Ball bitch? Really? You're going to use that term?"

"Don't mind him. He considers it a fun little inside joke between us. Don't you, Dick?"

Ricky rolls his eyes, but the guy ignores him and looks at me.

"You must be the new volunteer coach. I'm Kyle Mielewczyk." He sticks out his hand.

I shake it as I say, "Ah, Coach M's son."

His brows pinch together. "My second favorite name after 'ball bitch.'"

"Sorry. Trevor Matteny, but if you prefer to call me an asshole, that's fine, too."

He laughs and waves a hand. "You're fine. Certainly nowhere near the biggest asshole on the team!" he calls over his shoulder at Ricky.

I walk with him toward the dugout as Ricky grumbles in the background.

"Things okay there? I can make him run extra laps for being a pain in the ass if you want—I'm sure your dad would too, but I wouldn't make it look like favoritism. I learned from my high school coach that if you act like an asshole, you'll pay for it."

Kyle laughs but shakes his head. "No. It's harmless. We have some classes together. He's a pain in the ass but we're friends ish."

"Got it."

We grab a couple of bags from the dugout.

"So, what's your story? How'd you end up coaching?"

"Bounced my snowboard off a few trees and ended my chance at pro ball, but I'm becoming more okay with that. I'm remembering how much I love the sport even when I'm not playing. What about you?"

"I grew up loving the game without a shred of talent for it. I have horrible hand-eye coordination thanks to my mom, and by middle school I gave it up. But I like being a part of the game and spending time with my dad."

"But you don't help coach?"

He snorts. "I do a bit of everything. Whatever Dad wants me to help with. Since I understand the mechanics of the game, I'm good at sussing out problems, and Dad knows if I help out with that now, he'll hear less of it from the booth during games."

I perk up at that. "The booth?"

"Yeah. I'm the commentator for all home games."

"That's awesome. I had a chance to do a bit of that—"

"Ah at the game against the Metros."

"You know about that?"

"I was invited, but I was doing a semester abroad. I'm jealous I missed that, though I saw plenty of videos." He tilts his head and takes me in. "I've considered having a co-commentator before, but no one met my high standards of loving this game as much as I do. If you're interested, we could try it out."

"Fuck yeah, man. I'd love that."

"Cool. I'll grab your number from Dad and get you some details. Just so you know, one requirement is calling out dumb shit the players do, even our own team. You going to be okay with doing that to your friends?"

All I can do is laugh. "Trust me. I'll be fine. Hey, by the way, don't mention this to them. I'd rather let them be surprised."

He nods in understanding. "You're a shit-stirrer. Got it. We're going to get along fine."

He heads back toward the dugout as I aim for Coach M and Aaron, even more excited about the upcoming season than I was before.

I blow my whistle as the younger group of players fails yet again to nail a double play they had more than enough time to complete.

"Sanderson, Thorn, Sterling," I call out the first, second, and third basemen.

They trot over.

"Sorry, Coach," Thorn says immediately.

"I don't want apologies. I don't care about that. What I care about is fixing problems. You three need to spend extra time working on agility. You have the power in your throws and the chemistry as a unit, but your agility is holding you back. Sterling, you have to be faster getting the ball in your glove and then over to Thorn. Thorn, you need quicker turnaround time. Sanderson, you have to work on stretching and balance so you can extend farther off the base. Your throws have great precision, now you need to fine-tune the time it takes you to get through the play. Baseball games can be won and lost in nuance like that. I'm going to add on some agility work for you during practice, but I want you working on it outside of that too. If you work on it together, you'll end up even more in sync."

They look at each other and nod.

"Thanks, Coach," Sterling says.

"I'll send emails with ideas for drills to run. Now get back out there."

They all run back to the field, and Aaron blows his whistle this time, setting them up to run another play.

Coach M comes to my side. "If I could afford to pay you, I would. That was a good call."

"Thanks, Coach."

He smacks my shoulder. "Don't ever doubt that you have what it takes to be a part of this game in some way for however long you want. You have a good eye and an understanding of the game that a lot of people would kill for. Remember that."

I give him a nod, but he doesn't let me respond before he blows his whistle and yells for the team to bring it in.

I'm cold as fuck and I can't feel my nose or my toes, but today has been even better than I was hoping it would be.

I'm still in a great mood when I get to Chelsea's apartment and go inside. I have a key now, because my girl likes it when I'm here waiting for her after a long day.

I love it too.

"Hey, baby," I call as I walk down the hall.

"How was your first day of practice?"

"It went great. I'm looking forward to the rest of the season. How are you?"

I smile as I walk into the bedroom and take her in. She's in leggings and a baggy sweater, and just setting her book on the bedside table.

Her eyes lift to mine, a bit of trouble dancing in them.

"I want to have sex."

My bag hits the floor with a thud, and I blink a few times. "Right now?"

A slight laugh slips out. "Kind of?"

Walking over to the bed, I sit down next to her. "Talk to me."

"Okay, so, first of all, you should know I've been thinking about this for weeks, but chickening out every time I was going to talk to you about it. But at the Promise meeting on Tuesday night, a girl asked about having sex again and one of the answers she got was really helpful."

"What did she say?"

"Well, she mentioned making sure we're safe, which... obviously. I'm always safe with you."

My heart bursts at that, and I smile like an idiot. I love that it's second nature to her now. No wondering if she's safe with me.

"And I've been reconnecting with my body," she continues. "I feel confident in that. Then she mentioned something that worked for her... her partner being dominant. Whenever we talk dirty, it always relaxes me and keeps me in the moment, and I'm thinking if you take full control, maybe I'll be so focused on you that I won't think about anything else. If you're open to that."

I rub my jaw. I'm not against it. Dominant is my natural predisposition when it comes to sex. "I'm open to it. But I haven't been particularly dominant with you so far."

"I know. But I guess I see it as different. Like those things were my first sexual experiences, so taking control of them helped. But this is the way I was violated, and I'm worried that if I have to think about being in control, I'll get too lost in my own thoughts. I'd rather get lost in you."

I lean in and kiss her neck. "Good answer. Like I said, I'm open to trying."

She pulls back, dragging her teeth over her bottom lip. "Tonight? Wait."

"If you're changing your mind that quickly..."

She smacks my chest. "No. But there's something else we haven't talked about. Birth control."

"Ah. Right."

"So, I haven't been on the pill or anything in years because unfortunately, I always had bad luck with them. They made me sick or messed with my moods. My doctor said some people don't handle hormonal birth control well. I'm one of the unlucky ones. Which means we'll need to rely on condoms. I mean, there's like spermicidal lube and stuff like that—"

I cut her off with a kiss. "Condoms are fine. I can grab some—"

She throws open her bedside table drawer and pulls out a box. "I got some. They're supposed to feel really... natural."

Her cheeks tint pink in the most adorable way.

"You're very prepared."

She sighs. "I want to do this with you."

"I want to do this with you too. But I don't want it to feel forced or mechanical. That'll have you in your head more."

She tilts her head slightly, a wicked smile growing on those plush lips. "You better get me out of my head, then."

There's my girl. My wild, playful girl.

I stand up and hold out my hand. "Shower with me?"

"Yes, please."

I lead her into the bathroom, pausing to kiss her just inside the door. Then we take turns removing our clothes, watching each other. My fingers skim up her arms and she drags a finger down my chest.

Our shower is sensual as always. I wash and condition her hair, but then we take it a step further and wash each other's bodies, avoiding the most sensitive bits. I'm sporting a semi that morphs into a hard-on as I watch her towel off.

Anticipation coils in the air around us, and then we're kissing again, frantic this time. We ditch our towels and kiss our way down the hallway, hands roaming.

Every touch of her fingers to my skin is like a kiss of fire. A little burst of electricity.

Once we make it to the edge of the bed, I pull back, holding her face in my hands.

"You still want to do this?"

"Yes."

No hesitance, even if I see a flash of it in her eyes. But this is her call to make, so I follow her lead as she climbs onto the bed. I join her and then grab the box of condoms and some lube.

She reaches out and gives my cock a few hard strokes, making my brain misfire. All I can do is groan. And try not to come. If we do this, I want it to be phenomenal for her. She deserves that much. For it to wash away at least some of the uncomfortable feelings still burning deep inside her.

I slide the condom on and add a bit of lube, then turn to Chelsea, splayed out, auburn waves framing her flushed cheeks.

"Spread those legs for me, baby."

She does, and I nestle between her thighs, then lean down to kiss her.

"How are you doing?"

"Okay," she whispers.

Not the strongest vote of confidence, so I slip my hand between her legs and drag two fingers up her center, pausing to swirl them over her clit.

"Better," she breathes. "More of that."

I play with her pussy and her clit until she's nearly riding my hand, then pull back and line myself up at her center.

"What—what should I say if I want you to stop? Like do we need a safe word?"

I bring my face right over hers, brushing a whisper of a kiss to her lips. "If you want to stop, you say 'stop' or 'no.' I want you to know those words have meaning. If you say them, I'll listen and do whatever you ask."

Another bit of her uncertainty washes away, and I take that as a good sign.

Trying to keep her from getting lost in her head, I run my lips over her neck, kissing and sucking, while I tease her nipples with my fingers. When she relaxes even more, I move closer, then slide my hands down to her thighs, gripping them firmly as I move closer. Even through the condom, I can feel the heat of her.

My tip grazes her entrance, and I—

"Stop."

Chelsea's voice is almost painful, and I instantly pull back. Assessing her face and finding her ghost white, I leap off the bed and rip the condom off, then fumble to get my boxers on.

"It's okay. We won't do anything else tonight. At all. Until you're ready."

I grab her sleep shirt and hand it to her. She takes it, but doesn't make a move to put it on.

Fuck.

"I can go if you want."

That's the only thing that makes her move.

"No." She throws her arm out to me. "Don't leave."

I pull my sweats and a tee from my bag and put them on, then look at her, still lying there naked, holding the shirt.

In her drawer, I find a pair of soft, little boxer short things, and cautiously, I walk over to the bed and climb on beside her. When she doesn't move, I slowly lift one leg and slip the underwear over her foot, then do the same with the other before pulling them up, being mindful to keep my hands only on her outer thighs and hips. Then I pull the shirt over her head and help her put her arms in.

Not sure what else to do, I lie down beside her, keeping space between us, but gently resting my arm over her waist.

For a moment, she doesn't move, but then her body shudders with a sob.

My heart fucking shatters, and I'm about to get in my car, drive to Syracuse and hunt down every fucker with blond hair and hazel eyes until I find who did it.

But then she rolls over, throws her arm around my waist, and buries her face in my chest, and I know my only place is right here, holding her.

"Why is this still breaking me? I knew it was you. I knew I was safe. But all I saw was him. I was right back in that moment, barely aware of my surroundings, trying to scream and fight him off."

She sobs into my chest, and it takes real work to keep my rage contained.

Focus on her. What she needs.

"I don't think it's breaking you," I whisper. "I think this is the first time you've come anywhere near this line, and you made it really far without those thoughts creeping in. That shows how much you've healed. Tonight wasn't the right time, or the right way—or both. That's okay. There's no rush."

"But I want to be with you like this. I want to be with *you.* You make me feel safe and loved—incredible. I want to have that experience with you. Now I'm afraid he took that from me too."

"No," I growl. "He didn't take shit from us. We will get there, whether it's next week or next year. And whenever we do, it'll be that beautiful connection. But even without taking it any further, we worship each other's bodies and connect in a deep, intense way. When you feel ready, we'll refocus on that. If you feel ready to try this again, then we will. There's no timeline, just us. And we're pretty fucking spectacular together. So we're going to be fine. Own every single thing you're feeling. Feel it all. Process it how you need to. But don't *worry*. Especially not about us. Because we're going to be okay. We'll be amazing."

"I love you," she sniffs, not lifting her head.

I press a kiss to her head. "Love you too. Are you sure you're comfortable with me staying tonight?"

"Yes," she answers instantly. "I need you here. When your arms are around me, I'm safe. I need you to hold me and let me feel that all night."

"I'm all yours," I whisper, holding her tighter.

If this little bit of safety is all I can give her, I'll hold her forever if she wants.

19

CITYTTBABYATB

Chelsea

ME: GIVE ME A hint. Pleasssseeeee.
Book Boyfriend: You're relentless.
Me: And cute.
Trevor has been busy planning a whole special weekend for us to celebrate my birthday and Valentine's Day. But he won't tell me a thing about it and since I'm both nosy and excitable—and I like to rile him up sometimes—I won't stop bugging him about it.
Book Boyfriend: I will concede that point. And fine... here's the only clue you're getting.
Book Boyfriend: CITYTTBABYATB

I stop where I'm walking and blink at my phone. Did he really just send me an acronym? And is it a dirty one?

Me: You didn't give me a clue. You gave me homework!

Trevor: Good detectives know how to figure out a clue. Put your romance reading brain to good use.

Me: So is it dirty?

My heart beats a little harder. Trevor has that effect on me. With his words. His hands. His filthy mouth.

Thankfully, after trying and failing at having sex a couple of weeks ago, we eased right back into what we had been doing—basically everything else. The next morning as we laid in bed together, we kissed and held each other for more than an hour before we let our hands roam. Though it took a few minutes for me to push past that icky headspace, once I got there, I was fine. Better than fine. I was on fire for him, like usual.

While Trevor was right, and our physical connection is insane without sex, I still want that. I still crave it. I've spent time trying to work through more of my fears. I've talked about it with my therapist. And I want to try again. It needs to be different this time. Him taking control and going straight into dirty talk didn't work like I thought it would. I need to be gentler with myself, take it slower. I really believe I can do it, and I feel ready to try again. Maybe it can be my birthday present to myself. It's the only thing on my wishlist right now.

I look at the acronym again, trying to figure out what it could be.

Me: I see multiple As in there. Does it involve my ass? Because I'm not sure how I feel about that.

Book Boyfriend: Wow. You really took that to a place I wasn't expecting. It's not like I said I'd COTAEYPTYCOMF.

Me: Dirty! Also, I wasn't expecting you to know any of these acronyms except maybe STFUATTDLAGG.

Book Boyfriend: I didn't. But we've established you take control in the bedroom, so it wouldn't really make sense. Although you could tell me to STFUAETPLAGB.

Chelsea: I mean... you can consider that an open invitation.

Me: Right as I'm about to walk onto a baseball field with my friends? Mean. That's just mean.

Me: It'll be worth the wait? Especially when I'm splayed out on the bed for you later...

Book Boyfriend: I'll be at your apartment by 5.

Book Boyfriend: And for the record, with that first acronym, think less dirty. Take it back to our first date. See you tonight, baby.

Me: Have fun. Love you.

I put my phone away and continue my walk to class, going through the letters in my mind.

CITYTTBABYATB

Start at the beginning. C... C, I. Could I or can I? Can I what? Can I taste? Taste your... tits?

I laugh to myself as I get into the building. I know Trevor likes playing with my boobs, but enough to put it in an acronym? Wait, if it's related to our first date, that wouldn't make sense.

When I get to my classroom, I pull out my notebook and write out the letters again.

Can I? Can I take? Can I take your... teeth?

Okay, that's definitely not it.

I've only got a couple of days until our date. How am I going to freaking figure this out before then?

I look down at the paper again.

Can I teach? No.

Can I talk—ooh, tell. Can I tell you this... fuck I've got nothing.

What did we do on our first date?

We went to The Lake Shack.

Now I'm back to take.

Can I take you to the...

I have no idea.

When the professor appears at the front of the classroom, I reluctantly put my notebook aside. I can come back to it. Even though a part of me likes guessing. And maybe I want to let him surprise me.

He probably knew that and that's why he sent me that clue.

Damn, he's good.

"Yes. That'll be perfect. So we'll do the small booth and have a little area where people can sit and connect if it's something they've been through. And definitely a volunteer sign-up."

"I love that you're bringing this in. I know there will be some women there who would love to sign up to volunteer."

"Thanks, Nadine." I look up from the notebook in my lap and see Trevor walking down the hall and carrying a tray with food on it. "I've got to go, but I'll relay all that to Kristen."

"Sounds great. Talk soon. Oh, and happy birthday."

"Thanks. Bye."

I hang up, smiling, as Trevor walks into the room.

"Here I was going to wake you up to a fancy birthday breakfast, but no, you had to get up and work."

I give him my sweetest smile. "Not work. Planning for the women's festival. I had an idea to have a booth there for Promise, and Nadine was just getting back to me about it."

"I guess I can't complain too much. Especially when you're smiling like that. Even if it did mess with my plans to wake you up the fun way."

I arch a brow and sweep my hand over the spot next to me. "Should I lie back down? Pretend to be asleep? Then you can *wake me up*."

He lets out a long-suffering sigh, and I love that we've been together for enough time now that he can let out a long-suffering sigh because of me.

"I meant with breakfast, dirty girl." He leans in to kiss me as he sets the tray on my lap. "Happy birthday, baby."

"Thank you. I've been awake for less than a half hour and you're already spoiling me."

He kisses my neck as I reach for the small stack of pancakes layered with frosting. "And I'm only getting started."

"Mm. If you want me to get through breakfast, you better stop that."

He laughs and then has the audacity to stop. Rude. He grabs a slice of bacon from my plate and munches on it like he didn't start a raging fire between my legs.

The perturbed sigh I let out makes him laugh.

I frown in response. "Aren't you supposed to be spoiling me, not teasing me?"

"I can't do anything right today. Stop distracting you so you can eat, then start distracting you again?"

I give him a wicked smile. "I never said stop distracting me. I said *if* you wanted me to get through breakfast. If. You were the one who was very particular about breakfast, so I thought—"

My words die as his mouth slants over mine, kissing the sass right out of my mouth.

It's so much fun to tease him. Especially because it turns him on.

He drags his lips across my cheek and down my neck. "I promise you, I will give you anything you want, but it'll be a lot less messy if we eat first."

"Mm, fine. I guess I could agree to that."

"Good." He kisses my cheek, and we get back to eating, but one word is hanging in my mind. *Anything.*

"Did you mean it when you said you'd give me anything?"

Trevor was about to eat a bite of pancakes, but misses his mouth when I say that.

"Baby, what are you asking me?" He sets his fork down and turns to me.

"I want to try again. We'll do it differently. Go a lot slower. *A lot.* But I really want to. I've spent a lot of time thinking about it, and I'm ready to try again. With the mindset that it might not happen, but I'm being hopeful."

"If you really feel like you're ready, I will give you *anything.* Everything. Including that. And... okay, I don't want this to be weird, but one of your presents kind of relates."

He goes over to my dresser and pulls the three small boxes off it and brings them over, sliding the biggest of the three onto my lap. It's about the size of a hardcover book but much lighter. I'm a little confused, but I'm intrigued too.

When I pull off the paper and open the white box, I find something purple and silky staring back at me. I lift it out of the box and realize it's actually two things. Two... silk ties.

My eyes snap to him.

"Are these for tying someone up?"

He nods slowly. "I was thinking about how everything we did so far, you had control. Maybe extending that to sex would help. If you take control, you know everything that will happen because it'll all be your decision. Complete autonomy and no uncertainty. I figured what better way to do that than by tying my hands. You don't have to, but I read that sometimes..."

He keeps talking, but I don't hear the words anymore. His thoughtfulness knows no bounds, and he... he said he *read.* He's been doing research on this because, of course he has. My real-life book boyfriend. I slip my hand over his and give it the slightest pinch.

That stops his talking, then he looks down at his hand and smiles.

"Is that a yes?"

I throw my arms around him and kiss him. "I love you. And it's a definite yes. But this time, no forcing it. Whenever it feels right, we'll try."

He kisses me again. "Whenever it feels right."

I run my hands over the silky fabric again, my body flushing at the thought of tying him up. I've never had that level of control before. How sexy would he look splayed on the bed for me? A little chill rolls through me. Hopefully that means we're on the right track with this.

I set the box aside and look at the other two presents. "So, do I get to open the other two now?"

"Whatever the birthday girl wants. Just open the smallest one last."

I grab the medium-sized box, which is also lightweight, and tear off the wrapping paper to reveal a custom case for my Kindle. It's a pretty shade of deep pink with shimmery gold, silver, and white speckles. In the center are the words *well-behaved women seldom make history*. A quote—and the title of a book—by Laurel Thatcher Ulrich. It's become a popular badass feminist phrase.

"I love this. I can't wait to show it off by reading everywhere."

He laughs. "One of your favorite things to do."

Another soft kiss, then I pick up the small box and rip off the wrapping paper. When I pull the top off, I'm shocked to see a stunning yet delicate white gold bracelet with a beautiful charm in the center. I pick it up so I can get a closer a look.

"It's a phoenix," Trevor says. "Everybody always talks about a phoenix rising from the ashes, but that's just part of its symbolism. It can also be a symbol of renewal, hope, and transformation. All things I think of when I think about you. Your resilience is awe-inspiring, and I'm honored to be the person you share the deepest parts of yourself with. And the one who gets to celebrate your birthday with you."

I turn and brush my hand over his cheek. "This means so much to me. The way you see every version of me and always understand me... thank you. I want to show this off even more than the Kindle case."

We both laugh at that, then he helps me put the bracelet on.

"Perfect."

"Like you."

"Like us," I counter.

Our lips meet again, but only for a moment before we return to eating breakfast. I can't take my eyes off the phoenix charm. But I'm not the only one who's resilient. Who keeps rising.

I rest my hand over his. "How are you doing today? Is it strange celebrating my birthday when up until now you've always seen it as your dad's?"

Trevor gives me the sweetest smile and wraps a strand of my hair around his finger. "It feels good. Not just because therapy is really helpful in processing a lot of my feelings over losing my dad—what it means to me now—but also because this day never really felt sad. It was more of a day to honor him. Celebrating you and showing you how much I love you is the perfect way to honor him."

I make a strangled noise and reach for his hand.

"Do not pinch me again." My eyes flit to his, and he leans in closer. "I'd much rather you kiss me."

I set the tray aside and grab him by the shirt, pulling him to my lips.

I'm not going to argue with that.

Trevor

Spoiling Chelsea is my new favorite thing. She never really wants a lot, but seeing her eyes light up at a meaningful gift or experience is my new favorite high.

That's what I did all day yesterday, starting with the birthday breakfast in bed and the little presents I got her. Then I spent the rest of the day lying through my teeth, telling her we were just going to have a relaxing night in and order her favorite take out to continue her birthday celebration. That was until about an hour before we had to leave when I mentioned that I actually had some fancy dinner reservations.

Which was also a lie. There were reservations. For the party room at the amazing Mexican place downtown, where—with the help of Robbie and Amanda—there was a surprise party waiting for her with all our friends.

The sheer joy in her eyes was enough to undo me. We relaxed, ate so many tacos we could barely stand, and had the most delicious birthday cake I've ever eaten from the bakery in town. It had a frosting drawing of medusa on it that all the girls loved. The inside was filled with sprinkles and cake batter frosting. Which somehow tasted like Funfetti cake mix smells. Amazing.

We were so full and happy that we barely made it into bed before we passed out.

Today has been a Valentine's Day of fun, little dates, not unlike our first date. I haven't asked yet if Chelsea decoded that acronym, but we're headed for the stop that will reveal it all right now.

Chelsea smiles brightly as I find a parking spot near our destination. It's midafternoon now, and after this, we'll have a fancy meal, then head back to her place for the evening.

Chelsea smiles brightly when she sees where we're going. As soon as we get inside, she slowly spins around, then looks up at me with those dazzling eyes.

"Can I take you to the bookstore..."

"And buy you all the books?" I finish.

"Such a good acronym." She leans into me and brushes her lips over mine. "I hope you know what you're getting into."

"I'm prepared to leave with the entire romantasy section if necessary."

She just laughs and scampers over toward the romance section.

I swear I could live on that sound. Her happiness seeps into my bones and warms me to my core. If I could give her this happiness every second of every day, I would. She deserves all the joy in the world.

I tuck my hands in my pockets and follow her.

I'll do everything I can to keep that smile on her face for as long as possible.

We walk through the door of Chelsea's apartment, tension thick in the air around us.

All through our meal, we were touching. She'd slip her foot from her heels and run her toes up my leg. I'd brush my fingers over her hand, up her wrist, and trace the freckles on her arm. And then Chelsea interlaced her fingers with mine and left them like that while we ate dessert. They were the slightest touches, and yet they were powerful.

It's clear Chelsea feels the same because the second we've slipped off our coats and shoes, her arms are around my neck. Her lips find mine, hands roaming, untucking my shirt from my pants so she can get to the skin underneath. I curl my fingers into her hair, tugging her closer and deepening the kiss. She drags her fingernails down my back, then caresses the same spots with her fingertips, driving me wild. Every touch fans a flame of desire that stokes and grows inside me into burning desperation.

I back her up against the wall, and she hooks her leg around mine. Then I'm rocking into her, kissing her harder, then moving down her neck and sucking her tender skin into my mouth. A little gasp slips out, and she curls her fingers into my hair.

"Trevor..." And then she lets out a sultry little moan that takes me from ready to go, all the way to ready to fall to my knees and beg.

She catches my face with her hand and lifts my chin so she can see my eyes.

"I'm ready."

I scan her face. I always want to question it, but I've learned not to. She's in charge. It's always her choice, her decision, her in control.

"I'm yours. Be gentle with me."

She pecks my cheek. "Only if you're a good boy."

Then she wraps her hand around mine and drags me down the hall.

Usually, I try to put a mental block up and taper my excitement. Because I don't want my excitement—my goddamn need for her—to come off as pushy. But tonight, I'm staying in the moment. I think she might need that. To feel that desire from me. It might help her stay in this beautiful moment. One that's only meant for the two of us.

"Unzip my dress?" she breathes, slowly spinning for me.

I take my time, running my fingers over the fabric as she pulls her wild waves to the side.

My fingers brush the nape of her neck as I slowly pull the zipper down. Once I get to the bottom, I slip my hands inside her dress, caressing the soft curves of her stomach, then cupping and squeezing her full breasts. She drops her head back against my shoulder as I go for her nipples, but find pasties there instead.

"Can I help you take those off?"

"Please."

God, that *please* alone could destroy me.

I press a kiss to her neck. "I'll be right back."

The heat of her gaze is on me as I walk to the bathroom, undoing the buttons of my shirt along the way. I wet a washcloth with warm water, then head back down the hall, shrugging out of my shirt as I go.

When I walk into the bedroom again, I almost trip over my own feet.

She's lying on the bed in nothing but a barely-there thong and those fucking pasties.

A growl of desire slips out before I can stop myself, and I quickly shed all my clothes except my boxer-briefs, then climb onto the bed with her.

"I swear you get more gorgeous every day." Lying down next to her, I pepper kisses over her jaw and neck as I gently rub the warm washcloth over one of the pasties.

"I need those off," she whines.

"Working on it, gorgeous. Don't want to hurt your sweet nipples."

I get the first off, then shift on the bed, massaging the pastie on her other nipple while my mouth clamps over the now free one.

"Yes," she hisses. "More. I need more."

I suck, flick, and nip, and as the other pastie comes free, I tweak that nipple between my fingers.

"More." She arches and rolls her hips. "Take my thong off."

Again, I adjust my position, this time pausing to give my cock a quick stroke. Something to take the edge off. Then I slide the tiny scrap of fabric off her and slip my finger between her legs. The second I touch her wet center, she moans.

"Yes. I need you."

Fuck. I need her too.

I go back to sucking on her nipple while I work my hand between her legs, teasing her, swirling around her opening, and then stroking her swollen clit. Her long moan when I do that makes me hover there, playing with her clit as she writhes in pleasure under my touch.

It's a fucking ego trip to hear her moan like that and know it's my fingers, her desire for me, and the love between us that's creating it.

She shudders and grabs my hand.

"Stop. I'm too close." She swallows and meets my gaze as I lift my lips from her nipple. "Trev, get a condom."

Chelsea

This is the scary part, but holy fuck, I want it.

And the look of sheer desperation on Trevor's face says he wants it too.

He grabs a condom and sets it on the bed, then slips his boxers off and rolls onto his back, arms up.

"I'm all yours, baby."

With that, I grab the silk ties, anticipation whirling in me. I've never tied anyone up before. And while this is a very low-key version of it, I want to make sure it's enjoyable for him.

I take my time tying each wrist to a bedpost, making sure it's secure but not too tight.

Then I move to the end of the bed and admire my handiwork.

His muscular arms are splayed and tied. His chest rises and falls with heavy breaths. His cock is at full attention.

The cock that's going to be inside me very soon.

I want this.

And I refuse to let those other thoughts derail me again.

I'm here with Trevor. The sexy, book boyfriend of a man who takes care of me, protects me, shares his vulnerabilities with me, and lets me be his safe place while keeping me safe too.

So I focus on him, stroking him from root to tip, swirling the precum on his tip all over the head as I soak in the sound of his groans. Then I take the condom and tear the package open. Slowly, torturously, I roll it down his length.

"Fuck, baby."

A tremble rolls through me at that gravelly tone, and as I look at him, tied up and waiting for me, I can't hold back anymore. Running my hands up his thighs, I sit up on my knees, then crawl over his legs.

Then I move a little farther up, so I'm hovering right above him.

My body heats as the reality of it all sets in. And the memory of screaming and fighting—

"Baby, look at me."

Trevor's voice draws me back to the moment.

"Be here with me. Run your fingers through my hair. Focus on us. On our love. Nothing else can touch that. It's just us."

It's those words, that tether glowing brightly between us as it tugs my soul to his, that makes me sink down onto him, taking everything all at once.

He groans and flexes his hands like he's desperate to grab something, and I... can barely breathe. But in a good way. The best way. I'm choked up because it's him. Finally him.

His eyes roll over me, hazy and filled with lust, and I lift my hips, then slide down his length again.

Those intrusive thoughts try to creep in, but this time, the experience around me is so much louder, it drowns them out, and it's easy—*easy*—to get lost in Trevor. In us.

Every time I lift my hips and sink back down, he hits deeper, and it drives me crazy. I forgot how incredible it feels. The condom is more like a second skin, so tight to his cock I barely feel it. All I feel is his warmth coming through it. The heat born of pure lust and need.

That's when I let go and ride him, lost in the sensation of finally having him inside me. The connection that we've been building for months, deepening with every stroke. I want more. Need more. More of him. More of us.

"God, you look so good riding my cock, baby. No one has ever made me feel this good. And your beautiful body..." He moans. "You're perfect."

I was expecting more dirty talk, but I think I've broken him. Not that it's a bad thing. Trevor is always on. Always worrying, overthinking, or trying to process his trauma—usually more than one at a time. Getting him to truly relax is a challenge, and I've never seen him this free before. How utterly lost in pleasure he is makes me even hotter for him.

I'm determined to keep him in that place. And my focus on him keeps me there too. Gone are my fears and worries. There's only him. Only us.

My abs burn as I ride him, swirling my hips, changing up my pace, going tantalizingly slow until his abs tighten, or so fast he can barely breathe.

My body is on fire in the best way, and with every movement of my hips, my clit rubs against his pelvis. Again and again. Pressure and heat bloom inside me until I'm flying toward the edge.

That's when I reach up and undo the ties holding his hands.

"Baby?" he rasps.

"I need more. Grab my thighs. I want to feel you. Move with me."

"Anything you want," he groans. "Ah, fuck. Wrap your hand around my throat. Not tight enough to choke. Just enough to claim me. Own me. Use me."

So I do.

I wrap my hand around the side of his neck, my thumb brushing his throat.

"Perfect. So perfect."

I roll my hips again and again, gasping his name.

Like I was craving, his fingers dig into my thighs, and I know he's getting closer too. My eyes drop to his face again, and he's absolutely lost in a world of bliss. As I watch him, a chill rolls up my spine, and I transcend into a dominant goddess, taking what I want and letting myself be worshipped. I'm powerful and uninhibited as I ride him.

His muscles are tight, but his face is slack with pleasure.

"Fuck, baby. I'm so close."

I press my thumb tighter against his neck and whisper the words the guys in romance novels always say.

"Come for me."

"Eugh..."

"Don't you want to fill me up, show me who you belong to? Watch me fall apart for you while your cock pulses inside me?"

"Chels..." he gasps, his dark eyes hazy with lust. His fingers tighten on my thighs, and I'm so damn close. I move faster, desperate for the friction of his pelvis against my clit each time our bodies connect.

"You want it? Come. Right now."

"Fuck." It's a whimper and a moan as he comes apart for me. He clenches my thighs in his hands and bucks up into me, his pulsing cock filling me completely. But it's the unfiltered pleasure on his face that sends me over the edge.

Sparks burst inside me, igniting a flame deep within as I take everything he gives me and own my pleasure, reveling in it. Shame washes away, and there's a light in my chest shining through like rays of sunlight. I'm empowered and... free.

I ride him through every second of my high, not stopping until my muscles are shaking and I can't breathe. Then I collapse against him and his warm arms wrap around me.

That was everything I needed, and with it, one of the still broken pieces of me healed.

Shifting slightly, so we're lying side by side, I reach over and pull the condom off him, chucking it toward the trash can.

"Holy fuck," he groans, holding me close. "I've never had sex like that before. I've never been so lost in the experience before. I swear I saw God."

I bite back a laugh and nip at his ear. "So it was good for you?"

"Fucking amazing. I've never come that hard in my life. It's going to take me a week to get it up again."

"Is that a challenge?" I tease, running my hand over his stomach, just above his pelvis.

"Okay, maybe a day."

I graze my fingers up his chest, swirling them around his nipples as I suck on his neck.

He takes a sharp breath. "Okay, like an hour."

Satisfied, I lift my lips off his neck and smile wickedly.

A matching smile curves on his lips. "Why do I feel like I just opened Pandora's box?"

"Is that the new nickname for—"

He stops my words with a kiss. "That was amazing." Another kiss. "And I'll take more whenever you want to give it to me." One more kiss. "There will never be any pressure or expectation."

Pulling back, I meet his eyes. "The same goes for you, by the way. I want any sexual experiences to be fulfilling for both of us."

"Is this when I say I *filled*—"

Now it's me stealing the rest of his words with a kiss.

When I've kissed all the terrible dirty jokes away, I curl my body around his and rest my arm over his waist.

"Serious question... have you ever done that before? Not being tied up necessarily, but not being in control. Because it seemed like it worked for you."

"Honestly? I'm usually the bossy, more dominant one in bed. I never considered doing anything else because I enjoyed that, but what we just did?" He whistles. "It was more than me just enjoying myself. It got me out of my head. I don't know if you've noticed, but I tend to be overprotective sometimes and take my version of caretaking to new levels, to the point I forget about myself."

I feign shock. "You? Never."

"Letting go was a whole new high for me."

"Just like taking control at that level was for me."

"It's almost like we're perfect for each other."

"A perfect match," I breathe, twining my fingers with his.

"Perfect together."

Then he kisses me again, long and slow, and something restless inside me settles. With every piece of myself and my trust I hand over to him, the deeper our relationship grows.

We're so beautifully twined together now, I can't imagine anything untangling us.

376

20
Love of the Game

Trevor

"Fuck, baby. Yes. Just like that."

My head hits the headboard as I lean back, so turned on I can't fucking think. And that's the point.

My wrists are bound to the bed frame with those silky ties, and Chelsea is sitting on my lap, riding me, our sweaty bodies writhing together. There's nothing sexier than my girl riding me, her tits bouncing, and her long, sweaty hair framing her face.

I never thought I'd love being restrained or being out of control in the bedroom, but it turns out, I need it. I'd let her be even more controlling if she wanted to. Submitting to her takes all my stress away.

"Chels..." I groan, but then she stops. "Why?"

She leans over and grabs something from her drawer, then her lips are on mine. Still, she doesn't move, and I swear my cock is practically crying in desperation. He's definitely leaking. But then I hear the buzz of her vibrator, and then I feel the reverberations as she presses it to her clit.

She throws her head back and starts riding me again, and fuck, fuck, fuck... it's so good. Too good.

"Yes," she whines, riding me hard. I thrust into her, meeting her each time she sinks down on me.

I lean forward as much as I can and kiss her shoulder.

"I can feel your pussy tightening around me. You need to come, don't you?"

She shudders. "So badly."

"Keep working that vibrator over your sweet clit. I can't wait to feel you clench around me and milk me dry. I don't know if I can hold back. I might break the condom with how hard I'm going to come."

"Trev," she whines, then swirls her hips. "Yes, yes." She leans forward, her free hand curling into my hair as her forehead drops against mine.

Then her grip on my hair tightens, and she pulls as her body goes taut.

She cries out, and I watch her beautiful face as her pussy clenches around me in long, hard spasms.

"Fuck," I growl, eyes locked on her gorgeous face as I fill the condom, my fingers digging into my palms.

One of these times, I really might break the damn condom. I've never come so hard in my life as I have doing it with her.

And in the last month-and-a-half since we started having sex, we've *done it* a lot.

We're in the can't-keep-our-hands-off-each-other stage of our relationship.

It was a bumpy start for us, but it was worth it to be here now. Our relationship is easy. We rarely fight, and if we do, we usually playfully disarm each other and talk it through. It helps that we both really want to make our relationship strong, and we've both been through enough to not fuck around when it comes to communicating.

Things are good.

Which doesn't at all make the intrusive thoughts in the back of my mind say that all good things come to an end. But that's something for me to deal with at my next therapy appointment.

Chelsea unties my hands, and I wrap my arms around her.

Her mouth meets mine for lazy, sloppy kisses.

"I have to say, I'm loving this stage of our relationship."

I brush a kiss to her lips. "Me too. Seeing you wild and free... there's nothing hotter."

The alarm on my phone goes off, and I groan.

"Reality can suck it."

She laughs. "Don't act like you aren't excited for the game tonight. And I can't wait to hear you give the play-by-play."

"I'd be more excited if baseball didn't make me get out of bed with you."

"Sorry. You can't have your cake and eat it too."

"Or fuck it."

She laughs and climbs off me. "Come on. If you get up right now, I'll shower with you."

And just like that, I'm motivated to get my ass moving.

"Hey, Coach," I say with a knock on the door frame of his little office at the stadium.

"Matteny, you're here early."

"You asked me to be."

He smiles. "I did, but no one else is here yet."

"I know, but I wanted to talk to you about something too."

"Have a seat."

He gestures to one of the chairs in front of his desk, and I plop down.

"What can I help you with?" he asks.

"I'm applying for an internship at the Boys and Girls Club for the summer, and I was wondering if you'd write a reference for me. The internship is about helping to plan and implement their sports programs. It doesn't have to be long, but since I've worked so closely with you this year, I thought you'd have good insight."

"Absolutely. I'm happy to help. Send me an email with the details and I'll write one up. Actually, that reminds me... I spoke with the athletic director last week about you. You've done great work this year helping me, but I think you have more to give—and more to learn. Every year, the athletic director picks three interns to work with him. If you're interested, I can let his secretary know and she'll send a link to the application when it goes up next week."

"Wow. That sounds amazing. That would be great. Thanks, Coach."

"Of course. I'd be happy to write a reference for that one as well."

"I appreciate you helping me find a place with the team. It's helped me with moving forward."

"I'm happy to do it. Think you're ready for tonight?"

I swallow and nod. "Yeah. I'm not sure exactly how it'll feel—if I'll wish I was out there—but I'm excited to be a part of it in my own way."

"Good, because that brings me to the reason I wanted you here early." He nods behind me toward the door, and I turn to see Aaron, Miles, and Joel standing there.

"What's going on?" I ask, rising from my chair.

Coach does the same, a smirk on his face.

"We wanted to make sure you know you're an important part of our team," Coach says.

"The team goes beyond who's on the field. We all play a part in getting the players where they are, helping to build morale, and making the team what it is," Aaron says.

"We all know how much you love the game, but we've seen how you love this team too," Miles says.

"You've worked hard with a lot of the younger kids at practice, and being on the field with them, I've seen their improvement," Joel adds.

"So, this is for you." Coach hands me a box as the guys all smile at me.

I take it and pull the top off, revealing... a purple Finger Lakes Sea Dogs jersey.

"Thank you. This means a lot."

"Turn it over," Aaron says.

When I do, the air leaves my chest. I knew it wouldn't be my number. One of the guys on the team wears the number twelve. No, the number staring back at me is my dad's number. Six.

"How did you know?" I choke out.

"I asked Hyla," Aaron says.

Fuck. I really don't want to cry here, but it takes all my strength to keep the tears at bay.

"Thank you. All of you." My voice is rough, but it's the best I can do when I'm filled with so much emotion. "This means more than wearing my own number."

"Thought you might feel that way. We're glad to have you as a part of the team, kid."

As more guys filter into the locker room, Coach smiles, then walks out and yells, "Game in thirty. Get your asses moving!"

We all laugh, then I look over at the guys. "Thank you for including me in this."

"Hey, we've been on this roller coaster together for a long time. I have no idea what chaos you have up your sleeve today, but I'm glad you're still here with us," Joel says.

I glance at the time. "Speaking of which, I need to get out of here. But I'll see you all after the game." I pull the jersey over my head and smack Aaron on the shoulder. "Thank you all again. Kick ass out there."

Then I turn and head for the exit so I can meet Kyle in the booth.

I get there a few minutes early, but it's unlocked and set up already, so I set my water bottle down and get comfortable in one of the chairs. It's not fancy, but the view of the field from here is insane.

"Hey, man. Ready for this?" Kyle asks when he walks into the booth.

"I think so. I don't usually have a problem shutting up about baseball, so this should be fun."

Despite how big a part of my life baseball has been, I've never been in any kind of commentating booth. From up behind home plate, we have a view of the field I've never experienced before, and it has me itching with anticipation for the game to start.

"Remember, roast the other team harder than you roast ours, but don't be afraid to call out the guys when they do something dumb."

"Don't worry. I won't have any problems with that."

"The Finger Lakes Sea Dogs are fighting for the win, but Brockport is giving them a run for their money," Kyle says.

"It doesn't help that the Sea Dogs pitcher is starting to struggle on the mound."

"Between innings, the Sea Dogs sent Aaron Cooper to warm up," Kyle says. "This is his first game pitching in years. Trevor, what can we expect?"

I laugh confidently.

"You can expect a lesson on the skill and finesse of a pitcher. Look, I've been playing with him since I was old enough to hold a bat, and I can tell you, he knows his stuff. There's a reason he became a pitching coach at nineteen. And it wasn't desperation. He knows this game. He knows the mechanics of pitching. Hand injury or not, he has tremendous skill. Now that he's back at the top of his game, any batter going up against him should be worried. He still holds the state title for most shutouts ever pitched."

"Here's hoping we get to see him play soon."

I cover my mic and eye Kyle. "No shit."

He blows out a breath, as annoyed that they haven't pulled this pitcher as I am.

It's the top of the seventh, and this game has been way too tight. It makes for a lot more fun to call, but for the first game of the season, you want the team to get the W.

Rae is probably losing her shit over how badly this pitcher is doing *and* over worrying about Aaron. If anyone can turn this game around, it's him.

"With one on first and one out so far, this inning could go in any direction," Kyle says.

"First pitch now to Trent Adams of Brockport. Right down the center and it's... fouled off."

"Second pitch, and it's... high and outside."

"All this Brockport team needs is one good hit and it could change the outcome of this game," I say, the tension hitting me all the way up here.

"This is it," Kyle says. "Third pitch. Another fastball, and—it's a hit!"

"It's a grounder between first and second, but Wilkinson is there! He nabs the ball and sends to shortstop Brent Noyce covering second, and then over to Ricky Williams, who holds the bag, and it's a double play for the Sea Dogs to retire the side!"

"That's how we do it in Old Lake Town!" Kyle yells.

My heart is pounding with adrenaline, and something snaps into place for me. This might not be a career, but it's something I *know* I want to do in some capacity. This is as close to being in the game as I can get, living vicariously from my spot above the field, but it's more too. Because this takes it all back to my love of the game. It twines everything I know about the mechanics of baseball with my memories of watching the game with my dad. Doing this, I keep a little piece of him alive even more than I would if I were playing because his voice is in the back of my mind with every play I call.

Jesse texted me a couple of weeks ago with some information about the commentating gig for the Knights, and I'm willing to get on my knees and beg to make sure I get it.

"The tension is high here in the top of the ninth. The Sea Dogs are up by one, and Aaron Cooper has struck out the last two batters. If he can pull off one more strikeout, the Sea Dogs will start their season with a win."

My eyes are locked on Aaron as he gets ready to throw his first pitch to the next batter.

"He's got this."

"And he does. Strike one," Kyle says.

"Second pitch and it's... fouled off. Strike two. The crowd here is going wild, and I know we've got a group of Ida family here supporting our Ida Warriors alums. They want this win as much as the team does."

"Another foul," Kyle says, watching as Aaron throws the next pitch. "And another."

Aaron's shoulders tighten as frustration builds. I know how badly he wants this. But I've watched him do this hundreds of times. For a split second, he might not think he has this, but he does. Two more fouls, and he's ready to lose his shit.

"Aaron Cooper is looking more than a little stressed," Kyle says.

"Keep watching. If there's one thing he can do, it's tune everything out. He wants this win, which means he'll get it."

Kyle looks at me skeptically when there's another ball fouled off, but I see the change in Aaron's demeanor.

"Don't look at the number of fouls. Look at his stance. The determination in his eyes. And that brief communication with his catcher." Then his eyes drift over his shoulder, and I know without a doubt, he's looking at Rae. "He's about to win the damn game."

And just like that, the ball flies over the plate, staying right in the center of the box until the perfect moment when it drops.

"Oh my god. That's an immaculate two-seam fastball, leaving the hitter from Brockport almost falling over to hit it, but he can't! Strike three!"

"The Sea Dogs win," I say, eyes locked on the field, and for the briefest moment, Aaron's gaze flits up to the box before turning toward the stands, where Rae is running onto the field to get to him.

"First game down. What do you think?" Kyle asks. "In for a whole season of this?"

I give him my best cocky smile. "Put me down for next season too."

I've finally found what baseball looks like for me in the future.

"Hell of a game," I tell the guys when I get back to the locker room. I look at Joel. "That catch for the double play and you being a sneaky fucker stealing bases led to some fun commentary." Then my eyes go to Aaron. "And you were on fire. It was amazing to see, man."

"Thank you," Aaron says, humble as always.

"Sounds like you had a good time too," Miles says.

"I did. It was as close to being on the field as I could get."

"It kind of felt like you were," Joel says. "At least your sarcasm was there."

I give him a little shove. "Fuck off."

We laugh as they finish getting changed and Coach says a few words.

I walk out of the locker room with the team, and despite not playing tonight, I still feel the high of the game. That only increases when I see Chelsea waiting for me.

A year of playing at Syracuse, and I never had anyone waiting for me—besides occasionally my mom or Hyla. But never this. I never had someone I considered *mine* waiting for me.

Chelsea smiles so brightly it nearly knocks me over. Not that it's surprising. She knocked me on my ass the first day I met her, and I've never recovered.

She runs over and throws her arms around me, pressing a quick kiss to my lips. "You were amazing! I loved hearing your sexy voice all game." She lowers her voice. "Hopefully you're recovered from this afternoon, because I need more of you." Her teeth graze my ear lobe, and I almost moan.

But then she tilts her head and runs her hand over the jersey before looking around me to see the number on the back.

"Your dad's number?" she asks.

I nod. "Mine was taken, but—"

"This is even better, right?"

"It made me feel even more like he was here with me."

"He definitely was. I could feel it emanating from your voice. His spirit is part of your passion."

I sweep my hand through her hair, looking into her eyes, in awe of her.

I'll never stop being grateful for the way she sees and understands me. I wish I could've had this—had her—for so much longer. Maybe we weren't meant to find each other before now or maybe we missed out on the chances we were supposed to have, but whatever the case, I'm going to enjoy every moment I have her in my arms, hoping that's where she'll be for the foreseeable future.

Fuck, who am I kidding?

Chelsea Winters is my whole future, and I want her in my arms forever.

21
I Lived

Chelsea

BROWNIES ARE A FOOD of the gods.

Actually, screw the gods. They're a food of the goddesses.

And my current weakness as I stare down at the snack spread Rae and I just set out.

"Am I a terrible meeting hostess if I snag a brownie before the meeting starts?"

Rae grins at me. "If you are, then I am too. We made them. It's only right that we sample them. Quality testing." She lifts two off the plate and hands one to me, then she taps hers against mine. "Here's to us and how far we've both come this year."

"I'll eat to that."

We both finish our brownies in three bites or less—can't help it, Rae's recipe is so damn good—and look around the empty room.

"This time last year, I was still shrouded in darkness. I'd finally gotten out of bed, but I was angry and bitter. Looking back, it's hard to put into words how deeply I was hurting. How desperately I needed something like this."

"Going to my first support group changed everything for me. It helped me finally say the words out loud and tell my parents."

"I wish I would've found something like this during that time in my life, but the group wasn't what I needed most. It was more support. Friendship." My voice drops with the last word.

Unsurprisingly, Rae immediately wraps me in a hug. "I'm so glad I met you. I love my friends and my sister with all my heart, but you and I connect in a different way—and I don't just mean shared trauma. Your passion for helping people, uplifting women, and making your little corner of the world better inspires me. You know the first thing I thought when I saw you?"

"No. What?"

"That I had a total girl crush on you. Now I'm lucky enough to call you a friend, and I'm so grateful for that."

I bump my shoulder against hers. "Back at you."

"So, are you excited about the women's festival this weekend?"

I light up immediately. "I can't wait. I love that Promise has intertwined with it in a small way."

"Promise is a business built around supporting women. That's exactly why they should be there."

"I appreciate you all jumping on board and coming with me."

"Are you kidding? It sounds like it's going to be amazing. Possibly our most epic girls' night ever," Rae says with a laugh.

We'll both be working at the booth Promise will have at the festival for the morning on Saturday, then Amanda, Mackie, Sarah, and Hyla are meeting us, and we're going to spend the rest of the day exploring and having fun. After helping Nadine and the other wonderful women I met along the way plan this, I'm ridiculously excited to see how it all comes together.

More people wander in, so we focus on our meeting hosting duties. Like always, we introduce ourselves and then hand the floor over to whoever wants to talk. A few minutes into the meeting, I notice the girl in the hoodie from a couple of months ago—Maura—walk in with another girl, and my heart warms. It sucks that she was right and her friend went through something that would bring her here, but she's an incredible friend for showing up and now bringing her here.

After the meeting is finished, I end up in a conversation about the women's festival, which has been getting some great buzz. I'm looking forward to seeing what kind of turnout there ends up being.

When I excuse myself from that group, I turn around, hoping to find Maura and her friend, only to find them looking back at me from near the snack table.

I make my way over to them, the girl with Maura looking a little overwhelmed and uncertain. I've been there. And I've come a long way since then. It all happened so slowly that I didn't really notice, but it's like the steady climb up a mountain. You don't realize just how high up you are until you're looking back at where you came from.

"Hi. Maura, right?"

"Yeah. This is the friend I told you about. Harley, this is Chelsea."

"Hi," Harley says softly, though a bit of brightness appears in her eyes.

"Hi. I'm glad you came."

"I'm thankful you encouraged Maura to ask me about all of it." Tears well in her eyes, but she waves a hand away. "We actually went to Promise a couple of weeks ago, but you weren't there. Thank you. I was so afraid to even say the words. Talking to Maura helped."

"She's the one you should be grateful to. I gave her some advice, but it takes a great friend to recognize when their friends need help."

Harley reaches over and squeezes Maura's hand.

"Did you want or need to talk about anything?" I ask.

Harley shakes her head. "Not right now. Just being here helped."

"Good. I'm glad. I hope we'll see you again in the future."

"And it's always fine to bring friends for support," Rae says, coming to stand next to me.

"Thank you both," Harley says, then she and Maura leave.

"I wish every girl had a friend like that who they could truly rely on. Who would show up for them."

Rae loops her arm around mine. "Guess we'll have to make sure we raise the next generation that way. With strong friendships—especially female ones."

I chuckle at that. "With you leading the charge, we'll be in good hands."

No one makes or keeps friends quite like Rae Cooper. I'm honored to be one of them.

"This is such a beautiful thing you're doing. I've lived so close my whole life and never knew. I'm so glad you're here today. Would it be possible to get some business cards to keep in my shop downtown? You never know where someone might see exactly what they need."

The woman in front of me smiles warmly. She's dressed in a flowing bohemian paisley maxi skirt with a cropped tank top and oversized sweater. She runs a small shop in Old Lake Town selling soaps and handmade goods. She even teaches some classes.

"That would be amazing." I spin around and rummage through one of the containers we brought before pulling out a stack of postcards with information about Promise on them. "Take these, and if at any point you need more, you can call and ask."

"Perfect. Well, I'm so glad I met you…"

"Chelsea."

"Chelsea. Keep up the amazing work."

"Thank you. Take care."

"Many blessings." She bows her head and walks away, leaving us in a calm silence.

Rae is sitting at a small table on the counseling side of the booth, talking with a couple of women, but otherwise we're in a bit of a lull. Kristen joins me near the front of the booth and smiles. "You've helped do something pretty amazing here today. I hope you know that. And I appreciate you suggesting we be involved."

My cheeks heat at the compliment. "Thank you."

"You should be proud. You've come a long way this year, and I mean that. I have lots of interns who come in and out of Promise. We make it a point to try to pick people who are interested in and dedicated to our mission. The majority do a great job and continue on. Then there are a few who stand out. Who take Promise's mission and make it *their* mission. They bring a part of their spirit to everything they do and go above and beyond. Somehow, I got lucky enough to have two at the same time." She glances over at Rae. "We might not be able to change the world, but I'm certain you two can change your little corner of it."

Tears well in my eyes, but I blink them away. "That means a lot to me. You've taught me a lot, and I look forward to learning even more next year, then taking it all with me wherever I end up."

"Rae mentioned you'll be helping her this summer at the counseling center in Ida."

"Yeah, it's mostly volunteer stuff, but I'm excited. Especially since a lot of it is outreach and connecting with high school or college students. The earlier we teach girls about their strength and their power, the more strong females we have out in the world."

"Your passion for advocating and empowering women is inspiring. In fact, I was talking with a friend the other night. She's a professor in the women's studies department, and she's been working with the local high school to set up a program where women in their junior and senior years of college mentor girls who are in the junior and senior years of high school."

"Yes," I blurt out.

Kristen laughs.

"Seriously, how do I sign up? I would love to be a part of that."

"I'll pass her information along to you."

"Thank you."

I take a deep breath and let it out again, looking around at the tents and booths dotting the field, rooted in this moment. There were times when the darkness felt too overpowering to make it out of, but I made it.

Four beautiful, familiar faces appear, walking toward the booth.

"Rae, trouble's here."

Kristen looks at her watch. "Oh, you two need to get out of here and go have fun."

Rae comes over to join me as Amanda, Mackie, Sarah, and Hyla stroll up to the booth.

"Greetings, lovely ladies," Mackie says playfully. "We're here to escort you to the shenanigans."

"Oh, and we brought gifts!" Hyla holds up a bag and starts pulling out T-shirts.

"All from a shop a few tents down that sells all kinds of things with feminist slogans," Amanda says, holding up her T-shirt, which reads *Smash the Patriarchy* with a sledgehammer beneath it.

Mackie's has the same quote as my Kindle case, *Well-behaved women seldom make history.*

Sarah's says, *They didn't burn witches, they burned women.*

Then she holds one out to Rae that says, *Nevertheless, she persisted.*

"We got this one for you," Hyla says, handing it to me.

My body, my choice.

And for the second time in the last ten minutes, I want to cry.

"Thank you," I murmur. Then Hyla shows us hers.

Not fragile like a flower, fragile like a bomb.

"That's perfect for you," I whisper.

"For all of us," Hyla says.

I slip my shirt over my head and look around at my friends. My *best* friends. My tribe. If I'm taking cues from the vibes today, my coven.

With my coven of strong, wild, messy women, I head off to enjoy the festival.

"This is the coolest idea ever!" Hyla yells, throwing her hand up in the air.

In the middle of a large field is a pile of wood and palettes surrounding a huge plywood phoenix. Markers are scattered all around it so people can write things on the phoenix—good energy they want to put out into the universe or things they want to let go of. As the sun sets, they'll light it on fire, then there will be music and dancing—around the fire if we want—and people will be playing drums.

We have a blanket set up on the edge of the roped off area, and we slip underneath to get markers and write our words on the phoenix.

As I pick up a marker, I look down at the phoenix bracelet that's always on my wrist. The one Trevor gave me that feels like a representation of myself.

I find a spot on the left wing of the phoenix and write the word I'd most like to get rid of—to let go of in my life. I don't want it anymore and I certainly don't need it.

Shame.

I've carried it for long enough, and now it's time to let go.

"That's a good one," Amanda says.

"What's yours?"

She drags her finger under the word *worthlessness.*

"Let's leave it all behind tonight."

She rests her head against mine. "Hell yes."

We make our way back to the blanket and settle in with the girls, munching on some candied nuts. We had a fantastic time at the festival today. Even though I thought drum circles might be too hippie for me, we went to one and had fun. We learned about so many local artisans and practitioners as well as learning a lot about self-care and caring for each other. It's been an incredible experience, and if they decide to do it again next year, I definitely want to be involved again.

A few drummers enter the circle along with Nadine and they lead us through some chants.

I am strong.

I am brave.

I am powerful.

I am loved.

Then the fun begins. People start playing music and Nadine and a couple of other women start lighting the pyre. A place to burn away everything we don't need and claim what we do.

The women hurry away as the flames engulf the phoenix.

Let her burn and let her rise.

Small fireworks pop and crackle adding colorful hues to the wild flames.

"This is incredible," Amanda says.

"Seriously," Mackie says. "My mom would love this. I should invite her next year."

"All the moms," Sarah says, then elbows Rae. "Can you imagine how much trouble Mom and Katie would get into?"

I laugh too, picturing their mom and Miles's mom sitting here with us. And Liz, too. Gran would love this.

"I'm so glad you were a part of planning this and asked us to join you," Rae says. "I might never have known about it—or been brave enough to come—if it weren't for you, and I'm so glad I'm here."

"Yes to all of that," Hyla says. "I want to see this grow every year, with more incredible women. Maybe our tribe will grow too."

Even though it already is. Rae and Sarah recently added their cousin Dani to our Girl Gang texts now that she's living in Ida—and dating Joel's brother Jesse.

When the fire dies down enough to stand near it, Nadine appears again with a handful of other women and a group of musicians and drummers, who are playing and dancing by the fire.

"We invite you all to join us as we dance around the fire. If you want to feel completely free, we encourage you to leave your shirts behind and dance topless."

Leave it to Nadine... who strips her shirt off, then goes a step further by chucking it in the fire.

I'm not throwing my new favorite shirt in the fire, but...

"Are we doing it?" I ask.

"I'm in!" Hyla yells and whips her shirt off, making Mackie choke because of course Hyla's not wearing a bra.

Hyla winks at her, then Mackie shakes her head and pulls her shirt off too.

"I guess that's a yes," Amanda says, pulling off her shirt and bra and tossing them in the center of the blanket.

"You want to?" Sarah asks.

Rae stares blankly at her for a second, then smiles brightly. "Let's do it."

Without another thought I pull my shirt over my head and free myself from the confines of my bra, and we all make our way under the ropes and into the crowd of women—this beautiful sisterhood—dancing around the flames of the phoenix.

We hold hands and dance, singing along with chants and music, utterly free. The fire warms my skin as I dance with the women who have changed my life and helped me embrace all I've been through and who I've become, and in this wild, carefree moment, I've never felt more alive.

Our laughter is unhinged as we walk down the path back toward campus. Festivities are still happening, but with the girls needing to drive back to the lake house, we didn't want to leave too late.

I've lost track of what we're laughing about, but we're leaning against each other, cackling like we're drunk even though we're all sober, as we hit the parking lot by the student center and keep walking down the hill toward a smaller one where our cars are.

It's almost 11:00 p.m. and campus is quiet, though the sounds of music and drums from the festival still cut through the night air, which is rapidly cooling off. It was a warm weekend for early May, but the chill in the air without the sun is a reminder that it's not quite summer yet.

As we get closer to the edge of the student center, I notice a couple of figures under one of the streetlights. I instinctively reach for Amanda and Hyla, who are on either side of me.

"What is it?" Sarah asks as our steps slow.

"Probably nothing," I say, hoping I'm right. But two random people hanging around the student center that's been closed for hours is unlikely to be nothing.

Sometimes I truly wish I could go back to not assuming the worst in situations like this, but then again... have I ever? As women, we're trained from a young age to be aware of our surroundings, especially at night. If only we taught men from a young age not to attack and assault women.

Now that we're closer, I can make out that it's two guys, both smoking, though they put their cigarettes out when they see us.

"Should we walk a different way?" Mackie whispers.

"No." My voice is icy. Not toward her, but in anticipation of what's coming.

I refuse to back down. If I were alone, it might not be safe, but at the same time, I know how to use my body to my advantage and how to protect myself. If I hadn't been drugged that night, I could've gotten away. I'm certain of that.

That night I called Trevor because of that guy hanging around and acting sketchy after my class is a distant memory. The fear I remember, but I refuse to give in to it.

I'm done cowering from fragile men who try to hurt and control women to make themselves feel more powerful.

I'm done living in fear. Screw taking a bear over a man. Give me all the men. I'll *be* the bear. Let them decide if they'd like to meet *me* in the woods.

One of the guys whistles as they both prowl toward us.

"Where are you ladies headed tonight?"

"I bet we could give you somewhere more interesting to go," the second guys says.

"I can guarantee there's nothing interesting about either of you," Amanda says.

"Ooh, a mouthy one," the second one says. "I wonder what else you can do with that mouth."

"Besides tell you to fuck off?" I ask.

"Didn't your mother ever teach you not to swear?" the second guy asks.

"Nope. Just like your mother clearly didn't teach you not to harass women."

The first guy steps in front of me, and Hyla clenches her hand into a fist. God help anyone she swings at. She's gained a lot of muscle back in the last few months and there's nothing deadlier than a woman ready to protect someone she loves.

"*My body, my choice.* Hm. I was thinking *your body* would look good against mine."

I shift a step closer as a dark smile grows on his lips.

"Funny. I was thinking my knee would look good against your balls. Let's see."

"Wha—"

I lunge forward, grab him by the shoulders and pull him down as I shove my knee up into his balls once, and then a second time, just for good measure.

The other guy rushes to his side.

"You crazy bitch!"

"I prefer the term mad woman," I say coolly, even though my heart is beating a million miles a second.

Hyla stifles a laugh.

"What the fuck?" the first guy groans, holding his crotch as he tries to stand up.

"What makes you think you should ever approach a woman like that?"

A mix of anger and nausea wells inside me, and I find myself reaching for my phone.

I know I've said men are the problem—and they are. Men need to stop raping and assaulting women.

But society needs to stop allowing it to happen and hold them accountable. But they don't. Not often enough. So I will.

"Smile for the camera, boys."

"What the fuck are you doing?" the second guy demands.

"Making sure everyone knows exactly who to avoid."

"Let's get out of here and away from these psycho bitches," the first guy says.

"Have the night you deserve!" Amanda calls after them.

I'm shaking as I text their photo and some brief details to the campus police tip line, and then to Nadine, so she can let everyone know to be careful as they leave the festival. Not that I think those guys will be around again.

"Holy shit. That was badass," Amanda says. "I thought Rae and I were the ones trained in kickboxing."

I laugh weakly. "My grandmother taught me a long time ago how to hit a man where it hurts the most: his balls, his ego, and his sense of superiority."

"Nailed it," Hyla says.

Rae meets my eyes. "Are you okay? I've been there. Fighting back. It feels good, but also..."

I nod. I don't have words for how I feel either. Superhuman and yet incredibly small.

"I'm okay. But I'm ready to go home."

Hyla loops her arm through mine. "Let's go."

We got back to our cars without any other issues, though Hyla took my keys and drove my car back to the apartment building while the rest of the girls drove to the lake house. We all made strict promises to text when we got home so we know the others are safe.

As we stand in the lobby of my apartment building, Hyla wraps me in a hug.

"I'm proud of you. Your strength tonight was beautiful and powerful. I hope once you process all that, you feel the same way.

"Thanks," I whisper.

Hyla is staying with Robbie since he has two bedrooms, and as Hyla put it, she doesn't want to overhear sex noises.

Fair.

"Do you want me to walk you up to your apartment?"

"No, I'll be okay. I'll see you tomorrow."

"Okay. Goodnight."

And just like Trevor would, she makes no move to go into Robbie's apartment, instead waiting for me to go upstairs.

It's not until I'm right outside my apartment that I hear the click of the door downstairs.

My brain feels fuzzy, and I'm not sure if I want to laugh or cry or rage. But Trevor's waiting for me inside, and if nothing else, I need him.

I swing the door open and walk inside, quickly closing and locking the door behind me.

"Hey, baby," Trevor calls from the bedroom.

I'd be surprised he's still up, but it's Trevor. He would've waited all night to make sure I got home safe.

"Hi," I call in as even a tone as I can muster.

When I get to my bedroom, I find him sitting in bed reading, and damn if it's not a sexy picture. One I'd like to see every night.

"How was it?" he asks.

"I kneed a guy in the balls. Twice."

He's instantly on alert, but tries not to show it.

"Was that part of the entertainment at the festival?"

I shake my head and he launches off the bed.

"What happened?" he growls.

And for some reason, that makes me laugh.

He looks at me like I'm crazy, which I might be, because it doesn't take long for that laugh to morph into a cry.

He wraps his arms around me, angry energy vibrating off him.

"Tell me who I need to kill."

And there's another laugh.

"No one. I handled it."

"Or kneed it?" He pulls back slightly and cups my face in his hands.

"I love you," I murmur.

"Tell me what happened."

I gesture to the bed, and we sit, Trevor wrapping his arms around me and pulling me halfway onto his lap. I can't complain about being wrapped in a cozy Trevor cocoon.

He seethes as I tell him what happened, going through a range of emotions about it all. As they all pass, I'm left with a feeling of angry numbness. I'm not surprised it happened, but I'm pissed. And I'm proud I stood up for myself. Being careful is exhausting, and if I'm going to exhaust myself, I'd rather be fighting back, however I can.

"I fucking hate that this is how the world is for you. It's not okay. If I could change it, I would."

"You change it every day by being you. By being a good man. Because I know if you saw that happening to anyone, you'd step in. You'd shame the guys. You wouldn't let anyone get away with it. That makes a difference."

He sighs and rests his head against my shoulder. "I would... but I haven't always done that. I let the guys on my old team say shit I never should've let them get away with in the locker room. I'm not proud of it."

"We all have our own paths to walk and things to learn. Besides, hearing the shit guys say in a locker room is different from witnessing a guy trying to trap or assault a girl. Would you ever have allowed that?"

"Fuck no."

"Exactly." I brush my hand over his cheek. "Because you're a good man with a good heart."

"How do you have so much grace?"

"I have grace for the people who deserve it. People who have good hearts, who want to learn and grow, who want to fix the world, or who want to learn from their mistakes. And I have that grace because I've seen the darkness. You can either fade away and become a part of that darkness, or you become a star and be the light in that darkness instead."

He brushes his thumb over my cheek. "You astound me. I'm not sure if I could've become a star after all you went through—I'm not even sure I have after my own experiences. Maybe sometimes, but others? I have a visceral hatred for men who do that kind of shit—prey on women or anyone else. It's disgusting. And when it comes to you..." He drops his head against my shoulder. "I tried to find him."

"What?" I lean back and turn to look at him. He meets my gaze, his brows drawn together and eyes gleaming with hesitancy.

"After you told me what happened, I reached out to one of my few friends from my old team. A guy I trust completely. I asked him to check into it. See if anyone had heard anything about a report or even rumors that one of them might've done it. He never found anything. I'm sorry. I wish... I could've given you that justice. That peace."

Of course he tried to retroactively fix it. Only Trevor.

He still looks so unsure, and I can't help but lean in and kiss him. A simple kiss to reassure him.

"Thank you. I wish he could be held accountable. Actually face justice. But if I've learned anything, that's likely never going to happen, and while that's not okay, *I'm* okay, and I've learned sometimes moving on without closure is necessary."

He holds me tight to him as he slides down in bed and pulls the covers over us.

"There's that grace again. I'm angry about what happened to you tonight, but I'm grateful you're okay." He kisses me. "I love you. I don't want to lose you." Another kiss. Slower this time. Raw.

That fear is always there for him. Always ripping him apart. Losing someone else he loves terrifies him.

"I'm here." I kiss his cheek. "I'm safe." Then his nose. "I love you." His lips. "I need you."

Our lips meet again, but this time it's sloppy, desperate. We need each other to take away the hurt. We need to feel the depth of our love. Because it's real, so real and raw and utterly beautiful.

"What do you want?"

"Everything," I mutter against his lips.

Then we're peeling off clothes, hands roaming over warm skin.

He rolls onto his back and moves to pull me on top of him.

"No. Can you... I want you to take care of me."

A few simple words, but with them, I hand over the last remaining threads of my trust.

"Lay on your side," he whispers, then reaches over me to grab a condom.

He runs his fingers up my center, and I whimper at the touch. Then he gently lifts my leg and moves closer, until we're tangled together.

I gasp as he pushes inside me, my head dropping back in ecstasy.

I wrap my arms around his neck, one hand curling in his hair and the other digging into his back, and then slowly, we move. We find our rhythm. Slow and steady, our faces just inches apart. No teasing tonight, just us, focused solely on each other and the love between us.

It's different. So different from when I climb on top and take control.

This is an exchange. Two bodies, two souls coming together as one. Finally, there's nothing held back. We're complete now. Twined together.

I get lost in our love as we move together, both of us desperate for release but holding out as long as we can. It feels too good to stop, but I don't want it to be over.

It's not until my body is trembling, every thrust almost sending me into bliss that Trevor looks into my eyes and whispers, "Come with me. I want to feel you pulse around me while I come."

"Yes," I cry.

His hot mouth slants over mine as we move faster. Everything else slips away as we explode, our sweaty bodies heaving together as we ride our highs.

When we're finished, neither of us finds words. We just hold each other tightly as we lazily kiss, lost in bliss.

It's somewhere near two in the morning, and Trevor and I are lying in bed, naked, his fingers running through my hair as we talk.

We almost fell asleep kissing, then we got some food since we worked up an appetite, came back to bed and worked up some more appetite—this time with Trevor on top.

Now we're both too wound up—in the best way—to sleep. I'll never complain about lying in his arms though.

"What do you want from your future?" he asks, lazily drawing circles on my stomach with his finger.

"If I say *you* is that totally cheesy?"

He presses a kiss to my jaw. "More like sexy. And perfect. Because I want you as the center of my future too."

I bite the inside of my cheek because now is the perfect opening to ask the question that's been dancing in my mind for a while now.

"Does that mean you'll move in with me next year?"

We've already talked about summer. We'll be doing a mix of things from both staying with my family, to both staying with his mom, to staying separately at times. It'll probably be chaos, but in this transition period of our lives, it makes the most sense. But next year... I don't really want to live apart. He spends so much time here anyway, and—

"Yes. Fuck yes. I'd love to live here with you. Assuming Robbie's okay with that."

My cheeks heat a little. "When he asked me, I might've stumbled over some nonsense words before telling him that was the plan."

He laughs. "So, all this was just your way of getting me to confirm what you'd already decided?"

I shrug. "I prefer to call it manifesting."

His lips capture mine in a rough, hot kiss. "Whatever you call it, I'm in. I can't wait to live with you."

"Good."

"So, besides us, what's your future look like?"

"You know that song *I Lived* by OneRepublic?"

"Mhm."

"That's what I want from my future. Life is short and nothing is certain, and whenever my time comes, I want to know I lived my life to the fullest. Not jumping out of planes or traveling to far-off places. I want to live my truth and follow my heart and chase down all my dreams. For me, that includes having kids, continuing the type of work I do with Promise—wherever it leads me—being a mentor and role model to young women, and when I have kids of my own, raising them to be strong and compassionate and make the world a better place."

Awe shimmers in his eyes. "I'd expect nothing less from you. I noticed one thing you didn't mention, though. Marriage."

"I thought you said what I wanted besides us."

"Are we married? Did I miss that?"

I smack his stomach. "No, but... I don't know. Would anything change—besides living together full time—if we were married? Would you care or love me more than you do now?"

"Of course not."

"Then the way I see it, marriage is just a formality. A legal extension of our relationship."

"You don't care about the big wedding?"

I laugh and sigh. "I used to be obsessed with that idea. But over the years, it changed. I'd much rather have a marriage than a wedding. I'm open to anything, but for me, the wedding isn't a big deal."

"Hm. Good to know. So you're saying I can wife you up on short notice?"

"Not if you continue to say things like 'wife you up.'" I give him my sweetest smile and pat his cheek. "For the record, just in case you need to hear it, I want to do all the things I listed with the man of my dreams by my side… and he looks a lot like you."

He pulls me close, hand tangled in my hair as he looks into my eyes. "I want to build that life with you, Chels. There's no doubt in my mind you're it for me."

I don't have any words to respond to that, so I kiss him. I kiss him with all the passion and love inside me, as my heart beats to the rhythm of *forever*.

22
Rage
4 Months Later

Chelsea

"Perfect," I whisper to myself as I hang the last picture on the wall. It's one of us on the hood of Trevor's car at the Grand Canyon. The way the sun halos us in the shot gives it an old school '80s or '90s look.

Driving to the Grand Canyon was our big summer trip. Between me helping out at the counseling center in Ida and working at my family's campground, and Trevor doing his internship with the Boys and Girls Club *and* being a fantastic commentator for the Binghamton Knights, we were busy, but we made sure to have fun. Two weeks before school started, his internship finished, so we got on the road and drove to the Grand Canyon, exploring lots of the rest of the country along the way. We ate some fantastic food, saw lots of cool things, and listened to every Eagles album twice. It was the best vacation of my life—besides maybe going to Disney World when I was thirteen.

Summer flew by, and so has the beginning of the school year.

Trevor and I moving in together has been seamless, mostly because he spent so much time here last year and we spent most of our summer together, so it's not really new. We celebrated our one-year anniversary by recreating our first date, and our anniversary gift to each other was to go through and pick photos for each other to hang on the wall between the living room and the bedroom.

We've spent the last few weeks going through them all, framing them, and hanging them up.

I walk back toward the front of the apartment, aiming for the kitchen because I'm starving.

"All finished. It looks good."

To my surprise, Trevor doesn't look up from his phone.

He's fixated on it, typing away.

"Did you want anything to eat?" I ask, but still nothing.

I turn and head back toward the couch, talking the whole way. "I hear the Boston Revs are going to kick the Metros asses this weekend."

He still doesn't look up. Time to break out the big guns.

"I'm thinking about cutting my hair. Maybe a cute little bob or something."

His head shoots up, his eyes dancing over me, then he swallows hard. "If that's what you want."

I slide onto his lap. "Ah, you're so cute when you're trying to be respectful of my decisions, even if it's one you hate." I lift his phone out of his hand. "Like I want to cut my hair. Please. I love my wild woman hair."

He gives me a charming smirk. "So do I. Especially when it's wrapped around my hand while I fuck you into the mattress."

Yeah, that's something else we did over the summer—had a whole damn lot of sex. I've never felt as uninhibited and comfortable in my body as I do now. There's no power dynamic. It's all about what we're in the mood for. Which is usually having fun and getting as much pleasure out of it as possible.

"So, glad to know where my hair ranks in my importance since *that's* what it took to get you to look up from your phone."

He hangs his head. "Sorry. Got a text I wasn't expecting."

"Everything okay?"

He nods. "It's a good thing, actually, but..."

"You're being cryptic." I hand him back his phone.

"It's from my old teammate, BK. He's one of the good ones, and he and his girlfriend—they met during freshmen orientation—just got engaged. They're having a get together at a brewpub we used to go to a lot to celebrate. It's on Tuesday. In Syracuse."

"Oh," I whisper.

"Yeah. I—I'd like to go, and if you want to come with me, I'd love to introduce you to one of the few good friends I actually made there."

I bite my lip. "Will a lot of the team be there?"

He nods. "Anyone still on the team, which wouldn't be that many from when we were in school, since he's a senior now. And probably other friends from campus, plus friends of Sasha—his fiancée."

I suck in a big breath, then let it out. It's been a long time since I've been there. But maybe it's time. It's one of the larger cities in the state. I can't avoid it forever.

"I'll go."

"Are you sure?"

I give a firm nod, even though I don't feel firm. It's not that I don't want to go, it's just a place I have to push myself out of my comfort zone. The longer I build it up in my head, the worse it'll be.

"I'm sure. I'd love to meet your friends."

"Thank you." He brushes a kiss to my neck. "I love having you by my side, no matter what I'm doing." His phone goes off again, and he looks at it. This time, he smiles. "Good news. You won't just have me with you. Hyla will be there too."

"Really?" I say excitedly.

"Yep. She's got a couple of days free this coming week. I think she'll be here for your girls' night on Monday too, but don't mention it. I'm sure she wants to surprise people."

"More than likely."

Hyla's glow up since kicking her parents out of her life has only gotten better. She went to school to become a flight attendant, and with a connection from Rae and Sarah's cousin who plays professional football, she got a job working as a private flight attendant. Right now, she's working with a minor league baseball team. In even better news, she officially cut all ties to her former parents by having Liz adopt her. I had no idea adult adoption was a thing, but it's made them both—and Trevor—so much happier. We had a whole celebration over the summer when it was official.

I let out a little sigh. "It'll be good if she's there for girls' night."

Unfortunately, while summer was kind to us and Hyla, it wasn't kind to everyone. Amanda and Jamie hit a rough patch right as we got back to school. They're doing better now, but it was tough for a bit. But the worst of things happened to Sarah. Her biological parents returned, fucked up her life even more, then left in an explosive and dramatic exit. Sarah has been struggling since, and it's only getting worse. I'm hoping a visit with Hyla, who has always connected with her about the hard stuff, will help.

"Yeah," Trevor says solemnly.

"It sucks not being able to help your friends when they're hurting."

He blinks at me. "Sorry. Did we just switch places? That's usually my line."

I shove his shoulder. "Yes, I know, my wonderful protector." I sigh and lean against him. "It's strange to feel this happy when I know they're hurting."

He runs his fingers down my back. "I know, but we have to hold on to our happiness when we have it. We all go through dark times, and it's the joy and love from the people around us that help us heal and move forward."

I smile against his neck. "Who are you and what have you done with my grumpy, growly boyfriend?"

"Therapy, babe."

We both laugh at that.

"I like being happy."

He kisses my forehead. "Yeah, me too."

I'm not going to throw up.

Just because we're almost to Syracuse does not mean that my life is about to implode.

Good thoughts, Chelsea. Good thoughts.

Or any thoughts.

I flick my eyes up to the rearview mirror, catching Hyla's gaze. She must sense my panic because she jumps in with a question for Trevor, who is driving.

"How was guys' night last night? How's Joel doing?"

Trev sighs. "Not great. This stuff with Sarah is hard on him. I get it. I told him I'm here if he needs me. I wish I could help more, but I know what it's like when she gets to this place. Usually, she needs someone to call her on her bullshit. In high school, that was her grandparents—especially her grandfather—but she's shut down with everyone... I'm assuming. How was she last night?"

"Quiet."

"Yeah," Hyla agrees. "I tried to remind her of our mantra to spiral up and keep fighting, but she was really withdrawn. Maybe I should try to talk to her more."

"I think Rae is going to reach out to their parents... or already has? I'm not sure. She needs help. Hopefully, she'll get it. And Joel too."

"How's Amanda?" Trev asks.

"A lot better. Thankfully. It's mostly Sarah that's in a rough spot right now."

"Oh! Rae said she and Aaron are talking about trying for a baby. Probably not until next year, but that's exciting," Hyla says. "Speaking of which, when are you two going to give me cute babies to play with?"

I stifle a laugh as Trevor mutters under his breath.

"You know, if you want kids to play with, maybe you should have one," Trevor tells her, glaring at her in the rearview mirror.

"Yeah, I'm good. I'd much rather everyone else have cute babies that I can steal for a little while and then give back," she says.

"Has anyone told you that you're extremely selfless?" Trev deadpans.

Hyla sticks out her tongue at him, even though he can't see it. "Excuse me? I think babysitting people's kids so they can go out and have fun is selfless. Or at least not selfish. Either way, you're avoiding my question."

"Hyla," Trevor grumbles, but I just smile.

Talking about this stuff in front of Hyla doesn't bother me.

"I don't know. Trevor once said he didn't want to wait a long time to have kids."

"Really? We're going to do this now? With Hyla in the car?"

I shrug. "It's not like she won't know as soon as we start trying anyway."

He glances at me in surprise, then shakes his head. "Okay, love of my life, when would you like to start having children?"

"I've been thinking lately that I'd like to start having kids younger. I mean, I always wanted that to some degree, but with graduation in less than a year? I don't know. I'm open to discussion."

Trevor grumbles again. "Now I really wish Hyla wasn't in the car."

"Okay, if you're going to start dirty talking or reveal you have a pregnancy kink, I'm putting my noise canceling headphones on."

"No," I say quickly. "You're good." Then I rest my hand on Trevor's thigh. "We'll put a pin in that for later."

Even though I'm not putting a pin in anything. I'm thinking about what I want and when I want it. In fact, I'm channeling all my energy into it, hoping it'll distract me as Trevor pulls off the exit that leads us into Syracuse.

Okay, I've been in Syracuse for more than ten minutes, and I haven't spontaneously combusted, so that's good. I'm not triggered the way I thought I'd be, either. Maybe it's because we're not near campus, or maybe it's because I built it all up in my head, but either way, I'm fairly relaxed.

With Trevor on one side of me holding my hand, and Hyla on my other with her usual Hyla vibrancy, I feel safe.

Hopefully that means it'll be a good night.

As we round the corner from the street the parking garage is on to where the brewpub is, I immediately notice the group outside the building, and more of that fear creeps in, but Trevor holds my hand tighter.

"If you get overwhelmed, say the word and we'll go."

"Thank you," I whisper.

"We've got this," Hyla says, then she lowers her voice and leans in closer. "Remember, not fragile like a flower, fragile like a bomb. Hold your power and strength tight."

"Thanks," I breathe.

It's going to be okay.

When we get to the group, two people step away. The guy, who I assume is Trevor's friend, steps over and gives Trevor one of those bro-hugs.

"It's good to see you, man."

"You too," Trevor says. Then he looks at the woman. "Congratulations. Though are you sure *this* is the guy you want to marry?"

She throws an arm around his shoulders. "I like him sometimes."

"This is my girlfriend, Chelsea. Chels, this is BK and his fiancée, Sasha."

"Blake Klein," he says with an eye roll. "The BK thing will never die. It's nice to meet you."

"You too."

"If you didn't want it to stick, you shouldn't have gotten everyone to call you that freshman year," Sasha says, stepping forward to hug me. "It's really nice to meet you."

"You too. Thanks for inviting us."

"Absolutely," Blake says.

"Oh, and I don't know if you ever met my sister, Hyla..." Trevor says, nodding to her.

"I think once," Sasha says. "It's great to see you again."

To my surprise, they don't make a move to go back to the group.

"Do we need to go join everyone?" I ask.

"Nah," Blake says. "My idiot brother is in charge of all this crap. I'll let him handle the line holding duties. Half of those guys are his friends who kind of know me. A handful of the team will probably be here, and a bunch of our non-baseball friends, which are the people I prefer most of the time." He leans in. "I don't know if you know this, but baseball players are insufferable."

"So are baseball commentators." I give Trevor a cheeky grin, and he pulls me closer, pinching my butt as he does.

I jump a little, and he leans in. "You're not the only one who can pinch."

He always knows just how to flirt with me.

There's some yelling from the group behind Blake, then one voice rings out.

"Blakey! Come on!" the guy I'm assuming is his brother yells.

"We'll be there in a few minutes. Keep your pants on!" Blake calls back. Then he sighs. "I mean that very literally. Once he starts drinking... Sorry, I'm not exactly selling this, am I?"

"It's fine." I laugh, but Trevor groans.

When I look at him, his gaze is on a different guy approaching.

"You invited DJ?" he asks Blake.

"He invited himself," Sasha says, annoyed. "You know how he is."

"Your old roommate?" I whisper to Trevor.

"And the guy who ghosted me after my injury. I'll bet anything he pretends we're besties now. Not that we ever really were, but..."

He shuts up as the guy gets to us, and once Klein's not blocking his view, awareness shoots through me. There's something... familiar about him.

My chest tightens.

Blond hair. Hazel eyes.

Fuck, am I imagining it because I don't like his energy or...

Hazy flashes rip through me. Him tossing a baseball cap on the floor and his eyes becoming clearer like they just did.

And then he opens his mouth.

"Well, well, Trevor Matteny. Long time no see. How the hell have you been?"

Dread slices through me, icy and cold.

"What the hell is wrong with you? Stop fighting this..."

That voice. His voice.

My stomach drops, and I really think I might throw up.

"Who's this? You finally bag yourself a hottie?"

"I bet a hottie like you could keep me up all night."

I'm backing away before I realize my feet are moving.

"Yeah, this is my girlfriend, Chelsea." Trevor turns toward me, concern etching his features when he sees me.

"Hey, I'm Dane."

The name clangs through me as another flash from that night claws at me. Standing by a pool table. And then that voice. Him. Shaggy blond hair hidden by a baseball cap.

"I'm Dane. Baseball legend."

My head's spinning. It's too much. A sob rolls through my whole body and I wrap my arms around myself.

"It was you."

Trevor

Several things click together at once.

Chelsea standing there, face white, looking like she's going to scream.

She said he had shaggy blond hair and hazel eyes. Most of the time, DJ kept his hair short. Until sophomore year. And his eye color? Fuck, I never noticed it until right now.

She said he told her he was a baseball player.

"Hey man, can I borrow one of your hats tonight? You know how the girls feel about a baseball player."

Then she utters the most horrifying three words I could ever hear.

"It was you."

"Trevor." Hyla's voice is sharp, cautionary, but I barely hear it. There's only the sound of blood roaring in my ears as I lunge forward and punch him as hard as I can in the jaw.

He staggers backward, then dives forward and pushes me. "What the fuck, man? You that pissed I didn't call?"

I grab him and spin him around, shoving him against the brick wall and getting right in his face. "You raped her."

That smirky look finally slips off his face, and his gaze darts over my shoulder.

Then he puts up a cold exterior. "I don't know what the fuck you're talking about."

I punch him again. As hard as I can.

He punches me back.

"Trev! I know you're pissed, but you need to stop!" BK yells, but I ignore him.

Finally, I have this fucker in my grasp. He will pay. I will make him pay for what he did to her.

DJ shoves me again. "Fucker! This really how you want to play it? You're going to pretend you didn't help me?"

"What the fuck are you talking about? I'd never help you."

"When I asked you to cover for me if someone came looking for me? What did you think I meant? You're not naive enough to believe I was worried about a party breaking up, are you?"

I growl and shove him against the wall again, landing a punch to his ribs this time, even as his words eat away at me.

It never crossed my mind he'd mean something like that. Parties get broken up all the time. People fight. But I remember the few times girls came around the next day asking for him. I don't remember them looking upset, but could he have...? Once a guy came looking about damages for something at a party. I didn't lie and say he hadn't been there, just that I didn't know where DJ was. Why did I do that? Why did I ever fucking lie for him? Why? Horror coils in my stomach when I remember the time campus police knocked on the door looking for him. He wasn't there. Then they asked if he'd been at a party the night before. Campus police. Chelsea?

All those thoughts swirl inside me, deepening my rage.

He pushes me back, then gets in a punch to my face, sending me tumbling backward, but I grab his shirt and drag him onto the ground with me until we're in a full-fledged brawl. And though I hear BK trying to get me to stop, Hyla yelling at me, and maybe even Chelsea's soft voice too, I can't stop myself.

I'm lost in my hatred and rage. I was afraid someone I knew did this? But someone I lived with? Someone who might've used me to help him get away with it?

Fuck him.

But then hands are on me, and I'm being pulled upright and thrown against the wall.

"Hands behind your back. You're under arrest for disorderly conduct."

Fuck.

My chest rises and falls against the brick of the building as the officer reads me my rights. When he pulls me off the wall, my head is spinning, and reality is slowly settling in.

Out of the corner of my eye, I see DJ, and it takes everything in me not to growl. Not to lunge and make this all worse. I might've just fucked up a lot of things, but only one matters to me.

My eyes go to Chelsea, who is standing with Hyla.

A third officer stands in front of everyone—thankfully, the only other witnesses to this were BK and Sasha. Not that it matters.

"Who started it?" the third officer asks.

"He did," DJ spits in my direction.

"He was provoked," Hyla throws back, a murderous glare aimed at DJ. She has one arm wrapped protectively around Chelsea.

"How so?" the officer asks.

That's when Chelsea steps forward, a shaking finger pointed at DJ. "He raped me."

The officer blinks, then looks at the other two officers holding DJ and me.

"That's a heavy accusation," he says.

Chelsea stands tall. "It's complicated. More complicated than even I knew until tonight, but I had an exam performed after and DNA was found. I'm confident it will match his."

The officer drums his pen on his notepad, then throws his thumb out to the cars behind him.

"All right, take them both in." He turns to Chelsea. "If what you're saying is true, you'll need to come down and give a statement, talk to a detective. Possibly more."

Chelsea nods. "Okay."

"Do you have a way to get there?" he asks.

"I can drive her. If I can get the keys from my brother," Hyla says.

The officer holding me takes half a step back. "Where are your keys?"

"Left front pocket."

He reaches right in and grabs them, then hands them to Hyla.

"I'll call Mom," she says, meeting my eyes and conveying a hell of a lot more than words ever could.

She knows why I did it. She's got my back. She's got Chelsea.

Which is clear when she walks over to Chelsea, wraps an arm around her, and guides her back down the block, leaving me to contemplate how much I've fucked up my life.

It's the middle of the night when I walk out of the police station, battered and bruised, surrounded by Hyla, my mom, and Randall, the lawyer who appeared ten minutes after I got to the police station and told me he was there to help. Apparently, he's one of my mom's graphic design clients and had offered her twenty-four-seven legal help if she needed it. If I had more than half a brain cell left that wasn't thinking about how colossally fucked today—or tonight or yesterday, whatever—has been, I might wonder if he's got some kind of crush on her, but I've got fuck all nothing left to consider *that*.

"The good news is, the DA isn't interested in pressing charges," Randall says. "The other guy could potentially try, but with the information you've given me, he'd be stupid to do so, and I'm guessing he knows that."

I look back at the building, thankful they aren't pressing charges, but more worried about the greatest thing I have to lose. The girl inside, who has somehow been there even longer than me. From what Hyla told me, her dad and Robbie are both here, along with a lawyer.

"Thanks for your help," I say to Randall, then look at my mom. "Can we wait?"

"Of course."

"Do you need any help finding a place to stay tonight?" Randall asks.

"I booked a hotel," Hyla says. "But thank you."

The doors to the police station open, and my gaze snaps to them.

Chelsea walks out with Robbie, her dad, and a female lawyer, who is talking with her dad.

My stomach is in knots as they walk down the few stairs toward us, Robbie with his arm around Chelsea's back.

"I'll be in touch when I hear something," the female lawyer says. She gives Randall a warm smile. "Randall. If you need anything, give me a call."

"Thanks, Jacinta."

Jacinta walks away, and my gaze goes to Chelsea.

Did I completely fuck this up?

"Are you okay?" I ask. I mean physically, because who the fuck would be okay emotionally after all this?

"I... will be." She sniffs and grabs my hands. "I'm going to go home with my dad. I need a few days to process all this. And then we can talk."

"Of course. Whatever you need," I croak. Because what the fuck else do I say?

"Come on, I'll walk you to the car," Robbie says.

With a lingering look, she lets go of my hands and walks away with him.

Her dad steps in front of me, a serious expression on his face. Then Gene throws his arms around me, surprising the hell out of me.

"What's this for?"

"You look like you need it. And I told you I'd be here when you need some dad energy. Definitely needed tonight."

I force back the tears trying to burst out of me and hug him back. "Thank you."

"Thank you for standing up for her."

Even if I lost her in the process? Even if I enabled the guy who assaulted her?

He steps back and rests a hand on my shoulder, then he turns to look at my mom. "Call if you need anything."

"Thanks, Gene."

Gene walks away, leaving me with my mom and Hyla. Randall must've left. Not that I care. The person I care about is leaving, and there's nothing I can do to stop her.

"Let's get some shitty drive through food, go to the hotel, and get cleaned up," Mom says.

She wraps an arm around my back, then Hyla does the same, and together we walk back to the car.

I think we ordered one of everything on the menu at McDonalds, but I've barely eaten. Hyla practically force fed me fries before I took a shower. Now I'm sitting here, staring at the cold food on the bed in front of me. There's a frigid numbness deep inside me, shrouded in white hot flames.

I'm not sure I can say I regret punching DJ, but escalating it to the point I did? When Chelsea realized, we should've gone straight to the police station. That would've helped her more. Then maybe she wouldn't have had to listen to him talk.

Does she think I had any role in what happened to her?

Do I think that?

I try to remember that morning campus police came, but it's a blip among so many others from Syracuse that I didn't want to hold on to.

Reaching out with my foot, I drag the trash can over, then sweep all the shitty cold food into it with a growl.

"I would've eaten that," Hyla says playfully, trying to lighten the mood as always.

But I can't so much as muster a smile.

"Honey," Mom says, sitting down next to me.

Hyla sits down on my other side as Mom runs her fingers through my hair.

"Talk to us," Mom whispers.

The coldness inside me grows as I say the only thing I'm thinking right now. "I wish Dad was here." I choke back a sob, and Mom wraps her arm around me. "Or maybe I don't. I doubt he'd be proud of me."

"Yes, he would be," Hyla says.

"She's right. You stood up for someone you love. Nothing would make him prouder than that."

My jaw trembles as I try to hold back the emotion, but I can't. The dam cracks, and I break.

Hyla and Mom wrap me in a double hug.

"What if I destroyed things with Chelsea? What if she blames me or can't forgive me? What if I lose her?" I choke on the words between my sobs, but Hyla and Mom only hold me tighter.

"She loves you," Hyla whispers.

But what the fuck does that even mean? How much can love survive?

What if I put it through too much?

If I played any role in what happened to her—preventing him from being caught—why would she forgive me?

I'd never forgive myself.

I pull my knees up to my chest. Everything hurts and crying only makes it worse, but I can't stop myself. So, I let go, let Mom and Hyla hold me, even though they aren't who I need.

But I don't get to have that. Not when the person I need is the woman I might've unknowingly helped to break.

Chelsea

Trevor looked so utterly broken when I left him tonight, but I didn't know what to do. What to say.

He was arrested for fighting for me.

Because his former roommate raped me.

And I have no idea how to process any of that.

I usually love the little ways we're tethered together, but I'd break and burn this particular bridge if I could.

I flick on the light in my room, shaking and numb, and walk over to the bed. Then I drop down onto the mattress. The mattress with the thick gel cover on top. The gel cover Trevor bought. For me.

Because there's nothing he wouldn't do for me.

Including destroy himself in the process.

I lie down in the fetal position, tears in my eyes as a heavy, dark numbness washes over me.

I spent hours at the police station, recounting my story, having men gaslight me. Thankfully, Jacinta—a friend of Gran's who she immediately called for help—was there for the majority of it to help me through. By the end of it all, which included me doing a voice line-up, where I couldn't see the person, but could hear them. I had to select a sentence I remember him saying—only a handful, though seeing him made some things I wish could've stayed locked away come back—and listen to it repeated several times. I picked him without a second thought. All of it ended with the DA wanting to pursue a DNA warrant for DJ—Dane. Fuckhead. I wish I'd never have to hear his name again. Not a likelihood, though. As much as I want him to be held accountable, the thought that I'll have to endure a trial if his DNA matches—which I know it will—is gut churning.

And how does Trevor fit into all of it? Jacinta says they're not pressing charges against him, thank goodness, but since he knew this asshole and then punched him? How does that factor in?

It's too much.

It's all too much.

Tears stream down my cheeks, and I wish I could turn off my brain. Force myself to go to sleep. I'm exhausted, but there's too much rattling around inside me.

The bed shifts next to me, and I look up at Gran.

"I brought some tea."

A sob bubbles up, and she slides down on the bed and wraps an arm around me.

"Oh, sweetheart."

"I think I failed," I choke out.

"Failed at what?"

"You told me not to let anyone take my power, but I've never felt so weak."

"I don't accept that. I heard how you handled yourself tonight. With integrity and your head held high. That's not weakness. That's strength." She sweeps some hair out of my face. "Strength doesn't stop you from hurting or letting yourself break. It just helps you know you can rise again and be okay on the other side."

I glance at the phoenix on my bracelet.

Resilient. Invincible.

I don't feel either of those things right now.

In fact, I feel more like I'm burning up in all the flames as the fire suffocates me.

23
The Darkness

Chelsea

HELLO DARKNESS, MY OLD friend.

Apparently, my version of processing things is to... not.

All I've done for the past twenty-seven hours is lie in bed.

Oh, and overthink and replay everything that happened. One thing I never wanted was for Trevor to be twined into what I went through. Now he is. No matter what happens from here, he will be. Because he beat the hell out of the guy who raped me, and that will factor in somewhere down the line. Not to mention in his future.

I wish I could be mad about it, but I'm not. I always joked about that fantasy book boyfriend stuff with him, and it became clear early on that he'd do anything to protect me. If he could build a time machine and go back and make sure he was there to protect me that night, he would.

I feel bad not reaching out, but I have to work through this immediate stuff on my own. If I don't, I'm worried it will affect our relationship deeply. For the most part, I'm a solo processor. That's who I've always been.

Is that an excuse for lying in the dark and giving in to the darkness? Probably not. But the darkness is cozy. Like an old friend. And getting up means facing it all. Making it real.

Sleeping and ignoring life is simpler.

Gran's been in with tea and snacks multiple times, and both dad and Robbie have checked on me, but I haven't wanted to talk. I've been cranky and grouchy. No one can give me what I want because I don't know what that is. I want Trevor, but I also know I'm not ready to see him yet.

I just want the emptiness to go away.

I pull the sheet up over my head and close my eyes, ready to lose myself again, when there's a knock on the door.

Even though I grumble, it swings open.

"Sweetheart," Gran says, and I reluctantly pull the covers off my face. "There are two lovely young ladies here to see you."

I almost pull the blankets back up as I think of Lex and Bridget and them telling me to stop moping. *Get over it.*

But those thoughts drift away when Amanda and Mackie walk in, carrying bags of stuff.

I push myself up to sitting, tears welling in my eyes. "What are you two doing here?"

Amanda smiles as they climb onto the bed with me. "Friends don't let friends sit in the darkness alone."

"They crawl in and be the light that helps them find their way out," Mackie whispers.

Tears trickle down my cheeks.

This is what I needed. What I didn't know I needed.

"Rae wanted to come too, but with everything happening with Sarah, she didn't want to leave. But she sent these," Amanda says, pulling out a tray of brownies. There's a notecard taped to the top.

It's not pitch black in here, and with the door cracked, there's enough light that I can see.

I pull the note out of the envelope and unfold it.

Chels,
I've learned there are very few things in life that brownies can't help with. I added some extra magic to these (AKA salted caramel).
If there's one thing more powerful than brownies to help get you through the tough stuff, it's good friends. I wish I could be there, but sometimes the messiness hits more than one person at once. I just want you to know I love you and I'm thinking of you. I'm here if you need anything, so call, please.
And for the record, I think you're the most badass woman I know.
XO,
Rae

I sniff back tears. At my lowest moments, I craved this kind of friendship. It's healing to have it now.

"She's not the only one thinking of you," Mackie says. "This is from Hyla."

She hands me a box, which also has a note attached.

Chelsea,
My beautiful future sister-in-law. You are a bright, shining star in my life. Your strength and your willingness to fight are inspiring. I know you're hurting right now, but this is to remind

to remind you that even when you're breaking, you're not broken. Let that beautiful heart of yours and all our love get you through this.
P.S. Don't forget to smile... that's what Liz would say.
ILYSM
Hyla

I open the box and pull out a mug with the phrase *Not fragile like a flower, fragile like a bomb* on it. There's also an extra Post-it note from Hyla.

Don't be afraid to explode and set the world on fire.

I barely have time to process that before Amanda and Mackie start unloading the other bags, which include blankets, snacks, and a framed photo of the six of us at the women's festival back in May.

"Thank you," I choke out. "This means... everything."

Amanda wraps an arm around my back and rests her head on my shoulder. "We've got you."

Mackie grabs my hand. "Always. So we can talk or not talk. Lie here in the dark or watch a cheesy rom-com. Our only requirement is we will be ordering sushi for lunch. Consider it a healing ritual."

I laugh at that. "I'm in. For all of the above. No rom-coms though. I need an action comedy or a really cheesy '80s movie. Something to get me out of my head." I think for a second. "How about *Terminator?*"

"Sounds perfect," Mackie says.

Amanda makes some kind of pillow nest for us, while Mackie grabs my remote control, and outside of being with Trevor, I've never felt so safe.

"How's Trevor?" I ask.

"I don't know exactly. Struggling, but that's to be expected. Hyla was with him until she left this morning, but the guys will be checking on him. He'll be okay. Focus on you for right now," Amanda says.

That's hard, even though I know it's what I need to do.

"I need a brownie."

Amanda laughs and grabs the container.

I take a big bite, and I'm hit with the urge to cry again. This is how Rae takes care of people. She feeds them and makes sure they know they're loved. Even from a distance, I feel her energy here with me.

Mackie and Amanda settle in next to me, but before Mackie gets the movie going, there's another knock on the door.

Gran sticks her head in. "Hey, honey. I just spoke to Jacinta."

I sit straight up. "And?"

She pushes the door open and walks all the way inside. "They got the DNA sample from him. Now we wait."

Something about Amanda and Mackie being here with me and then hearing those words awakens something inside me. This is not who I am. I will not give in to the darkness. I will not let it dim my light.

"Gran, can you open the curtains?"

Trevor

I'm a moping, mumbling, cranky as fuck bastard.

Mom and Hyla came back to the apartment with me yesterday. While Mom left last night, Hyla left this morning. Now I'm sitting around in a pair of sweats with no shirt, my beard untamed, looking through Chelsea's romantasy books, and wondering how badly I've screwed up every part of my life.

This might be rock bottom.

A knock on the apartment door surprises me, but doesn't lift my mood. The only person I want to see wouldn't knock. Maybe it's Robbie here to tell me to get the fuck out. Though I haven't seen his car since everything happened.

It's a lot of effort to get off the couch, but when a second, firmer knock comes, I force myself to do it.

I throw the door open, and I don't know who I was expecting to see, but I wasn't expecting Nick Ardito to be standing in my doorway.

"Gonna invite me in, or do I have to beg?"

I move to the side because words don't come.

"I guess I'll take it."

He walks in and drops his bag on the floor as I close the door behind him.

"What are you doing here?" I finally ask.

He walks over and throws his arms around me. "This. You've shown up for me at the rockiest of bottoms. Now I'm here for you."

I dislike the tears that well in my eyes because I'm sick as fuck of crying. How do my eyes still have tears? Pathetic asshole has been my setting since Tuesday night.

"Now," he says, giving me a shove. "Go take a shower. You smell like ass. I'll make us some lunch. Turkey club is still your favorite, right?" He nods to the grocery bag next to his backpack.

"Yeah."

"I'll have them ready by the time you're done."

I stare at him blankly for a second. "Thank you."

He smiles and gives a quick nod. "Go on. I can smell you from here."

A slight smile curves at my lips despite the ache in my chest.

It shouldn't surprise me for a second that Nick came here. He's always shown up for me. When my dad died, he was the one who broke through the haze around me. He lost his mom when he was really little, and he made it a point to come spend time with me because he knew how I felt and he wanted to help.

Nick and I have been friends forever, but that was when we grew closer. Our bond deepened through high school, and whenever my childhood best friend ditched me, Nick was always there to cheer me up, take me out, get me smiling again.

I take a quick shower, letting the hot water soothe some of the tight muscles in my back, then make my way out to the living room where Nick is sitting with sandwiches plated up and the first *Terminator* movie queued on the TV.

"Remember when we discovered this movie and had to watch it every single sleepover?" he asks.

I laugh at that as I pick up my sandwich. "Oh, yeah. I think my mom was ready to throw the DVD away."

"Thank God for streaming," he says with a smile, then starts the movie.

We get comfortable on the couch and eat our sandwiches in silence. When we're finished, I lean back against the couch and run my hand through my hair.

"How did you deal with this with Leigh?"

Before they were married, Leigh went through some rough stuff that led to some distance between her and Nick.

He blows out a breath. "Well, it's a little different. Leigh was pushing me away, but from what Hyla said"—because of course she called him—"Chelsea isn't doing that."

"No. She openly said she needed some time to process. That's more than fucking fair."

"It is."

"I just don't know what process means? Process how she feels that my former roommate raped her? Process how she feels about me getting into a fight and getting arrested in defense of her? Process how she feels that the guy who raped her essentially said I helped him get away with it? Or maybe it's to process how best to break up with me—"

"Stop." Nick's voice is commanding in the way I only ever hear him use with his three-year-old son. "Hyla told me... everything. And I don't for one second think that Chelsea is figuring out how to break up with you. Her trauma was just thrown back in her face, and that's a lot to deal with."

"But—"

"No. No buts. I know how you are. I know how you care. And I know how you blame yourself and take on the weight of the world. But what happened was not your fault. I'll tell you that as many times as I need to for you to believe it. I know you feel like you failed her, but you didn't. You have done nothing but love her, wide open, with your whole heart. She knows that. Now you have to trust that she loves you the same way."

"What if love isn't enough?"

"If love is enough to transcend death—and we both know it is because we still feel the love of the parents we've lost—then it's enough to get you through this. It's more than enough. You can be hurt and angry and regretful all you want, but I won't let you give in to that darkness—that heaviness—inside you that says it's all your fault. So shut up."

With that, he gets off the couch, goes to the freezer, and brings back two pints of ice cream. The one he hands me is some kind of mint and chocolate.

"Sorry. It's not Mint-Ting-A-Ling, but it'll have to do. And if you're eating, you can't waste your breath blaming yourself."

I let out a whisper of a laugh at that. "I hate you."

He blows me a kiss. "Love you too."

Nick stayed the night last night and left earlier today. While his visit helped, I'm still mopey, pissy, and a bunch of other cranky dwarves. At least I got dressed in something other than sweats and went to the grocery store today. That's something. Still no sign of Robbie and no word from Chelsea.

I've wanted to call or text constantly, but she wanted space, and no matter how badly I want to apologize or talk to her or fix things, I will always respect her wishes. Even if it kills me.

With nothing else to do besides worry, stress, wonder if I've lost the woman I love, and rage over the fact that DJ might somehow still win in this scenario, I put on one of my favorite audiobooks earlier and started baking and cooking. Focusing on not fucking up a recipe means less brain space for intrusive thoughts and overthinking.

At least there will be plenty of treats for Chelsea to enjoy whenever she gets back.

Or for me to binge eat if she doesn't come back.

Nope.

I dish out a piece of the soufflé I made and as many of the oven baked fries as will fit on my plate, and head out to the living room, where I turn on the TV and scroll through streaming services, hoping for something to catch my interest, but nothing does.

I'm close to putting on *Terminator 2* when my phone goes off.

As usual, hope soars through me then promptly dies when I don't see Chelsea's name on the display. Instead, it's a text from Rae.

Rae: Hey, so Sarah and Joel had a thing a little while ago. She left and now she's not answering her phone. Can you just let me know if you hear from her or see her?

I growl and throw my head back. Because of fucking course. What does Sarah do when she's hurting? Push the people who love her most away. Rae's texting because she thinks Sarah might come here. One other safe spot away from the rest of them. But I doubt that. Alcohol is Sarah's favorite coping mechanism.

I pinch the bridge of my nose, trying not to scream. The last thing I want to do tonight is deal with my ex-girlfriend's bullshit. We'll always be close friends, but this is not my fucking problem anymore. I have enough problems. The second I think those words, I feel like a selfish prick.

With a sigh, I read the texts again, then send a response.

Me: I haven't heard anything, but I'll let you know if I do. Do you want me to check downtown for her car?

Rae: Maybe if we don't hear from her soon. I'll let you know.

I toss my phone back on the couch and shake my head because despite what Rae said and how shitty I'm feeling, I already know what I'm going to be doing tonight. Because I care. I fucking care about the people in my life, and that drive to help however I can won't let me sit here for long.

Hauling drunk people around is not my favorite activity, yet here I am on a Friday night, dragging my ex out of a bar so I can take her back to her current boyfriend. That is just par for the course of this shitty week.

How has it only been three days since I was sitting in the front seat of my car, having a conversation with Chelsea about having kids?

Before everything was completely fucked up.

Nick may not have let me say it was my fault, but he wasn't there. He didn't see the look in her eyes—he doesn't have to live with the guilt I'm drowning in.

How could Chelsea forgive me for potentially helping the guy who raped her?

There's a thread of hope still dangling inside me, but it's fraying with every day she doesn't come home or reach out. I want to go to her, but I've watched my friends fuck up enough shit that I'm scared to do that.

What if I push her before she's ready to talk and she ends things?

I'm running out of arguments for why she *won't* break up with me.

Who am I kidding? It would be what I deserve.

And this... this has got to be part of my punishment too.

I sigh in relief when we finally get to my car.

I throw the passenger door open and look down at Sarah. "Get in."

She looks at me for half a second, then flops into the seat. "That takes me back."

"What?"

"You being bossy. Demanding. Is that still your thing?"

I grip the car door, trying not to scream. Funny how that was always my thing with her, but with Chelsea, I actually prefer submitting. I love what we do no matter what, but when she's in control, I'm more present and not on.

Every part of me is better with her.

I'd give anything to have her in my arms right now. To go home and find her waiting there.

Fuck.

The only answer I give Sarah is, "Put your seatbelt on." Then I shut the door and get around to the driver's side, throwing myself into the seat and slamming the seatbelt into place.

"Are you mad at me?" she asks, like a little kid who's just been scolded.

I grunt as I put the car in drive and get us out of the parking lot.

"I'm mad about a lot of things," I say after a minute.

She reaches over and runs her hand over my thigh, giving it a squeeze at a spot she really fucking shouldn't.

"Jesus Christ, Sarah."

I lift her hand and put it back on her lap. I know she didn't mean anything by it, but it still pisses me off. It pisses me off that I'm dealing with her drunken bullshit because she's shutting everyone in her life out while I'm desperately hoping that I'm not losing the girl I love.

"What?" she asks in confusion. "I used to calm you down. We were good together once, right? Till I ruined it?"

Oh, fuck. This is bad.

Sarah was always firm about why we ended. It wasn't right. It took me some time to agree on that, but I eventually understood, and I get it even more now. I know it killed her to end it when she did since we were each other's first everything, but that she's still holding on to how hurt I was four years ago?

I'm still annoyed, but I soften my voice. "You didn't ruin it. We weren't right. We both know that now."

"I'm sorry."

"For what?"

"Everything," she whispers.

My heart breaks. I wish I had something to say to that, but I don't. And maybe that's a place where Sarah and I are similar because we both want to protect the people we love. We both blame ourselves for everything. We just go about it in different ways.

I flex my hand on the steering wheel, struggling for words, but still don't find any.

We settle into silence after that, and my only goal now is to get her home and back to Joel in one piece. By tomorrow, she'll be in a completely different state and want to fix this.

We're more than halfway to the lake house when she grabs my arm.

"Trevor. Pull over."

"What?"

"Stop the car. I'm going to be sick."

"Of course you are." Luckily, we're on a country road, so it's easy to pull over in some grass.

She flings the door open as I put the car in park, then she's puking everywhere.

Again, that anger roils inside me. Because with all the love and support she has in her life, she's still doing this shit. I reach over and pull her hair back as she continues puking.

"Jesus, Sarah. What the fuck are you doing?"

I let her hair go as she sits up and wipes her mouth, looking at me.

"Why is this your default?" I yell. So mad. At her. At myself. At fucking life. "Haven't you learned by now this only hurts everyone else? I just don't get it. I'm over here clinging to my relationship for dear life, praying that something I did before I even met her doesn't end it, and you're trying to throw away a relationship with a man who has loved you"—my voice breaks—"probably before I ever did."

She shuts her door and leans back against the seat, tears trickling down her cheeks as I pull back on the road.

Maybe I shouldn't have said that. Maybe it was too far. Maybe I shouldn't have been the one to drag her ass out of that bar when I'm this ugly combination of hurting and pissed at the world. But she has to wake up and see what's right in front of her. And I'm so mad that she has everything and is pissing it away while there's a good chance I've fucked up my life and my relationship, and I have no idea how to fix any of it. If I even can.

Sometime between the puke session and getting to the development the lake house is in, Sarah passed out. Not just sleeping, but drunk passed out. So when I get back to the lake house, I end up finagling her out of the car and carrying her up the stairs.

Joel swings the door open and runs out as I get to it, taking Sarah from my arms.

"What happened?"

Sarah is leaning into his chest and muttering something, half still sleepy drunk as I follow them into the house.

"She was at the bar doing shots." I almost wince at my words. Joel is hurting, and it's a pain I've been through. A pain I'm feeling again now—in a different way and on a whole new level. Only my pain is my own fucking fault. But as the person who wants to help my friends and make things okay, I tell him, "For what it's worth, she feels bad. And she thinks it's all her fault."

"What else is new?" he mutters, then begins the process of taking her upstairs as I stand there, numbly, watching.

"Hey," Rae says, stepping in front of me. "Thank you for bringing her back."

"Of course."

She looks at me for a moment, then gives me a quick hug before following Joel upstairs.

I close my eyes and lean against the closed door behind me, pinching the bridge of my nose. I'd laugh in misery over how fucked up this all is, but that makes me want to cry.

A hand clamps on my shoulder. "Thanks for finding her."

I open my eyes and look at Aaron, who gives me a grateful smile.

No matter how annoyed I am at her behavior, it wasn't going to stop me from looking for her. She was my best friend before she was my girlfriend, and after our breakup, we found that friendship again. I don't want to see her suffer. Just like I don't want to see any of my friends suffer. If I can help, I always will. At least I can help someone, even if I can't do shit about my own problems.

"It's fine," I say.

"But you're not."

I open my mouth, then close it again. Because I don't have anything to say to that. I'm not fine. I can't even pretend I am.

"Have you talked to her at all?" Aaron asks.

I shake my head. "She said she needed space." Probably space to figure out how best to get away from me. Whether she ever wants to see me again, or will just have Robbie kick me out of the apartment. At least I can always move back in here.

"Hey, Aaron!" Rae calls from upstairs.

"You should go deal with that. They need support right now."

"So do you."

"I'll be fine," I mutter.

"I call bullshit," Miles says, walking up behind Aaron. He smacks Aaron's arm. "Go take care of them."

Aaron looks at me again, then nods. "Call me if you need anything."

"Sure." Not that I'm going to. He's got enough going on.

Miles grabs his coat. "Come on."

"Where?"

"We're going back to your place and getting all the pizza we can eat. Which between the two of us is probably at least three large ones, right?"

I almost laugh at that. "You don't have to."

"I know I don't have to. I want to. You show up for everyone. Let someone show up for you."

My heart cracks a little more. I finally found my person to let in, let take care of me, and now...

"Yeah, okay."

"Such a warm invitation," he says with a smile. "But I'll take it. Let's go."

"Important question," Miles asks as we lounge on the couch watching *Terminator 3*. "How many times have you watched this movie in the last three days?"

I glance at him.

"I plead the fifth."

"Is it a comfort or a punishment at this point?"

"Fuck off. I love these movies."

"If you say so."

"Did you just come here to kick me when I'm down?"

He grabs the remote and pauses the movie, a serious look on his face.

"I'm here to make sure you don't drown in the darkness. Friends don't let friends be miserable alone. And contrary to what you think, you need support."

"Do I? I mean, I made my bed."

"No. Fuck that. That's what the little voice in your head says because you have an incessant need to help and protect people at all times."

I side-eye him because that hit a little too close to the head of the nail.

He chuckles. "Yeah. I know how that feels because I'm the same way. You and I are more alike than you realize."

"So wouldn't you blame yourself too?"

"Of course I would."

"Then... exactly my fucking point. I shouldn't have—"

He holds up his hand. "I would blame myself, but would you blame me?"

I open my mouth. Close it again. Because I don't know.

"I still blame myself for what happened with Rae," he says. "I watched that guy grab her on the dance floor, and my worst regret is that I didn't see she was alone before that. That I had to choose between fighting three guys or going to get help. I still wonder if I made the right choice."

"That wasn't your fault," I say firmly.

"And this wasn't yours. We are always harder on ourselves. Things that weigh on me are things I'd never ever place on my friends. You're feeling the weight of this because you care for Chelsea and you feel like you failed her, but what happened to her wasn't your fault. You know who's responsible for raping someone? Rapists."

"But—what if I helped him get away with it?"

He sighs and shakes his head.

"You didn't. I'd bet on it. You're a good guy, Trev. Believe that for a second."

"What if I was a *good guy* to the wrong person? Because I've been over it in my head again and again. I remember times that I covered for him. And I remember the campus police showing up at my door. They asked if he was there, if he'd been at some party the night before, and I can't remember when that was. I told them I thought he was home the night before. I lied to the campus police and it might've been about her. There's no coming back from that."

"Somehow, I don't think it's as bad as you think it is." He's quiet for a moment. "And you can come back from anything if you're willing to fight."

Maybe. Maybe I could. But it's not just me who has to be willing to fight. It's Chelsea. After everything that's happened,

I wouldn't blame her if fighting for me is the last thing she'd ever want to do.

Miles left around midnight after some convincing from me that he's more needed at the lake house.

It's true.

But I also needed to be alone. I needed time to think.

That's some bullshit, because I've done very little thinking.

Instead, I've stayed up half the night researching how arrest records affect your ability to get a job and talking myself out of calling or texting Chelsea even though I really, really want to.

Maybe tomorrow, I tell myself, as I finally throw my phone to the side and pull the covers over me, sinking into the cold loneliness.

Maybe tomorrow she'll come home. But knowing my luck, things are only going to get worse.

24
Every Broken Piece

Chelsea

WALKING OUT OF MY therapist's office, I feel myself stepping back into my power.

It's going to take time to process everything, especially if this ends up in a court case, but that dark haze around me is lifting. I'm ready to do the work. More importantly, I'm ready to go home and face how Trevor is twisted up in all this now.

Home.

Not my family's house. Our apartment. Trevor. Home is where he is.

I never wanted Trevor tangled up in all this, but the fact that his former roommate is the person who raped me means there's no chance of him *not* being wrapped up in it. Especially since he beat the shit out of him.

I wish I was the kind of person who could say I'm mad about that, but I'm not. Trevor defended me. Which is all the more reason I want to get home to him.

He stood up for me and got arrested, and I just walked away. I was so overwhelmed, I could barely breathe, let alone think. The most beautiful part of my life being connected to the ugliest one is the last thing I wanted, but I can't control that.

I can only control how I let it affect me, and I refuse to let this harm my relationship with Trevor.

My therapist said today if I had ended up in this situation without Trevor having any connection to it, he still would've become a part of it because he's my partner. And she's right. I was afraid of this creating a wedge between us, but that won't happen. I won't let it. Trevor and I are going to stand strong. Like we've done everything else, we'll face this hand in hand. I'm so ready to finally be in his arms again.

When my phone rings, I hope it's him. He's been respectful about giving me the space I asked for, but I miss him. I wouldn't have been angry if he'd called.

A glance at my phone screen tells me it's Amanda. Probably calling to check in.

She and Mackie left early yesterday morning, and I spent the entire day going through a weird version of the stages of grief. I alternated between ranting, crying, meditating, and stressing about what was going to happen, but by the end of the day, I felt better.

I answer my phone with the intention of telling Amanda I'm coming home, but when I hear her sniffling, I stop in the middle of the street, my blood running cold.

"Mands? What happened? Trevor?" Panic rises in my voice. I shouldn't have stayed away this long. I shouldn't have shut him out.

"No—he's okay. It's Sarah..." I take off running as she tells me what happened—some kind of overdose from alcohol and anxiety meds.

I need to get home to them. To my friends, my chosen family, the people who have shown up for me in the darkness and gotten me through the painful moments. And Trevor, who is undoubtedly hurting even more now. He needs me, and there's nowhere else I want to be than by his side.

Trevor

I hate hospitals.

I hate waiting rooms.

I can't remember a single time when I've been in one for a good reason.

Sarah's going to be okay. Whatever that means. Like Hyla was okay? Yeah, it started her on a healing journey, but she still hit that horrible place to begin with. Just like Sarah did, and I gave her a little nudge to get there. Joel doesn't blame me. No one here does, but I can't stop blaming myself. She was hurting and broken, and I pushed her over the edge. I thought she needed to hear it, but it only made things worse. Not just for her, but for everyone here. All my friends were affected by the words I said when I was pissed and hurting. No matter what I do, I keep hurting the people I love.

My chest tightens, my stomach twisting with nausea as I rub my clammy hands together.

I'm not okay.

Chelsea said she needed time to process everything. I don't know if she has, but I haven't. All I've done is spiral deeper into negative thoughts and the numbness of my anger.

I pull out my phone and go to my texts. Nothing from Chelsea—not that I'm looking, except I always hope to see one. I called her earlier but it went straight to voicemail. Which led me to leave her a tearful, nonsensical voice message I wish I could erase now.

Pushing those thoughts away, I click on the name I came here for. My therapist. And then I ask to schedule an appointment as soon as possible. Everything that has happened in the last five days has brought the shit I need to work on front and center.

Aaron drops into a chair next to me, scrubbing his hands over his face.

"How's Joel?" I ask.

Aaron chokes on an empty laugh. "Feeling like an idiot. He has an IV and nurses force feeding him peanut butter and jelly sandwiches."

Joel's as much of a mess as Sarah and after worrying about her and not eating or sleeping for the better part of two days, he passed out earlier.

What the fuck is happening this month? My birthday is in a week, and I'm less inclined than ever to celebrate it. Who knows what other fuckery the universe has in store for us.

"She's awake!" Rae says, as she walks into the waiting room. She looks at her dad. "Mom's in there. You should go too." He kisses her on the head and walks out of the room as the rest of us stand. "She's awake and she's... Sarah." A light laugh. "She knows she made a lot of mistakes and she's hurting, but she wants to heal. She's going to be okay, though." Rae sniffs and wipes her eyes. "I should go tell Joel."

"I'll do it," Miles says, then heads out of the room.

Rae lets out a long breath, then walks over to Aaron. "She's going to be okay."

He wraps her in a hug, holding her as she cries.

Everything hits me at once, and I'm so overwhelmed, I feel like I'm coming apart at the seams. I make a beeline for the elevator, but Amanda grabs my arm.

"Hey, where are you going?"

"Just need some air."

"Do you want me to come with you?"

"No, I'm okay," I croak, making it clear that I'm anything but. Either way, she lets me go, and I go right to the elevator, doing everything I can to keep myself from falling apart.

When I get outside, I realize I have no clue where I'm going, so I look around. Out of the corner of my eye, I see the small park across the street. A small park with a little baseball field. And like my feet have their own minds, I'm going that way without a thought.

Thankfully, there's no one at the little baseball diamond when I get there and plop down on one of the four-tier metal bleachers, letting my head drop into my hands.

The wind off the lake whips around me, sending a chill through me, but it's nothing compared to the cold ache inside me.

Everything is so fucked up, and all I keep wishing is that my dad was here. That I could talk to him. He'd have had an answer or just the right reassuring words. Even if they were the same words someone else said, I'd believe them coming from him.

If I were back home, I'd be sitting in the cemetery talking to his headstone, but this is the best I've got.

I look out at the baseball diamond, my eyes going to right field.

"Dad, I don't know if you can hear me. Anyone walking by would probably think I'm crazy, but I just... I miss you. Everything's messed up right now, and I feel like it's all my fault.

Or at least like I've made things worse." I sniff and wipe my face. "I wish I could hear your voice. Feel your hand on my shoulder. Feel the strength and warmth of one of your hugs. I'm so angry. There's all this rage burning inside me and everything that happens adds more fuel to that fire. I don't want to be that way. It's not how you raised me. But then I don't think you'd be particularly proud of me right now."

"I disagree."

I whip around and stare in disbelief at the sight of Chelsea walking toward the bleachers.

Chelsea

Trevor looks unbelievably broken, and it has me terrified about what's happening with Sarah.

When I got back to my family's house after Amanda's phone call, I packed the handful of things Robbie had brought for me, ready to get to Old Lake Town as fast as possible before realizing my car wasn't there. Then I had to get Robbie, wait for him to pack all of his stuff, and endure a three-hour car ride. My phone lost service halfway here and decided not to find it again—that's tomorrow's problem—which meant I haven't had any updates on Sarah for hours.

Robbie was about to turn into the hospital parking lot when I saw someone sitting in the bleachers, and I knew it was Trevor. Robbie crossed three lanes of traffic and I practically jumped out of the car.

"Chels?" Trevor asks, eyes full of tears.

My eyes are locked on his as I walk toward him. "I think your dad would be proud of you. You keep standing up and fighting for the people you love. You keep going even when things are hard. No matter how often you play the grump, you never actually become bitter. He'd be proud of that."

He stares at me, unconvinced. "I don't know how." Then he shakes his head. "I can't believe you're here."

"Where else would I be? I was planning on coming back today, but I hauled ass to get here when Amanda called."

"But... here. Not the hospital."

"I saw someone sitting on the bleachers, and I knew it was you. Is Sarah okay?"

He scoffs. "Okay is a relative term, but she's awake and yeah... okay."

"Are you okay?" Because something is very wrong.

"Probably not. But some of that depends on why you're here. If you're going to break up with me—"

"Break up with you?" I nearly screech in disbelief. "Why would you think that?"

"Because I..."

What is going on? Does he think I'm angry at him for defending me?

He shakes his head, running a hand through his hair. "You heard what he said. About me helping him. I'm so sorry. I swear, I never thought he did anything like that, and I would never have helped him. But the thought that I enabled him in any way to do that to you... I don't blame you if you hate me."

Well, that was not what I was expecting.

"Wait, you don't think you actually had something to do with him assaulting me, do you?" I stare at him, the realization hitting me all at once, that yes, he does. Of course he does. Of course my sweet, stupid, overprotective man, who only wants to take care of the people he loves, has been beating himself up thinking he hurt me.

I sink onto the bench next to him, feeling awful now that I didn't make it clearer I wasn't mad. I never thought he'd go to that place, but I should've known better.

"Trevor, look at me." He reluctantly turns toward me. "I'm so sorry. Sorry I didn't make it clear I wasn't angry at you. I wasn't thinking about that stuff at all. I'm sorry because all I thought about was myself. I ran away, and while I needed space to process, I should've been clearer about why and what that meant. I wasn't questioning anything between us. I just needed time alone to deal with it all."

He chokes back a sob. "You really don't blame me?"

I grab his hand, holding it tight enough to cause a bit of pain. I need him to focus, to stop thinking this shit.

"*You* are not responsible for what he did. Not in any way. You spent so much time proving you're worthy of my trust. I trust you. I know you. I know you would never hurt anyone like that."

"But what about the times I covered for him when people asked questions? There was a time when the campus police came and asked if he was around or if he'd been to some party, and I lied and said I didn't think so, but what if that was about you?"

I take his hands. "Then they didn't do their job. It's not like you swore an oath. It's normal you'd want to support your friend. That's not what he ended up being, but it's not like you'd known specifics or were actually questioned and then actively lied for him. Anyone who took your half-assed answer as the clear truth did a shitty job. Maybe it's a lesson learned about who you trust and who you're willing to cover for, but that's all. You have to let this go. Stop blaming yourself or convincing yourself you're hurting people because you're not."

"Tell that to Sarah."

"What happened?"

I listen as he tells me, and once again, I don't think he's in the wrong. Sure, he called her on her shit and maybe could've said it a bit nicer, but he wasn't mean, either. And he wasn't wrong.

"It sounds to me like you said what she needed to hear."

"But with the space she was in... I pushed her over the edge."

"Maybe it was a push, but something would've given her that no matter what. You're not responsible for her mental health getting to the point it was at, and walking on eggshells doesn't solve anything. Yes, you know her well. You knew what kind of state she was in, and you're letting that cloud your judgment now. You're holding yourself responsible for her actions simply because you didn't treat her with kid gloves. That's not on you."

"You give me too much grace."

"No. I give you the grace you deserve—the grace everyone deserves. You're too hard on yourself. Do you know what I see when I look at you?" He shakes his head. "I see a deeply loving, caring, *imperfect* man who would do anything for the people he cares about. The ultimate fantasy book boyfriend."

He lets out a weak laugh but doesn't say anything else.

After a few quiet moments, he runs his thumb over my hand.

"How are you doing?"

"Uh... I don't know. I feel okay. Besides worrying about Sarah—and about you—I keep going through a range of emotions. I'm angry about so many things, but I'm also proud of how I handled myself. Well, mostly. I let myself sink into that darkness again, but Amanda and Mackie showed up and helped pull me out. Now I'm preparing myself for a fight. They obtained his DNA."

"And?"

"Still waiting, but I know it's a match. I know..." My voice waivers and he wraps an arm around my back, playing with the tips of my hair.

"Are you mad that I fought him? I don't know if that could complicate anything with a trial."

"If it does, we'll handle it. You defended me. I appreciate you wanting to protect me, even if it was in a retroactive way. I hate that you were arrested, though. Is that going to cause issues for you with jobs and stuff? I don't know how any of this works."

"I read way too much online over the last few days, but hopefully, since no charges were pressed, as long as I'm up front about it, it should be okay."

"I hate that he's still walking around and you have to worry about this. It's not fucking fair. He deserves to face justice."

"There's not enough justice for what he did to you."

I rest my head on his shoulder, soaking in the feel of his body next to mine.

"Are we okay?" he whispers, voice rough.

"We're better than okay. I'm sorry I left you. There was so much going on in my mind, and I thought if I tried to face the ways you're now entangled in this story with you right there, it would've been too hard and confusing."

"You don't need to apologize. I read way too much into it because I was blaming myself." He rubs a hand over his face. "It's a good thing I made a therapy appointment. I can't believe I spent the week feeling like I ruined us. Our perfect relationship, everything we built..."

I lift my head and look at him. My sweet, messy man with all his trauma and heartache. I'll take every broken piece.

"You didn't ruin anything. But also, our relationship isn't perfect. It never has been. And despite how much you try to be, you're not perfect either. That's okay, because neither am I. There's no such thing as a perfect relationship. We're both messy, complicated humans who bring plenty of baggage and trauma and bad habits that we have to work through. We're going to fight and struggle and work on ourselves and our relationship a lot, but when we do that work, when we share those broken pieces of ourselves and learn to grow together, we build something that is perfect. Our love. The love between us is beautifully, messily perfect, and I wouldn't change any of the hard things that got us here. I love you."

He rests his hand on my waist as his forehead drops against mine and he lets out a rough exhale.

"I love you too."

Tears well in my eyes as I look at him. Some color is returning to his cheeks, but he still looks shattered.

"Don't ever think I'm going to leave you. I know you're terrified to lose me, but that's not going to happen. You're my soulmate. My person. The love of my life. No one sees me or understands me like you. There's nothing that would make me leave you."

"Nothing?" he asks with a laugh of disbelief.

"Sure, there are deal breakers in life, but you are not the type of man to do any of those things, so no. Nothing. This is it. You and me. I told you we may not be married, but whenever we get married, nothing will change. I'm all in. And I think I have been since that morning at The Lake Shack."

He pulls me into his arms and holds me, and I swear I can feel some of the cracks in his heart start to heal.

"I'm all in too. I'm yours forever."

"Good."

We hold each other in silence for a long time, letting our love wrap around us and heal some of the broken pieces. There are still plenty of things to talk through and figure out and process together, but as long as it's together, that's all that matters to me. We can face anything—we *will* face anything that comes our way. And we'll do it hand in hand, supporting each other the entire time.

After a long time spent wrapped in each other's arms, I convince Trevor to let me get him some food, then we make our way back to the hospital.

"I need to get Rae to eat something," Aaron says, running a hand through his hair. He's on the other side of Trevor and looks exhausted. Which isn't surprising. Given how deeply today has affected both his wife and his best friend, he's been busy trying to hold it all together.

"You need to eat too," I tell him. "Want us to go get something?"

He shakes his head. "No. I want to get Rae out of the hospital for some fresh air anyway. I just have to pry her away from Sarah."

"Why don't we go in?" I say. Rae and the girls are in there with her. I didn't want to join them all because I didn't want anyone's attention to fall on me. Sarah deserves their entire focus right now.

"Yeah," Trevor slowly agrees, though I see his hesitation. He's wanted to go in and talk to Sarah, but he still feels terrible. Which is all the more reason he needs to talk to her.

"Okay. Thanks," Aaron says.

We get up and head for the room, but halfway there, I pause and look over my shoulder.

"I need to run to the bathroom first. You go ahead without me."

"Are you sure?"

"Mhm. I'll be quick." I kiss his cheek and send him on his way, then find a bathroom.

I don't need to go, but I know Trevor needs a few minutes with Sarah alone so they can talk.

I let five minutes pass, then slowly make my way toward her room, only to find Trevor walking out of it.

"Hey, everything okay?"

"Yeah. She's... more herself. She told me to take you home."

I let out a weak laugh. "I'm not against that idea. Should I stop in first though?"

He shakes his head. "Joel's in there now, and I think they need some time together."

So do we.

I thought that might happen, though, so I took a page out of my friends' playbook and had Robbie go to the bookstore and grab the first few books in one of my favorite lighthearted, fun romance series and then wrote a note to go with them and left them with Aaron to give to Sarah.

Trevor still looks a little disoriented, so I grab his hands and draw his attention back to me.

"How did the conversation go? Did she blame you for anything?"

"No. She was apologizing to me." He sighs and ruffles his hair with his hand. "But I never want to be a person who hurts the people he cares about."

I rest my hand on his cheek. "You're not. I wish you could see yourself through my eyes so you'd know what an incredible man you are. We all make mistakes, but you are mindful and caring and always trying to help the people you love. Like I said earlier, you're a man your dad would be proud of. And for what it's worth, I'm proud of you too. I just wish you'd be proud of yourself."

He leans in, pulling me closer, his hand tangled in my hair, and kisses my forehead.

"I missed you."

I let out a shuddery breath. "Can we go home?"

He musters a smile, though his eyes are glassy. "Home."

Nothing seems quite as heavy when I'm wrapped in Trevor's arms.

As soon as we got home, we took a shower, then Trevor pulled out the insane amount of food he cooked over the last few days and we loaded up plates to eat in bed.

We've been talking for hours about everything that's happened and all our struggles. We both have a lot of things to work through, whether it's our emotions after everything or harder stuff that we need to focus on with our therapists.

The biggest thing we agreed on is that while all this affects us individually and affects us as a unit, it does not and will not affect our relationship. It will not enter into that in any way. We're a unified front, and that's how it'll stay.

"I'm tired," Trevor sighs, and I know he means more emotionally than physically.

"I know," I whisper. "So am I."

He kisses my neck, across my throat, and then the other side of my neck.

His breath tickles my ear as he whispers, "I need you."

Then we're kissing as we fumble with our clothes, desperate to feel the connection between us that we've both missed this past week.

When we're naked, I cup his cheek, looking into those deep, dark eyes. "What do you want?"

He sits up against the pillows and pulls me onto his lap. "I need you right here. Like this."

I grab a condom, then roll it down his length, not waiting longer than a breath to slide down him.

Face to face, with my arms wrapped around his neck, I ride him as he holds me close.

He buries his face in my neck. "Fuck, I need you. I missed you. I love you. More than anything in this life, Chels. You're mine."

"And you're mine."

My body shudders with need. His lips find mine, and we move together, letting everything else fall away. All the pain, all the anger, all the uncertainty. It doesn't matter right now. For this moment, it's just us, our souls intertwining and dancing together as we forget about the world around us and get lost in our love, letting it heal us. Finally, we can both breathe again. We have each other, and that's all that matters. Whatever comes now, we'll face it together.

Trevor

Waking up with my girl wrapped in my arms is the best feeling ever. Especially after how shitty this week has been.

We stayed up half the night talking, cuddling, and having sex. Reconnection in every way.

There's still a heaviness hanging over me, but it's slowly lifting. I have a therapy appointment first thing Tuesday morning, and I'm hoping that will help even more. Though I'm still expecting it to take time for us to process all this—individually and together as well.

My heart is calmer as I watch Chelsea sleeping peacefully. Her resilience is breathtaking and her grace continues to astound me. She likes to call me her book boyfriend, but she's my dream girl, only now instead of it being because of the things I found attractive or I thought I wanted in a partner, it's because of her. Her heart, her soul, her brilliant smile, her wicked sense of humor, her intelligence, her kindness, her fortitude, and her strength. There aren't enough words to explain how lucky I am that she's mine and how hard I'll fight to make sure she always knows how loved and cherished she is.

Fuck, she takes my breath away.

A dream that's a fantasy some days. Smiling to myself, I slide my hand over and gently pinch her arm.

She stirs and looks at me, eyes squinty.

"Did you just pinch me?" she asks, a sleepy rasp in her voice.

I lean in close and whisper in her ear, "I had to be sure you were real."

Her gorgeous smile cuts through the haze still hanging around me, like the sun through parting clouds.

"I'm real. This is real. And we're okay. We're here together. Happy. Or we will be, even if we still have to work through some hard stuff."

"I'll do anything as long as it's with you."

She rolls over and buries her face in my chest, her mess of auburn waves strewn everywhere.

"I missed you."

"I missed you too. We're better together."

"So much better. I promise I won't run away from you to process something ever again. Everything is easier when I'm in your arms."

I press a kiss to her head. "And I promise to try not to assume the worst and blame myself and take on the weight of the world."

She chuckles and lifts her head. "I have faith in you. Mostly."

"Gee, thanks. So much love."

"All the love." She kisses my nose. "But I also know you are always going to be someone who takes protecting the people you love and caring for them seriously, which means you'll always put some extra weight on your shoulders. Luckily, I'll be here to pull it off or help you carry it."

I open my mouth to respond, but her phone rings. After turning it off and on three times last night, we finally got the service to connect right again—at which point I asked her to delete the pathetic voicemail I left her yesterday. Thankfully, she did it without question. Now, I'm definitely putting a new phone on the Christmas list for her.

She grabs it off the bedside table, eyes going wide when she sees the name.

"It's Jacinta."

She scrambles to answer it and puts it on speaker.

"Hi, Jacinta. What's going on?"

She laughs a little. "Good morning, Chelsea."

"And Trevor. He's here too."

"Is he? Good. I called your grandmother first, but she said to call you. The results came in this morning, earlier than expected. The DNA was a match."

Chelsea lets out a shuddery breath. "So... what does that mean?"

"The DA will prosecute the case. There's a warrant out for his arrest."

"And then what happens?" I ask. "Do we need to be prepared for a trial?"

"Eventually," Jacinta says. "But bureaucracy takes a while. There's a good chance it'll take at least a year to get there. From here, he'll be arrested, arraigned, and have to put up bail."

"I hate that he still gets to walk around," I grumble.

"I know. But innocent until proven guilty by a jury of peers. No matter what the DNA says."

"And I'll have to testify and all that, right?"

"Yes. There will be a lot of prep work, but for the time being, anything that pops up is in my hands. You have a very strong case, Chelsea. It would be highly unlikely for this not to go in your favor."

"Even with me getting into a fight with him?" I ask.

"Anything like that can be spun. It's just about how convincing we are to the jury. Again, that's my job. For now, I want you both to breathe. Relax. Recoup. You've been through a lot. Heal. Get to the strongest version of yourselves, so you're ready when the time comes."

"Thank you," Chelsea says. "For everything."

"You're welcome. We're going to get justice, Chelsea. I really believe that. Have a good rest of your day, and take care of yourselves. I'll be in touch with any new information."

"Thank you," I say.

"Have a great day, Jacinta."

We say our goodbyes, then hang up, staring at each other in stunned silence.

"It might actually happen... justice. I let go of the hope of it happening for so long. The fact that he could actually pay?"

She blows out a trembling breath.

"Here's hoping he gets exactly what he deserves. And more."

"When I moved here, I hoped that karma was on my side. I had no idea how much that would end up being true. I'll always hate what happened to me, but I look at my life now, and I have everything I could want or need. I have a beautiful life. With you."

"And we're not even at our best now," I say with a laugh.

"No. But we will be. We'll heal and keep growing together. And no matter what, we'll be okay."

"Nah. We'll be better than okay." I softly kiss her lips. "We'll be perfect."

25
Upgrade You
6 Months Later

Trevor

"That's right, baby. Just like that."

"Yes," Chelsea throws her head back, hands clenched in the sheets.

"So pretty when you come for me."

With a grunt, I pull out, replacing my cock with my fingers and stroking myself hard and fast until I come all over her perfect tits.

I keep my fingers buried inside her until she stops spasming, then brush my thumb over her clit one last time before lying down next to her.

"I'm not sure what's hotter. Wearing a condom and letting you milk me dry, or taking you bare and covering you in my cum."

She laughs and runs her finger through the mess on her chest, then licks it off her finger.

I drop my mouth against hers. "Okay, that's definitely hotter."

We've gotten a little looser with birth control lately, switching it up between using a condom or the pull-out method depending on the time of the month. During her period, I get to finish inside her without a condom, and that is the best feeling in the whole fucking world. Even though there's probably some microscopic risk, we've both agreed we want to have kids early on, so we're not stressing about it. Granted, we'd like to be out of college before we start trying, but there's only two months until graduation.

The last two years of my life have been an insane whirlwind, but being here with Chelsea makes all of it worth it. We're both in good places with our mental health after everything that happened in the fall, though we're preparing for more stress in the coming months. The trial is set for November, so we're trying to enjoy our lives right now and not let any of that filter in.

"Oh, did I tell you I saw another apartment listing? It's available the first of May, but since we're done halfway through the month, that makes sense anyway," Chelsea says.

"Good to know hot as fuck sex makes you think of apartment listings."

She pushes me over and rolls on top of me. "I was thinking about how we'll have a new apartment to christen, but if you're going to be sassy about it—"

"I take it all back."

"Good." She leans down until her lips are hovering centimeters above mine, then leans over and grabs her phone.

"Tease."

She licks up the side of my neck. "You love it."

She's not wrong.

"This one's closer to Ida, but that probably makes more sense. I won't be working at the campground as much. Plus, your job is in Ida."

To my surprise, the Boys and Girls Club where I interned last year reached out to me last month because the Adolescent Program Director for the county is leaving, and they were impressed by the work I did as an intern.

I still had to go through the interview—and explain my arrest record—but it ended up working out. I'll start right after graduation, and since the current director is leaving a few weeks before me, I'll be thrown in the deep end, but after interning with the college athletic director this year, I'm confident and up to the challenge.

Chelsea will be doing a mix of things. Helping out here and there at her family's campground over the summer—likely the last summer she'll help out there—preparing to start her counseling master's degree in the fall, and doing outreach for Promise, with a twist. The center in Ida where Rae has volunteered for years lost a lot of its funding and closed its doors, but because of how passionate Chelsea and Rae are, their boss from Promise convinced the board of directors to connect with colleges and high schools in Ida and work with them to have Chelsea and Rae do outreach there. And because my girl has no chill, she'll also be working part time as part of a mentorship program run by one of the local colleges. She is determined to change the world, and I couldn't be prouder of her.

Chelsea shows me the pictures, which look nice, meaning it's probably just okay because the pictures make it look better, but okay is a step up from a craphole. She adds it to the list of potential options, but I haven't seen anywhere yet that gives me the feeling of home. Anywhere would feel like home as long as I have Chelsea, but I want something that feels right.

I remember how my dad talked about his dream house—the one he never got to see—but even without that, he loved the little house I grew up in, and it had a strong sense of warmth and home to it. But maybe that was just my dad.

Missing him will never get easier, but I'm finding more ways to celebrate him.

Chelsea keeps Loganberry in the fridge all the time now. She got more pictures from my mom of me and my dad and hung them up without telling me. She's always thinking about little things like that.

She's so far past being my dream girl at this point. She's my everything. Sometimes that still scares the shit out of me, but I refuse to let the part of me that's scared to lose again prevent me from enjoying what I have now.

Chelsea throws her leg over me and rests her head on my chest. If I could stay like this forever, I would.

"I'm happy," she sighs.

"That's good. Glad to know you haven't tired of me yet."

"Never. You're sweet, you smell good, you cook, you're the best cuddler ever, and you'd do anything to protect me."

"Wasn't kill my way across a continent one of the requirements?"

She waves a hand. "That was for *fantasy* book boyfriends. You're my real life one, and that's so much better." Her eyes flit to mine. "In fact, maybe I should upgrade you to a book husband."

My eyes fly wide.

Did she just...

"Baby, did you just propose to me?"

She smiles innocently, pink dusting her cheeks. "Maybe? I don't know. Didn't we kind of do that already?"

I stare at her in disbelief. "I think I would've remembered that."

"No, I mean… we agreed that marriage matters more than a wedding, but regardless, a piece of paper won't change how we feel or act. Then I think we said we'd just do it whenever we felt ready. So haven't we sort of been engaged?"

"No. Literally no. Not at all. An engagement should be… well both people in the couple should know. Probably should have a ring."

"I have this." She wiggles her middle finger where a rose quartz ring that I got her for her birthday sits. It was handmade by a local artisan and meant to reflect strength, love, and compassion. "And it means a lot more."

At that, I roll over, pinning her hands above her head. "Are you telling me you want to get engaged or that we are engaged?"

She smiles that slightly devilish smile that makes me crazy. "The second one. But not in a let's tell everyone and plan a wedding way. In a we're both open to the next phase of our relationship, and when it feels right, we'll get married."

"Bold of you to assume I won't drag you down to the courthouse right now."

She laughs. "It's Sunday afternoon."

"I'll find a judge. Or a boat captain."

"Trev…"

I capture her lips in a rough, sloppy kiss. "I love you. And I will marry you anytime, anywhere. But you're right. Not today. I don't want the big crazy wedding either, but it would be good to have your family there and my mom and Hyla."

"Agreed," she whispers. "Until then, I'm yours. But I'm pretty sure I have been for a while."

"You've been mine since the moment we met, even if you didn't know it yet."

She takes my face in her hands and looks into my eyes. "Some part of my heart knew. That's what kept drawing me to you. That tether between our souls was always pulling me right to you."

"Right where you were supposed to be."

"Right where *we're* supposed to be."

She kisses me again, and I'm lost to her. But then again, I always am. I'm always ready to get on my knees, crawl to her, worship her, treat her like the goddess she is.

Hitting those trees and upending my entire life was worth it to get to her.

I will never lose sight of how lucky I am to have all this—to have this sort of love. I'm grateful to my dad for teaching me what it means to be a man—to protect, care for, and love deeply. Loving without anything held back and being grateful for every day is the greatest way to honor him and keep his memory alive. Chelsea and I do that, and I can't wait to see how that love continues to grow and how it'll shape the future neither of us saw coming, but that we found and dreamed of together.

Epilogue
Profound Peace
4 Years Later

Chelsea

"And what are you going to be when you grow up?"

"A boss."

"Of what?"

"Whateva I wanna." Our three-year-old daughter, Brooke, toddles away, pleased with that answer and herself.

Trevor and I look at each other and laugh. Raising a fierce little girl who knows her power is not for the faint of heart. I challenge anyone to deny Brooke something and not be on the business end of a very, *very* sassy glare.

"You're already the boss, aren't you?" Liz says, walking into the kitchen and sweeping Brooke into her arms.

When we first moved home from college, we lived in an apartment near Ida for a bit, but once I was pregnant with Brooke, Liz asked if we'd consider moving into the house with her.

I watched the emotion on Trevor's face and knew he was thinking of his dad's dream of their family living together and taking care of each other. I said yes before he could.

Liz built the house with two master suites and purposely took the one on the far side of the house. While it's all accessible, that side is where the back staircase leads and where her library is, so it feels more like her space.

There were some adjustments after Brooke was born—like when Liz needed to take off her grandma hat and walk away so we could be parents, but otherwise it's been pretty smooth. And on days when any of us needs extra support or help, it's nice that we're together.

"Do you want to go play with some balloons with Grammie while we wait for everyone to get here for your party?"

"Balloons! Birthday party! I can have cupcakes?"

"Later," Liz says. Then she disappears into the living room with Brooke.

Trevor stalks over to me and wraps his arms around my waist. "Well, I won't complain about a little alone time with my wife."

"Mm, I love when you call me that."

His laugh rumbles in my ear. "I think you just like that you can officially call me your book husband. Or better yet, your very own shadow daddy."

"I think you're more of a bat boy. I can get you some wings. Halloween costume idea."

"Anything for my mate," he teases.

I laugh, but I cut off quickly when his lips press into my throat. He smiles against my skin, slowly dragging his lips up, then he runs his fingers through my hair and slants his mouth over mine, owning all of me with his lips and tongue. And just like always, my mind floats away on a cotton-candy cloud while my love-drunk body melts against my husband's.

In addition to it being Brooke's birthday today, it's also our wedding anniversary.

Once I got pregnant, life was a whirlwind, so while we kept intending to get married, we didn't even get a marriage license until a month before Brooke was born. While we were in the hospital, waiting for Brooke to make her entrance, we decided to get married right then and there. With my dad, Hilary, Gran, and Robbie there for me and Liz and Hyla there for Trevor, we asked the hospital chaplain to marry us.

It made the day extra special, but we still consider our first date to be our official anniversary, though we'll take any opportunity to celebrate our love, whether it's a random Wednesday afternoon or the anniversary of when we got married.

Trevor lifts me onto the counter, somehow not breaking our kiss, and I rake my fingers through his hair. Like always, I'm desperate for more. We've been together five-and-a-half years and I still can't get enough of him.

Which must be why I let out a soft moan like we're alone in this house when we're very much not.

"Happy Brooke's birthday—ah! My eyes! Save me!"

Trevor and I break apart, stifling laughter as we look over at Hyla, who is standing in the entrance to the kitchen. Mackenzie is behind her with her hands covering Hyla's eyes.

"You're safe now," I say.

Hyla reaches up and pulls Mackie's hands down, resting them on her waist instead.

"Are you determined to scar me for life?" Hyla demands.

Trev shrugs and sends her that classic brotherly asshole smirk. "Figured that's been handled about ten times over by now."

Hyla sticks her tongue out at Trevor while Mackie laughs from behind her.

I hop off the counter. "Good to know some things never change."

"Nope. He'll clearly never stop harassing me." Hyla pretends to be miffed.

"I—"

An ear-splitting shriek interrupts me, and we all dash from the room. There's nothing like your kid screaming like they're dying to give you a minor heart attack.

But when we get to the living room, we find the reason for the *happy* shriek. Sadie. Sarah and Joel's daughter and Brooke's favorite person in the whole world. She's almost a year younger than Brooke, but Brooke doesn't care. She adores Sadie. Along with Rae and Aaron's son, Carter, and Miles's daughter, Emmie, they're an adorable little foursome.

Trevor puts a hand to his chest and lets out a breath. "Good to know everything's okay."

"Except our eardrums," Joel deadpans.

Yeah, truth.

"I'm all dona." Brooke shoves the presents piled in front of her away.

"Honey, there are a bunch more to open." I tap the one on top of the pile.

She shakes her head. "No. I want cupcakes. My birthday. I pick."

I sigh and look at Trevor, who smiles and shrugs.

Our girl has him wrapped around her finger. Because it's her birthday, I'm inclined to let her do what she wants, but Trevor is happy to bow down to her demands most days. He can be a disciplinarian, but he always looks like a kicked puppy when he watches her cry or have a tantrum.

"Cupcakes it is, then."

Brooke's already halfway to the dining room, everyone following her with the kids in the lead.

Rae falls into step with me. "Well, at least you know you're raising a girl so strong, she'll never be afraid to speak up for herself."

I laugh at that. "Yes. Here's hoping she uses it to lead and help others, not to run a drug cartel."

We both laugh at that.

But really, I'm grateful. I want her to walk out into the world empowered, with her head held high, knowing she can make a difference and help create a better world than the one I grew up in. Every day I fight for her and all the other little girls growing up right now, but change takes time, especially in a world so filled with vitriol for women.

I want it to be better for her. While I hope she's as compassionate as she is fierce, I don't want her to have to walk my path to get there.

It doesn't hit me as hard anymore when I talk about what I've been through. But seeing the person who raped me brought to justice helped with that. It took the shame off me and put it all on him. He deserves to carry every bit of it.

The trial ended up being when I was five months pregnant, and Jacinta used that to our advantage. Pregnancy makes a woman seem more vulnerable, she said, and while I think he would've been convicted easily either way, the jury only deliberated for ten minutes before returning with their verdict. He was sentenced to fifteen years in jail. I was shocked, but we had a judge who has always been a strong proponent on women's issues. He deserves every day of the sentence. Though I'm sure he'll get parole sooner. Either way, he gets to carry around the title of sex offender for the rest of his life. Good for him. He earned it.

Now it's my mission to make sure there are fewer girls out there like me. I will fight every day of my life to make this world a better place for my daughter.

As I watch her, I know she'll fight the same way.

I pull out my phone, ready to take pictures, but Liz waves me off. I appreciate that. Being present as a parent is important to me. I want to be in the pictures, not just take them. Though for a moment, I hang back and watch. The kids are all sitting around a small table, and Brooke is putting cupcakes in front of each of them while Emmie reminds everyone not to eat them until we sing happy birthday to Brooke.

I grab the lighter and hand it to Trevor once Brooke is seated with a cupcake in front of her.

After he lights the candles for her, he joins me again, all the while reminding her to wait to blow them out until we've sung.

Trevor wraps his arms around me from behind, and I lean against him as our family and friends surround us, singing to Brooke. My heart could burst at the amount of joy in this room. We are so lucky to have each and every person here in our lives.

I'm lucky I found Trevor when I did. Or maybe it was all part of fate's plan. It's hard to believe that when I think of the ways we could've met sooner, and how much longer we could've loved each other. But it doesn't really matter. We're here now. Right where we're supposed to be.

We all clap and cheer as Brooke blows out the candles on her cupcake. Trevor goes to pull them out before she bites one like she did last year, and Brooke latches onto him, giving him a giant hug as he whispers to her.

He is the most amazing father I could've imagined for my daughter, and the best husband. Sometimes I can't believe this is my life.

As Trevor comes to stand beside me, I reach over and pinch his arm. He turns to me with the best glare he can muster—which isn't much.

"Are you ever going to stop pinching me?"

"Nope. When I have a moment where I think this can't be real or it's too good to be true, I pinch you. Then I see your smile and I know it's real. The only fake thing about you is your grumpiness."

He tries to put on that grumpy pout, but I see a lot less of it these days and I think he's lost his touch.

"If it makes you happy and reminds you how special what we have is, you can pinch me every day."

"And you won't complain?"

"Oh no. I'll complain. But only because then I see *your* smile."

He leans in and steals a quick kiss, setting my heart on fire and making me feel all gooey inside.

"I love you."

"Love you too, baby."

He pulls me closer, slipping his hand in my back pocket and giving my butt a little pinch. I laugh and lean into him, gratitude overwhelming me.

When I moved to Old Lake Town for college, I couldn't have imagined how much I'd gain—friendship, love, a better understanding of myself. Gran told me not to let anyone steal my power or my peace. Little did I know I'd grow into an even more powerful version of myself and find a profound peace with my path in life and the beautiful tribe surrounding me.

One day, when Brooke asks how it all happened, I can tell her the world didn't break me. I grew. I healed. I fought back. And

I'll keep fighting to protect my friends, my family, the life we're building, and the perfect love at the heart of it all.

The End

Learn more about Bethany's books, find bonus chapters and freebies, sign up for her newsletter, join her Facebook group Bethany Monaco Smith's Book Besties, and more here:

A Note from Bethany

Thank you so much for reading Trevor and Chelsea's love story!
Is Trevor your newest book boyfriend now?
Writing this story was an emotional roller coaster (I'm just along
for the ride with my book babies), and I hope you loved how
their story ended up.

If you want more from them, you can grab a bonus chapter
featuring Chelsea's pregnancy on my website.

And if you want to know the stories of some of the side
characters in this book (including Hyla), check out the Friends
Like This series (Rae & Aaron, Sarah & Joel, Miles & his girl, and
Hyla & Mackenzie), the Freaking Love trilogy (includes Nick
and Leigh's story), and the other Ida Heartthrobs books—The
Forever Fight (Jesse & Dani) and The Future Play (Amanda &
Jamie).

Thanks again for reading!

Bethany's Books

Friends Like This series
Friends Like This
Falling Like This
Broken Like This
Love Like This
Married Like This
(a Friends Like This bonus novella)
Together Like This
Heartbreak Like This
Family Like This
Future Like This
Nothing Like This
Trust Like This
Always Like This

Ida Heartthrobs series
The Forever Fight
The Perfect Love
The Future Play

Freaking Love series
First Love
Real Love
Forever Love

Baker Girls series
The Last Lie
The Last Key
The Last Love Story

Ida Romance series
Reckless for You
Faking It for the Holidays
Everything for You
Running Back to You
Caught Up In Your Love

Lacy Creek series
Finally Yours
Always Mine
Only Ours
Complete Trilogy

The Perfect Love Playlist

You can find The Perfect Love Playlist on Spotify

- Uncharted- Sara Bareilles

- Boston- Augustana

- My Mind & Me- Selena Gomez

- My Church- Maren Morris

- cut!- Maren Morris feat. Julia Michaels

- invisible string- Taylor Swift

- I'll Never Break Your Heart- Backstreet Boys

- From The Jump (Duet Version)- James Arthur, Kelly Clarkson

- Scared To Start- Michael Marcagi

- TRUSTFALL- P!nk

- Broken & Beautiful- Kelly Clarkson

- Heart's on Fire- Passenger

- Call It What You Want- Taylor Swift

- Snow On The Beach- Taylor Swift feat. Lana Del Rey

- FEMININE RAGE- PEGGY

- Good Woman- Maren Morris

- Fall Into Me- Forest Blakk

- One Bedroom- Yellowcard

- Used To Be Young- Miley Cyrus

- Stand By You- Rachel Platten

- Say You Won't Let Go- James Arthur

- Carry You Home- Alex Warren

- because, of course- Maren Morris

- Girls- Rachel Platten

- LABOUR (the cacophony)- Paris Paloma

- I Lived (live from One Night In Malibu)- OneRepublic

- Little Bit Better- Caleb Hearn, ROSIE

- GIRL- Maren Morris

- Beautiful Things- Benson Boone

- I Shall Believe- Sheryl Crow

- Perfectly Broken (Acoustic Duet)- BANNERS, Lily Meola

- Ghosts That We Knew- Mumford & Sons

- Karma- Taylor Swift

About the Author

Bethany Monaco Smith is a writer-mom. When she's not busy hanging with her boys, she's writing beautifully messy love stories.

She loves happily-ever-afters and cries at every emotional moment, whether reading, writing, or watching. When she's not mom-ing or writing, you can find her binge-reading on Kindle Unlimited, supporting fellow indie authors, and having sushi dates with her SIL. Bethany survives on coffee, rewatching the same TV shows over and over, and her KU subscription. She lives in the Southern Tier of NY with her husband and two sons.

For more about Bethany and what she's working on, follow along on Instagram (@bethanymonacosmith) or on her website, www.bethanymonacosmith.com. Stay in touch by joining Bethany's exclusive Facebook group, Bethany's Book Nook & signing up for her newsletter.

Acknowledgements

Cassie & Lacey, thank you for helping make this and every book possible.

To my betas, Shani, Ryann, and Mel, thank you for giving all your thoughts (and your love for Trevor!).

To the reader team group chat, thank you for always being so wonderfully supportive.

The BOD squad for being a safe & supportive space.

Special thanks to Jenni Bara for letting me borrow a few of your characters.

And to all my readers for being here. You're the best!

www.ingramcontent.com/pod-product-compliance
Lightning Source LLC
Chambersburg PA
CBHW061036310726
48969CB00004B/974